The Justice in Revenge

Also by Ryan Van Loan

The Sin in the Steel

The
JUSTICE
in
REVENGE

Ryan Van Loan

TOR

A Tom Doherty Associates Book
New York

THE JUSTICE IN REVENGE

Copyright © 2021 by Ryan Van Loan

Maps by Tim Paul

A Tor Book
Published by Tom Doherty Associates
120 Broadway
New York, NY 10271

www.tor-forge.com

Tor® is a registered trademark of Macmillan Publishing Group, LLC.

Library of Congress Cataloging-in-Publication Data

Names: Van Loan, Ryan, author.
Title: The justice in revenge / Ryan Van Loan.
Description: First edition. | New York : Tor, 2021. | A Tom Doherty
  Associates book.
Identifiers: LCCN 2021009122 (print) | LCCN 2021009123 (ebook) | ISBN
  9781250222619 (hardcover) | ISBN 9781250222602 (ebook)
Subjects: GSAFD: Fantasy fiction.
Classification: LCC PS3622.A5854945 J87 2021 (print) | LCC PS3622.A5854945
  (ebook) | DDC 813/.6—dc23
LC record available at https://lccn.loc.gov/2021009122
LC ebook record available at https://lccn.loc.gov/2021009123

Our books may be purchased in bulk for promotional, educational, or business use. Please contact your local bookseller or the Macmillan Corporate and Premium Sales Department at 1-800-221-7945, extension 5442, or by email at MacmillanSpecialMarkets@macmillan.com.

First Edition: July 2021

Printed in the United States of America

0 9 8 7 6 5 4 3 2 1

For Melissa, who saw true

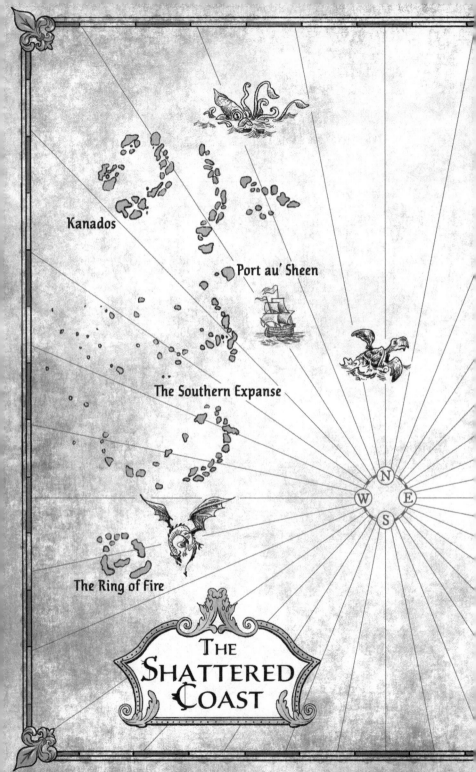

Kanados

Port au' Sheen

The Southern Expanse

The Ring of Fire

The Shattered Coast

The Free Cities

Northern Wastes

Servenza

Frilituo

Colgna

The Burning Lands

The Southeast
Island

Normain

Cordoban Confederacy

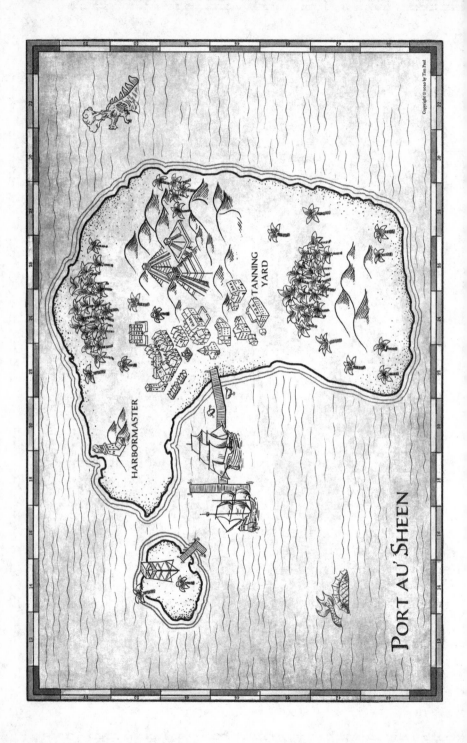

PORT AU' SHEEN

HARBORMASTER

TANNING YARD

Imperial Isle

Gilded

Royal

Blossoms

Kneeling

Mercato

Kanados

Spired

Castello

Grand Canal

Painted Rock

Foreign

The Tip

Foreskin

SERVENZA

The Justice in Revenge

1

I once saw a condemned woman try to escape her fate by swimming for a ship setting sail in the Crescent. It was full winter; high tide and storms turned the waters into roiling waves that broke again and again as they swept through the harbor. The drowning waves, they were called. Before long the waves had earned their name and the hangman had no need for his noose.

Half a year ago, my life had been a sea I knew well and navigated like an old salt. Now I swam in a sea of boardroom intrigue and backdoor politics that continually took me by surprise: the drowning waves. I'd no intention of slipping under, but isn't that what everyone believes?

Philosophers say war makes for strange bedfellows, but in the streets it's said that necessity makes whores of us all. I had thought them liars, but a living shard of a Goddess in your head has a way of changing your perspective. That's why I'd come to the Cathedral of the Dead Gods and put myself in the heart of their power even though they suspected much about my involvement with the disappearance of their precious Ghost Captain. Rightly so, given I'd killed him. That the bastard had nearly killed both Eld and me likely wouldn't have dissuaded them from parting our limbs from our bodies. I'd risked it anyway. Necessity.

"You're no demi-God."

"Demi-Goddess, then," I whispered mentally to Sin. "Hush, I want to hear if that Veneficus decides we're easy meat and comes running, changed into some monstrous creature or other."

I fingered the gilded lace that crept out from beneath my

green—of a shade almost light enough to be blue—jacket, then pulled the garment tight around me, the bottom flaring at the waist to show off my pants. Eld led the way out of the side oratory, an arching cavern of stone shipped in from Normain centuries ago. The cathedral was modeled on one of the Dead Gods, I'd forgotten which, and the stone was a not-quite white, not-quite grey color, supposedly the hue of the Dead Gods' bones. The supporting ridges in the arched ceiling of the oratory jutted out like the short ribs they were supposed to mimic. As with everything with the Dead Gods, it was meant to give life to creatures that had been dead for millennia. *Yet they still manage to fuck the world up.*

Sunlight swept across my face. My eyes burned with Sin's magic as he kept my vision sharp despite the contrast with the dark halls we'd just left. Eld didn't have Sin's magic and he grunted at the light, putting his back against the stone wall. As I moved past him, he used his powder-blue coat to hide his hand gripping the hilt of his sword. Now that we were outside, the chanting of the worshippers within sounded like a hive of bees.

"They weren't happy," Eld said, still blinking against the harsh light of late morning. He brushed a stray, blond strand of hair back beneath his tricorne. "I thought that younger one . . . Ulfren? Thought he was going to transform into some nightmarish beast right then and there when you told them to fuck off."

"I told them they'd best keep their distance if they wanted a profitable future," I reminded him.

"I think there was a 'fuck off' in there, too."

"Implied only," I assured him. He snorted and I shrugged in my jacket, feeling my blades dig into my sides at the movement—blackened blades just a shade darker than my hands so that most would miss the heartbeat when I drew them. A razor-thin lead, but with Sin's magic that was all I needed.

"They're on edge."

"Losing a war will do that," he agreed, his eyes on the door we'd just used.

"The New Goddess doesn't take prisoners. With Ciris's mages now offering healing . . ." I watched a woman in a dress too thin for the weather—but likely her finest—ushering two children into the cathedral. Both were bent with wracking coughs. Likely her purse was nearly empty.

"With Sin Eaters offering that," I continued, "and without the price of coin or service to Gods dead millennia ago, they've lost the last big lever they had."

"Aye, and losing the Ghost Captain cost them their best shot at Ciris's throat," Eld said.

"Which is why they're so desperate." Desperate enough to poison our tea. "We can use that."

"If we can get the Godsdamned Board to listen to us."

"Big if, that." Sin's voice was low in my ears. "Were you to allow the ritual of Possession to be complete, perhaps—"

"I'd be a mindless automaton in service to your Goddess," I told him mentally.

"That's not how it works."

"Says you. I didn't let you talk me into it this past summer when Eld was dying on the sands. I'm damn sure not going to let you do it now," I whispered in my mind.

"Do you believe them?" Eld asked, pulling me out of my head.

"The Sin Eaters?"

"No." He gave me a strange look, his blue eyes troubled. "The Dead Gods."

I shivered, remembering the heat in that Veneficus's voice when he asked to taste our blood. He wanted to discern the truth of our words in return for giving us the name of whoever murdered my spy. The boy wasn't the first of my little fish—children I paid to deliver messages or just to keep their eyes and ears open—to turn up with this throat slit.

Govanti, the biggest of my little fish, had convinced me to bring the lad on less than a fortnight ago, in part because he thought the lad would be safe, since he lived with his parents. Their hovel was close to the finer Quartos; rare for a murder to take place there and rarer still for a child to die by the blade within sight of the Doga's Palacio. Out farther, in the Painted Rock where I'd grown up and toward the Tip, life was cheap, but the rich preferred to keep their illusions. The Constabulary had been called out to investigate—procedures had to be observed—but his parents had no money and they'd stopped before they scarcely started.

I remembered the boy's shock of dark hair poking out beneath his cap, his lifeless eyes—not the first I'd seen staring back at me since returning to Servenza—and clenched my teeth to keep from snarling. Govanti had been distraught, but I paid him an extra coin as if that would ease his mind. And I? I'd pay the weregild for all. *What hope do I have to save the world when I can't even save my own?* That, more than anything else, had brought me to the Dead Gods today, but their promises were as false as their deities.

"'Show me the truth and I'll show you a shadow cast by the sun. Both are blinding, both unknowable save for the shade they provide,'" I quoted after a pause. I'd read Gillibrand after Ballwik and always wished I'd read her first because then I'd've had no need for the latter.

"Never trust a mage," I added.

A shadow passed over Eld's pale face and I felt a flash of guilt, but he just touched the edge of his tricorne and nodded. "Now that, I do believe."

The steps to the main entrance to the cathedral, two dozen paces away, began to teem with a flood of worshippers. All to the good. Servenza took a dim view of magic in the streets, and if the Doga was in attendance—for today was the start of the increasingly elaborate celebrations that would culminate in a fortnight with the Feast of Masks on Midwinter's Day—she wouldn't tolerate a Veneficus attacking citizens. *I hope.* As if my thoughts were a command, the woman appeared at the head of the steps with half a dozen guards, bright in their crimson-and-gold ceremonial uniforms.

Eld straightened his coat so it aligned with the red vest beneath and looked at me. "How'd you know they poisoned the tea?"

"Oh—that."

I'm quick on my feet and even quicker in thought. I used to have to smoke kan to keep my thoughts from tumbling into one another and driving me half-mad, but with Sin I was able to harness those thoughts and keep them pulling evenly in their traces. Save when it came to talking about magic. Eld and I had had one almost-but-not-quite-open conversation about what I'd done back on that island, and Eld hadn't spoken to me for a fortnight after, until I invited him to see my plan for taking over the Company. That plan had gone up in flames and by the time the ashes settled, the opportunity to discuss my magic was little more than ash itself. Eld hated all magic; he'd hate mine, too, despite our friendship. I searched my mind for an answer to his question, but none came, and Sin didn't help either, the bastard.

"You told me to stay clear of this," Sin reminded me.

Eld was still looking at me expectantly, his eyes a brilliant blue in the sunshine. For a moment I considered not answering, just staring, but he deserved a reply. I couldn't give him the truth. . . .

"I, uh, let's just say a little voice told me?" I said finally. "And it turned out to be right."

"Oh," Eld said, then realization bloomed in his eyes. "Oh." He looked away, his cheeks turning a red that had nothing to do with the sun.

I bit back a curse and turned to look toward the stairs. An un-ending stream of people parted around the Doga, who seemed to have taken up residence at the top of the steps, her dark hair and skin nearly a match for my own, though I guessed much of her color came from the sun. I had to give it to the woman, she had presence, her gold crown placed within her ochre locks so that it looked a part of her. Thread o' gold braided in as well made her hair shimmer in the light, and while she eschewed the latest fashion—a flaring jacket over tight trousers—her dress was still

6 • Ryan Van Loan

in style. The fabric, in a purple soft enough to be lavender, spilled down to her heels and was sewn up at one side to reveal gilded lace.

The crowd, some carrying crutches or heaps of bloody bandages they no longer needed after receiving healing by the Dead Gods, bowed as they passed. Judging from the Doga's smile, their obeisances were deeper than the ones they'd given to their Gods.

Beyond the Doga, a man and woman were working their way against the crowd, perhaps heading for the next healing service. They were fools to not wait until the cathedral had cleared out. The man was jostled by another and nearly fell, his dark jacket billowing behind him, drawing a few curses from those around him. He pulled his jacket back around him and I saw a short-barreled pistole in his hand. Past him, a score of paces away, strode a woman in a similarly dark jacket, gaze fixated on . . . the Doga.

"They're going to assassinate her."

"What?" Eld turned away from the canal; he'd been watching for our gondola to arrive.

"The Doga." I pointed. "Those two in the brown rags are trying to kill her. Sin, let's go," I said, the last spoken only in my mind.

I leapt into the crowd, letting Sin guide me deeper into the swirling maelstrom of humanity. I kept my eyes on the man. He was past middle age with an unkempt look; bristling hints of a white beard and greasy grey hair jutted out from his ill-fitting tricorne. Even with Sin's help, it was difficult to move against the crowd. Two steps forward, one up, one back, and another two steps forward wasn't going to get us there fast enough. *Right hand inside left jacket pocket, left hand down to pouch sewn in the belt.* Eight paces. The great thing about being able to wear a jacket and pants was that the pockets gave me so many options that I didn't need to carry a purse unless I needed extra ammunition. Or makeup. Today I needed neither. "Ready?" I felt Sin's nod and smiled. "Then let's do this."

I dropped my left hand inside my jacket and found the smooth handle of my new slingshot, its dark wood reinforced with bands of steel so it could handle the stronger rubber draw I could pull with my Sin-enhanced strength. My other hand went to the small lump hidden on the side of my belt and twisted the pistole ball free. I kept marching forward, Sin guiding my heeled boots. The assassin had no clue I was coming for him—his attention was focused on the Doga—and I couldn't keep the laughter from my lips as I drew the slingshot up in line with his head.

"Easy," Sin said as I drew back on the band. "That far and you'll take his head off and hit another beyond him." I let slacken the rubber and Sin grunted, "Better."

My eyes burned with his magic, the rest of my senses disappeared, and everything slowed for a single, crystalizing, perfect moment. The man had the pistole half-raised, preparing his shot. I released the ball and heard its angry whine, followed a breath later by the sound of the assassin's skull cracking. A spray of blood and bone paired with a plume of smoke and flame as the pistole boomed against the stairs. A woman screamed, followed by a chorus of other voices. People decided bolting was the better part of valor, and suddenly I found myself fighting to remain close to the woman in the brown jacket, who had broken into an awkward run, still trying to reach the Doga.

"Again, Sin," I muttered, drawing another ball. I felt my eyes burn and movement still, but a lad with a shock of red hair blocked my shot. "Let it go." Time and sound returned with a fury and everyone began running again. "Now." This time it was a woman in a ridiculously tall, heavily feathered hat who saved the would-be assassin. "Let it go," I growled. "We're going to have to push through the crowd."

"Can't," Sin said.

"Why?"

"Because, the strength required would mean you'd seriously injure, perhaps even kill, at least half a dozen people in getting to the woman. And she's going to reach the Doga in a dozen paces while you've more than thrice that to cover. Wait for the shot, it will come."

"Aye, or it won't," I muttered. I shifted my vision, let myself take in the full scene, and grinned. *Of course.*

"Eld!"

He was standing above me, near one of the columns that formed the entryway to the cathedral. Where I'd leapt right in, Eld had worked his way to the top of the stairs by moving along the edge. Sin growled and I laughed.

"Eld!" I shouted again, gesturing toward the gilded cistern that stood between him and the Doga's guard. This was where worshippers cleansed their hands, mouths, eyes, and ears before entering. But it'd do for a distraction as well. Eld leapt over a woman who'd tripped and fallen, and bellowed as he lifted the monstrosity overhead.

The Doga's guards had drawn blades and circled her protectively. Oblivious to the real threat, they took note of Eld, who jumped down a pair of steps with the cistern held overhead. He teetered on the landing, then heaved the massive vessel. Water sluiced out in an arc and the cistern crashed down the steps. I cursed when I realized it would land short.

Most of the water crashed against the guard, but a bit of spray carried on past, hitting the assassin full in the face. She was running toward the Doga, hands reaching for something in her belt. She cried out in surprise when the water hit her, drawing the attention of the Doga's guards.

Finally.

A moment later the woman's cry turned to one of pain and something shimmered through the air around her. Smoke? The woman ignited in a hissing, sputtering ball of flame that surged into the air and sent the Doga's guards scurrying back with cries of their own. The woman fell, collapsing in on herself as she turned into a ball of pure fire. Eld caught up the cistern from where it had come to rest and, with another roar, tossed the remaining water onto the woman. She went out with a smoldering hiss. A breeze carried the perverse scent of spiced meat toward me.

Eld's grunt was loud in the crackling silence that followed. "Well, that's new."

2

The Doga's eyes bored into mine, her proud, hooked nose making her look a sea hawk observing its prey. Around us the last few score of worshippers were fleeing in absolute pandemonium and the Doga's guards were shouting at people to keep back, steel leveled, searching for the next attack. I inclined my head slightly. The Doga's lips twitched and she returned the gesture. Between us, the woman's corpse sent wisps of smoke into the air.

"Buc, it's past time to be gone." Eld grabbed me firmly but gently, despite all the strength he'd just shown, and turned me around. From the corner of my eye I glimpsed the Doga's guards doing the same with Her Grace, moving her quickly away. We ran like the few fools still remaining down the steep, marbled steps of the cathedral and onto the stone dock beside the canal, leaping into our waiting gondola.

At Eld's shouted instructions, Joffers, our gondolier, pulled the tie rope loose and shoved the gondola away from the dock, making it tip from side to side. Eld and I stumbled into each other, more falling than ducking beneath the tented canopy in the center of the boat. For a moment neither of us spoke and I let myself relax into one of the dark crushed-velvet seats. It wasn't as soft as I'd have liked, but while we had money now, after our summer adventure, we weren't made of minted coin and this gondola had come third- or fourthhand. Still, better than walking or trying to find a carriage for hire at this hour. If only the guild would allow private carriages. My thoughts drifted for a moment until Eld cleared his throat.

"What was that about?" he asked.

I released the breath I'd been holding. He didn't ask about my magic. Tension lifted from my shoulders. "I'm not sure," I said. "Someone wants the Doga dead."

"Clearly," Eld said dryly.

I made a noise in my throat and closed my eyes. "The man was ill dressed and unkempt—was he disguised or a distraction so the real assassin, the woman, could get close?"

"She seemed the more dangerous of the two."

"She did that," I agreed. "Women usually are." I heard him shift and bared my teeth without opening my eyes. "But I don't understand how she went up in flames so quickly."

"An explosive device of some sort?"

"Likely, but if it was then she must have rigged it wrong because she didn't explode so much as implode."

"Unless that was the point," Sin chimed in my ear. "A suicide mission to burn the Doga alive."

"Perhaps," I whispered back in my mind. "That would certainly send a message."

"But to whom?" Sin asked. "For what?"

"Those are the questions."

"If you allowed me to Possess you, Buc, we could share our knowledge with the Goddess. It has been one hundred and eighty-seven days without her guiding hand. Unlike those undead fools, her knowledge truly is legion. She'd have the answers."

"Not a fucking chance," I said, pushing away his mental protestations.

I'd taken Sin from an artifact in a centuries-old shipwreck, doing it to save Eld from magic that was killing him and to defeat the Ghost Captain who'd used said magic. It had worked, but only just. Sin claimed his powers were at a fraction of their usual strength and that I was cut off from a huge base of knowledge and wisdom because I wouldn't allow him to Possess me and complete Ciris's ritual. I couldn't tell if he was lying or not, but if he was, even the fraction of power currently granted to me was frightening.

"No—" I cut him off before he could start again. Persistent little fucker.

"So a coordinated attempt with some mechanism to ensure the Doga was only leaving the scene in pieces," Eld mused, bringing me out of my head.

"Crispy pieces. That failed when our valiant hero dumped cold water all over her plans," I added. "Literally."

I opened my eyes and laughed at the look of consternation on Eld's face. "I'd only hoped you'd distract her long enough for me to get a clear shot or for those loutish guards to notice her. You continue to impress, Eld."

"I try," he said, unable to keep the smile from his lips. Or his eyes.

"It's been an eventful morning," I said, settling back against the seat again. "The Board will want to hear of this."

"Aye." Eld dug into his vest and pulled out his pocket watch. "And we're already late, so maybe the exciting news will assuage them."

"You know it won't." I sighed.

"Remind me, why do we care about them again?"

"Because, my dear, simple Eld, I—we—intend to use them to drive the growing wedge deeper between Ciris and the Dead Gods, to force them into open war. But that won't happen unless we get them dancing to our tune."

"They don't seem to like the music we've been playing so far."

"That's because they've no ear for genius," I growled.

Now it was Eld's turn to laugh. There was something in that sound that never failed to make my heart leap. *It's a Godsdamned thing, Sambuciña Alhurra, to be in love with a man who sees you like the sister he never had. A sister tainted by magic he hates with every fiber of his being.*

"Fuck me," I whispered, my words lost in Eld's laughter. Tension settled around me like a cloak pulled so tightly that I could barely manage a breath. It was a weight I'd grown used to over these months and I hated both the tension and its familiarity.

Fuck me.

3

Our heeled boots clicked against the fine marbled hallway, echoes chasing after us as we followed the liveried servant—in gilded suit from head to toe, of course—down the fresco-lined hall. Every time we walked this corridor I remembered the first time we'd come, at bayonet point. These days the only knives were of the verbal kind, often hid behind silken tones and fawning smiles, but meant to cut as deeply as steel.

The Board worked toward one purpose and one purpose only: profit. Each and every board member thought they knew best how to achieve said profit and so while they all pulled at the oar, they pulled in a dozen directions. For all of that foolishness, they weren't fools themselves, merely infected with the disease of wealth that made them believe they were born better than those mere mortals who sat outside their hallowed ranks.

Needless to say, having an orphaned street rat and a mercenary—or whatever they thought Eld was—sitting at their table did little for their humor. I'd be damned if I let them think us afraid or, worse, weak. Still, my stomach tightened as we reached the ornate white doors that rose from floor to ceiling, inlaid with the gilded sigil of the Kanados Trading Company.

"Never let the bastards see you sweat," Sin whispered in my ear.

"That's my line."

"Then you know it's a good one."

He'd timed his rejoinder just right, so I couldn't keep the smile from my lips as the doors swung open, admitting us to the already-in-session meeting. As always, the room was dominated by the massive table, though half the seats stood empty, waiting for a time when the Company ran the world and needed to admit additional board members.

At the head sat the Chair, an older woman whose skin looked like a quill drained of ink. She was flanked by the rest of the Board, a dozen or so men and women who were theoretically allowed to sit where they chose. In reality, those with more power or who were close to the Chair sat nearer her, while those who had less influence or were newer to the group sat farther away. Their finery sparkled beneath the great chandelier overhead and I was suddenly conscious of the dried sweat on my brow, the dust on my jacket and boots. I'd intended to change before coming, but that was before we saved the Doga's life.

Salina, sitting nearest our seats, motioned hurriedly for us to join her. She shook her head, blond braids barely moving where they were piled down the left shoulder of her green jacket, failing to keep the disapproval from her face. Half a year ago she'd threatened us with hanging if we didn't solve the mystery behind the Company's disappearing ships, but I'd managed to turn the tables on her. Still, if we had any to thank for our newfound seats here, it was her . . . a fact she hoped the rest of the Board would forget. When it became clear they wouldn't, she'd become an unexpected ally, but she still leapt when the Chair said "jump," and the Chair liked that word an awful lot. I slid into the seat beside her while Eld took the longer walk around the unoccupied end of the table to sit opposite me.

"What'd I miss?" I whispered.

"So kind of the pair of you to grace us with your presence." The Chair's voice, high and lilting like chimes on a summer's afternoon, belying the steel beneath, echoed through the room. "What's put the smile on your face, Sambuciña?"

"Buc," I reminded her, although we both knew she needed no reminding. "I'm just thinking of knowledge and that old ditty about it and power and how profit follows power. I know that's what we're all here to discuss, right? Profits."

"Profits." The Chair shook her head. Her dark hair, sprinkled with white and gathered loosely behind her, tinkled with the jewels she'd threaded through them.

"How quaint," the woman seated at the Chair's left said. She was the Parliamentarian and as old as the Chair, as dark-skinned as I was, face unlined despite a clear love for the sun. "Do you have any new ventures to put before us? Perhaps less flammable than your last?"

"Ah, yes, the child's redesign of our sugar factories," the Chair said, raising her voice to be heard over the laughter reverberating from the rest of the members around the table.

I heard Salina's breath hiss between her teeth: she alone of them all knew what I was truly capable of. If looks could kill, the Chair would have been in her grave already. I opened my mouth, but the Chair didn't give me a chance to draw steel, verbal or otherwise.

"You put forward interesting schematics, true, child," the Chair said, flashing her teeth when I bristled. "Then you rushed them into production without consulting our engineers, without testing, so eager were you to prove your genius to us. And what happened?" she asked, spreading her thin arms.

"Poof," said the Parliamentarian.

"Always back to this, eh?" I asked. I'd reengineered the way the sugar the Company brought back from the Shattered Coast was refined and forced the Board's hand into letting me pilot the new designs in the Mercarto Quarto. We'd been riding high after saving the Board from bankruptcy and the Ghost Captain's piracy and this was meant to clinch my position atop the Board. It had worked, until it hadn't. I suspected the fire had had something to do with the spacing of the new machinery and the excess heat generated—sugar is highly flammable, after all, so one spark and—

My memory of the fire itself was vague; Eld said I'd taken a knock and a lungful of smoke—but my memory of what came after was clearly sharper than theirs. "The venture proved profitable, did it not? The insurance payout was vast. I don't remember any tears when our shares increased."

"Aye, it was larger than anticipated," the Chair said. "One almost would have thought you planned to fail."

"The adjustor from the banks certainly did," the Parliamentarian quipped. The woman was full of herself this morning. Even more than usual.

"Your eagerness to show us all your genius not only burned our operations to the ground, it took nearly half the Quarto with it," the Chair continued. "The bribes required to keep the guilds off our backs, to say nothing of the Doga, erased much of the aforementioned profits." She rested her thin forearms on the table. "Were we to follow your strategy we'd be out of business within a fortnight."

"As I recall, the last time you were within a fortnight of losing everything, it was I who saved your arses."

Eld's groan was lost in the uproar that followed my words. I mouthed "whoops" to him and he buried his face in his hands. Weeks earlier, I'd started the first meeting we'd been part of by reminding the Board how much they owed us. It'd gone down like an overladen treasure galleon in hurricane seas, then and now. The rich don't enjoy being reminded of their failures, but then again, neither did I.

"You've a guttersweep's grace—" the Parliamentarian growled.

"Grace!" Eld's shout cut off the sniping and brought every eye to him. His cheeks flushed. "That is to say," he added in a milder tone, "we've news of the Doga. News you'll want to hear."

"News?" Lucrezia—a tall woman of Eld's years, willow-thin, with a figure I'd never have, and perfectly curled brown hair that fell in unbraided waves down her sun-kissed skin—leaned forward. She was newly raised to the Board after her father's unexpected passing and rarely spoke, but Eld always seemed to draw her out.

Her eyes sparkled as she leaned toward him, her marriage hand hidden by an overlong sleeve. While others might wonder about her marital status, I knew she was single. So did Eld.

"We must hear your news, sirrah," she said breathlessly.

Salina snorted softly and Eld's cheeks burned brighter still. He stammered and gestured to me. "Buc?"

"Oh, that," I drawled. "The Doga was nearly assassinated this very morn. It would have succeeded if not for yours truly. And Eld," I added, nodding at him in acknowledgment.

"Always an afterthought," he muttered, a smile ghosting his lips.

There was a sprinkle of murmured conversation around the room, but nowhere close to the hysterical outpouring I'd been expecting. I studied some of the faces nearest me. Interesting.

"You aren't surprised," I said.

"Fools try to kill the Doga every few years," the Parliamentarian said. "It's been that way ever since Servenza gave up our Grand Republic for a single ruler." She made a small gesture with her hand, as if swatting at a fly. "Besides, the Doga is merely a pawn of the Empress."

"Now, unless you and Eld wish to tell us all why you were at the Cathedral of Baol, treating with the Dead Gods, I suggest we move on to more pressing matters," the Chair said.

"Not even a rat trusts itself to one hole," I said. That they also knew where the assassination attempt had taken place told me they had spies everywhere—and spies fast enough to beat me back here with the news. The former, I'd known; the latter, I hadn't. "You know my position on whoring ourselves out to Ciris," I added, to offer a reason for our being there.

"And wouldn't we be even greater whores if we treated with both the Dead Gods and Ciris?" someone from the middle of the table asked. There was a titter of laughter at that and I felt my cheeks burn.

"The Doga may be a pawn, but she's still the Doga of Servenza," I said, fighting and failing to keep the heat from my voice.

"Sambuciña is right." The Chair's voice, thin steel, cut through the room. I froze. The woman never agreed with me. Ever. I had Sin check I hadn't dropped dead and he confirmed I hadn't. My eyes burned with his magic and her features leapt forward so that she appeared a palm away from me. I saw a bead of sweat slick down the edge of her hairline. Her left eyelid twitched and her lips were pressed together in a way that told me she didn't trust herself to say more.

The woman was the head of the most powerful trading company in the world and, depending on who you asked, second in power only to the Empress herself.

Yet she was clearly terrified by what I'd said.

Why?

"We are of Servenza, the most powerful city-state in the Empire, and to those outside these islands there is little difference between us, the Doga, and the Empress herself," the Chair continued after a moment. "The Doga's a pawn, true enough, but perception matters in the marketplace and given the recent . . . troubles, we can ill afford questions about our reach."

There was truth to that: Servenza was the most powerful of the city-states in the Empire and the Company owed its beginnings to Servenza's success. Or perhaps there was something more? The Chair had dozens of eyes and ears; all of the members did. My contacts were of the streets and while that was useful in some ways, they weren't likely to tell me what hold the Doga might or might not have over the Company. Still, I did just save the Doga's life. Possibilities raced through my mind. Delicious ones. Something caught my ear and I pulled myself out of the daydream and back to reality.

"The disturbances around the Tip are spreading," Salina whispered as the Chair kept on, saying something about the need to remind the world who they owed their prosperity to.

I leaned forward; now this was something I might ken better. The far edge of Servenza tapered to a point and it was said all shit emptied out at the Tip. A rough Quarto, and I knew it like the scars on the back of my hand. *Scars?* I glanced at the teardrop marks on my hand, unable to remember where I'd picked them up.

"They are just sparks, so far, but our reports say that with murders nearly doubling since the fall and the gangs fighting for territory, they are catching." Salina glanced at the parchment before her. "The Company shifted much of its operations farther west after your experiment went awry."

"Burned to the ground, you mean," I said. She nodded. "Moved our operations west?" She inclined her head again. "So," I breathed, "right where the gangs are fighting." That's sure to be blamed on me. "Bloody great."

"Then we are adjourned," the Chair said loudly, interrupting our sidebar. She slapped her gavel lightly onto the table. "We'll hold Congress again after the Masquerade on Midwinter's Day."

Everyone stood up, Lucrezia practically leaping out of her seat, trying to catch Eld's arm before he rounded the table to join me and I felt something twist in my stomach. He seemed politely confused at her attention, leaning down to catch whatever mindless flattery she was trying on him this time. The woman was harmless—I saw her fingers dance up Eld's arm to his bicep—practically harmless. But she was an annoyance. The whole damned Board was an annoyance. As I stood up, trying to ignore the jealousy stuck in the back of my throat, a hand touched my shoulder. Spinning around, I caught the hand in a wrist lock; Sin caught me before I broke the offender's wrist.

"Ow! Easy, Buc," Salina said, trying to keep the pain from her voice. She pulled her hand free and smiled as if nothing at all was wrong. "The Chair would like a word with you." She glanced past me to where Eld was trying to extricate himself from Lucrezia's clutches. "Privately."

"Sorry, 'Lina," I said after swallowing the heat in my voice. "Startled me is all."

"Aye, well, I'll announce myself next time," she said with a hollow laugh, rubbing her wrist. "You'd better go," she added in a lower tone. "You've kept her waiting once already today, twice may make her explode."

"Wouldn't be the first woman I've had that effect on today," I said absently. Salina stared at me but I shook my braid and stepped around her. The Chair awaited me at the head of the table with a smile on her lips that made me wish for one of my hidden blades.

4

"You know how to provoke, Sambuciña," the Chair said. "Always pressing, reminding them"—she gestured at the now-empty table—"of who you are, where you came from. Keep it up and you'll find yourself censured. The Parliamentarian was on the verge of calling for it when your hulking friend distracted her with your news." She shook her hair, jewels chiming against one another in pitch with her voice. "I'm not sure what you've done to deserve him, but I can respect Eld. I can respect loyalty."

Up close, I was reminded that she avoided the sun because if she ever came out she might catch fire like a scrap of paper under a magnifying glass. I knew she was old, but up close it was obvious that "old" was too small a word for the years she'd lived. Ancient and wizened, but with a rod of steel through her back that kept her straight in her chair even if her dress nearly swallowed her thin frame. I'd have admired the Chair, save that she was content to see the world enslaved by the Gods so long as it meant the Company turned a profit. What was the world to her and the rest but common rabble, existing to serve, to purchase, to be purchased?

"I—"

"Am about to give me the famous side of your profane tongue?" She made a sound in her throat that might have been amusement. Or merely clearing phlegm. "I'm sure that would make you feel better, but I'm not here to indulge your precious feelings, child." Her smile was warm, her eyes harsh winter, full of storms waiting to break against whomsoever dared sail their seas. "You keep basking in our failure last summer without seeming to realize that now it's your failure as well."

"Pardon?"

"You and Eld are of the Board, Sambuciña. Our success is your success and our failure . . ."

"Is ours," I muttered.

"Precisely." She licked her lips. "You say you prevented the Doga's assassination?" I nodded. "Tell me. All of it."

"Not much to tell. Two raggedly dressed parishioners tried to kill her on the steps of the Dead Gods' cathedral. One with a pistole, the other with a grenado of some sort. Eld and I intervened."

"You and Eld intervened," she repeated. "Well. I need you to intervene again."

"Intervene? How?" I felt the hair on the back of my neck stand up. I'd never heard the Chair ask anyone to do anything. Demand, sure, but ask?

"I'm not sure she considers this a request," Sin whispered in my mind.

"Semantics," I told him.

"Salina told you of the unrest in the Tip?"

"Aye. Murders," I said, thinking of the lad I'd found in the alleyway two days ago, a rusty black line drawn acrost his throat, his lifeblood soaked through the new coat my alms had bought him. "Gang rumbles."

"I fear there's more to it than that," the Chair said. "Taken with the attempt on the Doga's life, I smell smoke."

"And where there's smoke . . ." I muttered.

Her lips creased in a hint of a smile. "You know all too well about that, don't you?" She held up a hand to forestall my reply. "We're all in this ship together, Buc. Rich . . . and poor." She didn't sound happy about the last. "Every ship has cats to keep the rats belowdecks. Usually, that's enough, but when there's a fire the rats become afraid, and fear is a powerful thing, powerful enough to overcome their fear of the cat, of the crew, of anything that isn't the flames at their back."

"I'm not quite sure I follow where you're leading," I said.

"You must have been a child the last time the gangs of Servenza went to war," she said. "You wouldn't remember—"

"I remember," I growled. I was the reason for that war, though none knew it. I'd pinned the leader of the Krakens, Blood in the Water—La Signora, as she was known to her followers—to a wall with a whaling spear and burned her manse down around her corpse. The power vacuum had turned the canals around the Tip red with blood for a full season.

"Then imagine that along with the death of the Doga. She's the cat in this scenario, her and her Constabulary. With the cat gone and the flames rising higher, the rats will overrun us all."

"Interesting way to think of your fellow Servenzans."

"They aren't Servenza," she snorted. "Servenza is of the sea and ships and trade and coin and power. Servenza is the Kanados Trading Company."

"So you want me to be your ratcatcher?"

"Who better?" she asked.

"Fuck you."

"There's that tongue," she said. The Chair ran a hand through the jewels in her hair. "You want your hand on the tiller right away, child, but my locks are more white than black and I didn't gain true power until they were grey. I'm in this seat not just because I am intelligent and cunning, traits we both share," she admitted, "but also because I understood what this Company required of me: loyalty and service. You come to us because of a shrewd bargain you struck and seem to imagine that we'll hand over the ledgers and the gavel with it, but what you fail to appreciate is that your bargain was just the price of entry."

Her lips curled. "You're looking for power in all the wrong places. Treating with the undead in their macabre temples may seem to you a way to gain that, but every time you go near them you risk putting your head through the noose."

She put a purple-lacquered fingernail to her chin. "If they were to somehow find out the truth of what happened to that Ghost Captain of theirs, what would they do to you? I hear the Veneficus have a raging bull's own temper. But you know that better than I, eh?"

"So kind of you to care."

"I care about the Board, Sambuciña." She sighed and for a moment looked her years. "And despite what I would wish, I told you, you are of this Board. We protect our own." The Chair straightened. "And that brings me back to loyalty. It's something the Board demands. Something I demand. A lesson Eld learned long ago. And one you would do well to learn now. Do you understand?"

"Perfectly," I said, the grinding of my teeth loud in the silence. *Do your bidding or the Dead Gods will find more reasons to want me dead.* Loyalty at bayonet point. Half a year on and nothing had changed. Here I was, still with a blade at my back.

"I wish I could believe that were true," she muttered. Shaking her braids, she drummed her nails on the tabletop. "I gave you a chance, just now, and you didn't leap to it. You didn't even come to it grudgingly." She looked up, her eyes hard. "I'm done making offers. The trade winds will shift after Midwinter's Day and when they do, I'm going to call the Board to vote on expanding our operations throughout the Northern Wastes. I'm going to send you as our representative to oversee the expansion."

"I don't have time to go haring off to that frozen ice bucket," I growled.

"I wonder what exactly you were hoping to gain through us?" the Chair asked, her lips downturned. "Power without the knowledge of how to wield it is more dangerous to the owner than any other. I gave you time to learn and you did not, so now I will teach you. You know our bylaws. What happens if you refuse an approved request from the Board?"

I closed my eyes and saw the words before me. "'Saving illness or malady, should any seated member of the Board decline a request having the voted and approved consent of the Board, they shall be removed forthwith, reduced to shareholder status, and banned from a seat for life.'" I opened my eyes and bared my teeth in a grin. "Try it, old woman, and I'll request unanimous consent, as is my right . . . which you won't have."

"Mmm, you could try that," she admitted. "But do that and I'll ensure your mission keeps you away until the ice fields freeze over again. It will be two years or more before you return to Servenza. Do that and I'll see Eld sent to the Burning Lands." She matched my grin tooth for tooth. "And you'll never see him again."

"I would care?" I sniffed, Sin hiding my racing heart. Not just threatening me at bayonet point, but running me through. "You don't know me very well, do you?"

"Well enough, child," she murmured. "Well enough. Now, run along and enjoy the few weeks you've left," the Chair said, dismissing me with a wave. "Oh, and, Buc?" Her use of my actual name pulled me back around to face her. "This is the last chance you'll be given. See that you don't burn this one to ground, too."

The Chair's threats still echoing in my ears, I jumped into the gondola, ducking under the canopy that covered three-quarters of its length, and Joffers nudged the boat out into the canal. Somehow, after discovering the Chair had been following us even more closely than I'd imagined, and had discovered a way to fuck us over in the bargain, the newfound awkwardness between Eld and me didn't feel as important.

"I think we have a way to control the Board," I said quickly, taking the seat opposite his before the strength of the current sent me tumbling. I crossed my legs. "If they don't strangle us first. Our news about the Doga has broken some things loose. . . ." I quickly filled him in on what the Chair had told me about the Doga, leaving out the part where she threatened us both with exile. "I don't trust her sudden concern about the Doga, but I'll be the first to admit feelings are a foreign concept to me."

"She sees the Doga as chief mouser."

"Aye, I get that, but she's given us something we can use—if the Chair is worried, the Doga must be frantic."

Eld nodded. "There's got to be a catch."

I snorted. "Of course there's a catch. Probably several. She already brought up the Dead Gods. Again."

I opened my mouth to tell him the rest and caught the words on my tongue before they could pass my lips. The Eld I knew before I returned to Servenza filled with magic would have been at my side, finding ways to thwart the Chair's move, but the new Eld, the Eld who'd kept his distance since he realized what I'd become, that Eld I wasn't so sure of. What if he thinks I should go? Worse, what if he chose to fight beside me in front of the Board and the Chair followed through on her threats? If we gave up the Board we'd lose everything we fought so hard for over the summer. The Gods would win. The Chair thought me a willful child grasping for power like it was a lolly I wanted to swallow whole. That was fine, I didn't want her to ken my true purpose, but I couldn't wait a year or two to make my play for control of the Kanados Trading Company. The Gods were already closing in; this morning's meeting with the Veneficus had shown the truth of that. Turns out killing the Ghost Captain and Chan Sha had put us in the sights of Gods both undead and new.

"We need to have something to hold over her, but if we're going to use the Board, Eld, we have to support them, aye? Or at least be seen to support them." I tapped my lip. "I wonder how we can get an audience with the Doga? Leverage our saving her life this morn into controlling the Chair from the shadows?"

He plucked at his tricorne on the seat beside him. "We don't have to do this, you know? We could give back the seats, or keep them and collect the dividends without showing up. Go do something else."

"Eld, this is everything we've been working toward for years. Gods, man, we both nearly died half a dozen times alone this summer to get here. Aye, it's not as straightforward as I thought it'd be, but we've a seat at one of the places of power. We're going to need that power to destroy the Gods."

"We have been at it for a long time," he admitted. "I guess I just imagined it all happening . . . differently." Rain began to fall softly against the canvas top, then harder as the winter winds picked up, and the gondola drifted for a moment, pulled to the side as Joffers paused to huddle beneath his oilskin slicker. With the pause came silence.

This was what we—I—had been working toward. Once I'd realized who was really to blame for the suffering I'd grown up in. A disease plaguing the world, one that allowed any manner of evils so long as the war was won, a war begun ages before Eld or I were born, that wouldn't end until either Ciris or the Dead Gods no longer existed. But if one had to die for this to end, why not both? Why not give the world the chance it never had: to be free? I didn't think freedom was the magic that would cure all ills, but it would give us the chance to try. We were so close to obtaining the resources required to make that dream a reality and . . . Eld was right. We were failing.

Failure. A bitter word no matter how much coin we had to sweeten the deal. The Chair might not understand my motivations, but she could be counted on to follow through on her promise. Unless, of course, I could pin her down, though I wasn't sure anyone had ever managed that. I'd always be a commoner to her, and even if I weren't, I'd be little better than Salina, condemned to wait until I was old and grey before I'd have my shot at being the Chair. Which meant I had to find another way. A way that either forced the Chair's hand or forced her bony arse out of the seat. I'd reached this conclusion before, several times, but how to achieve this continued to elude me. My schemes to improve sugar production and leverage those profits against the Chair had gone up in flames, taking my chance for a quick coup with them. Failure.

"Say, is the gondola drifting?" Eld asked.

"The gondola's drifting," Sin said right on top of him. His curse reverberated through my mind—he hated when Eld beat him to anything. "It shouldn't be possible," he muttered.

"Joffers?" I called, sitting up in my seat. The old man didn't answer. Shit. I met Eld's eyes, saw his widen, caught the shadow against the canopy at his back, and threw myself into a roll. He did the same, passing me as we rolled across the cushion-covered deck. I came up lunging, Sin's magic making my arm tingle, my fingers both simultaneously numb and dexterous as the blade up my sleeve slid into my palm.

I punched it through the thin canvas.

Right into the shadow on the other side.

A throaty gasp sprayed the canvas with dark drops. Blood. I jerked the blade out, slammed it home again in the opposite lung, withdrew, and began carving the canopy open, revealing a figure in a full sealskin suit, still dripping wet from the canal's waters. The man, dark stubble like gunpowder burns blackening his cheeks, gave a bloody gasp and collapsed to the deck with a dull thud. Behind me I heard Eld's rotating pistole bark twice, but I had no time to see how he was faring as two more would-be assassins, in dark-grey, fur-seal suits, levered themselves out of the winter-dark canal waters. One leveled a speargun while the other drew a blackened blade the size of my forearm.

Without Sin they would have pinned me to the gunwale and eviscerated me. With Sin, his magic flooding my veins so that my entire body burned like liquid steel, they never had a chance. I leapt forward, time stilling as my mind sought the path for my body to follow. *Shoulder to rib cage, wristlock, squeeze, blade falling at an angle with the current.*

"When?" Sin asked breathlessly.

"Now!"

I moved like chained lightning, jumping the low cutout of the forward seat and slamming into the taller one—the one with the speargun. I heard his breath hiss from between clenched teeth at the impact as I kept moving, intertwining my hands over his wrist. His bones cracked with a snap before my supernatural strength and then his arm was my plaything. I turned his speargun—still in his grasp—toward his compatriot, barely a pace away, and squeezed the trigger. The barbed harpoon punched through the fur suit and sent the other flying over the side of the gondola with a strangled grunt. Their legs hit the gunwale and they flipped backward, their blackened blade scything through the air.

I caught it by the hilt, a finger's breadth above the deck, and stepped backward, driving it up hard behind me. The tall one tried to scream but the blade had impaled his tongue to the roof of his mouth. For a moment we rocked back and forth, the gondola perilously close to overturning, then I found my footing and my leverage and ran the blade up through his skull. He dropped like a puppet with its strings cut.

"Eld! Blade?"

"Please," he cried, his voice thick with effort.

"On your left."

I ripped the blade free in a wave of gore and flung it behind me, Sin guiding the throw. I spun around, finding the canopy collapsed under the weight of three more invaders. Eld was using his now-empty pistole to parry the blows of a fourth wielding a shortened trident. Eld's sword was half out of the scabbard, but too long for the close quarters. His pale arm shot out and he caught the hilt of the blade I'd tossed without looking. He swung it up low and across and the woman with the trident shrieked, dropping the weapon to the deck, both hands abruptly busy trying to keep her intestines from spilling across the deck. Eld smashed her in the face with the butt of his pistole and she went over the gondola's edge. He swung around to the three facing him and growled.

"Who's next?"

I took a step forward, nearly tripping on the spare gondola oar strapped to the deck. It gave me an idea. The oar was fastened down in half a dozen places, too many to cut quickly, but with Sin's magic I didn't need to cut anything. Muscles, tendons, ligaments, and I all screamed as my magic-infused limbs ripped it free. The heavy oak oar was nearly the length and weight of the gondola itself. I whipped around in a circle, dangerously close to overbalancing as the entire boat pitched and rolled from the violence and the waves.

"High! Low!" I shouted.

Eld dropped to the deck a fraction of a breath before the oar swept through where he'd been standing. I felt the thick beam reverberate as I caught one of the figures in the head and sent the body spinning into the choppy canal waters. Still spinning, I dropped the oar, grinding my teeth with effort. Eld jumped high as the other two attackers were sent overboard, shouting in pain and fear until they hit the water. I let the oar's momentum spin me half around again, then dropped it; it rolled back and forth in the bottom of the gondola before coming to a stop.

My breath came in ragged gasps as Eld and I stared across the wreckage of the canopy at each other. He raised his eyebrows and I shrugged and gave a weak laugh that caught in my throat. The shattered canopy shifted and Eld drew his sword; then Joffers's head appeared, followed by the rest of the man, bloody dirk in one hand, broken pole in the other. He pulled his oilskin cloak back into place around him and blew his twin mustaches out, rainwater and blood flecking his lips.

"Killed your man?"

"Woman," he said after a moment. He took a shuddering breath and nodded. "Aye."

"That military service doesn't leave your bones, does it?" I said.

"I was your age when I left it behind, child." He cleared his throat. "Signorina."

"It was there when you needed it," I told him. Eld clapped the older man's thin shoulder and whispered something in his ear that made Joffers's face break for a moment before he regained his composure. "I'll get this canopy righted while you get us back into the center of the channel. I think you'll want to use that pole," I added, pointing at the one I'd dropped. "Yours has seen its final fare."

The two men stared at me as if I were some strange lights the Northfolk claimed to see dancing in the night's skies. Show me a job to be done and I'll show you men waiting for a woman to do it, so Sin and I got to work. My limbs were trembling by the time I got the poles back in their sockets and the canvas halfway straightened out—probably as much as it could be righted, given the rents Eld and I had carved in it. By the time I slipped back inside, my hands were pruny.

"W-what was that?" Eld asked, teeth chattering, when he came in—I had heard him and Joffers drop the remaining body over the side. I offered him one of the blankets that was only half-damp and he took it, shrugging it around his shoulders as he dropped into his seat.

"I'd say someone wanted us dead."

Eld rolled his eyes.

"It could have to do with us keeping the Doga alive this morning," I said after a moment. He nodded, wiping back a sodden, blond lock of hair. "Or—"

"Aye?"

I shook my head slowly, sloughing water from my braids across my chest. Or, I didn't know. A few months back I'd found myself in an alleyway with no memory of how I'd gotten there. Strange, but I'd managed to nearly convince myself it was just my imagination when it happened again. Off and on, since, but it was long enough since my last lapse that it seemed possible it was well and truly past. Sin swore it wasn't anything to do with him, but I knew how far I could trust him—still, I couldn't think of a reason he'd lie about this. Which meant I'd no idea what was wrong with me, just that every few weeks I suddenly had amnesia and not even the useful kind that made me forget bad shit. Could the assassins be connected to that, somehow?

"How bad a knock did I take when the sugar factory went up in flames?" I asked. That wasn't when my memory issues started, but it was the only injury I'd taken since we returned to Servenza. "I still don't know how the thing managed to catch fire."

"I don't think anyone plans for fires," Eld said, his eyes fixed on a point over my shoulder.

"Tell that to the insurance adjustor."

His lips twitched and he returned his gaze to mine. "What's that have to do with who tried to kill us today? The bank already paid out."

"It's just that . . ." I hadn't told Eld about Sin or about the issues with my memory. Without knowing what was wrong with me, and more importantly, what I wasn't remembering, there was no way to know if the suppositions I was making were accurate. Gooseflesh ran down the back of my neck. If I couldn't trust my own mind, what could I trust? My mind was the whole reason I'd gotten to where I was.

"You can trust me," Sin whispered.

"Sure, I can trust you," I told him. "Just as soon as I let your bloody Goddess inside my mind."

"And I'd like to think I played a role on the sands against the Ghost Captain," he continued.

"A supporting role," I assured him.

"Does your head still hurt?" Eld's question brought me back to reality and him leaning toward me, worry bright in his blue eyes. "Or is it something else?"

"It's nothing," I lied. "I just thought that—" I faked a grin. "I'm just trying to figure out who wants us dead badly enough to send a dozen toughs after us in the middle of a wintry Servenzan canal."

"Long list?"

"Pages," I said, and he laughed.

"Where were we going now?" Eld asked, shrugging off the blanket.

"Back to the palazzo," I replied. The rain pounded on the canopy like a thousand nails dropped by a God. *Is that you, Ciris?* "Before anything else happens today," I added.

"Wise, that." He nodded over his shoulders. "You scared Joffers, just now."

"Why?" I frowned, looking across at him. "He was buried under the canvas with the first that jumped him the whole time. He didn't see—" Didn't see me put down half a dozen without half a thought. Didn't see a little woman heft a pole it takes two men to get into the oar socket. Didn't see my magic. *But you did, didn't you?*

"I saw you," he whispered as if hearing me.

"Do I scare you, Eld?" I asked him.

"I think it was your nonchalance more than the killing that unnerved him," Eld said, ignoring the question.

"We faced a horde of undead this summer, Eld. What's a few fools draped in seal fur compared to that?"

"Aye, I understand, but Joffers wasn't there and doesn't."

"So long as he understands the coin we pay him, I care not," I muttered. I ran a hand over my damp braid and squeezed a few drips of water out of my hair. "I don't know if this"—I gestured at the gaping hole in the canvas—"was due to the past summer, us saving the Doga this morning, or something else entirely."

Eld's lips moved but he didn't say anything. His brow furrowed as if a thought had just struck him, but he was a bad poker player at the best of times and I could tell he'd been sitting on something. "If we are being followed, it wouldn't hurt to make their jobs harder for them, would it?"

"No, I suppose it wouldn't," I said, staring at the scrap of day-light just barely visible through the torn canvas.

"And it'd be even better if we were able to identify who is shad-owing us, perhaps even have a discreet word with them?"

"You mean like just now?" I chuckled and punched him gently in the shoulder.

"Ow!" Eld rubbed his shoulder, glaring at me.

"I barely hit you," I chided him. "Growing soft."

"Why I said 'discreet,'" he laughed.

"Uh-huh."

"What I'm saying, Buc," Eld said after a moment, shifting from rubbing his shoulder to fingering the tear in his jacket that could have been a blade through the ribs if it'd been just a little more to the right, "is that it might make sense for you to slip out of the gondola at the next intersection and catch a hansom cab while I take this around a few of the Quartos . . . you know, in case we're still being followed?"

"Finding out who is keeping tabs on us at the street level isn't a bad idea," I admitted. "But I don't know if you've heard"—I pointed at the sagging, soaked canvas—"it's pouring like a motherfucking monsoon out there. I'm already wet, so I don't really fancy climbing out at the moment." I palmed a knife. "Besides, if you want to have a word with these folks, discreet or not, you're going to want me there."

"I can better defend myself than you, if it comes to an out-and-out fight," Eld said.

"Did you see me with the oar? With Si—" I wanted the words back as soon as I said them, the image of me whipping a hunk of oak the length of a gondola around like it were a barrel stave—something even Eld would be hard-pressed to do and not something a thin woman who barely came to his chest should be capable of—bright in my mind.

"With me in you, we're the most dangerous being in this city," Sin said. He didn't boast, merely stated fact.

Aye, but Eld didn't need reminding of that. Avoiding that conversation was likely why he suggested splitting up despite the rain. Suddenly I wanted nothing more than to be away from the reality staring at me: that Eld and I were heading down separate paths. If we weren't now, we would be soon enough if the Chair had her way.

The silence achieved peak awkwardness.

"Buc—" Eld began.

I ducked back under the canvas opening and whatever he said was lost in the sounds of the storm breaking against the canal waters, hammering the stone sides of the canal where it narrowed at an intersection. Sheets of icy rain cascaded down, driven horizontally by the wind. Joffers didn't see me, or if he did, didn't see me signal him to slow down. Luckily, with Sin I didn't need him to. The magic was in my bones, which was where I wanted Eld to be. I choked back something warm in my throat and leapt.

The rain was as cold as my soul.

5

Eld watched Buc disappear into the rain. He almost called after her, to tell her to come back, that it was okay to tell him what was going on in that mind of hers.

Theirs.

The thought made him hesitate and in that moment, Buc was gone. He'd lost his chance—which pretty much summed up the past six months. He bit hard on the corner of his lip and sank back against the cushioned seat. *Have to tell Joffers the plans have changed.* He winced at the thought of forcing the old man to stay out longer in this downpour. The man had likely been out in worse before Eld was born, but he'd just nearly died and that had to make a difference. Eld would tell him in a moment; first he wanted a breath to think. *Perhaps that's my problem, I've thought too much.*

He snorted at what Buc would say to that. Would have said . . . if he hadn't bungled things up since the summer. She'd changed so much after they got back. She wouldn't have tolerated the Dead Gods' threats this morning, let alone shrugged off their poisoning attempt. The old Buc would have lost her shit and likely killed the pair of mages and somehow turned it all around so the mages were to blame in the first place. Today, instead of freaking out, she'd been polite—tactful, even, for her, at least. *And isn't that what you wanted? To see her mature into the formidable woman she was capable of being?*

"But is she changing or is the Sin inside her making her different?" he whispered. He could say the words out loud, in the privacy of the gondola, shielded by the rain; he could ask the question he feared the answer to. He rubbed his bruised shoulder ruefully—Buc had thought she just tapped him, but she didn't recognize her Sin-enhanced strength. "Which leaves me analyzing her, studying her, and never knowing if she's finally coming into her own or if I'm losing her." Losing the woman he was in love with. Had been in love with—past tense. He had to keep reminding himself of that.

It all came back to summer. Weeks after they'd escaped the Shattered Coast, he'd realized what he'd done by nearly dying on that beach: he'd forced Buc to choose between watching him die or using magic to save him. To her, he was the younger brother who needed to be looked after, the way Buc's sister had taken care of her. Of course she'd chosen to save him—and in so doing, damned herself with that kiss. That kiss.

He pushed the memory away. *Even then, if I'd told her that I knew . . .* That he knew that she had magic inside her? Or that he'd seen, in the military, how magic could twist a mage until they were merely a pawn of Ciris, doing her bidding with no thought for their own ambitions, own dreams, own life? Buc seemed to be fighting off that fate for now, a credit to her strength, but Eld knew where the path of the Sin Eater led: rot and ruin. For a moment, despite the chill in the air and the pouring rain, he felt the scalding sun of the Burning Lands on his skin, smelled the burning charnel house the mages left in their wake.

Sin Eaters betrayed me, Buc. They cost me my whole command. Seventy souls who trusted me. I led them all to a bloody death. I failed them because I didn't account for the twisting magic of Gods. I shouldn't have trusted mages then and I can't trust them now. I can't fail again. Blinking back tears, Eld shook his head.

"I swore I'd never tie myself to their magic again, Buc. I should have told you that, should have walked away. But I was a coward." He gripped the edge of the seat with all his might, squeezing until his fingers began to scream from the pressure. It was better than screaming aloud. "And then after the warehouse fire . . . you nearly died, Buc!"

Joffers coughed loudly over the falling rain and Eld spoke more quietly, for his ears alone. "Nearly died. And I kept thinking about that kiss on the sand. The pressure of your lips against mine. That's when I knew it wasn't infatuation." His tears fell freely now. "It wasn't infatuation, it was love. I—I was selfish, and when you needed a friend, all I could think about was becoming your lover. Of finding a way to expunge the magic from your soul and have you to myself."

When the sugar refinery burned to the ground around them, Buc had become trapped in a nightmarish memory of the previous time she'd been trapped in a burning warehouse. When she'd lost her sister and nearly her life. Sin had insisted that if Eld wanted Buc to recover, he had to swear to never be more than her friend, and, desperate, he'd agreed. He'd promised Sin—and himself— that he'd move on. Let time heal the rift between them.

Every time I hear his voice from her lips. Eld choked back the bile in his throat. He wanted to tell Buc about that, that the voice in her head could take her over, could speak with him. *And if it speaks to me, is it talking to anyone else?* But he'd been down this path once before and that time, Buc had nearly lost her mind. *I just need to keep my distance. Till this blows over.* Do that, and he and Buc could return to being the partners they'd been before all the fuckery happened in the Shattered Coast.

Lately, he'd begun to wonder if he had moved off too far, if he hadn't lost Buc forever. In most of the ways that mattered, anyway. He hadn't realized it at first. Not until it was too late. The distance between them had grown and now he knew the space she'd taken wasn't one of healing, but one of hurt. The past. Magic. Silence. Rejection. The warehouse and all that she'd lost with it. The Board. A long list of hurts that had been hammer blows to the wedge between them, driving them farther and farther apart.

The Board was the worst of it. Eld had had a taste of bureaucracy in the army, but the machinations and politics and the intentionally slow, grinding process of the Company had caught Buc flatfooted. Buc didn't know how to handle it, and that had led to the warehouse incident, which destroyed what little progress she'd made with the Board. They no longer saw her as a prodigy, merely an annoyance.

"And I can't tell you any of that, Buc, because we hardly speak for more than a few minutes these days."

Eld swallowed the lump in his throat. *And because I don't know if I'm speaking to you or to the Sin inside you.* Rubbing his eyes with the back of his sleeve, he drew a shuddering breath. There were other worries there, about who had taken up the space left in his wake—Salina, Sin—but they were cares for another day. He had to tell Joffers to take the long way home or the man would have them there before Buc. Perhaps that would give him enough time to think of a way out of this mess, a way back to Buc. His lips tingled with the memory of her taste.

No. As a friend. It was hoping for more that had landed him in this mess in the first place. And now it was on him to get them back to right.

First Joffers. Then to think. Eld stepped into the rain, his eyes on the gondolier, but his mind was on a rocky, sand-swept beach, dead to within an inch of his life, but never having felt so alive. He longed to feel that way again the way a drowning man longs for a lungful of air. Just one gasp, one taste. One more.

Once more.

6

I watched the gondola disappear into the rain, Joffers expertly poling around the bend in the canal. Joffers. I bit back a curse. I
promised the man he'd have no trouble, steering for two of the
Company's own. I should have reminded Eld of that; we should
have gone straight home. It would have been one time Eld's polite
streak might have come in useful. But I'd been too slow to see it
and now he was gone and poor old Joffers with him. The gnawing pit within my chest sunk in on itself, sending a throbbing
throughout my body. If need was a noose around the neck, then
feeling what I did for Eld was like a blade in the guts. At least the
noose was a clean death; I'd seen a man once who lived a week
with a hand of steel in his stomach before he finally died. This particular shard had been there for months. *Gods, it hurts.*

"I think he enjoys the rain," Sin said. "Joffers, I mean."

"I don't care about Joffers," I muttered, pulling my jacket up
against my neck, and made for the crossroads a dozen paces away
from the canal's edge. "Not really."

True, the man had forgotten more about the back channels
of Servenza's canals than most smugglers had ever known. He'd
handled himself well today; the woman had smashed him in the
throat to keep him from crying out but he'd brought her down in
the end. And I liked the way he snorted into his mustaches whenever I complimented him. But in the end, he was a tool, no different than the pole he used. To Eld, he was something more, of
course, but then to Eld, everyone was something more.

Eld. I tried to keep my jacket tight against my neck, but by the time I reached the protective overhang of the cab station, I was soaked from hair to stockings. At least it would wash any blood from me. I hadn't been touched, but Sin and I had touched a fair number and the last thing I needed was the Constabulary asking questions. A newspaper crier had beaten me to the station, a lass in the faded grey, threadbare jacket and trousers that served as uniform for criers and messengers alike. She looked up expectantly, water dripping down her face in muddy rivulets, and shook a paper.

"Care for the news, signorina? There's word from Normain, just a soldo!"

"Easy, lass," I growled. "I'm soaked, not deaf." I glanced at the stack at her feet and the one in her hand: all the words had run out with the rain, staining the yellowed paper black. "Why don't you tell me the word and I'll give you a coin for it?"

"Silver?" the girl asked. She ran a hand through knotted, unruly gold locks and tried not to shiver in the wind. "I does it for a silver."

"You'll do it for whatever I give you," I told her. "Or not."

I turned away, studying the empty street, waiting for a hansom cab to show itself. In this rain it would be slower than a gondola but drier, and I was done with boats for the moment. "I've a ride to catch."

"Inventor wanted in connection to a noble's assassination from this summer past! The man, called the Artificer, was known for his gearwork architecture and private school. A close cousin to the noble's paramour, he was working on a secret contrivance that was meant to upset the balance of power in Normain. According to this paper's sources . . ."

The lass shouted every other sentence, but she was quick enough about it and I'd naught else to do while waiting. The story was intriguing, but I'd a notion that this inventor had invented himself a new identity or been offed along with the noble. Any noble fool enough to have one man on the side was surely fool enough to have two, and loose lips besides. To say nothing of creating gearwork without Sin Eater oversight. I'd heard Normain didn't require Ciris's mark on gearwork, but I didn't think her mages recognized borders either. This Artificer wasn't going to be found. I glanced back at the girl and arched an eyebrow.

"You can read, girl?"

She paused, midsentence, glanced down at the water-streaked paper in her hands and back to me before answering. "Uh, no, signorina. I have the printer tell me the front-page story every morn and I memorize it."

I shook my wet hair; I could already feel my braided strands beginning to crinkle. "Learning to read would be easier."

"I—I don't know what the symbols mean, signorina."

"If you're smart enough to remember all that—" I frowned. "You didn't make that shit up, just now, about the Artificer, did you?"

She shook her head quickly.

"Good. If you had I'd have told you to go be a writer and I wouldn't wish that fate on anyone." I pointed at the paper. "Anyway, if you can memorize that, you can learn to read. Just need to get yourself a primer. That's a book with pictures that help show you what the symbols—they're called letters—mean."

"Thanks, signorina, for the advice," she said, her tone meant to be sincere, but to my ears I could hear the loud "fuck off" that she'd left unspoken.

My lips twitched in spite of the Eld-sized hole in my chest. "What's your name, lass?"

"Quenta," she said.

"Big name for a small girl." In the Empire that was the name for the schooners that held one-fifth in storage what a galleon could.

"I'm not small!"

"There you go, shouting again."

"I'm not small," she repeated in a more normal tone. "I'm nearly as tall as you."

"Aye, and I'm small," I said dryly. "But size counts for little un-less you're dealing with fools and if you are—then why care what they think?" I shrugged in my sodden shirt. "You usually hang around this Quarto?"

"Sometimes," she said. "Here and farther along toward the Tip, in the Painted Rock Quarto."

"Ah."

"Isn't that where you grew up?" Sin asked.

"You know it is."

"You ever get into the Tip itself?" I asked Quenta.

"I—I live there," she said in a much quieter tone. "But I don't sell papers there, t'a'int no one that can read in the Tip."

"I'd have thought the nobles going whoring would," I said.

"They, uh, have other things on their mind, signorina."

"Fair enough." I produced a coin, seemingly from the air, but she was too busy wiping her runny nose to notice, and let it flip across my fingers. "Point is this, Quenta: I've a need for a smart lass who can keep her eyes and ears open and her mouth shut. I'm looking for news of Servenza, the kind that won't find its way to your pages. If you hear anything of interest, anything at all, you come to the Blossoms Quarto and ask for Sambuciña—what?" The girl had perked up.

"I've just never been to that Quarto before, signorina."

"Uh-huh, well, it may smell like flowers, but remember all those motherfuckers shit just like you or I. And their shit smells like shit. Aye?"

She nodded.

"I'm interested in all manner of things, but you hear anything about the Gods or their mages, or talk of fighting amongst the gangs, and I'll give you another coin."

I tossed it to her and she snatched it out of the air fast enough that I half wondered if she wasn't a pickpocket, too. Her eyes wid-ened when she saw gold where she'd expected silver.

"If I don't hear from you in a fortnight, I'll send a lad named

Govanti around to have a word . . . might be there's other uses for your ears, if you ken. Another coin, same color as that one. Deal?"

"A whole lira?" She spat on her hand and held it out. "Deal."

I laughed and Sin groaned, but I was already wet and dirty, so I spat on my hand and shook hers. A hansom cab came around the corner and I stuck an arm out into the downpour and waved until it slowed and pulled over. "Until next time, Quenta."

I couldn't stop thinking about Eld and magic as the cab carried me through the streets to our palazzo. The rain hadn't slackened, rather the opposite, a precursor to one of the infamous winter storms blowing in from across the seas. It'd be pissing rain for the next couple of days at least.

I'd known how Eld felt about magic, but somehow I thought he'd feel differently if I was the one with magic, rather than some random mage. The sudden chasm between us had knocked me on my arse, last summer, and the Company had done everything it could to make sure I stayed there. Which led to my plan to restructure the sugar factories and force the Company to give me a true seat at the table. Preferably the Chair's.

Only, that hadn't happened. I'd woken up a week later in my bed, surrounded by physikers and an Eld who wouldn't meet my eyes. That was when I realized I'd lost him. That was when the sharks, smelling blood, began to circle. Females ones, like Lucrezia. I wasn't sure what she hoped he'd see in her, truly.

"She's charming, pleasant, well-read—" Sin began.

"I wasn't asking for a list."

"Attractive."

I growled.

"I'm just saying she's got some qualities that, in my experience, men would find appealing."

"Have you ever been inside a man's head?" I asked him.

"Of course," Sin said. "Though as a woman, because there's a balance that's better maintained with your kind by being opposites."

"W-wait, you're a woman?"

"I'm neither a man nor a woman," he said. "I'm magic. I'm me. But your kind get tripped up by that sort of shit. Honestly, why gender matters at all is beyond—Anyway," he said, sensing my mood, "typically we take on the characteristics of the opposite of our hosts."

"Interesting," I lied. "What were we talking about?"

"Lucrezia."

"Ah, that bitch."

None of the women eyeing Eld could do what we'd done. Gods, they'd have been dead on the gondola, let alone facing the Ghost Captain and his undead crews of Shambles. I remembered the stench of them, the hundreds that I dodged, fought, destroyed. That was my first time with Sin, and I was driven half-insane by my sudden power. Now we were a well-oiled machine. Together with Eld, we were a force to bring the Gods to their knees. Today, during the assassination attempt and again on the canal, we'd been unified, the way we'd been before.

"Relationships built on adrenaline and danger don't seem inclined to health or longevity," Sin noted.

Relationships. Eld and I could scarcely call what we'd become a relationship, but Sin was right, we'd had one today.

"That wasn't what I meant," Sin said.

"That's perfect, Sin." *I need to find a way to bring more of that into our lives. Remind him what we're capable of. And then he'll have to see that we're better together.* "Thanks."

"That's not what I'm saying!"

"Hush," I told him. I stepped out of the cab and tossed the driver a coin. Two lire in a few hours, but it was a small price for what I'd won: a way back.

7

As I walked through the wrought-iron gates between the head-high, white-plastered walls, the rain began to slacken and I bit back a curse. It would stop now. Many of the palazzos in the Blossoms Quarto had meandering paths leading to their entrances, meant to show off gardens and topiaries and the like. I wasn't one for bullshit and our budget wasn't either, so our pathway only had one bend in it and our garden—if you could call it that—was dominated by a few hedges. Wide marble steps led to the modest three-story building we'd bought after our first Kanados dividend payment. It was dwarfed by its neighbors, hulking behemoths five or six stories tall. I didn't give a wrinkled fig. I liked our palazzo, with its marble pillars flecked with streaks of green that reminded me of summer and its recently painted plastered stucco that shone in the sun. In the grey of the storm it was diminished, true, but it was home.

"Home."

A foreign word to me and one I'd only just begun to savor when Eld and I fell apart. Lightning flashed overhead and for a moment the palazzo shone in its light. I smiled as the door opened. Scratching absently at the scar on my wrist, I shrugged out of my jacket and handed it to Glori. I could dress and undress myself, but after our first fortnight in the palazzo, Eld had reminded me that there are some hills to die on and some to concede . . . and Glori had dug in for a final stand. The woman had come with the house so it shouldn't have been any surprise that she knew when to hold the high ground. Even a demi-Goddess had to bend and with Glori, one bended or was bent. A season and a half later and I was used to her ministrations. Mostly.

Taking the still-wet garment, my head housekeeper made a sound in her throat, disapproval writ large across her plain, weathered features.

"That bad?" I asked her.

She held up my jacket so I could see the stains on it.

"Your jacket's bled green all over your sleeves, signorina," Glori said.

I almost told her at least the blood had bled itself out in the rain, but I didn't think that would impress her. Glori's black servant's uniform was spotless, making her faded tan skin look almost white. She shook her long, thick-braided grey hair. "If you'd only wear dresses, as is proper for a lady of your station, this wouldn't have happened."

"No, it'd be worse," I agreed. "The Doga likely would have died today, for one thing. And besides, all the ladies of my station are wearing jackets and trousers."

"T'ain't proper," the old woman muttered under her breath, slipping a mint leaf into her mouth. I'd explained the wisdom of brushing her teeth instead of chewing a leaf that did wonders for her halitosis and nothing at all for the debris rotting her teeth, but she was stubborn as a donkey past its prime.

"Takes one to know one."

"Shove it, Sin. I'm not stubborn, just set in my ways." I felt him roll his eyes in my mind.

"No one proper ever made history, Glori," I told her, marching past, suddenly shivering in my shirtsleeves.

"Those in the history books rarely died happy, either," she said.

"You're a seer, woman!"

"Signora Salina is in the drawing room, yon," she called after me.

"Good, maybe she can make sense of the Chair," I muttered beneath my breath.

I made for the drawing room, taking a quick detour through the door on my right, its edges hidden in the painted plaster, the cracks drawn over with thick ivy that climbed to the as-yet plain ceiling, poking my head into the rear of the library. A maid in livery matching Glori's, and just as clean, compared two books before shelving the one with a green leather binding. She stepped back, mouthing the title slowly, before nodding with a faint smile of satisfaction.

"Marin!"

Marin squeaked and spun around, nearly dropping the other book. "You're soaked through, Buc!"

"You've a fondness for the obvious, girl," I told her. She blushed and I laughed. "What I really meant to say is you sound like your grandmother."

"Now that is insulting," she said, dark face stern before her cheeks dissolved in laughter.

Marin was my favorite chambermaid. Originally from the Tip, she'd been adopted by one of Glori's daughters. When the fever had taken that daughter and her son-in-law, Glori had taken Marin in and treated her like her own. Marin reminded me of what I might have been, if I'd known Sister longer or met Eld sooner. I'd been teaching her to read, although our lessons had grown spotty of late, but she knew enough to maintain the books I ordered. The dark mahogany shelves, nearly as black as either of us, shone in the chandelier light, burnished by Marin's cleaning. Over two-thirds were filled with books and I had enough in my bedroom to fill the rest, but I was trying—and mostly failing—to take my time in filling the house from floor to rafters with tomes.

"I thought you'd have been at the Board meeting, signorina," she said, hefting the book in her arms.

"I was, but nothing's so boring as the rich, unless it's the old and rich." Again she tried and failed to hide her laughter. "Is that Kolka's *The Mind Fears the Body*?"

"It hasn't arrived yet," Marin said, shaking braids that fanned down to her waist. "Maestro Roulin says he should have it from Normain on the next ship."

"Aye, I've heard that before," I muttered. I had hopes for the tome. I'd read mention of Kolka in the afterword to Verner's *Disciple of the Body*, one of the first books I'd read, number twenty-four, and the first on anatomy. If the transcriber was to be believed, Kolka laid bare the maladies of the mind the way Verner did with the body. "Well, I'll leave you to it, Marin."

"Signorina?"

"Aye?"

"Will we have another lesson soon?" She nodded toward the shelves. "I can read almost every title now, but I'm afraid to try to open them."

"Books are knowledge and knowledge can be scary, Marin." I flashed her a smile. "But books are also friends, the kind who hold you closer when you need it most. You've naught to fear from them and I'll prove it to you. Soon," I promised.

"What game are you playing at?" Sin asked when I slipped back out the secret door, heading for the drawing room.

"What do you mean?"

"Teaching a chambermaid to read is just going to illuminate the severe limitations of her position."

"Better she live ignorant?"

"And happy," he said.

"That's the problem with you religious types—you're all convinced education is pain when it's the cure. After I throw off the yoke of the Gods, Marin will have the opportunity to improve her position if she wants to."

"When you murder Ciris, you mean," he said, disgust warring with disbelief.

"Think of it as me putting her back to whatever sleep she was in before she awoke three centuries ago. Only, this one she won't be waking up from," I added.

His silence was loud in my mind.

"You look like a twice-drowned cat," Salina said, grinning. Back to finding me amusing, I saw, after the unpleasantness of the meeting. She was all right, when she wasn't being an insufferable prig.

"And you look . . . remarkably dry," I said. "How?"

"Magic," Salina said, her eyes taking on the light they did whenever the mention of magic came up between us. Salina had seen us first after the Shattered Coast and while she didn't know anything, she suspected much.

"Will Sirrah Eld be home shortly?" Glori called from the doorway. I saw Salina twitch slightly in surprise, though she hid it well, but I'd heard Glori's swishing skirts following me into the drawing room. Glori firmly believed servants were not to be seen or heard unless their service was required. Glori also firmly believed she didn't count amongst the help. Despite that, the woman was a ghost when she wanted to be. "You said there was some excitement with the Doga this morning?"

"He's fine," I told her. "With Joffers, catching rain."

"He'll be soaked through, too," she muttered. "In need of a bowl of whitefish broth. And another for Joffers. Signorina, should I bring you one, too?"

I rolled my eyes. "Since everyone's telling me how fucking wet I am—and no one between my legs either"—Glori's eyes popped and Salina's laugh sounded scandalized—"I think I'll pass and go find some dry clothes. Coming, 'Lina?"

"Not like that," she muttered, and it was my turn to laugh.

Glori seemed to have lost her capacity for speech. I stepped around the older woman, motioning for Salina to follow, and made for my rooms on the second floor. My stomach rumbled and I regretted refusing the soup. Sin's magic came at a cost and had me eating for three, and after fighting off would-be assassins—twice—I was going to be ravenous soon. Sometimes my tongue was too fast for my own good. Sin's snort was loud between my ears as we climbed the winding stairs and passed through the doors into the main hallway and only then did I realize that my hands were clenched into fists. Eld. He and Joffers could take care of themselves, but they would have been overwhelmed by the lot that tried us earlier. It was unlikely they'd try again so soon, but everything about today had been unlikely. Then why'd he send me away?

"Off to visit one of those sharks. The female kind?" Sin asked.

"If I put an ice pick through my ears would it take you with it?"

"Perhaps, but you'd be lobotomized."

"It might be worth it," I told him; I felt his smile melt in my mind.

"What did the Chair want with you?" Salina asked as we walked.

"Oh, just to find out who is causing unrest across the rougher parts of Servenza," I said, running a finger along the cream-colored wallpaper that Eld had picked out. Glori had helped ensure that it fitted our new station, so there was gilded filigree worked into it. "Reading between the lines, she wants me to feed her information that will give her a leg up on the Doga."

"She wants you to ask around the Painted Rock Quarto?" She glanced at me. "Because you grew up there?"

"No, she wants me poking around the Tip because I grew up in the gutter and the rich imagine we all huddle in that Quarto when we aren't waiting on them."

"You must be pissed," Salina said.

"I was," I muttered. "Still am. Told her to fuck off."

"You didn't—"

"Close enough," I said, glancing at her. "You can imagine how she took that?"

"No one refuses the Chair. Not more than once, anyway," Salina said.

"Aye, well, you're not wrong." I told her what the Chair had planned for my future, and she winced.

"You can't do that, Buc!"

"Is everyone going to tell me what they already know today?"

"Easy, Buc. There has to be a way around this." She scrunched her nose slightly, as she did when deep in thought. "It's going to require something from outside the Board, though . . ."

"Don't worry," I told her in a tone that was far lighter than the pain in my chest. "I'm on it."

"Of course, but I can help," she said. "I'm not the Chair, I'm your friend."

"Friend?"

"Ally, then." She snorted. "It's the same thing with you in the end, so what's the difference?"

"Words matter," I told her. Like when I told Eld I'd do anything for him and he tossed me aside because I took Sin to save his life. "And I'm sorry," I said after a moment, "it's just been a trying morn and the afternoon isn't looking much better."

"Fair enough," the other woman said. "But at least I'm here now."

"True, though you did nearly kill my servant of apoplexy."

"Listen, you may share this little place with a man bearing a nice pair of shoulders and an even better arse, but I share mine alone." She sniffed. "I don't know what you get up to, I just know I'm not the one getting off."

Her face heated all the way to her forehead and we exchanged looks and then exploded into laughter. If you'd have told me at the start of all this I'd have wound up laughing with Salina, I'd have thought you mad, but war isn't the only thing that makes for strange bedfellows. And if I didn't laugh, I'd scream or reach for steel and neither was going to give me what I wanted. Yet. The Doga's attempted assassination was the opportunity I'd been waiting for and the Chair's threat the incentive I needed to shift my arse—if I could only figure out how to twist them to my advantage.

We were still giggling like a pair of drunkards when we reached my room. I pushed the door open, took a step in, then paused in the doorway.

"I hope you're not planning on changing completely before our dancing lesson," Salina said as she nearly bumped into me after my sudden stop. She snorted and stepped back. If Eld were home, she would have made a joke and tried to look over my shoulder to see if he was in my room. A reason to be glad he was out. "Not unless you've brought on a dressing maid when I wasn't looking? You'll never get those buttons undone and done up in another pair of pantaloons in time."

"Time?"

"Aye, just throw on a dry jacket, anything will do at this point, and run a comb through your hair." She glanced at my hair and sighed. "Well, maybe just leave that. I have some ideas on where to look for ways to shift the Chair's decision. Not that I'm familiar with the Northern Wastes, but I know the Doga." She pulled a small watch from her pocket and bit back a curse. "We're going to have to talk on the run as it is if we're to meet the dancing maestro on time. We can't be late—he's a holy terror if you're late, Buc."

I stepped into my room, keeping the door between us, and stuck my head back out. "I don't think I'm going to make lessons today, 'Lina."

"You're joking." She growled when I shook my head. "You can't keep skipping out on learning the Company's—society's—ways."

"Do you really think the Chair would have assigned you the task of refining me if she wanted either of us to succeed?"

"That's precisely the point, fool woman! She wants to see you the same callow girl that sauntered in here six months ago." She shook her blond braid. "Buc, not bothering to learn how to use the Company doesn't make you better than them, it just leaves you out of favor and open to the manipulations of the likes of the Parliamentarian and the Chair. See today for a bright fucking shining example." Her eyes popped, more for her language than anger.

I opened my mouth, surprised at her vehemence, and she gave me the other barrel.

"When you're ready to grow up," Salina growled, cutting me off, her button nose twisted up, cheeks red, "come calling, won't you? Until then I'm done wasting my time. You can dance like a fish at the end of market day when the Masquerade comes, for all I care," she said, spinning around.

She glanced back over her shoulder. "But every woman swooning at Eld will dance like a Goddess. And they'll still be here when you're off on your great ice expedition because you thought yourself too good to play the game. Remember that the next time you want to blow off a lesson." Salina stalked away, booted heels clicking loudly.

"What's that about?" I asked Sin, mentally.

"She did tie her ship to the pair of you after you returned," Sin pointed out.

"Aye, through little choice of her own."

"I don't think that's factoring in here. She just came through a storm to meet you, too."

"Aye, well—" I cleared my throat. "I've matters to attend to," I called after her. "Damn it! I'll be at the next one, 'Lina!"

She raised her hand in the air in reply.

"I didn't think a lady of her stature would know that gesture," Sin muttered.

"Don't let that cute face fool you, she's the mind of a sailor," I told him.

"Now," I said aloud, turning to face into my room. "What the fuck do you want?"

Half a dozen men and women in the midnight-blue, nearly black, uniforms of the Secreto, the Doga's secret police, faced me from across my bed, pistoles leveled. I should have been shocked, given they'd apparently snuck into my bedroom undetected, but today had been one unpleasant surprise after another. Their captain, gold bars the only mark to single her out, stood up from where she'd been lying on my bed.

"Comfy," she said, patting the blankets. She sauntered across in that lazy way those good with a sword have, until she was a pace away, eyes level with my own. Her amber eyes matched the rank on her collar, and her hair was pulled back and tied up; otherwise she was as unremarkable as any woman you'd pass on the street, which was likely the point.

"Surprised to see us?"

"Well, you are the secret police, so I guess I'm surprised you live up to the reputation?" I let my false grin go. "Now, what do you want?"

"I'm here about a body."

"Aye? Which one?"

"How many do you have?" Her throaty chuckle echoed in the stillness. "Didn't think you'd say," she continued when I said nothing. "The Doga would like a word."

"I thought she might," I said. Perfect. "Tell you what, you lot clear out and I'll be down in half a bell."

"I've a better idea," she said. "You come with us now and my Secreto don't decorate yon plain walls with your brains."

The way she said this, as if commenting that the rain had picked up—which it had, smashing against the windows loudly enough that none were likely to hear the Secreto execute me—told me she was serious.

"Well, when you put it that way . . . Lead on, Captain," I told her, stifling a joke about my designer saying the walls wanted some color.

She laughed. "You've stones, girl, I'll give you that." She grunted and jerked her head, and one of the men holstered his pistole and crossed to the fireplace, where Glori had built a roaring blaze in anticipation of my return. I opened my mouth to tell him he wasn't the only one who needed drying off when he did something to the brickwork and the entire fireplace shifted back three paces and canted at an angle, revealing a dark passage.

"Where the fuck did that come from?" I asked. "Sin?"

"I—I . . . I don't know," he said finally. I could hear anger warring with astonishment and grudging respect at the level of skill required to leave no trace of the opening. I'd come home to prevent any more shit from happening to me and now I'd stepped into it up to my waist. My stomach growled. And I hadn't even eaten lunch yet.

"Well, that's just not fair," I snarled.

8

They brought me out into the middle of the Doga's Palacio, from behind a bookcase that slid back into place amongst the other shelves. If the Doga thought to impress me with her library, she'd erred: it was good enough, but the Grand Library of the Company dwarfed it in both breadth and scope. I'd been more impressed by the series of underground passageways the Secreto had guided me through. The trip had taken nearly an hour, almost double what it should have, but I suspected they doubled back time and again to make finding my way back impossible.

"Not impossible," Sin said.

"Not with you," I answered mentally. "But they don't know I have you, do they?"

"A secret from the Secreto," he said.

"If you take up puns, I will lobotomize myself," I told him.

Half the Secreto slipped away as the captain marched me down one aisle and up another before leading me into the center of the room. The dark, well-polished shelves reflected the bright, crystal-chandelier lamplight. The air smelled of some warm spice and that ephemeral hint of parchment, a scent that set me at ease despite the captain's hand on the hilt of her sword. Two chairs faced one another from either side of a small round table that held a tall stack of books, a pitcher, and two glasses.

"Her Grace, the Doga of Servenza, seat of the Servenzan Empire," the captain intoned. The Doga stood from her chair and studied me for a moment before indicating the chair across from her. "I know you've a blade or two on you," the captain whispered in my ear as I moved past her, the warning loud in her tone. "Touch it and my sharpshooter will blow that pretty little head clean off your shoulders.

"I knew I liked you," I whispered back. I glanced up and my eyes burned with magic for a fraction of a moment, long enough to focus on a panel in the ceiling, beside where one of the chandeliers was attached. Two blackened gun barrels stared down at me. "If I wanted her dead I wouldn't have saved her, now, would I?"

"Perhaps, perhaps not."

I swung wide of the table as the Doga settled back into her chair, shaking out her plain white skirts and pulling her crimson robe more tightly around her, though there was no chill in the air. Her hair, eyes, and skin were almost a single color, a shade lighter than the ebony shelves of the library, the gilded crown still threaded through her braids as it had been this morning: an extension of herself and the only mark of royalty she wore. Suddenly conscious of my color-bled shirtsleeves and soaked-dark trousers, I sat down carefully, partially to reassure the captain and her sharpshooter and partially to allow myself a glance at the books on the table. *Of Powders and Their Properties, Elements of Fire, Guns and Other Arms,* and others with similar titles. Clearly the Doga had been as unsettled as Eld by the woman immolating in front of her.

"I admire your proactivity," I said, gesturing at the books. She arched a thin eyebrow. "Your Grace," I added after a moment.

"Forewarned is forearmed," the other woman replied, her voice deeper than I'd expected. "Thank you for agreeing to see me."

"Aye, well, Your Grace's Secreto are . . . persuasive," I said. "I hadn't realized such an extent of passages lay beneath the streets."

"Have you read much of Servenza's history?" she asked.

"I've read much of world history," I said, "and some general takes on Servenza. I must have missed the part where we were founded by a warren of rabbits."

The Doga said nothing for a moment, then chuckled, her hawkish features softening, though no warmth reached her eyes.

"Careful, Buc. You speak of my family and half of the nobles who sit on your Board. Rabbits? No, but the Noble Quartos—the Blossom, the Gilded, and the Royal—were the first built on the island. Centuries ago, we often came under attack from both pirates and mainlanders, and our forebearers thought it wise to have methods to move and retreat out of sight, so hidden passages riddle the streets and sewers. And the palazzos."

"I'm surprised it's such a well-kept secret," I said. "I've never heard of them and I grew up on the streets."

"But not a gang member?"

"You could say gangs were allergic to me," I said.

"At least Blood in the Water was, eh?" she asked, eyes twinkling when she saw me stiffen. "My great-grandmother's father was assassinated when his guard held off the attackers while he fled to a secure room, only to be murdered there," she said, moving on as if she hadn't just told me she knew I murdered one of the most infamous gang leaders in Servenzan history.

"Not so secure after all," I said.

"No. After that, my great-grandmother ordered maps to be made of many, if not all, of the hidden passages. She intended it as a security precaution, so her forces could hold the tunnels against their enemies and she had an actual secure way off Servenza."

"I don't suppose I'd find those maps at the corner booksellers?"

"You'd suppose right." The Doga adjusted her skirts. "I've the sole master copy. It helps on days like today, when I need a discreet word without the audience that comes from attending me in the throne room."

"That's handy," I admitted. "Damn it"—I slapped my knee—"you've a private channel to every palazzo in the Quarto, don't you?"

She smiled her predator's smile. "The Kanados Trading Company isn't the only one with secrets, Buc. I can give you a copy of the map, if you'd like? It will be a partial only, I won't lie."

"A gracious gift, Doga," I told her.

"Speaking of secrets and gifts . . . you've a problem, Buc. The solution of which could be mutually beneficial to us both."

"I'm sorry, Your Grace, but I've many problems," I told her. "Which one is this?"

"Careful," Sin hissed. "I've met any number of dangers in my many lives, but this woman makes me nervous."

"You don't say," I whispered mentally. "I didn't think any knew of me assassinating that old hag, La Signora. Not that many looked hard—she had it coming and the vacuum left by her consumed the streets for the better part of two years—but if the Doga knew and did nothing . . ."

"She's playing a long game," Sin agreed.

"You saved my life today," the Doga said with a frown. "My guard is good at their job, but in the chaos after that piece of filth missed his shot, they missed the woman. If she'd gotten any closer . . ."

"Poof," I said. Sin sighed.

"Poof," she agreed, with no amusement in her voice.

She reached for the pitcher, which had a hint of steam wafting from it, and filled the two glasses with what smelled like mulled wine. She gestured but I shook my head; I was starving and the last thing I needed was to get drunk in front of one of the most powerful women in the world. Her expression said, "Some have no taste," before she took a sip from her glass and made a sound in her throat.

"Today's wasn't the first attempt on my life, Buc. Recently, there've been several. My body twin died last week, though none know it. That involved a couple of pistoles and a gondolier taking the wrong turn—"

"Accidental or on purpose?" I asked. "Sorry to interrupt, Your Grace," I added.

She softened her glare. "No, I brought you here because your reputation precedes you, Buc. Ask your questions."

"Well, I'm wondering if the gondolier was in on the attempt or not."

"It's a possibility we've considered."

"What'd he have to say for himself?"

"She didn't say much of anything after one of the assassins put a pistole ball through her throat," the Doga said.

"Makes conversation difficult," I agreed.

"But I think it was accidental. There was an overturned boat and she was trying to make up time by turning down a side canal. There was another attempt before that, and each one has grown increasingly sophisticated." She waved a hand. "Someone's always trying to kill me, that's not the issue, but the frequency is concerning."

Crazy bitch. I was no stranger to people wanting me dead, either, but I didn't seek it out nor was I so sanguine about it. Were our positions reversed, I'd've had the Secreto scouring the streets for answers—which was what I intended to do as soon as I got a meal in me. I had the feeling I was going to need Sin's strength for whatever I found. And Eld's sword at my back.

"He's becoming a bit of an afterthought, isn't he?" Sin whispered. "With our strength we don't need anyone."

"Stow it," I growled, then said out loud, "Who attacked your body twin, Your Grace?"

"The one who pulled the trigger was a beggar, dressed in the same rags as his compatriots from this morning."

"She served her purpose then," I muttered. "Misdirecting the assassins," I added at her expression.

"Perhaps, but he was quite fervent—he shot her with two double-barreled pistoles and stabbed her a dozen times with a blade before the guards prised him off." I whistled through my teeth. "I had him tortured of course," she added. She shrugged as she took another sip from her glass. "The usual hot irons and pliers and even some less usual methods involving rats and syrup and—well, you don't care about that, do you?"

"And you were worried she wasn't taking it seriously enough," Sin whispered. "What do you imagine they did with the syrup?"

"I've an idea," I told him, suppressing a shudder. After nearly being tortured to death in the hold of a pirate's ship last summer, I'd done some reading. As the Doga said, forewarned is forearmed and now I had a much deeper appreciation for how truly fucked the human mind is. Number 382. Despite its mundane name, Corewell's *On Pain and Its Application* had given me night terrors for a week. What's wrong with a simple blade twixt the ribs?

"Believing me dead, his mission accomplished, the man had no reason to lie," she continued.

"What'd he tell you?" I asked, leaning forward in spite of myself. "Who'd he give up?"

"No one. That was the frustrating part. There was hardly anything left to him and he still wouldn't talk save for some doggerel."

"Doggerel?"

"'The drowned rise.'" The Doga's nostrils flared. "What does that even mean?"

"What'd you do?"

"Revealed myself, to see if that would change his story at all."

"I take it that it didn't," I said.

"No, it did not."

"They were dressed as beggars," I pointed out. "Were they of the guilds, freelancers, or was it a disguise?"

"Oh, they were of Servenza," she growled. "The guilds wouldn't claim them."

"Of course," I said.

"Of course," she agreed.

"You try flashing some coin about the rougher Quartos? Gold has a way of opening even the clammiest of lips."

"Aye," she said. "But there's unrest in the streets of late and even gold stays lips when steel is sure to follow."

"Unrest? The gangs squabbling over territory?"

She laughed mirthlessly. "Of course the Company would be worried about that, a turf war that keeps workers from showing up to the factory on time because they are worried that taking the wrong turn will land them in the gutters with slit throats."

She shook her dusky brown hair. "Fighting over street corners isn't the half of it. Gang leaders have been vanishing and none seem to know where they've gone. The gangs run everything within their territories: the factories, the stores, and that's not even getting into the more criminal aspects of their organizations. Their leaders are necessary. Yet the Constabulary and even my Secreto—whom I've been running ragged through the Tip to find answers—are hearing nothing. Silence." She slammed the glass down and wine splattered one of the books. The Doga took no notice but it took everything in me not to leap on top of it to save it.

"I'm blind and deaf in my own Godsdamned city," she growled. "The only thing I know for sure is that there are sparks, Buc. Sparks looking for tinder, and if those sparks grow much more they could catch fire. All of Servenza could . . ."

"Does the Empress know of this?"

"The Empress?" The Doga took a deep breath, studied me for a long moment, and then something loosened within her. "The Empress is busy with the affairs of running the Empire. There's possible war with Normain to consider and prepare for and if one of her lackeys comes asking for help, she'd as easily replace them as pitch in."

"Even for the Doga of her home province, center of the Empire?" I asked, feigning innocence. I could practically taste her bitterness, so I knew the answer.

"Even then." She picked up her cup and sniffed its contents but didn't drink. "The Kanados Trading Company used to be of assistance in such matters, but ever since their little ghostly sugar scare this summer, their attention seems to have slipped."

She knows. About this summer.

"She knows," Sin agreed.

"Which brings me back to you, Sambuciña 'Buc' Alhurra." She smiled and set her glass aside. "I know of your connections from your time on the streets, and the fact that you managed to gain not one but two seats on the Board, when those seats are only open when there's a grave to be filled, speaks to your effectiveness."

Her dark eyes latched onto mine and I was once again reminded of a sea hawk hunting over the open water, its eyes bright on prey. "You've proved your interest, if not your loyalty, by saving my life today, which makes me inclined to believe you're just the woman I need."

"Your Grace is kind," I said after a moment. "And I did help the Company out . . . but they also had something I wanted at the time."

"There were some who thought the Board had lost their touch, you know, after this summer," the Doga said, ignoring my unspoken question. "First, in allowing the sugar crisis to get as bad as it had and then, to allow a slip of a girl with the stench of the streets still on her to con them out of two seats." She smiled. "Their words, not mine. I'm merely a shareholder in the Company, one voice amidst many others. I'll tell you, those whispers have quieted since. The Board has gone back to business, the girl kept on a short leash."

I stiffened and she chuckled. "Of course, shareholders don't know about some of the more interesting meetings you've been having lately, off the formal Company minutes and perhaps without the knowledge of even the Board?"

"They tried blackmail," I told her.

"What—?"

"The Company, they tried to blackmail me into solving their sugar problems." I leaned forward. "But I don't respond well to threats, Your Grace. Growing up on the streets showed me what comes of bending from fear. You just keep bending. Until you snap. I've come up in the world since then, so I've a feeling more pressure would be required, but some think that having more means having more to lose." I let a smile touch my lips, but not my eyes. "Don't make that mistake with me."

Silence stretched razor thin after my speech.

"You've a grand marshal's nerve, girl," the Doga said finally. She laughed, edging forward on her seat as if she hadn't sat back at my words a moment before. "And a sailor's tongue."

"So I've been told," I murmured.

"So you don't respond to blackmail, that's good to know." She tapped a finger against her lips. "But I'd no intention of blackmailing you, Buc. If I can turn you, who else can?" She shook her head. "The Company sees everything in terms of leverage, but as ruler I don't care about balance sheets and profits. I have to weigh them, aye, but I'm judged on the welfare of my people. Plain and simple. And you're one of my subjects, are you not?"

"I hadn't thought of it in those terms before," I said. "I mean, the welfare part," I lied. "I am, Your Grace."

"Then here's what I propose. You know how difficult it is to unseat a Chair?"

"Intimately," I growled, bringing a smile to her face. The bylaws were one of the first things I'd studied after our disastrous introductory meeting. Sin winced. Unseating the Chair required a two-thirds majority vote, which would never happen, or the death of the Chair, which seemed as likely to occur. Or the death of a Board member, but that just triggered another vote that would have the same result. The Godsdamned bylaws were the reason why the Chair had a better than even shot at carrying through on her threat.

"I don't imagine you sailed to the Shattered Coast and went through all that shit just to put the Company's purse strings at your disposal," the other woman said. I nodded. She moved a hand up to the edge of her circlet. "You want power and that is something I can understand. But you'll never have it while the Chair sits her bony arse at the Board's head. I can help with that."

"Say on."

"I'm not on the Board—it would conflict with my dogeship—but my family has been a shareholder since its inception and I've ties to the members through blood, marriage, and society. It will not be easy, but I've recently come into some knowledge that will allow me to arrange to have the Chair cast down." Her eyes shone in the light as she pointed at me. "And you raised in her place."

"Th-that's an awfully large favor, Your Grace," I said, my throat suddenly dry. Eld and I had nearly died a dozen times over the summer to get seats on the Board and here was the Doga, offering me the whole damn Company on her family's silver. Aye, there were strings attached, like keeping the Board from voting me out, and I'd have my hand on a tiller that everyone was pulling in every fucking direction. Still, it'd be my hand. Mine. "I don't suspect this comes as a thank-you, for saving your life?"

"You'd suspect right," she said. "I did say I'd give you maps of the underground," she reminded me.

"A partial set." I licked my lips. "You've books aplenty on whatever that bomb was this morning," I said, speaking slowly, then picking up speed. Without kan, my mind used to race out of control. With Sin, it's more focused, but it's still a struggle at times to keep to normal speeds. I've never wanted to have anything at all to do with normal, but there's a whole world of them and just one me, so sometimes I have to.

"And you've one slipped in there on doggerel and nursery lines from the street. That beggar got to you, didn't he? With that line about the drowned rising." I ran a hand back across the right side of my head, feeling the shaved skin there, and smiled. "You want me to find out who's behind the attempts on your life, aye? They only have to get it right once, you have to get it right every time. And I might not be there next time."

"Careful, Buc," the Doga breathed after a moment. Her face gave nothing away, but I could see her chest rising and falling beneath her robes—I'd gotten to her. I tend to do that. It's a gift.

"Or a curse," Sin said.

"My apologies, Your Grace. I simply wanted you to know that

I understand the enormity of your offer to me and the similar enormity of the task before me."

"Uh-huh." She cleared her throat, taking a large sip of her wine. "I want you to find out who is trying to kill me, Buc, and then I want you to do to them what you did to Blood in the Water. Do that, and I'll see you Chair."

"And the old crone won't be able to stop you?"

"How do you think she got the Chair in the first place?" Her expression was sharp enough to draw blood. "Do we have an agreement?"

"Sin—"

"Time dilated . . . but not for long—you really should eat something if you're going to call on me so often."

"If I'd known that today I'd prevent an assassination, fight off a bunch of canal pirates, and go mental rounds with some of the scariest women in the world, I'd have eaten a Godsdamned buffet," I told him. "Now, let me think."

I was getting nowhere with the Board. The Chair put paid to whatever fantasies I'd conjured up today. I would find a way to swing the odds back in my favor, eventually, but that would take time that I simply didn't have. When I was ten-and-seven I dreamed of finding a means to end the Gods. Now I'd found that means, and if I was going to make good on my promise by the time I was ten-and-ten that meant ten-and-eight had to be one holy motherfuck of a year. To say nothing of ten-and-nine. All the holy motherfucks. I felt Sin mouth "motherfuck" in my mind. It wasn't going to happen if I kept adding up the same sums. The Doga clearly had something on the Chair, or more likely, something on all of the Board, and she was willing to call those debts due to save her life. That made sense. What didn't make sense— and true, I'd nothing to go on as of yet—was who wanted her dead so badly. And was it connected to the recent unrest in the streets? Of course it was. Which the Chair wanted me to look into. Several thousand thoughts began crowding in, but Sin held them back. Information first, theories later. All of that was well and good and true, even, but what tipped the scales, and I hated myself for it, was Eld.

Eld.

I'd always laughed at those who made fools of themselves for love and I'd no intention of being a fool, but set love aside for now: I needed my friend back, at the least.

I wasn't planning a damned life with Eld. Not yet. I just needed to get him comfortable sharing a gondola with me for longer than one Quarto's ride. Worry about the rest later. I didn't know where the Doga's case was going to lead, but this morning had ended in gunfire and a woman burned alive. I was willing to bet that the rest was going to be as bloody and violent, and there was no way Eld was going to let me have all the fun alone. Together we'd taken down the Ghost Captain and won seats on the most powerful trading company in the world. Together, with the Doga as a blade, we could win control of that company and then the Gods would be within my grasp.

It will work. It has to.

The world rushed back to greet me as Sin dropped his magic, and with it came a deep, coring hole within me. Hunger, of several kinds, and only one way to satiate it.

"You've a deal," I told the Doga. "Let's go find whatever batshit crazies are willing to blow themselves up to see you dead and give them a burial at sea with weights around their necks."

The Doga's eyes twinkled. "I think I'm going to enjoy this partnership, Buc."

"I was wrong, before," Sin said. "She makes me nervous, but you? Buc, you're terrifying."

We all three laughed.

9

"You dare to threaten me, Ulfren?" the Doga asked, talking past the burning at the back of her throat. Standing slowly so that the Veneficus, pale enough that his robes looked blacker than a moonless midnight, had to look up to meet her eyes, she leaned forward. "Within my own Palacio? After everything I've done for you and yours?"

"Not threaten, Your Grace," the mage said, showing his teeth in a way he likely meant to be reassuring, but made her want to signal her woman hid above to put a silver ball through him. The Doga worshipped the Dead Gods, but their servants had grown drunk with their blood in the millennia since the deities' slumber had begun. *Without Grandmama they'd never have had a bloody square span of Servenza, let alone half the Quarto their cathedral takes up. And without me—*

Ulfren's pallid features twisted as if the effort of being civil physically pained him. "I merely suggested that with the information we've passed to you on the Chair, it's time you made your move and returned the Kanados Trading Company to serving the Empire."

"Ulfren, you're from Normain," she said, not bothering to hide her smirk. "Speak plain: you want me to remove Ciris and her ilk from our island."

"To start," he agreed, running his long fingers through the fine hair, as pale as moonlight, that hung past his chin. He gripped it hard, nearly pulling a clump free. "We gave you enough on that old crone to see her unseated tomorrow."

"Aye, but that does nothing if the next Chair elected also serves the Sin Eaters," she reminded him. "We must weaken the Company as a whole, first. Then, when they are wounded, we'll go in for the kill."

She'd thought to deal the blow earlier, when she'd ordered a squad of her Secreto to send that girl and her brute of a partner to the bottom of the canals. Not just because she found their apparent interruption of the assassination attempt suspicious, but because it would force the Chair to hold elections for two new Board members to fill the sudden vacancies. *And I have just the arses to fill them.*

Her secret police were on edge now, having lost half a dozen of their brothers and sisters in a single operation. Only the captain knew Buc had killed them and wounded more. Had the others known the truth, the girl wouldn't have made it here alive. Still, the failed attack had confirmed what all the unbelievable rumors said was true: they were special. *Special, I can use.*

"Surely," she said, now that the silence had built, "your kind above all others can understand the value of patience. Our Gods breathed their last millennia ago, but here we kneel, faithful to their commands."

"The war goes poorly," he growled. "With the disappearance of one of our own, we must expend resources to find them."

"Who now?"

Ulfren's raw snarl sent a chill down her back. "Our brother in the Shattered Coast."

"I thought you found the Ghost Captain's body on the shore?"

"There were signs that he'd already left it," Ulfren said. He snorted. "Some believe he may still be alive, weakened in his new form, aye, but with the knowledge we need."

The Doga fought the urge to draw her robe tighter around her and nodded instead. Half of being a ruler was looming and the rest, wit, and she knew how to employ both to great effect. *Thanks again, Grandmama.*

"If you were going to find him, he'd have been found by now," she told the mage. His eyes flashed, but she waved his retort away with her hand. "He wasn't the only one on that beach, Ulfren. I let you watch my audience with the girl so you would know I serve faithfully, but since it wasn't clear enough, let me make it plain: Alhurra will give me everything after I've let her wrap herself around my thumb. I know her kind from the gutter, I see them at every Feast of Justice, when I pronounce judgments. Push her and she'll push back for no other reason than she can. But let her pull and she'll set the hook so deep within her she'll think it her own idea when I reel her in.

"I'll get the knowledge you seek, Ulfren, but in return you'll continue on as we've agreed. I need the Company wounded and I need you ready to move on the Sin Eaters when I give the command. I won't hear about lack of priests, not when I'm so close."

She allowed him a deep breath, then added before he could say anything else, "Do you understand?" He straightened, tall and whipcord thin, saying nothing, his expression reward enough.

"Yon's a firebrand in need of quenching," a voice growled in the Doga's ear.

She bit her cheek hard to keep from screaming, taking a partial breath to smooth her features before turning. The girl was a palm of steel that she needed to steer before it stabbed the wrong person, and the Dead Gods' priest a chipped stiletto that wanted refining, but this one was an unsheathed sword with blood still wet along the blade . . . and no way of knowing whose blood dripped from its length.

"He's a Veneficus," she said, studying the figure who stood in the shadows cast by the library shelves. "They're always like that."

"He thinks you weak, dependent upon his Gods," the woman countered, her voice rough and grating, like an unfinished blade plucked hot from the coals and drawn tight across the throat. She shifted, her jacket more of a cape that nearly hid her gender.

"If he does, he'll be disabused shortly."

"You really think the girl will bend to your whims?"

"No," the Doga said, surprising herself with the truth. "No, I don't think she will, but she may find the bastards who keep going for my throat." She left unsaid that either way, the Alhurra girl had a funeral in her future. *I need those seats.* "I've a feeling Ulfren and his kin will have their hands full with Ciris shortly," she continued. "After the events in the Shattered Coast, war is coming. Even without that, Ciris allowing her mages to provide healing with no strings attached will cut the Dead Gods' priests deep. That will keep him distracted."

"And if it doesn't?"

"Isn't that why you're here, my friend?"

The woman laughed, a sound harsh enough to make the Doga wince.

"Buc was the one you wanted, aye?" the Doga said. For a moment she considered sitting down again, but there was something in the figure opposite her that suggested caution. *Gods, I hate caution.*

"She was." The figure shifted, its wide-brimmed, slanting hat turning up slowly until a single, amber-glowing eye was revealed, staring at her. "Remember our agreement, Doga. You've made a lot of them today, but ours is the only one that matters. No matter how this plays out, the girl belongs to me!" Her voice rasped as if about to catch fire. "To Sicarii."

"Of course," the Doga said, mentally saying a prayer that her voice remained even. "You can have the slip of a girl."

The other laughed. "She's a slip that won't stay slipped, but by the end she'll find me. It's not in her nature to fail often, aye, or for long, and that will be her downfall." She grinned, her eye burning like a coal in the shadows. "You say she's mine, but if your Secreto had gone straight for the pair of them instead of taking the gondolier out first, she'd have belonged to the fish and I would have been deeply . . . upset." The word slipped from her tongue like poison dripping across a hot blade.

Something lurched in the Doga's chest, sending pins and needles and an overwhelming desire to vomit through her body. She
fought it back, tasting bile through clenched teeth she tried to form
into a smile, but the other's twisted lips told her she'd failed. She
swallowed hard, unable to find her breath.

"But leave that—as you said, I will have the girl. The Veneficus
will be back, Doga," she said, suddenly changing subjects as she
was wont to do. "This is one scrap caught between their teeth that
they won't let go. Can't let go. Then there's the Company to consider. Whispers say the Chair is thinking of making an offer that
the Empress—who sees war with Normain on the next wave—
can't refuse."

"You mean that the Company and the Sin Eaters should form
a merchant alliance to rule Servenza in the Empress's name, with
the Empress named Doga?" She wanted to laugh at Sicarii's startled look—it was the first she'd seen the creature discomforted.
"Next you'll tell me that you have heard whispers of the Chair's
infidelity to the Board. That she owns shares in several other companies, including a not insignificant holding in Normain's newest
start-up? That many would name her traitor to the Company, to
Servenza, to the Empress herself?" She didn't bother hiding her
smile or the heat in her voice. *The mages may be growing weaker,
but the Dead Gods provide. Always.*

"We may have an arrangement, you and I, but never forget I
ruled Servenza before you found your way to our canals and I'll
rule Servenza long after you're gone."

"An island surrounded by enemies," Sicarii said after a moment,
but her tone had shifted fractionally, acknowledging the Doga's
victory. "You may want to consider consolidating, begin building
your own power so that you—Servenza—can stand on her own,
free from Veneficus . . . or the Empire."

"Careful," the Doga hissed. She glanced around, but her guard
had mysteriously vanished, just as they had every time Sicarii paid
a visit to her private chambers. They'd reappear after Sicarii was

long gone, convinced they'd stood by her side the entire time though unable to recall any details. It made her wonder: If Sicarii could find her, alone in the chambers meant to keep her safe, were her family's secret passages actually secret anymore?

She needed to tread carefully with Sicarii. Sicarii had ideas, ideas that the Doga could use to shape the future of Servenza and her line in ways Grandmama never would have dreamed. *If we're careful. Caution. Again.*

"You never know who might be listening and that was close to treason."

"I know exactly who is listening," the other countered. "No one."

She licked her lips. "If I increase the size of the Constabulary or my Secreto, the Empress will become suspicious."

"You increased it by one just now," Sicarii said, pointing a gloved hand toward the chair opposite the Doga's.

"Buc? She wouldn't accept my offer of muscle, not with that hulking brute she had with her this morning, so I had to give her something . . . unless you know who is so desperate to see my throat slit?"

"Why wasn't her man with her now?"

Of course you don't know who has been trying so damned hard to kill me. Because all you care about are the answers you seek, to questions I can't ferret out. Yet. But I can't answer you if I'm dead. So why don't you see that? A thought slipped through her that perhaps Sicarii did know and simply didn't care.

Aware that the silence was lengthening, she said, "My eyes and ears indicate they often go their own ways."

"Find out," Sicarii said. "I want to know why Eld wasn't at her side." She made a noise in her throat.

"She's a means to an end. And at the end—you'll have her."

"I will," Sicarii growled.

She fell silent again and the Doga felt sweat pooling at the back of her gown where it tightened around her waist. "If there's a good reason for the recruitment," Sicarii continued, "she'll never blink an eye."

"P-pardon?"

"The Empress," Sicarii said, as if speaking to a simpleton.

Anger flashed through her. Sicarii often leapt around from topic to topic, then grew irritated when the Doga couldn't follow her twisted logic. Twisted, but brilliant. She swallowed the retort. "A good reason, you say? Like what?"

"I've put my finger to the pulse of the streets and there's something there," the figure rasped. "Something that we can use, you and I. War."

"Between the Gods?"

"No, though that's coming soon enough." Sicarii sounded pleased at the thought. "That will distract the Empress, but until then, I was thinking of something beneath her attention but well worth yours. A gang war."

"Gang wars are to be prevented," the Doga said. "There would be blood in the streets."

"Blood has a way of covering all manner of sins, Doga," Sicarii said. "Something that girl learned a long time ago and something you'd do well to learn now. You told her you understood what she wanted: power. I've a feeling you're kindred spirits, though yours may be more . . . Imperial."

Sicarii's laughter made her skin crawl as if in anticipation of a blade. *She knows.* But then, she'd known Sicarii knew from the first time the woman had appeared in her bedchamber with an actual blade to her throat and a finger pressed to her lips. Without this creature, her dream would have remained just that, but now, she had possibilities. Servenza had thrived under her rule; surely the Empire deserved that success writ large?

"Blood it is, then."

"It always is, sooner or late," Sicarii chuckled. "And Buc's will be last."

10

———— ⚬⚬⚬ ————

"I don't remember the streets being like this last time we were here," Eld said.

"Like what?"

"So . . . prickly," he said, sidestepping a woman who gave him a look that would have drawn blood if it had been a blade.

The streets were loud around us; the Quarto was coming to life as the noon sun began to break through the grey storm clouds of the previous day. I scratched absently at my left hand; the tear-shaped scars there felt as if they should hurt. I was damned if I knew how I came by them. Likely running on streets like these. The Painted Rock Quarto wasn't the Tip—fewer of the cobble-stones were gone and the buildings, though poor and missing plaster in many places, were still standing instead of leaning or fallen over. But it wasn't that far a run to the Tip, so most of the swirling humanity around us wore patched and ragged clothing. More than one pickpocket gave us a sharp glance before deciding that Eld's hand on his sword and the open blade I only half concealed against my wrist were more trouble than our purses were worth. In the Tip, any purse was worth the trouble, and trouble there often meant the crimson kind.

"Last you were here was when you ran into me. Almost three years ago, now," I reminded him.

"Aye, when you went for my purse, as I recall," he said.

Still, even here, there was a tension that I only recalled feeling once or twice when I'd called this Quarto home. One woman shouted an epithet at another, whose face was smeared with ash from one of the Dead Gods' rituals. A man in a torn coat shoved the shouting woman, and I caught a glimpse of his ash-streaked face before the crowd swallowed them and their religious argument. The Sin Eaters reaching out to the Dead Gods traditional congregants, the poor, was setting everyone on edge. Servenza had always been full of worshippers of both deities, but there'd been an uneasy alliance amongst the populace, something one didn't hear of from Normain or other places the Dead Gods' actual bones rested. Since this summer, that had disappeared.

"You were big and tall and sunburnt as fuck," I said, smiling at the memory.

"You thought me a rube," he laughed.

"I did," I admitted. "But you'd damned fast hands for them being the size of hams."

"They are not," he said, glancing down at them. "Few scars, sure, but we've all them."

"True." I scratched again at mine absently. When had I picked these up?

"These beggars are hard to find," Eld muttered, pausing on one of the few corners lacking a hawker to get a look down the alleyway that intersected it.

"And harder to buy," I agreed. We'd tried a few already, who had as much as told us to go fuck ourselves, albeit with a lot of bowing and scraping and knuckling of the forehead. A beggar might try to slit your throat, but they'd be polite doing it, in hopes you'd cough up a coin with your lifeblood. "Damn."

"Eh?" Eld glanced down.

"I remembered when I've felt this feeling before."

I plucked at my amber jacket, wool despite Salina's insisting that my clothing should be silk. Eld, who had taken her advice, had been shivering the whole morning. *Show me a noble and I'll show you a fool.* A common saying on the streets, though only whispered in the finer Quartos.

"The first time was right before Sister died and the second was after I slit Blood in the Water's throat," I said, dropping my voice. There were some who still remembered the old bitch, and no telling if those were fond memories or not. "It's the feeling of change, when rivalries flair and would-be leaders vie for control."

"War," Eld whispered.

"Aye, amongst the gangs." I remembered the scuffle from a moment before and added, "And the Gods, too."

He cursed and half drew his blade before letting it slide back into its sheath. "No wonder we're drawing every eye . . . everyone's wondering which side we're on, which God we bend our knees to—we'd do not to linger. How long did the Doga say we had to find who wants her dead?"

"She didn't." *Before the Chair forces me to choose between you and my dreams.* I shrugged. "I'm assuming we have until whoever it is succeeds? I imagine a corpse would have a hard time honoring her half of the bargain."

Eld cursed again and blushed when a passing man shunted the girl-child with him—probably his daughter—to his other side with a recriminating look that softened when he took in Eld's frame. "We'd better be about it, then. If the next attempt is like the last, we may not have that long."

"Aye," I grunted. I had felt the phantom heat of the flames spouting from the would-be assassin when she went up. "A few paces closer and she'd have taken the guard and likely caught the Doga's dress on fire."

"Ugly, that," Eld said.

"I saw a lamplighter once, that happened to," I said. "Plying her trade. A coal fell off her pole and landed in her skirts and she didn't realize until it was too late."

"How'd she not see that falling?"

"Just lit the lamp," I told him. "Night blind and it was a windy night, so when she went, she went fast."

Two of the Constabulary, dressed in their powder uniforms,

strode by us with a grunted, "Citizens," but not pausing and observably not looking at anything around them, which seemed both disconcerting and wise. *Something is definitely afoot.*

"That woman went fast, too," Eld commented.

"Aye, I'd've given a pretty coin to have been able to investigate her corpse." Now it was my turn to curse. "And I could have, if we'd stayed."

"We didn't know if the Doga's guards were going to assume we were part of it," Eld reminded me.

"After saving her life?"

"There's an old soldier's trick," Eld said, speaking slowly, bright eyes shooting down to study mine, then flicking away. When I didn't stiffen at his mention of his time in the army, he continued, talking faster. "Let the enemy rout a small number of troops, maybe not even a small number, and set an ambush farther back. Then, when they relax their guard, thinking the battle done and dusted, you hit them hard."

"Risky," I whistled. "What if the routing troops don't stop? Or if they infect your ambush with fear and they all rout?"

"Always a possibility," he agreed. "But if you've veteran troops with nerve and can pull it off, you're practically assured victory."

"So probably just as well we didn't stick around," I mused. "But I'd still like to know what set her off."

A newspaper crier called out the big story from around the corner. Deeper into the Quarto, another voice, higher in pitch, took up the cry and farther off, another, like a group of gulls sounding out where the fish had gathered.

"I'd settle for finding someone willing to do more than glare at us," Eld said. "We should have started closer to the canal."

"Why?" I asked him. "You want to find that dilapidated flat we called home?" We had lived in half a dozen in the years we'd been friends, most along the canal, where the smells wafting from the edge of the Painted Rock Quarto kept the prices down. The last had been nice, a place I'd fancied we could one day own outright.

It would have fit into the drawing room and library of our palazzo. Sometimes I wondered what happened to the girl who was excited about that tiny apartment.

"She didn't dream big enough," Sin said.

"She dreamed big enough to capture you," I reminded him, and he fell silent.

"I didn't know you were so nostalgic," I told Eld.

"I'm not, at least not about that," he said. "Only now I'm remembering why you always kept us on that side of the Rock. We're beginning to attract the wrong kind of attention, Buc," he added softly.

"I told you not to wear silk," I muttered, following his gaze to where three urchins in brown jackets and mismatched trousers stood in an alley. Ostensibly they were tossing bits of driftwood and betting on the cast, but I saw them sneaking glances our way, and their jackets, while rough, were too uniform to be anything but a gang's colors. One's eye was blackened and another tossed her driftwood with a limp shoulder, but I could see bulges beneath their ragged jackets that indicated they were armed and clearly ready to fight again.

The newspaper criers sounded once more, and one farther in, where the Painted Rock would turn toward the true Tip of Servenza, caught my ear. "Lucky for you, I've a plan," I told Eld.

"Does it involve us beating up children?"

"It most certainly does not," I told him in a mock shocked tone that made him roll his eyes. "At least, it doesn't if we move."

"When?"

"Now."

"Where?"

"There." I pointed toward the Tip.

"But that's deeper into this mess, Buc," Eld said, following my finger.

"Aye, but there's a paper out there calling my name. Unless you'd rather fight?"

"You know I wouldn't. I just don't see how we're best served moving into an even rougher part of the Quarto. We should have come in disguise."

"I thought you swore off disguises after the Downing incident."

"I—I'd forgotten that," Eld admitted. His face darkened again and well it should, as he'd been a thin pair of cotton underpants away from showing half of Frilituo his most private parts. Neither of us had realized Downing wasn't a doctor but a male prostitute famed for his ability to maintain an erection no matter how distracting the moment . . . and the lady's betrothal party had come prepared to distract. Eld saw my face and stiffened and I couldn't keep the laughter from bubbling up.

"He still cares for you," Sin said suddenly, his words cutting through my mind.

"Why do you say that?" I felt my laughter catch in my chest.

"He looks at you more often than anything else, including those gang urchins—who are following us, by the way—and I've not seen him smile this much in a while."

I didn't dare to believe Sin, but he was right that things felt lighter between us than they had in weeks. Maybe it wouldn't be such a bad thing if that gang did try us. . . .

"I thought it was you."

"Signorina," Quenta said, dropping the papers in her hands.

"Surprised to see me?" I asked.

"I-it's not often those of your station come to this Quarto," the girl said, falling to her knees to collect the scattered newspapers.

"Here, let me help," Eld said, bending over her. Quenta looked up through her knotted gold locks and squeaked, turning a shade that matched Eld's red collar.

"Only one or two got wet," he added. "And we'll buy those from you, since Buc here was the cause of you dropping them."

"Easy with the accusations," I told him. "You didn't waste

time hoarding that coin, did you, lass?" Quenta managed an even deeper shade when she met my eyes. "Might have been a little too enthusiastic."

"The seamstress said this was the latest fashion," the girl said quickly, dropping another paper as she touched the edge of her new jacket. When I'd last seen her, she'd been in the thread-bare greys of most criers and messengers, but now she wore a jacket nearly the same cut as mine. The fabric, though truly fine, was a shade of yellow close enough to that of a gold lira that it was borderline garish. Her trousers were tight and a little short, but unpatched and a black dark enough that it'd take a few months for sun and rain to fade them to grey. Her boots, trimmed in faux gild that caught the sunlight, put her over the top.

"With these clothes I can sell my papers in the nicer Quartos," she concluded.

"Your maestro give you permission to have a corner there?"

"He will! When he sobers enough to see I've come up in the world," Quenta said.

"Uh-huh. Until then, how'd you like to earn another coin?"

"I ain't heard nothing what you were asking of," she said. "It's only been a couple of suns since you asked!"

"Easy, lass," Eld said, standing up with an arm full of news-papers. "You don't have to shout, Buc's not interrogating you."

"That's her normal voice," I said.

"Oh."

"Aye." I sighed. "I just need to know who is running the head beggars' guild these days," I told Quenta, turning back to her. She took the stack of papers from Eld, avoiding his eyes while her ears turned pink. "And where they can be found."

"B-beggars guild runs out of the Tip," Quenta said. A man in an orange-and-green plaid coat that was so patched with other colors the plaid was beginning to look like a rainbow interrupted to slip her a copper and take a paper. "Thank you, sirrah!" she called after him.

"The Mosquitoes," she said out of the corner of her mouth, "have their hall, well, it's an alley, really, along the Foreskin."

"I beg your pardon," Eld hissed.

"What?"

"The Mosquitoes call their home the Foreskin?" Eld snorted. "Gods, I can't believe I just said that sentence in front of a young woman."

"I'm not offended," I said.

"Not you. Her!"

"And here I thought you were being a gentleman," I mocked. Quenta giggled. "The Foreskin is what locals call the southern bend of the Tip, where it curves down and hangs a bit," I explained.

"And the Mosquitoes are what beggars call themselves," Quenta added. "They name themselves that, sirrah, because they only take a little bit at a time, but enough of them take and it adds up." Eld's face was still crimson from a moment before, but he laughed at that.

"She's not wrong," I said. "I read a book on the Northern Wastes, about where the Quando clans lay claim. The author said that in the late spring, when the bogs have unfrozen, the mosquitoes come out in swarms large enough to eat horses alive. Even griffins have been known to fly south until true summer arrives."

Eld whistled. "Mosquitoes, eh?"

"Aye, but that presents another problem," I said.

"What's that?"

"You. You can't walk into the Tip in all that silk, not unless you're heading straight for a brothel, and even then you'd want to have half a dozen others with you for, uh, moral support," I said, glancing down at Quenta.

"You're joking."

"She en't," Quenta said.

"Well, you can't go alone. Not to the Foreskin. I'm coming with you," Eld said.

"That's what all the prostitutes say."

Quenta burst out laughing and Eld's face turned purple.

"You can come along," I said, "but it's going to need something."

"W-what?" Eld asked, his voice still tight from my joke.

"A disguise."

Eld went apoplectic.

"For a gentleman, he sure knows a lot of curse words," Quenta said in an awed voice.

"It's a failing," I agreed. Eld's tongue tripped him up and he began choking out gibberish, which was probably just as well, given Quenta's presence. "A real failing."

11

"This is turning into a Godsdamned waste of a day!"

"Hey, at least you're comfortable," Eld grumbled. "I knew we should have gone to a proper tailor and not that thirdhand thrift hawker—this coat is too short." He fought to cross his arms and the grey wool made an ominous tearing sound. "And too damned tight."

"That's because you've too much muscle, which I've never heard you complain about before. Besides, there's an upside you're missing."

"Aye, and what's that?" he asked.

"It shows off your arse to great effect."

"Pardon?"

"You don't have to apologize to me," I said. "Come on," I added, slapping him hard on the butt.

"Buc!"

"Do you always call my name when a woman slaps you?"

"Buc!" he rasped.

"Don't worry, I won't ask you what they say when you do. Wouldn't be polite."

I kept walking, and after a moment he caught up with me, his face a study in marble that gave nothing away, but I noticed a trickle of sweat on his brow despite the gusty wind that had returned. Even in our woolens, we stood out here, where every third person wore rags and the rest a hodgepodge of stained, patchwork jackets, trousers, and dresses.

Women wore trousers not because of fashion but out of necessity; many wore faded army pantaloons from a few campaigns back, paired with ill-fitting sandals in place of boots. They gave us a wide berth and an even wider one to a small group of nobles who laughed uproariously as they marched down the center of the street, hands on swords or pistoles, faces ruddy from drink. Either getting an early start or a late walk home.

I stepped in a puddle and bit back a curse at the acrid stench of urine that rose from it. It hadn't been a feast day yesterday, but when the sea storms broke that hard upon Servenza there was little to do but batten down the hatches and wait it out, and all work stopped as a consequence. This being Servenza, nothing stopped the drinking. Or the whoring. Or the begging. We'd tramped all through the Foreskin—much to Eld's chagrin—and seen not a scrap of beggars. The motley collection of folks who leaned against hovels along the harbor front or sat on rickety porches of homes missing windows or, in some cases, roofs, claimed not to know where the Mosquitoes were—despite the coin we'd implied was in it for them. None of them were begging either. Drunk or sleeping it off or too poor to have done either and sullen for it, not a single one could tell us where all the fucking beggars had begged off to.

"It's enough to make me want to tear these clothes off, make a bonfire of them, and scream," I muttered.

"Now that might get their attention," Eld agreed. "But I'm not sure if yon ladies of the night would appreciate the competition."

I almost asked him if he would appreciate it, but that was a canal too far. I'd already pushed him as hard as I could and, from the tautness in his shoulders, he half wanted to storm away. *But you can't leave me now, Eld. Not here.* I smiled at that, put my arm through his, and steered him up Redlight Row. Here the cobblestones weren't missing and the houses had fewer holes, and all had roofs. The Tip was the latrine of Servenza and used as such, but none wanted to fuck where they shat, so here, at least, was a modicum of decency. The whole Quarto set a fire within me . . . if not for a few stray chances seized upon, this could have been my home. Nearly was, until Eld found me.

"Now home is a place famed for the perfumed air of the trees," Sin said.

"I'm not going to feel guilty about success," I told him. "Not when it means I've a chance to give every soul here what I have today."

"Do you really believe that?"

"You know I do."

"I know you think you do, but you really believe that you'll destroy the pillar that is Ciris, the pillar that the world is built upon, and suddenly lire will rain from the sky and everyone will live happily ever after?"

"I'm not a fool," I growled. "There is no happily ever after—but there will be a chance. Something we've never had, thanks to the Gods. And now your religious war threatens to destroy us all. Ciris is no pillar . . . she's a chain around our necks. No, killing her and the Dead Gods won't fix this," I agreed.

A small boy, half-naked and pallid from the cold despite his bronzed skin, darted amongst the nobles ahead of us. They were making for one of the houses, where half a dozen men and a few women in scraps of silk and lace stood invitingly. Another child played with a headless doll, her look so vacant I hoped she was gazing on another reality.

"Your Gods don't care about the Painted Rock Quarto or the Foreskin or the Tip—they probably find the names amusing and proof of these people's lot in life. But I'm going to disabuse them, Sin. All of them. I've already started with you."

"How did you arrive at that conclusion?" he asked. His presence was ash and sparks in my mind. He hated everything I'd just said.

But you didn't call me a liar.

"Because you know I'm right and you're listening, aren't you? Enough." I cut him off. "We've a Mosquito to find."

"Eld."

He glanced down at Buc's harsh tone and arched his eyebrows.

"It's me." Buc's voice grew deeper, more languid, and Eld felt his breath hiss between his teeth. "Sin."

"I—I thought we agreed you weren't going to do this again," Eld growled.

"I hadn't planned on it," Sin said, his words coming through Buc's mouth sending gooseflesh down Eld's arms. "Yesterday, between saving the Doga's life and then saving our own, I used too much of my magic. The wards I placed around Buc's mind faltered in one or two places."

"The places your magic can't heal?"

"I could fix them"—Sin's voice grew frustrated—"if she allowed me to Possess her."

"She'd rather die first."

"Which is why I haven't been able to fix her mind. Not completely. Your not keeping up your end of our . . . arrangement hasn't helped either."

"The fuck I haven't," Eld snarled. A would-be hawker, who'd stepped away from the tattered canopy she'd rigged against a pitted, grey building, saw his face and threw him a hasty curtsy before ducking back amongst her rusted pots and pans. "You said if I told her the truth, like I did the last time, that you wouldn't be able to contain the madness in the broken part of her mind."

"True," Sin said.

"So I haven't told her the truth. I've kept my distance." That last tore at him. Mages had killed everyone he was supposed to protect, they'd tried to kill Buc and him half a dozen times, and he hated magic to his core. *I don't hate you, Buc. I should have told you that as soon as we touched Servenza's shore.* Only then, he had thought that she needed space—and he certainly did, if his newfound feelings for her were to cool. She needed a friend, not some doe-eyed schoolboy. After the fire he'd realized his mistake, but it was too late. So Sin said, and Eld was forced to take him at his word.

"Aye, but you're a terrible liar," Sin said. "Every time the fire is brought up, your presence seems to remind her of what happened and threatens to send her back to the wreck she was after."

"We can't allow that." Eld swallowed the lump in his throat. Finding Buc's still form buried under burning rubble had been the scariest moment of his life. Scarier than watching his friends and comrades destroyed by magic and his folly. Scarier than feeling the creeping death of the Ghost Captain's spell as it turned him into a mindless Shambles. Or so he'd thought. Until she awoke a week later and the raving began. "What do you want me to do?"

"Keep your distance. Aye," Sin snapped, "I know you've been trying, but it's not enough. You need to find a reason why you shouldn't be at her side constantly. A reason she'll believe. Maybe that Lucrezia?"

"I fucking hate you," Eld muttered.

"But you love her," Sin whispered, and hearing those words on Buc's lips, her emerald eyes boring into his, Eld felt his heart burst from half a dozen emotions. He nodded. "Then try harder," Sin said, grinding Buc's teeth. "I'm not sure I can erase her memory again."

"I'm never not going to be there for Buc," Eld said, his cheeks flushing. They both knew what Buc would think if she knew the truth . . . because Eld had told her the truth once before. "You told me to hold her at arm's length, to not talk about your magic, to play the fool. I've done that. Yet here you are, saying you can't protect her. If you can't protect her, Sin, then I will."

"I am protecting her," Sin said. "Without completing the ritual I'm not as powerful as I should be. I need time, and with the Doga's offer and the Chair's new threats I don't have that luxury."

"The Chair's new threats?" Eld asked. *Buc didn't say anything about that.* He frowned. "You mean telling the Dead Gods we offed the Ghost Captain?"

"What else?" Sin asked. "I know you don't trust me, but we both care for Buc, Eld. Do this and with enough time, I'll find a way to fix her, but until then . . ." Buc sighed. "I've got to go before she realizes what's wrong. Her mind is the strongest, most pain-in-the-arse of its kind I've ever encountered." Grudging admiration softened his tone.

"What can I do?" Eld asked.

"She needs food, or rather I do," Sin said. "Plenty of it. And for you to keep any mention of the fire from her."

Eld studied the short woman at his side, black braids piled down one side, scalp shaved bare on the other, dark, delicate features in sharp relief beneath the amber jacket and trousers that were tight enough that he had to look away before his mind wandered. He wasn't fast enough, looking away, to not see Sin in her eyes. Buc was infected and he wasn't sure a cure existed. Until he found one he'd have to trust the creature lurking beneath her skin.

"I'll do what I can," Eld said, finally. *I'm sorry, Buc.* "Anything for her."

"Well, are you going to tell me?" Eld asked.

His question passed through my mind, dispersing the sudden fog that had clouded it. *Where are we?* A woman sauntered past, her skirts clean and bright, marking her out where every other soul I could see wore rags. Beyond her and the row of collapsed hovels I could see the faint glow that indicated brothels nearby. Redlight Row?

"Tell you what?" I couldn't remember. The headache building along my temples was a now-familiar feeling. Something was wrong with me. With my mind.

"You said you'd enough of these liars and you'd a plan to find these beggars here and now."

"Beggars?" I pulled up beside a building with a half-worn-away painting of a clog on its door. "What nonsense are you spouting, Eld?"

"Buc, if you're having a go—" Eld glanced down and frowned, his bright eyes dark with concern. "It was your idea to speak to the beggars after one of their own murdered the Doga's look-alike. For all the good it's done us so far," he muttered. "And then you said you had an idea that might lead to answers we couldn't find on our own."

"When?"

"Just now . . . don't you remember?"

"I—" My mind was a blank. I remembered this morning, sharp as a paper fresh off the press: the Painted Rock Quarto, Quenta and the Mosquitoes, and our plan to search the Tip. But the moment before this one was a fog that kept slipping through my fingers no matter how I grasped at it. Sin?

"I remember us leaving Joffers at the canal at noon," Sin said. "But past that, I don't think we've done much beyond walk the streets awhile."

"Noon was hours past," I reminded him.

"I know," he said slowly, "but I don't know what else we did. Which is strange."

"Is this like last time?" I asked.

"No—that was truly strange," he said. "I still don't know how we ended up in the middle of the Crescent in that boat."

"Or where the blood came from?"

"Or where the blood came from," he admitted. "At least it wasn't ours."

"I'm fine," I told Eld, whose worry creases had grown deeper in the wake of my silence. "Just testing you," I lied, forcing a laugh that I didn't feel. My head hurt, but the ache was dissipating. He smiled uncertainly and I touched his elbow, which provided the distraction I knew it would. "I think I just lost my line of thought there, for a moment. Probably need some lunch."

"After that lot you put down before we left the Painted Rock Quarto?" Eld asked. "Gods, Buc, you ate enough of that hot pepper fish and bread for three."

Now that he said it, I did feel a little full, but I needed the energy for Sin's magic. *Magic.* "Can you use your magic to figure out what the fuck's going on?"

"On it," Sin whispered back.

I stepped hard on the fear in my mind and it squished out along the edges, filling me with a dread that made my mouth twist. My intellect had gotten us this far. And Eld's brawn. And a little bit of luck. All right, a lot of luck. For all that, it began with my mind, and now the sharpest blade I owned was losing its edge.

"We'll figure it out," Sin told me. That made feel a little better; if I couldn't lie to him without him knowing it, at least he couldn't lie to me either.

"We walked Redlight Row," Eld said patiently. "Asked a few of the whor—prostitutes, but they said they haven't seen a beggar in a fortnight." He frowned. "They didn't seem to find that strange."

"Given the atmosphere, I'm not surprised," I said.

"So you do remember?"

"Of course," I lied. Fuck it. Digging into one of my inside pockets, I pulled out a gold lira, buffed it quickly against my sleeve until it shone, and held it up high, so that it caught the afternoon's waning light. "Piece of gold to the first of you lot that can tell me aught of the beggars known as the Mosquitoes!" I shouted.

"Blood of the Gods, Buc!" Eld reached inside his jacket where I knew he kept a rotating-barreled pistole. Half the street had turned at my words and several of the more ragged types had come to a complete stop, gazes fixed on the coin in my hand. It represented a month's wages to some, perhaps more. "Are you trying to get us killed?"

"Full lira to the lucky one what tells me what I want to know!" I glanced at Eld. "I'm done playing games."

"Are you?" he hissed. "Because this seems like a game to me. A damned stupid one."

"You wound me, Eld." Still, my arm had been up for more than a moment now and I was worried I might have been a bit too hasty.

"You don't say," Sin snorted.

A woman strode past, her legs shown off to great effect by tight, bloodred trousers tucked into dark, calf-high leather boots, and the rest of her figure obscured by a long, green jacket that flared at the waist. She plucked the coin from my hand, tanned fingers flashing in the sun, long, unbraided locks swirling in the wind so her face was obscured. "Done and done," she said throatily. "The Mosquitoes were overrun by an upstart guild a fortnight ago. Those that didn't end up in the Crescent"—she jerked her long brimmed hat in the direction of the bay—"fell in with them."

"So, a gang war," Eld said.

"A guild war," I corrected him. "Not uncommon for the Tip. Who is them?" I asked her.

"The Gnats."

"The Gnats overwhelmed the Mosquitoes?" Eld asked.

"Your friend seems a simple type," the woman said.

"He is," I agreed. "You have my coin," I reminded her. "Where can we find the Gnats?"

"Three or four streets over there's an old factory that serves as a gambling den these days. Can't miss it. Head back up toward the base of the Tip and it's the fourth alley on your right. Savvy?"

"Aye." She dipped her hat, her hair still hiding her features, and kept walking, a slight limp to her step. A strange, spice-like aroma seemed to follow her. Or maybe I'd just burped up some of that fish from lunch.

"Should have done that an hour ago," I told Eld.

"I'm not going to remind you that I suggested a similar plan," he told me, shaking his head. Luckily he took my impertinence as part and parcel of who I was and not another missing memory. "Although I'd something more circumspect in mind."

"You can't be circumcised when it comes to the Foreskin," I said.
"I—I—"

"Uh-huh," I told him, brushing past and pulling him along by the arm. "Am speechless when confronted by my brilliance, I know." Eld said something that made one of the prostitutes we were passing blush and I laughed so hard he had to hold me up as we walked. "Come on," I said when I finally found my breath. "Let's go squash a gnat."

12

"I'd have thought they'd have the factories working double time after that storm," Eld said.

"It is a bit quiet," I agreed.

We stood beneath a lamppost that had no lamp—it had probably been stolen, who knew how many seasons past—looking down the street at several factories, including the one that the stranger had pointed out as being a gambling den. Most factories were in the Mercarto Quarto, but there were others sprinkled throughout Servenza, though any this deep in the Tip were likely to be sweatshops. They should have been bright with activity, but the windows were boarded over and the chimneys cold. The street was emptier than the ones we'd left, despite several carts set up to cater to workers with bread and soup. The aroma was enough to make me simultaneously glad I'd already eaten and horrified that I might have eaten something as rotten as whatever they were selling.

"Likely something to do with the gangs," I said after a moment.

Eld grunted agreement, detaching himself from the post. Three children in clean but faded threadbare clothing ran past, the lead one whooping that the last to catch them would turn into a gull—which seemed a good thing to turn into if you wanted to escape. The rest were hard on his heels, but the girl in the middle pulled up with a squeak that made him stop and turn. She and the deep-tanned boy beside her stared at me. She whispered something and the boy nodded. The taller one sketched a bow.

"Pardon, signorina, sirrah, she didn't mean no harm. C'mon, Zul," he growled. "Don't be staring, no matter the finery."

"No, it's her," the girl said. "She's the one."

"The one what?"

"The one from the burned factory."

Eld half stepped between us, but I stilled him with a touch on his arm when I saw the boy's eyes widen, the whites bright against his dark skin. *He recognizes me. How?* This time he took the time for a proper bow.

"Signorina, ye shouldn't be here." He coughed hard, phlegm rattling in his throat, and added, "It's dangerous."

"Because of the gangs, aye?" I shrugged and let the thin stiletto I'd palmed dance across the backs of my fingers in a flash of steel. "I appreciate the tip, lad, but we can take care of ourselves."

"The gangs and more besides," the boy said.

The girl said, "They's in the—"

"Zul!" he hissed, spinning on her. "Enough—less you want the streets to hear?" The thin boy, mute, grasped at her arm, but she shrugged it off, opening her mouth defiantly. "No," the first boy warned. He turned back to me. "We know what you done, signorina, but this street's gone bad today, savvy?"

"I do," I told him. What I savvied was that somehow I'd gathered a reputation amongst the street urchins as one who paid out coin. I wondered which of my informants had loose lips. Quenta? She was the newest and her new clothes spoke volumes even if her lips didn't. Apparently none of them told them the other side of that coin: you could end up in alley with your throat cut wide like Habert. "And thank you for the warning, lad, but I only give coin out when I'm the one doing the asking. Savvy?"

"What's she talking about, B—?"

"Zul, leave it," the boy said. He shook the frizzy, black hair out of his eyes and shrugged. "Didn't ask for handouts, signorina, just paying debts is all. Gods watch you . . . whichever you serve," he said, the last added hastily as if it were still new to his lips.

"And you," Eld said, and then they ran off down the street, Zul already making the harsh cawing sounds of a gull by the time they turned the corner. "What was that about?" Eld asked.

"I think I'm going to have to have a word with Quenta about discretion," I muttered. I explained my reasoning and Eld nodded slowly. Sin made a noise in my mind but I ignored him. Sin didn't trust anyone, which was something I could get behind, but these kids were no more a threat than Quenta had been.

"I don't think that's what this was," Sin said.

"Then what?"

He was silent.

"Uh-huh. Let's find these beggars and be quick about it," I told him.

"I don't know," Eld said as we passed the dark doors of the gambling hall, "maybe those children were right." He tried to pull his coat down farther, but it rode right back up and he threw his hands into the air. "This better have not been a waste of time, Buc, you know I hate disguises."

"Shh, I'm counting," I told him. Not that I needed to concentrate, but there's nothing worse than a man's whinging. Eld wasn't usually given to that particular fault, unless he was sick—show me a man who doesn't turn into a mewling baby at the first sign of a sniffle—but the coat was getting to him, apparently.

"We're fine; if folks are frightened off the streets, that just means we're less likely to get our pockets picked. This alley's the one," I added, pointing at the black, yawning mouth in front of us.

"I don't know how it managed to find so many shadows," Eld muttered.

I tried not to roll my eyes but he had a point; it was dark between the buildings even though the afternoon's sun was just beginning to slip from the sky. "More to the point," I said, "there should be some lookouts, even if the streets are quiet. Especially then."

"Maybe the Gnats got what the Mosquitoes did," Eld said. "What's the next level down from a Gnat?"

"Bite-me."

"Beg pardon?"

"Bite-mes," I told him. "Smaller than a gnat, but I think you'd have to go pretty far south, as far as the Cordoban Confederacy, to find any." Number 286. Semsin's *Flying Insects and Their Proclivities.* The twisted alleyway bent out of sight, likely running between the buildings of this street and the next, which made it a sensible meeting place for beggars. I took a step and my foot came down in another puddle that splashed all over my trousers.

"Gods, that smell." Eld retched. "Was that—?"

"Day-old piss?" I growled. "Aye, well, there's a pair of boots ruined."

"Now I'm thankful for this damned short coat," Eld muttered.

"If you keep moaning about that jacket, Eld, I'll begin to think you're—"

Something slid against metal with a grinding sound and my ears burned as Sin flared his abilities, heightening my senses so that I heard the sound a pistole's firing mechanism made when the wheels spun.

"Down!"

I pushed him so hard he tripped backward, caught himself against the edge of the building, and swung out of sight. With Sin's abilities trained elsewhere, my momentum and the day-old piss made me slip and I fell flat on my arse.

The pistole erupted in the darkness, an explosion of fire and thunder, the roar replaced by a high-pitched ringing that took my Sin-enhanced hearing with it. Something angry tore the air over my head, right where I'd been standing. The plume of smoke obscured faces, but I could still see half a dozen pairs of legs rushing toward me. I put a hand down for leverage—right into the piss puddle—and growled. *You motherfuckers.*

"Sin!"

"On it," he spat.

Slingshot into the pack to break them, twin stilettos when they do, and then we dance.

"And I will call the tune," I muttered.

My muscles burned with magic and I went from arse-on-the-ground to standing in a single motion, hands a blur as I found my slingshot by feel. My other hand plucked at the pouch hanging from my belt and a lead ball fell into it. I couldn't see the attackers now but Sin showed me where they should be in my mind's eye, based on the glance I'd had of their legs.

I let lead fly.

A man shouted and I felt him fall in the smoky darkness, the impact of his body against the street reverberating through my piss-soaked boots, relayed to me by Sin. I let fly again. And again. One last shot and then I felt the vibrations change as they broke. I dropped my slingshot into a pocket and reached for my blades. *Left, away from the entrance, use the wall as leverage, and come back across.* I flipped the stiletto in my left hand so that I held it with an overhand grip. Ice-picking all the way.

Someone fired another pistole, a bright flash and bang, this one smaller than the first, but they were still firing at where I'd been standing when this all started. I laughed and one of them turned toward me, but it was too late. My eyes burned, Sin pushing my pupils wider than humanly possible, taking my ringing hearing with it. I saw a lad a few years younger than myself rushing toward me, swinging a glass-studded club. He didn't see me until it was too late and I let him run onto the end of my blade. He tried to scream but I'd already buried the knife in his throat so all that came out was a throaty gurgle and a spray of hot blood that coated my face.

I slammed my head into the bridge of his nose, knocking him back to free my blades, and spun. *Wall.* I kicked off and flew back across the alley, using my shoulder to send a shorter figure stumbling to the ground, then leapt onto the back of a tall man in a tattered cloak. Wrapping my legs around his waist, I ice-picked him half a dozen times through the top of the shoulder, severing the artery that lay there while my other blade found a home in his groin. Screaming, the man tumbled to the ground. I rolled free just as Eld appeared in the alleyway, a pistole in each hand.

"'Bout time you showed up!"

"Aye, better late than never," he said with a grin that didn't touch his eyes. A pistole bucked in his fist, belching flame, and I heard another body hit the cobblestones behind me. Something flew through the air, whistling past my shoulder, and broke, with the sound of shattering glass, in the puddle I'd stepped in moments earlier. "Missed!" he shouted. Then a wall of flame erupted from the puddle and Eld's shout was drowned in a fiery roar.

Fuck.

"Nooo!" The scream tore at my throat as I leapt from the dead or dying man and onto the figure that had tossed the grenado. The girl went down beneath my weight with a scream, her hands struggling to push me back, but fighting was not new to me even before Sin. I caught her arm, smaller than my own, at the elbow, and pulled it into my armpit, twisting until I felt the bone break. The girl screamed again, her gilded shirt tearing and fountaining blood from where Sin and I had nearly torn her arm completely off. *You tried to murder Eld.* She screamed and I howled.

We rolled over on the cobblestones, the girl shrieking and clawing at my face with her good hand, me red with rage and filled with Sin's magic. When we came to a stop, with me atop her, I'd already buried the blade in my right hand in her guts. I felt her body jerk beneath my own, the whites of her eyes and her gilded shirt the only colors I could make out in the blackness of the alley. I stabbed her again. *Eld.* And again. And again. I didn't stop.

Eld's roar brought me to. He flew through the guttering wall of flames, tripped over the man I'd killed, and sent the last one—a thickset man in a dirty bowler—spinning against the wall with a grunt. "I. Hate. This. Effing—!" Eld twisted around, shedding his jacket, which was now on fire in several places. "Coat!"

He wrapped the last attacker in the smoldering fabric, took a step back, leveled his pistole, and pulled the trigger. My vision went with the muzzle flash, but I didn't need to see to feel the thump as the man fell.

"You know," I panted, pushing myself up to one knee, "you might be onto something with these disguises."

Eld slumped to the ground beside me, pistoles resting on his knees. "N-now you listen?" he gasped.

"Better late than never?" He chuckled and I joined him, adrenaline setting our limbs to shaking.

13

The flames from the grenado died, leaving behind an acrid scent of gunpowder and something . . . spicy? in its wake. I glanced around, taking in the scene now that everything had calmed down. Sin gave me a little bit of magic, so I could see clear as on a bright morning despite the shadows. Blood ran in pools from the lad with the glass-studded club. More blood, growing cold, reached my right hand where I leaned back on the cobblestone; it was from the man I'd butchered. Farther back, I saw the mostly headless torso of the one Eld had shot, and beyond that, the marks left by the first I'd downed with my slingshot. He'd run off in the mayhem, but I wasn't in the mood to go chasing. Let him tell the story—maybe that'll make them think twice next time.

I was avoiding looking at the body beside me. I could still feel the ferocity of that violence in my limbs, the phantom sensation of ramming a blade through another. I'd killed before. Gods, this summer I'd killed enough to make a small army . . . but most of those had already been dead, I'd just been helping them stay dead. This was another matter. A bunch of children led by some foolhardy adults who'd targeted the wrong pair and paid the price. But it was more than that. I had a Goddess's magic now and that granted me power I'd never known before. The power to tear a girl limb from limb.

"Only after she nearly killed Eld," Sin reminded me.

"True, and I don't regret killing her," I whispered mentally. "Just the way I did it was . . ."

"Awesome? In the true sense of the word," he added quickly.

I felt a shiver run down my back. "I was going to say frightening."

I took a deep breath and caught a note of that strange spice, a scent similar to cinnamon, but sharper. I recognized it immediately: the same smell the woman assassin gave off when she burned alive trying to kill the Doga.

"Not a mistake, then," I said aloud.

"What's that?" Eld's gaze was on me, his mouth twisted in concern.

"This," I said, gesturing around, "was no accident." I explained about the flames and Eld nodded thoughtfully. "Lucky I shoved you out of the way, Eld, or you'd have more than singed eyebrows."

"Are they?" He put a hand to his eyes. "Are they singed?"

"Blacker than my own," I confirmed. I snorted. "You're fine, you vain bastard."

"Not vain," he muttered, still feeling his eyebrows cautiously. "Just mindful."

I grinned and he smiled and then we both laughed. *All right, let's find out what these corpses can tell us.* I levered myself up, preparing for what I knew I'd see, and looked at the girl I'd killed.

The laughter died on my lips.

"Quenta."

"Damn it," Eld muttered, cursing softly, bitterly. He squeezed my shoulder. "This isn't your fault, Buc."

"Why would I ever think it was?" I asked him. "I didn't set her on this path, she chose where to set her boots." I glanced at the garish pair she'd bought with my lira and sighed. "The real question, Eld, is: Was she bought before I ran into her in that storm, or after?"

"Did someone lay a deep trap for you or have they been following you close all along?"

"That's it," I agreed. "I'm going to have to be more careful in how I handle my informants moving forward."

"I'll handle them," he suggested.

"No, you won't, they're mine."

"But why?"

"Because."

Because as strong as your arm is, mine's stronger now. And my will's always been the stronger. Would you have let a girl slip a blade between your ribs rather than hurt her? You almost let me once. I looked around the alley, at the half-dozen dead, and remembered the way those flames had leapt up as if to consume Eld's soul. *Because I can't lose you.*

"Because they are of the street and, for better or worse, so am I. But I'll take you along if it makes you feel better," I added.

"It does."

I hid my smile at the realization I'd just hooked him into staying by my side. "You were right, Sin." He perked up in my mind. "This was a good way to win him back. All it took was murdering some children." I swallowed hard to keep the vomit in my throat down.

"They weren't all children."

I didn't say anything.

"Self-defense is never murder," Sin protested.

"Aye, but they never stood a chance against me, let alone Eld and me together. So good as."

"Your problem, Buc, is you never know when to take what you have and be satisfied. Sometimes a win is a win, no matter the price."

"Satisfied? What's that?"

"I suppose dead drops are out," Eld said, pulling me out of my head and away from Sin.

"What's that?" I asked.

"We can't run all information through cyphers and letters?"

"We could if they taught street rats how to read," I said. "But actually, that does give me a thought." I forced myself to look at Quenta again. Her hair was as tangled as it had been the last I'd seen her, the blond stained red in places; with her eyes closed she looked as if she could have been related to Eld. Her remaining jacket sleeve—I'd torn the other off along with her arm—was a mess of blood and gore, but the inside of the jacket, which gaped open, was perversely blood free. I saw a bulge in her pocket and reached for it. Paper crinkled against my fingers. It was wrapped around something hard and I pulled the whole thing free.

"Not sure what to make of that," Eld muttered.

"Neither am I," I said, staring at the full lira in the palm of my hand. The paper was blank save for a single drawing.

Of a stiletto.

14

Eld and I cut through back alleys, moving at a quick walk to put distance between us and the bloody scene we'd left behind, sometimes sprinting when none could see us. The last thing we needed was to draw attention to ourselves. I was less worried about the Constabulary—they didn't give a rancid olive for street toughs who ran out their luck on the end of a blade, and I had the Doga's sigil coin to flash if it came to it—and more worried that whomever tried to kill us had others lurking around to finish the job. My limbs were a strange combination of mini jolts of lightning from adrenaline and numbness from Sin's magic wearing off. I saw Quenta's dead face whenever I blinked, so I kept my eyes open wide, staying ready for the next attack. This was the second time they'd failed and I'd a feeling they wouldn't stop now.

"Whomever tried that was following us," Eld said.

"Clearly," I said, pausing at an intersection that formed a T. I kept my palm-length blade concealed against my wrist as Sin searched for enemies through my eyes. "Turns out offering coin to strangers is dangerous, Eld." I glanced down the left-hand side, which was empty save for a pile of rotting fish guts and a scrap of cloth that likely belonged to a body. "Who would have thought?"

He snorted. "No one tried to kill us until we saved the Doga's life yesterday, so that must have been what drew attention to us."

"Someone really wants to see her dead," I agreed. "And now us with her," I added. "But careful in your assumptions there . . . recall I've been losing some of my little fish to blades for weeks now, long before we knew anyone was trying to assassinate the Doga. I thought it was the Dead Gods, but she's one of their biggest supporters, so that's out."

"Wait," Eld panted, catching his breath. "You thought the Dead Gods murdered your informants?"

I nodded, brushing my braids back over my left shoulder.

"Then why in the Gods' names did we meet with them at Baol's cathedral?"

"I wanted to see if they'd own it or what kind of liars they were if they lied about it," I said. Pointing to the right, which was free of rancid fish and bodies, I added, "This way, c'mon."

I darted forward, my clothes starting to stiffen from the piss, water, and blood I'd rolled through in the fight. Sliding to a halt, I felt Eld bump into me and step back as I peered around the corner and spotted the dark glimmer of a canal between two buildings. The Foreign Quarto lay just beyond . . . or we could double back and use the canals to go through the Tip toward Servenza proper.

"W-what kind of liars were they?" Eld asked, his lips close to my ear.

I suppressed a shiver and tried to focus. "The inscrutable kind," I said. "Doesn't matter."

"It doesn't?"

"No," I said, watching the flow of traffic. Most of the passersby were foreigners. Some wore the dark furs of the north, thrown open at what they felt were mild temperatures; others, from the south, had piled on layers of thin woolens to form bulky jackets and still shivered in the chill. A northerner and a southerner were brawling while half a dozen others had stopped to exchange bets. Judging by the curses being hurled, it'd started as a religious disagreement and come around to a gambling opportunity. So . . . normal. The flows and eddies seemed natural, no would-be murderers lurking. Yet.

"Whatever incendiary that was they planned to use on the Doga was the same as the one that nearly took your eyebrows. Which rules out the Dead Gods. For now."

"What about the ones who jumped us on the gondola? Don't assume they're of the same," he added.

"Aren't you the smart-arse." I glanced back at him and frowned at his grin. "I wouldn't dream of it," I added. "The real question is, do we keep chasing down this lead on the Gnats or try to figure out who turned Quenta and see what canal that takes us down?"

"Both," Eld suggested.

"Both," I repeated. I closed my eyes and Quenta stared back at me. It's one thing to find someone killing my little fish, it's another to gut them myself. "You're not wrong. We have to find Govanti and see if anyone's been whispering in his ear or slipping coin in his pocket."

"Govanti?"

"The first little fish I hooked," I reminded him. "When we returned this summer. He's not so little, a few years younger than me. I watched him pick a woman's pocket so smoothly she never felt his tug, and when I followed him back to the little cellar he calls home, I found five score or more empty purses he'd set up as trophies."

"Damn," Eld said.

"Indeed. We had a word about hoarding enough evidence to send him to the gallows without bothering with the judiciary, and ever since he's been running my eyes and ears out of the Rock and the Mercarto. He was the one who heard about the last of mine who got their throat cut."

"I'll go," Eld said.

"We'll go together."

"No."

I opened my mouth to tell Eld where he could shove his head and he touched my arm.

"Buc, say what you want, but you just fought a girl you tried to save. What if instead of a coin Govanti reaches for a blade? What if he's already been bought and is waiting for you? Does he know me?"

"He'd recognize you, but likely not right away," I admitted.

"So let me go in your place. I won't run your informants," he protested quickly, "but I can find out if he's been turned and if he hasn't, if others have been. I'll keep my distance, watch him, and approach him in the open. That way if he's planning something, he can't spring it."

I wasn't sure I trusted Eld to have the subtlety required for what he proposed, but I could still feel the phantom shiver in my arm from the impact of stabbing Quenta to death and I wasn't especially eager to repeat that with Govanti. I could do it, and I would if it came to it, but perhaps Eld was right.

"You'll find him near where the canal cuts past the Painted Rock and Mercarto. You remember that bakery that called their muffins scones?"

Eld chuckled. "The one whose maestra threatened to throw you into the canal if you corrected her pastry naming one more time?"

I felt my mouth smile against my will. "Aye, that wench. His cellar is the next building over. He'll be somewhere around there."

"What's he look like?"

He looks exactly like you must have when you were a lad.

"You'll know him when you see him," I said, avoiding Eld's eyes. "He's got blond hair just below his ears, pulled back in a half-arsed ponytail, pale skin that doesn't tan, and if he ever grows into his shoulders he's going to make the toughs think twice before trying him. Blue eyes and a broken nose," I added.

Eld opened his mouth, paused uncertainly, and shook his head. "Where will you be?"

"Home, of course. I'll take a gondola."

"I'll find you there later?"

I nodded and Eld squeezed my arm, started to say something, gave me another squeeze instead, and stepped out of the alley as if he'd been heading toward the canal all along instead of lurking in the shadows with me.

"You sent him away," Sin whispered.

"Did I? Or did he want to leave?"

"You think he'll find Govanti?"

"Of course," I said, watching Eld go. I glanced at the now-dried blood on my fingers and realized I didn't want to go home. I didn't want to be alone either. I wanted a friend, but the only friend I had was walking away.

15

"Buc?" Salina looked confused for a moment, but hid it behind a smile. "Mara said it was you, of course, but I wasn't expecting—is that blood on your clothes?"

"What?" I glanced down at the dark stain on my amber sleeve. "Oh that? Aye, someone tried to kill me."

"K-kill you? Mara didn't mention that. I'd heard there was another burglary at the Fortescues', in the Blossoms, but that's what they get for living on the edge of the Quarto. I never imagined . . ."

Salina glanced at the young man in livery holding the door open and rolled her eyes. "Come in, won't you?" she asked in a tone sweet enough to give me a toothache.

I stepped over the marble threshold, into an expansive foyer glittering with gilded filigree that shone in the chandelier light. The space was large enough to fit our own foyer thrice with room to spare. Like so many aspects of life around the rich and powerful, it was meant to make you feel small, if you were fool enough to let it. Salina motioned for me to follow, already speaking commands in that absent way that I knew meant she was anything but absent.

"Will you tell Mara we'll be in the east sitting room? We'll want tea and biscuits and warm water to wash up afterward."

The servant bobbed his head, but seemed inclined to dawdle until Salina sniffed. Then he practically ran.

"I'll have to learn that trick for my maid."

"Won't work—she's too old to give a shit," Salina said. "Servants are like children or dogs, you've got to get your bluffs in early."

"It was children."

"It was children, what?" Salina asked. She paused in the brilliant fire-maple-floored hallway and studied me. "Are you all right?"

"Sure, and children that tried to kill me. In the streets," I said, answering her in reverse order. "I killed them instead."

"Gods' breath," Salina whispered. "Not a burglary, then. And Eld, was he with you?"

"Aye, but he's gone now. At my suggestion, I suppose." I snorted. "He didn't protest, though."

"Ah, I see." Salina's brown eyes were surprisingly soft, not a word I usually attributed to her. "Well, let's go back to my sitting room, where there's less chance of my servants eavesdropping and carrying the tale back to the Chair or whomever else is buying them off."

"You think they're spies?"

"I think they're all spies," Salina said. She motioned for me to follow and kept walking, skirts swishing loudly enough to mask our conversation in the narrow hall.

"That's the trick to not having your life gossiped about in back hallways—treat them all as if they were carrying tales, although most of the older ones aren't on the take . . . that's another reason why gestures, harsh looks, and sniffs don't work on them."

I nodded and let the rest of Salina's words wash over me. Despite trying to blackmail us this summer, she wasn't that bad, as far as merchants and nobles went. They all loved to hear themselves talk, though, and she was as susceptible to that flaw as the rest. Still, I'd come here for that, in part—to let someone else fill the silence for me.

And because Eld left instead of insisting he stay by my side as he would have done, once.

This morning I thought I could take a more direct approach in ways the Doga and her ilk never could. After all, I grew up on those streets; I certainly understood them in ways the Doga never would. But today had shown me the truth: even if I understood them in theory, I didn't know them anymore. It felt strange, like a dress that had shrunk in the washing and now didn't fit quite right. Or like rereading a book you'd read as a child and finding that your memory didn't match what was on the page. It'd been a few years since I let Eld rescue me, and time had changed all of us. Which meant I needed to be more careful, more discreet. *Which will take more time.* I felt my mouth twist at the thought, but there was nothing for it.

"What were you doing in the Tip?"

"What if I told you the Chair gave me a way out of being sent off after Midwinter's Day?" I asked her.

"I'd call you a liar," Salina said.

"What?" I took a gulp of my tea and cursed as it scalded my throat. "There goes tasting food for days," I growled. I blew across the top of the purple porcelain cup and glared as she grinned. We were alone; the servant who had brought and poured the tea had left.

"What do you mean you'd call me a liar? Does the woman never change her mind?"

"Only when circumstance or others force her to. I don't think you appreciate the levels to the woman, Buc. Now, the Chair can make an example of you," Salina said, taking a cautious sip of her own brew. "We haven't recovered as quickly from this summer as any of us would like and she needs a distraction, something to focus the Board on that will then trickle down to the shareholders at the next Company Congress."

"Something like me," I muttered.

"Aye, something like you." She pursed her thin lips, bright with lipstick against her powdered cheeks, and made a noise in her throat. "You're different, Buc, and they all know it, but none of them like being reminded of it. It's like an oarlock that's not quite symmetrical, so whenever you pull, there's a bump that throws your rhythm off. It's enough to irritate, not enough to stop you from reaching your destination."

With her free hand, she adjusted her blond hair so her curls were off her shoulder. "And it's not like you've done yourself any favors in reminding them at every opportunity that you aren't like them."

"Fuck the Board," I said, setting my cup down.

"Precisely how the Chair expects you to act," she agreed with a nod. "I often wonder what happened to that strange girl I hired to hunt down pirates and mages in fathomless seas." Her smile wasn't happy. "She'd never have played right into their hands like this."

"'Hired' is an interesting name for it," I told her. "That girl would have told you to fuck yourself," I added. I sniffed. "She's become a woman and that woman found out quickly how far acting like she came from the gutter got her in this society. You remember the first months I was back? What were they like before the Chair gave me the chance with the warehouse?"

"Aye, and what was that, Buc?" Salina sat forward, her eyes flashing. "An opportunity."

"It was," I agreed. "Until it caught fire and burned itself to the ground." Somehow. "And burned my chances with it."

"More than just your chance burned," she said in a low tone. "Since then you've been a different woman."

"You tell me I need to change and then hate what I've become?" I shook my hair, felt some of the dried blood caked there crack, and stopped. Salina had already grown queasy at the stain on my dress—if I tossed blood in her face, she might actually pass out. "You're right. The Chair didn't change her mind," I said, taking a careful breath. This had to be handled delicately. "What if I don't need the Board? Or the Chair?"

"W-what do you mean?" She straightened in her low-backed chair, the ancient dark wood creaking at her sudden shift.

"What if . . ." I paused, taking in, as if for the first time, the frescoes carved and painted into the walls of the cozy sitting room. There were scenes of Servenza in different seasons, with a few landmarks that pointed to a common theme throughout: power. The Kanados Trading Company, the Doga, and the Empress. In that order, but Servenza's flag seemed to be brighter, to stand higher, than the rest. Meaningless symbolism to most, and maybe it had just been the artist's own opinion, but I'd a hunch that no matter its relative prominence, that flag said something. The question was . . . did it say something of Salina? "What if I had a means of superseding the Chair such that I didn't have to worry about her sending me away?"

"I'd want to know what you were doing in the Tip then," Salina said. "And why did a bunch of children try to murder you?" I didn't say anything while she studied me for a long moment. She cleared her throat. "I've heard you're quite popular with them, the urchins, for reasons I can't fathom, so I'll ask again: What do you mean?"

"I sometimes forget how intelligent you are, Salina," I told her. "If you'd been half as arrogant as you were when we first met, you might have kept me from the Board after all. I mean that as a compliment, by the way," I added.

Salina shook her hair. "I stand by my original impression, Buc." She grinned. "You really are the most perfect arsehole."

"Guilty," I admitted. "You ask what I mean, but let me ask you a question: Do your walls have a rodent problem? One that comes and goes and you never know if they're gone or still there, listening? Through the walls?"

Salina had been about to take another sip of tea, but froze at my question, the cup seemingly motionless in her hand; with Sin's magics I could see the slight tremble there. She set the cup down carefully and sat back in her chair, though I could see the whites of her knuckles as she clenched the gilded arms.

"If I take your meaning aright, and I think I do, then I'll say this: these do not, but my family built this palazzo nearly two centuries before. The original architecture in the center? That's been around for nearly as long as Servenza herself."

"I see," I said.

"Do you, Buc?" she asked, almost as if asking herself rather than me. Salina crossed her legs, crimson and pale rose skirts flashing. "Do you really? Well, then, let me tell you a story.

"My family sat on the Board since the Kanados Trading Company's founding, bankrolled the first plantation that grew kan. My father was nearly made Chair despite his extreme youth until Servenza intervened and the Chair got it instead . . . but it was a close-run thing despite that. Something the Chair never forgot."

"I'll bet she didn't," I agreed. "The bitch keeps receipts."

"In triplicate." Salina's smile was unamused. "Under her reign, the Company expanded exponentially, but that required capital, which required taking on more shareholders, more debts, and the Board began to grow worried. Opposition coalesced around my father—I was just a child, but I remember the late-night dinner parties—and when word came that some of the kan plantations had a blight . . . well, things looked grim for the Chair."

"And yet she's still the Chair," I said.

"And yet." Salina sighed. "Father went to see the plantation personally, nominally at the Board's request, but all knew if he returned with word the kan was failing it would bring about a vote of no confidence in the Chair." Picking up her cup again, she took a long swallow, then set it down, empty. "They said it was a storm, one of those hurricanes that gave the Shattered Coast its name. None really know, though, because nothing was ever found save part of the figurehead from the prow."

"You think he was murdered?"

She hesitated. "It would take much for someone to send an entire ship and her crew to the depths over one man, but—"

"If that one man could unseat one of the most powerful women in the world?"

"Aye," she said sourly. "After that, I was promised his seat as heir, but the Chair convinced the rest of the Board that the stakes were now too high, given the Company's success, to trust a seat to mere inheritance. It grew easier once more favorable reports on the kan's yield began coming in, but even so I found myself forced to prove my worth to obtain that which I was owed. Last summer was supposed to be my chance."

"Then you're welcome," I said.

I could hear her teeth grinding together. "It didn't look as if you were going to deliver, Buc. Recall that you came in at the very last moment?"

"But I came," I added, holding back the double entendre that leapt to mind. Salina seemed a bit on edge.

"You did come," Salina said after a pause. "After I'd already made alternate arrangements."

"To get your seat on the Board?"

She nodded.

"Which would require someone outside the Board," I said slowly, everything sliding together in a flash. She nodded again. "You said before that Servenza intervened to keep your father from the Chair. Did Servenza intervene again, this time against the Chair?"

"Aye," Salina whispered. "So I have my seat and with it the knowledge that should I fail, they will blot me out like one does an ant scurrying across the page and pay more mind to the ink marred than the ant's death."

"I see," I said. And this time I did. I wasn't the only one who'd made alliances, or, as they were likely seen, deals, debts incurred to be held for future interest. "Whose ship did your father sail on, Salina?"

She closed her brown eyes and when she opened them again they were filled with anger and unshed tears.

"One of Servenza's. One of the Doga's own."

We sat in silence for a time, me mulling over what I'd learned while Salina collected herself. The Doga had moved against Salina's family twice, but then had helped her when she was at her most low—a position engineered by the Doga in the first place. In the end, none of what Salina told me surprised me, just that if both of us were ensnared by the Doga—and in my case, possibly the Chair, as well—who else was? I said as much and Salina shrugged.

"Not Lucrezia. She's got her father's estates to fall back upon, which makes her powerful enough to be her own woman, though she doesn't seem to realize it. Likely the one or two others of her stature are free as well. After that, it's anyone's guess." She met my eyes. "I'll just tell you this, Buc: you can bargain with the Doga, but you must be careful to never owe her. Once you find yourself under her thumb, it will be too late: her kind never relax their hold."

"I'm not one to just bend over and take it," I muttered.

Salina smirked. "Now there's the woman I met this summer."

"Maybe once I'm through with them, they'll be the ones bent double and me behind."

I made a gesture, Salina snorted, and we both began laughing. I felt something loosen in me, something that had been drawn taut around my heart after this afternoon's mess. It'd felt like a wire cutting into me, one that had been there since Eld and I lost our way, only now it was slack and I could breathe. And feel. And laugh. As I wiped tears away, I finally realized what had been strange about Salina. Not that she wore makeup or had her hair styled, but that her dress looked uncomfortable for sitting, the skirts too extravagant, too long, especially given the latest trend of jacket and trousers.

"Y-you're wearing a ball gown?" I shook my head, still giggling, "at this hour? Do you sleep in the damned things?"

"I do not," Salina said quickly, blushing. She shook her head. "And there are some newer dances that are especially made for the latest fashions, but that's not what tonight is for."

"Dances?" I frowned. Suddenly the sums were beginning to add up to a figure I didn't like. "And just what is tonight for?"

"Well," Salina said, her eyes sparkling, "that's why I was so surprised to see you. I thought for sure you'd blow this off, too."

"No," I groaned.

"Aye, we've another dancing lesson for the Masquerade," she said, pushing herself to her feet. She opened the door and called past me, "Mara! Were you able to find a gown for Signorina Buc?"

"Aye, signora!" Mara's voice echoed from down the hall. "And the maestro has just arrived, so there's still time for her to change. I've got the powders and irons ready!"

"Instruments of torture, more like."

"Up," Salina commanded. "We've work to do."

I groaned, but let her draw me up and followed her toward the door. I glanced at Quenta's lifeblood dried on my sleeve, and for a breath, that wire was back and cutting hard. "You never asked me about the blood," I said quietly.

Salina glanced back. "I didn't. You would tell me or you wouldn't, Buc. I was just here to listen."

"And then did all the talking," I said.

"Maybe that's what you wanted?" She smiled. "Isn't that what friends are for?"

"Friends?"

The word caught me off guard and she smirked at the look on my face. "If you came here after what happened, what else are we?"

"Aye," I said slowly, wondering what this new sensation was. I'd never had any friends other than Sister or Eld. I'd never felt the lack, either; people were weak in the end, waiting to buckle when you needed them the most. Though without Eld to talk to and with Sin trying to convert me every other moment, I could use an ally or three.

"You've the power of the Gods, Buc," Sin said quietly. There was an urgency to his voice. "That's all you need."

I brushed him off, but I couldn't help thinking about someone else who'd had the power of the Gods and tried to use that and their wit to play all sides off one another. It hadn't ended great for Chan Sha. There was an itch between my shoulder blades, almost as if I could sense the blade coming. I shivered instead.

Allies?

"Friends," I said out loud, and reached for Salina's hand. She took it and shook it seriously before a teasing grin swept across her features. I met that grin with one of my own as I let her shepherd me down the hall toward the waiting horrors of learning to dance from an aging maestro who barely came to my chin. That word kept reverberating through me. *Allies.* But I'd had another name for it over the summer. One I should have warned Quenta about.

Cannon fodder.

16

Eld let Glori shut the copper-and-leather embossed door to his bedroom behind him. The servants who didn't reside in the palazzo were long gone to their homes; those who lived in had gone to bed hours before. Guilt for keeping the old woman up rather than any real desire for sleep had driven Eld from the drawing room and its flickering fireplace. Buc was still out; Salina had sent a note that Buc had decided to take tea with her. A rather late tea, and something Eld had trouble imagining Buc being interested in.

Was Buc changing or was Sin changing her?

A chill gripped him at the memory of Sin's deeper voice coming from her mouth. Afterward she'd seemed fine, right up until they ran into that ambush. For a moment there—more than a moment, really—she'd seemed completely confused, unsure where they were or what they were doing. Like before. Only, before had been worse. Far worse.

He slipped out of his robes and made for the bed, taking care not to extend his right arm too far. It ached with the promise of a bruise on the morrow, though in the moment he hadn't felt it any more than he had the flash of flame that had nearly engulfed him. He'd looked a sight when he found Govanti, right where Buc had said he would be—the lad had taken one look at him and lit out like a seal before a shark. *I was in a singed jacket speckled with blood.* He smiled ruefully and scratched the stubble on his chin with his good arm. Luckily the past few months had forced him to find distractions in reading and, more often, in swordplay and calisthenics. He was in the best shape of his life, while Govanti was still young enough to be more limbs than dexterity. He'd caught the boy easily.

Eld eased down onto the edge of the bed, hearing the frame creak from his weight. Eventually the lad realized Eld wasn't trying to kill him—an interesting conversation, that, involving a blade and the inside hem of Eld's trouser. Buc had clearly shown the boy a trick or two. Once Govanti knew he was safe, the boy had practically begged Eld to take Govanti back with him. He would have, too, if he hadn't promised Buc he wouldn't run her informants. Taking Govanti in wasn't quite that, but given the tension between them, he couldn't risk it. Not without checking with her first.

He couldn't keep the growl in the back of his throat. Someone— likely Glori waiting to see his lamp go out—shifted on the other side of the door. Eld levered himself into bed and rolled over, blowing out the gilded lamp on the bedside table. Darkness consumed him and with it came Govanti's stories. About gang leaders found brutally murdered, entire gangs disappearing, mages in corners of the city they'd never been before, and the whispers of a flaming-eyed demon who burned their enemies alive and laughed and danced over the ash heaps of corpses. Fanciful stuff, but Govanti was no child . . . he'd grown up on the streets, same as Buc. Buc wouldn't have believed the half of it. Not then. Not now. Still, something had scared the lad. . . .

The air kissed his skin with a chill and Eld pulled the blankets up, thinking of another kiss. Was it so wrong to want more? More than just a friendship? *To have that I'll have to tell her. Everything. Do that and I might lose her. Do that and she might lose herself.*

The pressure of all the lies felt like a weight on his chest, threatening to cave his lungs in, so heavy he was continually surprised his ribs didn't crack.

"Without you, I wouldn't be alive today and without me, you might not have made it out alive today."

His tongue tripped over the lie. She'd been more than capable, enough that had he not put his brace down, she'd likely have torn the pair of would-be assassins to shreds with her blades and carried on without a thought. *Magic.* His skin pebbled for another reason. Perhaps the young woman whom he had always known didn't need anyone, had finally realized that truth herself? *It's what Sin believes.* Not that he trusted Sin, but he had to trust a little or else none of the past few months made sense. He missed the time when sense was something that existed in his world. Now everything was smoke and lies, blood and betrayal. *Buc's facing something larger this time.* Not Chan Sha, bereft of her crew, not a Ghost Captain with a mindless army. She just had to manipulate two compromised people. *Now she's compromised, even if she doesn't realize it. Worse, the Gods know her name. So do the Chair and the Doga. And if it's not one of them trying to kill us, someone else knows her name as well. This summer we were an unknown, often overlooked quantity, but no one's pulling any punches now.*

Eld rolled onto his back, stared up at the inky blackness above him, and bit his lip. *If she's compromised, then I have to be the rational one, even if it's at a remove. I need to find out who wants us dead so badly they tried to incinerate us in broad daylight, same as the Doga. Before our luck runs out.* There was a saying in the army about luck only applying to grenadoes and mages, and he had a feeling they were facing both.

Tomorrow.

He didn't expect to sleep, but the decision released some of the weight from his chest and he slid below the covers and into dreams before he realized he was tired after all.

Dreams of dancing on the sand, lungs full of hot coals as his breath came in gasps. His limbs felt like water, yet he forced the blade in his hand to strike like a sand adder, darting in and out, the charred pirate queen before him struggling to keep his steel from her throat despite her magic and twin blades. Each blow reverberated through him and he saw her movement, felt her intent, let her catch his shoulder, and fell, hand vainly trying to staunch the wound. She stepped past him and he let go of himself, let the blood flow freely, and hacked at her leg. Chan Sha cried out, fell back, and the dead swarmed over her like a skeletal wave.

Dreams of dying on the sands, waiting for Buc as his flesh flayed itself from the inside out, blackening with rot and decay. In this dream she never returned and he heard the Ghost Captain's chortle at what a fool he was to trust that slip of a girl. Eld opened his mouth to tell the Dead Walker he was a fool, but the only sound that came out was a dried hiss from his long-since-desiccated tongue. There was a voice, bright in his mind, familiar, reminding him he was a Shambles now and that he lived to serve. He drew his arm back, saw the rusted blade clutched in his fist, and studied the thin, black girl in rags at his feet. She looked up, unkempt braids twisted and tangled, a bruise marring her cheek. Her green eyes were bright in the island sun. There was no question in their depths, simply calm assurance.

Buc.

Again that laugh, but this time a different tone, deeper than he remembered.

Sin.

The sword moved of its own volition, struck with the weight of a monsoon. Eld, blind panic exploding through him, fought the momentum with every decaying fiber of his decrepit being, but the sword only moved faster, his limbs trembling, dried tendons cracking from the force of the descending blow. The blade hummed as it scythed through the air and Eld wanted to tear his eyes out, but he was a prisoner chained within his own body and Buc's gaze held him fast. The blade flashed between them and his mind screamed until everything burst in an impossibly bright white flame. The world tore apart and rained black ash down, and darkness consumed all save for two gems, shining in the black ink.

Emeralds.

17

"Smoke filled the alley from the shot," the man said quickly. "Couldn't see arse nor shit, but that demon fired some pistole what made no sound. Was her shot that lamed me," he added, pressing a hand against the dirty linen bandage that covered his leg above the knee.

"But not so lame that you couldn't run away when it was over, eh?" she asked.

"Maestra?"

She growled in her throat, saw her gleaming eye of fire reflected in the man's terrified gaze, and spat. "Use my name, that's honorific enough."

"S-Sicarii—please!" He shook his greasy locks and wiped at his forehead, leaving a bloody smudge across his tanned features. "By the time I got to my feet it really was over. They was all dead or dying an' the only reason I got away was because she was too busy turning that lass you paid off into a pincushion."

She studied the man for several moments, letting the silence build and, with it, the tension. Silence was something oft undervalued, something she'd not realized the importance of herself until it was nearly too late. Here, it was a tool, to let the man's imagination run until he was convinced she was going to slit his throat. Then—when she didn't—he'd talk and the truth would come. But was it the same truth as what he told the first time? Or something else? And if else, would she kill him or not? With his shattered leg he was useful for little more than begging, but beggars had proved their worth already, hadn't they? Sicarii chuckled and the man winced at the sound of her harsh voice.

"Tell me again. From the beginning."

"The paper lass lost her nerve. Gave us away, savvy? We was in the alley where you told us to be, already half-lost to the night what with the buildings there . . ."

Sicarii listened with half an ear—he was telling the same story after all, so he'd live to beg for his coin. Nothing was a surprise; it would have been pure luck if that lot had managed to kill Buc and Eld. *But who knows the value of pure luck better than I?* She reached without thought, tapping the glowing stone she'd fashioned into a makeshift eye. No, killing them today would have been too easy, though an injury or a wound wouldn't have been an unwelcome outcome. *Does that fool think I don't know Quenta never held a pistole? He probably pissed himself and pulled the trigger early.* But then, he'd paid for it if he had, along with the rest.

Quenta had been eager for more coin, though surprisingly less eager to do what had been asked of her. That Buc girl had a way with people, when she wasn't driving them to distraction or killing them. Laughter bubbled up in Sicarii's chest . . . she knew she wasn't entirely sane, but no sane person would attempt what she was doing. *As long as I don't lose myself like I did when—*Her mind went blank for a moment, then refocused on what mattered: revenge. Perhaps Buc hadn't taken a physical wound, but she'd murdered Quenta and that would eat at the girl as much as Quenta's betrayal.

"Whom do you trust, when you can't trust anyone?"

She began to laugh, a horrible sound even to her own ears, but she was unable to stop, even as she drowned out the rest of the man's story. It didn't matter. He didn't matter. All that mattered was the pain Buc was feeling now. It was but a taste of what was to come. Sicarii's throat burned with laughter as tears flowed from her single real eye. It was all too perfect. By the time Sicarii was through with Buc, the girl wouldn't be able to trust anyone.

Not even a corpse.

"When will you move against the girl and her brute?"

Ulfren watched his Eldest, but her ebon-marbled visage gave nothing away. She stood still as a corpse, her silver braids motionless, though the creature opposite them made his skin crawl. *I wonder if she made Sicarii meet us here in the crypts to balance the scales?* Unlike his own pale skin, which made his robes seem blacker than midnight, the Eldest's skin nearly matched the shadows in hue. With her dark robes, it would have been difficult to discern discomfort—if she had any. He had plenty.

"I told you where they would be twice now, helped lead them right into the seat of your power on the island, and yet they still draw breath?" Sicarii's growl echoed through the chamber. The figure opposite them blended into the shadows nearly as well as the Eldest, save for the fiery orb peering at them from beneath the broad-brimmed hat that was pulled low to hide her features. In the dark the orb should have illuminated Sicarii's face, but it almost seemed to eat the blackness around it instead. "Small wonder Ciris is taking your territory by the armful if a small girl and a washed-up sellsword give you pause," Sicarii added.

"Blood and bone," Ulfren snapped, meeting Sicarii's growl with one of his own. The flaming eye turned toward him and he hissed and reached for the pouch that hung from his belt before he realized his hands had moved. *Not yet.* Aborting the gesture, he crossed his arms instead of grasping one of the glass vials that held holy blood and the hairs of a wolf, goat, and saber cat—rare, that one—and saw his Eldest's thin lips crease in a smile. "You are the one that stands within our power now, Sicarii."

"But I'm no little girl," the woman said, her harsh voice purring as if she was that saber cat, and he felt a chill run through him.

"No, you are not," his Eldest said; her breathy voice sounded like a dying woman's final gasp.

She tapped the bone-white pillar beside her that supported the latticework ceiling above them, carved to look like the bones of their Gods, which lay in Normain. "So you should know this war is still being fought by proxy. To move against her in our true forms would be to invite the notice of the Kanados Trading Company, and we all know whose proxy they are."

"The mind witch," Ulfren snarled, clenching his hands, his filed nails bit into the flesh of his arms hard enough to draw blood. "Ciris."

"We have begun to draw her in," his Eldest continued. "She came to us because the dross from the gutter she's been paying for their large ears have been turning up in those same gutters with their throats slit."

"Blood calls to blood," Ulfren whispered.

"It does and it has," she agreed beside him. "Soon this Buc and Eld will realize the mind witch's mages do not protect them."

"But perhaps you can?" Sicarii's chuckle sounded like logs crackling in a fire. "Veneficus, did that girl strike you as one who wanted protecting?" When the Eldest said nothing Sicarii's eye bobbed in acknowledgment. "She's a lone shark, sharp teeth, aye, but only hers and that brute of hers to bite with. Though it seems like they've done a lot of biting, haven't they? Was what happened this summer by proxy?"

The Eldest shifted. "Do you know what happened beyond the islands of the Shattered Coast?" Her tone hardened like the grating of bone against bone. "What happened to our brother?"

"Ah, your blood calling to you?" Sicarii asked. "Did Sambuciña Alhurra"—her voice burned like liquid flame—"ever tell you how is it that she and her partner returned when the most powerful pirate in the Shattered Coast and a Dead Walker of the Gods did not?"

Ulfren leapt forward, one hand reaching for a vial, the other for the cord that would set his cloak free as Transformation took him, but his Eldest caught him in midstride. Her midnight-black arms were like whipcords, suffused with the pure blood of their Gods, and far stronger than his own. He jerked to a stop as something in his wrist broke; the pain distracted him long enough to get his bloodlust under control. *If I change it will be the saber and my fangs will spear that creature through her eyes, flames or no flames. I will feel her skull in my jaws. I will—*

His Eldest shook him hard, slamming his heels against the floor and snapping his mouth shut with a click of his teeth. Perhaps he wasn't as in control as he thought. The Ghost Captain had been their best chance of assassinating Ciris, channeling all of their resources into one surgical thrust that would have severed the magical brain stem of her priesthood and left their corpses to molder. *Now Ciris turns our own practices against us, feigning to care for the masses when she was ever a creature of the elite, and the blind fall into line.* It couldn't continue. It couldn't be allowed to continue. And if this creature knew . . .

"You're angry," Sicarii said. "I understand. Anger is what fuels us to do what we must, despite the cost. Still, the girl may not cost as much as your spies would have you believe."

"Say on," the Eldest said after a moment, only the slight rise of her eyebrows betraying her interest.

"The Kanados Trading Company has no love for Sambu-ciña Alhurra or Eldritch Nelson Rawlings," Sicarii said. "Why would they? The girl is from the gutter, same as the ones you've been throat-slitting, and the Company has always prided itself on its exclusivity. The Sin Eaters seem to love her, true enough, and again you must ask yourselves why that is. . . . But," she continued, despite Ulfren's growl, which was loud enough to cover the one from his Eldest, "this is a war of proxy, as you said. The mind witch and her mages may not wish to see the girl dead, but the Company does, so should she find herself faceup in an alley one morn, throat opened ear to ear, they won't be the ones appealing to Ciris, and Ciris won't be able to do much more than snarl about it."

"Perhaps it is as you say," the Eldest said. She cleared her throat, a sound like a sarcophagus's lid sliding open. "But if the child is dear to the mind witch, we would need to take care. This couldn't be traced back to us. The methods by which we'd use to obtain the answers to the questions we need to ask of her would be . . . mortal."

"I understand," Sicarii said. "She has been taking risks of late, traveling to the seedier parts of Servenza."

"We hear," Ulfren said, forcing the anger from his voice, "of gangs fighting with one another in the Tip and beyond. Should one of these battles erupt while she is there, I don't think we could be blamed," he suggested.

"Gangs?" Sicarii chuckled. "I may be able to help with that."

Sicarii's laughter intertwined with Ulfren's and the Eldest's until the crypt echoed with the grating, fiery sound that would be, Gods willing, the last thing Sambuciña Alhurra and her partner would ever hear.

18

"We've arrived, signorina," Joffers said in his gravelly voice.

"Arrived?" I asked, suddenly aware that what had broken my concentration was the vibration of the gondola against the dock.

"Aye," the old man said, skillfully tying a line to the iron cleat jutting out from the stone dock. "Home, as you asked."

As I asked? My mind was a blank canvas with not even a sketch of a memory to be found. I could remember the night before, trying to tease that old skinflint of a dancing maestro before he gave me the rough side of his tongue and threatened the lash. After that, well, we'd come to an accord of sorts. I think by the end, I'd surprised him with my footwork.

"We surprised him," Sin added.

"Aye, but what came next?"

"Sleep," he said slowly.

"Aye, and then?"

"I—I don't know."

"Is aught amiss, signorina?" Joffers's long braided mustachios, bright white against his dark-tanned leathery skin, jiggled with the twisting of his head. He began shrugging out of his oilskin cloak. "Are you cold? You don't look well."

"That's what a night of dancing will do for you, Joffers," I told him, forcing a smile. If Salina was right, and I'd no reason to doubt her, any of my number of servants could be spies. I couldn't afford to let them pass on tales of my absentmindedness, or worse, weakness. "Best beware."

"I've no fear there, signorina," he said with a laugh, letting his cloak settle back around his shoulders. "My dancing days are behind me, and my husband, Longinous, was never one for parties. And that was even before the war."

"Which?"

"Which what?"

"Which war?" I asked him.

"Oh, they all blend together after a while," he said, smile slipping from his lips. "This was decades ago, probably the one with the Free Cities?"

"Mmm." I'd been hoping he might have been an avenue into Eld's past, but old as Eld was, that war probably happened before he was more than a suspicion in his mother's eye. Who was his mother? "Make sure you breakfast well. I don't know when I'll be needing you again today."

"Breakfast? It's nearly time for lunch." I followed his gaze up to where the sun was partially hidden behind a sullen wall of grey. "But I will grab a bite," he said, bowing his head slightly. My stomach growled. "And mayhap you would be wise to do the same?"

"Mayhap, Joffers," I said as I jumped up onto the dock and realized I was wearing the same bloody, torn clothes as yesterday. "Mayhap."

"What the fuck is wrong with me?" I asked Sin as we walked down the dock, shivering in the winter winds that pulled at my torn jacket.

"You know," he said absently, "I think that's the first time I've seen Joffers laugh."

"Well, bully for Joffers," I growled mentally. "I don't see anything to laugh about here, showing up places with moldering holes in my memory. Our memory."

"No, me neither," he said, his voice grown tight. "Possession would fix this, you know. Ciris would be able to give us the right magic within moments of becoming aware of us."

"Being able to do something and actually doing it are two different things," I reminded him.

"Aye, I know you won't do it, Buc. Her name, I wish you would. Until then I'm trying, but it's like catching smoke." There was a note to his voice that hadn't been there before, something desperate and almost . . . frightened?

I didn't give him the satisfaction of letting him know that made two of us. Then again, he was inside my head, so he already knew. A shiver ran down my back that had nothing to do with the wind as I mounted the steps that led up to the garden and the rear of our palazzo.

My mind was clearer by the time the kitchen maid heard my knock and let me in. I gave her a smile and a kind word, but it must not have been kind enough, because she practically ran away from me as I entered. I glanced down at my sleeve, nearly black with dried blood up to my elbow. Quenta's blood. Maybe the maid had her reasons.

"So much for keeping up appearances," I muttered sourly.

"Signorina Buc!"

"Marin!" I said as I turned around. She had a book tucked under one arm, a feather duster under the other. She looked resplendent enough that if not for the color of her servant's uniform, a bystander might have mistaken who was owner and who was servant. I glanced at the book and remembered my promise to give her a reading lesson. Not now, though.

"How is your day going?"

"Well enough," Marin said. "Sirrah Eld left early this morning and with you being out of the house, Glori gave me the afternoon off."

"He left already?" I asked.

Marin nodded, her black braids swinging behind her. "You know, if you don't stop making all those faces, you'll have wrinkles before you're twenty. Leastwise that's what Glori says."

"I'll worry about that when twenty arrives," I said. With Sin's magic, wrinkles were an impossibility. "Did you see which direction the maid ran off to? I'm starving."

"I will send her up right away, signorina." Her nose wrinkled. "You may want to bathe first? I could have another draw hot water. To help with the blood and all."

"None of it mine, fortunately," I said, picking at my sleeve. "Still, it wouldn't do for Glori to see me in this state."

"It wouldn't," Marin agreed. "She's already been in a fit over Sirrah Eld coming home bloody all the time."

"What do you mean?" I frowned.

"Well, he came home last night looking like he'd been to the wars."

"And it wasn't the first time?"

"No, last week he had a streak of blood across his cheek and didn't even realize it until I said something."

"If someone cut him, he realized it," I assured her.

"It wasn't his blood."

"Sin, can you remember what happened last week? Any holes there?"

"None. And"—he leapt ahead with my thoughts—"every time we were with Eld, he was fine and there was no, uh, excitement like the past few days. But we were only with him thrice."

"Likely a footpad that wouldn't take no for an answer," I told Marin.

"That's what he said."

"Well, then, that's solved, aye?" Marin opened her mouth and I held out a hand. "I appreciate the concern, Marin," I lied. I liked Marin, but her concern was an annoyance. I glanced at the book tucked beneath her arm. "I'm not going to have time for a lesson today. In fact," I added as if the thought just occurred to me, "I think I may hire a tutor for you."

"A tutor?" She frowned. "I enjoy our lessons, signorina. You're a fine teacher."

"And you're a better liar," I told her with a false smile in an effort to take the sting from my words. "But if you wait for me, you'll be the one with wrinkles before you learn to read." I moved past her. "Let's both of us think on it, aye? For now, how about that bath?" I heard her mumble an assent, and I added, "And send that kitchen maid along with a bite as well?"

"I don't understand you humans," Sin said.

"Of course you don't," I told him, sinking down into the bathwater so that only my nose and eyes were above the surface. Its heat was slowly leaching the tension from my muscles. "You're a shard of a Goddess, how could you?" I ducked my head under and came up dripping. "What don't you understand?"

"The falling-out you've had with Eld. Over me. It's causing you pain, Buc. Why try to fight it? Why keep him close if it's like a knife in your ribs?"

"Pain? There's pain and then there's pain." I nodded slowly. "Aye, I understand pain. I understand the gnawing hunger of the streets, the constant edge in your mind that knows if it doesn't keep itself razor sharp you'll awaken one morning choking on your lifeblood, the blade already drawn across your throat for the crust of bread or scrap of copper in your pocket. Eld saved me from that.

"And I know what it's like to see him tied up and tortured and near death, where every blow is as painful to me as it is to him . . . knowing that the next blow could well land on me. We saved ourselves from that.

"I know what it's like to see every woman and man jack of them that laid fingers on us dead and buried at sea or lost in bloodred sands. To fight and kill to reach him, to sacrifice my life, my very soul, to see him live another day. I saved Eld from that."

Tears burned the back of my throat. "I saved him because he saved me, aye, but after so many times you give up counting and then it becomes about something more. There's a new pain, now."

"You expected better from him? After all of that," Sin suggested, "why wouldn't you? If he but asked you could tell him." I felt a pressure in my chest, knew it was Sin. "His face, his voice, his soul lives there, but you've never told him that. He's never asked."

"Were you listening to what I just said?" I asked, my voice breaking.

"I was," his voice said in my mind. "I've been listening to others try to tell you what you don't want to hear. That Eld leaves without you, comes back without you. Bleeds without you.

"I've been watching, too. Watching your back because Eld isn't there anymore. You need to move on, Buc, if you're to have a hope of freeing this world. Shackled to a man, you'll never achieve that. You'll drown first."

His words hit me like a hammer blow, pulsing through me in time with the beating of my heart.

"You don't understand," I whispered, cursing Sin for doing something to cloud my vision, and heard him say it wasn't his doing, his voice sounding far off. Closer and louder than my silent tears was my voice. "I started this for Sister. For me. I never planned for him, but I've come to realize that I can't do this alone." I choked out the rest. "It has to be with him. Together. Us against the world!"

"That dream ended when you took me from the altar," Sin said. "I'll help you realize your dreams, but Eld can't be part of them any longer. There's no changing that."

I plunged beneath the bathwater, trying to shut his words out, but they were inside me, just like he was. Worse was the certainty that he was right. Eld's hatred of magic ran deeper than I'd ever imagined. Because I never thought to ask. Never really knew him. Never really cared to. And now that I did, it was too late. My back hit the bottom of the deep tub, but I couldn't drown out Sin's words nor their import.

There's no changing that.

19

"Y-you saved my life!" Govanti gasped, staring down at the two corpses at his feet.

"It was a near-run thing," Eld agreed, forcing an evenness into his voice that he didn't feel. The lad looked about to faint and the last thing he needed was to realize that Eld had gotten distracted—always a risk when he thought of Buc—and had missed the pair trailing Govanti until he turned into the alley. *I thought those urchins going at it hammer and tongs a few canals back were the danger, but fighting's just become part of the scenery now. Need to stick tighter to Govanti if this is what the streets have become.* With half a block between them it had been closer than Eld anticipated and if it hadn't been for the pair being completely focused on stabbing the lad to death, as well as Govanti's vigorous protests against being filled with holes—he wouldn't have been able to take them unawares as he had.

"I can see why Buc's little fish have been disappearing," Eld added, bending down to clean his basket-hilt sword on the man's rags. There was some blood on the hilt lining, but it was close enough to the crimson-dyed leather that it would pass muster until he could attend to it tonight. The body shifted from the blade and a sharp-chinned face with a lancing scar from eye to throat came into view, making his breath hiss between his teeth.

"What is it?" Govanti asked.

"I've seen this one before," Eld said slowly. Figures were piling up in his mind, but he couldn't calculate the sums. *I hate mathematics.* "A fortnight past, someone tried to pick my pocket, wouldn't take no for an answer, and nearly slipped a blade through me, save I beat them to it."

He pulled the man's jacket and undershirt back to reveal a dirty bandage. "Seems you're not the only one they want dead, lad."

"Is that supposed to make me feel better?"

Eld glanced up and saw that some color had returned to Govanti's face, though the lad's pallor still nearly matched his strawberry-blond hair in its single ponytail. Eld shrugged. "Look at it this way: if they're going after me, that leaves them less time to go after you. And"—he stood up, sheathing his sword as he did so—"there's two less of them after today."

"But why?" Govanti asked. "Why now?"

"When did the first of your informants turn up missing?"

"Not missing," Govanti said, drawing his thin jacket, faded to a dull brown, around his shoulders. His frame was wide, but with no muscle to go with it, the jacket hung on him like a scarecrow's garb. "Dead. It was the last full moon? Deedee. Found her on the edge of the Tip after she missed meeting me." His mouth worked into the semblance of a smile that didn't reach his eyes. "She never missed a free meal, sirrah."

"Eld," he reminded him.

"Sirrah Eld," Govanti said.

"After this"—Eld gestured at the bodies—"I think just Eld will do.

"More than a month, then." He scratched at his chin, noticed some flecks of blood on the back of his hand from swinging his blade after running the first through, and made a mental note to clean up before he returned to the palazzo for dinner. Blood on his sword hilt was one thing, but on his hands? Buc would be home by then and she'd want to know where he'd picked up someone else's blood. *Godsdamn Sin and his keeping my distance.* Godsdamn him for likely being right, too. Someone had started murdering Buc's people before they got involved with the Doga, but the timing coincided with the unrest on the streets and canals. So, were the murders byproducts of the latter or a precursor to the former?

"I don't know those words," Govanti said, pulling Eld back to the moment and making him realize he'd accidentally asked his question out loud.

"Are your friends dying because they were in the wrong place at the wrong time during a rumble over turf, or were they targeted for murder?"

"Does it matter?"

"For Deedee, no," Eld said. "For the rest of us, it might. Are we faced with two mysteries or one?"

"You mean, finding out who wants us dead and who wants the Doga dead?"

"Careful!" Eld glanced back toward the main street and canal beyond it, but so far none had come down after them. "I told you that last can't leave your lips. Buc would eviscerate me if she knew I'd let our working for the Doga slip." Too many lies to keep.

"Best we were gone," he added. "Before someone finds us standing over these two and has questions."

"Shouldn't we search them for clues? Buc would, aye?" Govanti asked.

"She would and we should." Eld chuckled humorlessly. "I'm just the brawn, Govanti." They knelt down together, avoiding the growing pool of blood. It was the work of a moment. Both corpses were clean save for the daggers they'd planned to use on Govanti. Eld gave both blades to the lad—he could use them or sell them and either way Eld had more than enough steel on him as it was.

"All right, you're going to take a carriage back to your cellar, aye?" Eld directed when they were finished. Govanti opened his mouth but Eld tossed him a silver soldo to forestall his question. "No point in tempting fate and getting stabbed on the way home. I need to get back before Buc starts asking where I've been.

Knowing her, she already has plans to ferret out the answers to questions the likes of you or I haven't even fathomed yet."

"Thankee, sirrah—that is, Eld," Govanti said, pocketing the coin. "Will you do me a favor?"

"Sure, lad."

"Will you tell the servant girl, Marin, that 'G' said hello?"

Eld adjusted his tricorne and smiled at the lad. "You and Marin get on?"

"I—I don't think so," Govanti said, his cheeks flaming. "At least I wouldn't call it that. I saw her once, when Buc had me stop by to deliver my report. She, she seemed nice."

"She's a fine lass," Eld agreed.

"More than fine!"

"You ever tell her?"

"That she's more than fine?" Govanti choked.

"That you think she's nice," Eld said, unable to keep from chuckling.

"Oh." Govanti's face was as red as Eld's coat. "No, sirrah—Eld. I've only spoken to her once."

"Well, next time you're by the palazzo, consider telling her." Eld put his hand on the lad's shoulder and squeezed. "The canal waters are dark and full of blades these days, Govanti. You don't take the moments you have before you, you might never get another chance and there's no edge sharper than regret. Take my word for it."

"I will, sirrah."

"Good, now go hail that carriage," Eld said, motioning for him to head back the way they came. "I'll be in touch in the next few days. I've a feeling that washerwoman we spoke with earlier knew more than she was letting on."

"Aye, as you say," Govanti said. He inclined his head and then moved down the street, his worn boots silent on the cobblestone. "Eld?"

Eld glanced back over his shoulder and the lad blushed and looked away.

"You're pretty savvy yourself. I see why Buc's your friend."

Eld studied Govanti for a moment and nodded, lifting his hand. He turned away before the lad could see his face crumple. "I was once. I wish I knew for sure I still was."

20

"You brought us to a brothel?" Eld's voice was low, pitched for my ears alone, piped full of indignation. He pushed himself up from the gondola's seat and steadied himself against the back. "You said we were just going to dip into the Tip today."

"Aye, dip your tip in the Tip."

"Buc," he growled, looking around the crowded street where a mix of factory and dockworkers streamed by. Those returning from working overnight looked haggard and worn, and those heading out for their shifts looked little better. It'd rained last night and the bars, dives, and taverns had been overflowing. Seemed like every third worker had just come from such a place, for aside from one or two shooting an envious gaze our way, the rest were fixated on the chore before them: walking. "We're not even wearing disguises."

"I thought you hated disguises."

"I bloody well want one if I'm going to a whorehouse," he snapped.

"Easy on, Eld—that term's offensive." I sniffed and he muttered something under his breath, but I could see red creeping up his neck from the collar of his powder-blue jacket. "Besides we're not even in the Tip yet, until yonder bend." I nodded toward where the canal bent in front of us, forcing traffic to loop wide around the water's edge. "This is still the Painted Rock Quarto. And in the Quarto brothel workers are . . . Joffers, would you call them courtesans?" I asked, looking back at the old man, who held the gondola up against the canal's crenellated, stone edge with his oar.

"Time was courtesans had to come from the finer Quartos," he said after a moment. His face was inscrutable, but I saw his lips twitch when he glanced at Eld. "These days all the bordellos have been turned into palazzos, so I suppose you might call them that. Better than 'harlot,'" he added, bending his knees as a passing barge sent waves against our boat.

"Better than 'harlot,' Eld," I said.

"Buc—I can't go in there," he choked.

"Gods, man, we're not here for that. I don't need to buy a fuck"—I glanced sidelong at him—"and I gather you don't need to either, anymore."

"What's that supposed to mean?" Eld asked in a voice several octaves higher than his usual baritone.

"Just that you've been out late recently and I assumed a fine bachelor like yourself wasn't spending those nights cold and alone."

"I haven't been sharing my bed with anyone," Eld gasped.

"Aye? Well, you do you."

A sound behind us made us both turn, but Joffers avoided eye contact, making a show of tying off the boat now that he knew we weren't leaving immediately.

"We're here for information."

"Information?" Eld asked carefully.

"Aye, loose trousers tend to translate to looser tongues."

Eld blushed.

"You've a filthy mind, Eld," I told him. "No wonder that Lucrezia Rorigo keeps throwing herself at you."

"Buc . . ."

"Bridge too far?"

"Several canals too far," he said.

"Fair enough." I took his arm and he startled. "You're my escort, remember?" I laughed.

He eyed me suspiciously, but I knew his polite streak would win out, and sure enough a moment later he stepped ashore, tapped the heels of his dark calf-high boots together, and helped me step up. Not that I needed his help, especially now that I didn't need to worry about skirts tripping me up, I just wanted him well in tow before we began. Give a man an order and he balks, ask him to do something simple and he does it without question. Ask a few times more and the next time you give him an order, he's leaping to obey before he realizes it. I'd been trying to put him through his paces ever since reading *On Hounds and Their Training,* number 371. Turns out training men to your touch isn't all that different from dogs. And I needed Eld used to my hand to lead him back to my side.

"You had this planned all along, didn't you?" he asked, pulling me out of my thoughts.

"Of course."

"Is that why you wore red?"

"We'll be back shortly, Joffers," I called over my shoulder. The old man grunted an assent, already busy polishing the woodwork. "Crimson," I said, turning back to Eld. "The jacket's crimson." I tugged its already tight cut across my chest tighter, making the most of my bosom, and his eyes widened. "The blouse is rose," I said, fighting to hide my smile, "and the pants are mahogany." I glanced down. "Or black, it's hard to say. You should know these things," I added, "coming from a noble family."

"The only thing I know about fashion is that it's been scandalous of late," Eld muttered. "Those trousers you and all the other signorinas insist on wearing do things to your arses that are . . . distracting."

I snorted. "Aye, imagine how it must feel to be Joffers."

Eld frowned.

"Loving men, you fool." I rolled my eyes. "He's had to stare at your arse for months and keep us from sinking at the same time. No easy feat, that."

"Th-thanks, I think?"

"You're quite welcome," I said, steering us around some of the street hawkers who had pitched tents and stands along the canal side. Across the street a large palazzo—probably built before it became clear the Painted Rock Quarto was not going to rise much further in station than the Tip—shone with lights. None knew when it'd become a bordello, but over the years, it had been run by a score of maestras and maestros. Its pale, marbled columns marched across a crimson-streaked façade that was made true red by the sundry chandeliers that hung overhead.

Street wars came and went and so did the management, but the courtesans remained. Two men and a woman leaned beside gilt-painted windowsills, evenly spaced so that their being there was clearly intentional, if one was too dim to realize what the swords at their belts were for. Patrons treated these courtesans with respect or they spilled their lifeblood into the canal. The guards were also part of the reason why any street rivalry never made it past the doors. It'd been a while, but it looked no different than it had all those years ago. I explained this to Eld as we drew closer.

"Y-you lived here?"

"Gods, man, no." I patted his arm. "After Sister died I was on my own and there was a time or two where food was tight and the Crimson Corsets and Gilded Lilies did me a good turn when they had no cause to."

"So that's why you're wearing red."

"I thought you'd prefer that to a corset," I told him. I didn't tell him I'd waited to see what he was wearing and fitted my outfit so that we made a pair: him in light blue and me in darker red. "My thinking is if someone's been following me of late, they're unlikely to know this connection."

"So the courtesans will tell us what happened to the Mosquitoes and the Gnats and whatever else we need?"

"For a price, aye."

"Crimson Corsets," he muttered. "Seems a bit on the nose." He glanced down at me, his blue eyes bright and sharp as a winter's morning. "Full of secrets, aren't you?"

"You're one to talk."

"What's that supposed to mean?"

I licked my finger and reached up and touched the lobe of his ear and showed him the shiny red blot that I'd wiped off. "Why's there blood on your ear?"

"Er, shaving?"

"Eld."

"Footpads won't take no these days," he said quickly.

"Uh-huh." I remembered what Marin had told me. "Footpads don't linger to bleed themselves dry on the likes of you. Certainly not in our Quarto and not when you only stepped out for a morning walk."

"I don't know if you've noticed," he said as I made for one of those lounging against the bordello, "but Servenza's lousy with cutthroats these days, Buc."

The guard, a short woman with biceps that looked to rival Eld's despite her frame, returned my nod and detached herself from the wall long enough to pull the door open for us. Eld started to hand her a coin, saw her glare, realized what offering that meant in this place, and blushed.

"If you didn't walk around looking like the Goddess of Murder all day long, they'd be trying to put a blade in you, too," he growled.

"Well"—I frowned—"resting bitch face comes in handy now and again. Let me do the talking," I added as we stepped over the threshold. "There's a lot of jargon here and I don't want you to accidentally order yourself an orgy."

"Too right," Eld muttered. "Be the death of me."

"But what a way to go," Sin whispered.

It took a few hours, starting with the Corsets and moving down the red-lanterned row to end with the Lilies, to find the answers we sought. A few hours where Eld's eyes popped so much I half expected to see his eyeballs chasing after us, where we saw women and men in various states of undress and more than a few in acts I hadn't even considered possible until today. I'd forgotten that time we'd been in Colgna searching for the countess's missing daughter that it'd been me who slipped into the Winking Lass—a bordello that was tame by Servenzan standards—aiming to find her daughter's suspected flame.

The daughter, it turned out, didn't care for men and was working her way through the bawdy house's skirts. Eld had gotten suspiciously ill beforehand, which had forced my decision to infiltrate the place, but now I realized he'd never set foot in a brothel, even before we'd met. Sometimes I wondered how he managed to make it in the military, but then I remembered he hadn't.

Despite being in virgin territory, Eld tried to help, and accidentally asked one of the courtesans to ply her tongue in a place he'd likely never touched before. It took a few coins to pay the lass off. After that, Eld's face matched my jacket and even I was beginning to feel a little . . . warm.

It was worth it for the stories we heard, over and over again. The nobles were just beginning to hear rumors of something that had started a season ago, but the strong always target the weak and vulnerable. The violence—the murders and infighting—had started here, in the brothels. Again and again we heard of prostitutes found in back alleys, clothing and bodies torn to shreds as if a dozen blades had found them all at once. The brutality, more than the murders themselves, had them all afraid, but it'd gone on long enough that fear was giving way to anger. The maestras running the bordellos were willing to bargain with any who promised to find the killers of their slain daughters and sons.

I didn't even have to dig in my pocket for coin before their suspicious glares softened and a different sort of tear shone in their eyes. Eventually, the stories commingled, centering on a layabout constable around the corner who was likely on the dole from half a dozen gangs but knew the criminal underbelly well enough to have our answers.

I laughed mentally as we left the last bordello, Eld trying not to stare at the sultry dark woman who led us out, her jacket open and nothing beneath it. Despite his skepticism, as ever, I'd been right.

"How's that?" Sin asked.

"Honesty is shortsighted. And overrated."

"You're not going to find their killer?"

"Perhaps, but I've my eyes on saving the world, Sin, not avenging prostitutes who chose to let the wrong client in their skirts."

"So let the powerless die, so long as you save the rest that's left breathing in the end?"

"If that's what it takes . . . aye."

Sin's silence was loud in my mind.

21

"Why didn't you just say you were Secreto?" the constable asked. His bicorne was crooked, revealing a shock of dark hair already turning grey; stubble dotted his narrow, vulpine cheeks. A few stains on his faded uniform, its color giving the constables their nickname of the blues, made for an unkempt appearance, but I noticed his cudgel was oiled and looked well used and the pistole tucked into his boot looked similarly cared for. Those were the only reasons I hadn't treated him like the drunk his breath smelled like and put a knife to his throat. That, and the kanhouse we were in had enough patrons that threatening one of the blues might have led to some of his compatriots showing up. Someone always wants to play the bloody hero.

"Because mayhap the Doga doesn't want it known she's asking questions." I tucked the sigil I'd shown him back into my jacket and shrugged. "And mayhap I didn't know you'd be such a pain in the arse."

"Then you don't know Rafiro," he said with a grin that revealed crooked but sharp, kan-whitened teeth even brighter than my own. He sat up in his seat and indicated the chairs around the small corner table he occupied. "Sit, you. We'll have a round of kan!" he hollered at the short man with a stained apron and a harried look on his face behind the counter. The man rolled his eyes, but turned around quick enough that the few wisps of hair on his head flew up like tendrils of smoke. Rafiro chuckled. "They hate a blue, but they can't do nothing about it." His smile slipped. "And these days, there's worse to hate than us."

"What's that mean?" Eld asked, setting his tricorne on the table. He pulled back a chair and sat on the edge, making it tip dangerously. A glance told me he was trying—and partially failing—to avoid a large stain across the bleached wood. "What's going on?"

"Lot of questions yer asking," Rafiro said. "What's happened to the Mosquitoes, where are the Gnats, what's going on in the streets? Which one you want first?"

"All of them," I said, resting my forearms on the table. I wasn't intimidating, like Eld—I couldn't loom—but something in my eyes made him flinch. "The Doga requires all of them."

"If you've any sense at all you know what's on in the streets," Rafiro grumbled. He took off his bicorne and ran a shaky hand through his dark locks. "Can smell the bodies left in the back alleys, those that were too far off to be tossed into the canals. And we're pulling out the ones that were tossed by the hour now," he added. His dark eyes shot up, caught my glance, and looked away. "Can hear the clickety-clackety of the clubs against the lampposts calling the gangs to rumble every other night, it seems."

"A gang war," Eld said.

"Wars," Rafiro corrected him. "Started a fortnight or so ago?" He shook his head. "Blues didn't think much of it at the time, seemed like the regular infighting that happens every so often. Began with the Cobblestone Corners."

"Corners?"

"It's a knock-and-grab strategy," I explained. "Have a lookout following a target, they signal to another waiting around a sharp corner, and when the target turns, they're blindsided by something like a club or a stick . . . or a cobblestone," I said dryly. "Then you search their pockets and run before they wake up. If they ever do," I added.

"Lovely," Eld muttered.

"She's got it exactly," Rafiro said. "The Corners used cobblestones 'cause they got their start as lads an' lasses without a cuparo to their name, but as they grew up their numbers did, too, and they'd begun to move their trade into some of the finer Quartos. Anyways, their leader was a lad turned man name of Jek Longshaft—"

"Bet he was a popular one with the ladies," I joked.

"Lads," Rafiro corrected. "He was; the moniker wasn't just for his hand with a cudgel, if ye take my meaning. Though he had a Godsdamned temper when drunk, which he was more often than not. Was that lack of judgment that led him to take them out of the Tip." He cleared his throat. "One night, Jek went out drinking in the Mercarto Quarto with a few of his top cronies and was found torn apart the next day. I didn't see it myself, but they said it looked like someone had taken a dozen cleavers to him—the others were just shot through the head."

"Execution?"

"Looked like," he agreed. "Then what was left of the Corners got it into their heads that the Sharp Eagles was the ones that did the murdering and went seeking revenge."

"Card sharps and backstabbers," I told Eld.

"Eloquent names, these gangs have," he said, shaking his head. "Should be poets."

"There's a poetry to the streets." I snorted. "Just not the kind most have an ear for."

"After that," Rafiro continued, shooting us both looks as if we'd interrupted one of the great tales told by bards in taverns across the world, "the whole lid came off. Mosquitoes were overrun by the Gnats, as you know, and then someone began taking out the leaders 'cross gangs all over the island. Krakens and Blackened Blades have always been at one another's throats, but both lost their entire ruling lines and splintered into half a dozen small factions," he said, ticking them off on his fingers. "The Poisoned Eels were hit last night and that's going to be the blow that will shatter any semblance of peace. Today's the quiet before the storm. Tomorrow the streets are going to run red."

"Why's that?" Eld asked.

"The Eels were the overgang that came up after Blood in the Water passed," I said slowly. That had been right before I tried to pickpocket Eld, so my connections to what happened after that were essentially nonexistent.

"The Eels ran all the rest," Rafiro confirmed. "'Bout Gods-damned time," he growled when the short man appeared with three mugs of steamy kan and set them on the table with a bare hint at a bow before dashing back behind the counter. Rafiro blew foam off the top of one and took a long draught of what surely must have been a scalding hot brew. Kan was a funny plant, capable of slowing down or speeding up thought depending on if it was smoked or drunk, but I'd noticed the drinkers had a harder time letting it go than the smokers, and Rafiro's shakes made sense now. If the man wasn't a full-blown addict already, he would be soon.

"The gangs are a necessary evil. Without them, we'd have a thousand different thieves doing all sorts of Gods know what 'cross the city," he explained, taking another gulp from his mug. He belched, sending a noxious wind of kan and booze our way, and Eld choked. "With them, we can keep them confined to the lower Quartos, know where to go looking if one of them steps too far, an' they en't half-bad at policing their own. Without them—"

"Chaos," I muttered. "Worse than that," I added, glancing at Eld. "Gangs are all about turf, but the larger ones control factories, stores, hawkers, and the like. If that gets upended, it's going to be felt beyond the Tip."

"What the Doga, beggaring Her Grace's pardon, and her lot don't understand," Rafiro said, "is that you grab a man by his tip and squeeze and the whole body's going to feel that kinda pain." He reached down below the table and winced. "Too right, they will."

"More poetry from the streets?" Eld asked dryly.

"So that's what is happening out there," I said, sharing a look with Eld and fighting to keep from laughing. It wasn't funny, Rafiro was right, but the idea of Servenza being one big dick was too rich a joke not to laugh at. "What about the Mosquitoes?"

"What about them?" Rafiro shrugged. "Listen, I've been keeping my head down, my eyes forward, and my ears closed."

"Bullshit."

"Listen, I—"

"Bullshit," I repeated.

Rafiro slammed his now-empty mug on the table and leaned forward, eyes narrowing. "You lot don't know what you're asking after. Haven't the faintest. I told you folks were scared, but not because of the gangs. Unless you're unlucky to be in the wrong back alley at the wrong time, so long's you're paid up on your dues, you're fine."

His voice dropped to a whisper and he licked his lips, gaze darting past us. Eld and I both followed his glance, but there was nothing to see. The rest of the kanhouse's patrons were on the far side of the space, doing their best to avoid the blue and his company. We leaned in at Rafiro's gesture.

"It's not just gang leaders that have shown up murdered. Couple of shopkeeps, a merchant here and there, and more prostitutes besides. My leftenant tried to get to the bottom of what happened to the Corners once she realized that was where things first got their sails crossed."

"What'd she find out?"

"No one knows. A lamplighter found her in the gutter with her throat slit and her body carved apart with strange little cuts so that her uniform hung off her like bloody ribbons. Bianca, one of the Gilded Lilies, were found the next morning. She likely died the same night as my boss, from the way her corpse smelled." He grinned mirthlessly. "I guess whores take longer to find than constables." His grin faded. "She'd been cut up the same way, same as my leftenant, same as those gang leaders, and same as those others I told you about."

Bianca. I had stiffened at the name, but Rafiro missed it, his eyes on the table. One of the names given to us earlier by a maestra who had more anger than grief in her eyes when telling us the tale of her murdered girl. I reached out and touched Eld's knee. Maybe I wasn't lying to the maestras after all. If Bianca was somehow connected to everything else going on in the Tip, and if that was connected to the attempts on the Doga's life? A lot of ifs. "Why, though? Why cut up a courtesan like that?"

"Didn't I say?" He shook his head. "Bianca had been informing for my leftenant. They were together the night they died, but Bianca's body wasn't in this Quarto or the Tip."

"Where was she found?" Eld asked.

"The Blossoms Quarto."

"Oh, I remember that now," I said. "Or I remember reading about it, but it was just a line that a woman had been found dead at the bottom of some steps leading to the canal docks." I frowned. "The article implied it was an accident."

Rafiro snorted. "Only if she fell down a flight of razor blades." He sat back and pulled his jacket straight, the brass buttons reflecting the noon sun's light from the window. "She wasn't the first to die, signorina, and she wasn't the last, nor are the rich Quartos being spared."

"You mean the robberies?" I asked, remembering that Salina had mentioned a palazzo had been tossed.

"Robberies and some killed, like the whore that tripped into those razor blades. The people are scared an' that's why they're more willing to tolerate a blue like me around these days." He tapped his club and nodded at the pistole in his boot. "We don't carry razors."

I nodded slowly. It was all beginning to make sense, not clear enough that I had a fully formed painting to consider, but the horizon was taking shape, the background filling in. The center was still blank canvas: Why? What purpose? Fear could be useful, but the fear I'd felt in the streets wasn't the kind that came from being taken over, exchanging one would-be tough for another. *What kind is it, then? And who's carving people up into ribbons?*

If I couldn't see clearly, I could still infer, and it was impossible that what was going on here wasn't in some way connected to the attempts on the Doga's life. It strained credulity to believe the attempts on our own lives weren't interwoven as well. Someone was making a power move here, even if what that move entailed was still hidden deep in the shadows. It all amounted to one giant fucking knot. And us at the center.

"Ask him about the beggar," Sin suggested.

"Good call," I said.

"Don't sound surprised," he muttered.

"Hey, you've been quiet of late."

"I've been trying to figure out what's going on with our memory," he said. "And you've been doing fine, I've been watching."

"I'm beginning to forget what life was like without a dead voice inside my head."

"Boring," he said. "And I'm not dead."

"Uh-huh."

"Rafiro, let me ask you something." I waited for his gaze to meet my own so I—Sin—could see any lies that might be there. "Does the phrase 'the drowned rise' mean anything to you?"

"No," he said immediately, and Sin confirmed he was holding something back. Rafiro hesitated, then shrugged. "Fuck it." He glanced around for the dozenth time. "Sicarii."

"Bless you," Eld said.

"You don't recognize it?" Rafiro asked. His eyes shifted between us. "Really?"

"Sicarii," I mouthed the word, and something whispered in my mind, but I couldn't quite hear it. I shook my head and he bit back a curse.

"I think you're leading me on, signorina." He stood up abruptly, knocking his chair against the wall loudly, then leaned over the table. "Everyone says they don't recognize the name, but they're all liars." His booze breath washed over us. "But I'll tell you a truth, just the same. You keep asking these questions, signorina, and you'll recognize it, sure enough."

He lowered his voice and whispered, "Sicarii," then turned away, calling loudly over his shoulder, "Thanks for the drinks, Secreto!"

For a moment both of us sat there silent, then Eld made a motion, and I realized that the rest of the patrons were staring at us and the short man behind the bar had reached beneath the counter in the way that barkeeps have when they feel they're going to need to break out the blunderbuss. The blues might not carry blades, but the Secreto did . . . all manner of them. Rafiro's parting gift. "Past time for us to be gone," I whispered.

"Aye." Eld dug into his pocket and pulled out a handful of silver soldi that more than paid for our drinks. He made a show of counting them out and stacking them on the table. As he did so, the kanhouse relaxed by degrees and the owner's hands came back up from behind the bar—empty. We quickly made our exit.

"It's a damned thing to nearly get caught up in a brawl over being the Doga's own," I told Eld as we walked down the street, "especially since we're not technically Secreto."

"Aye, but Rafiro thought we were, when you flashed that sigil she gave you, and I think he was hoping we'd solve his riddle for him," Eld said. "Took his revenge when we didn't."

"By outing us," I muttered.

He adjusted his tricorne and shrugged, rolling his shoulders in his powder-blue jacket in a way I recognized, getting the feel for where his pistoles were placed. I'd done the same with my blades before we'd stepped into the street. There was something comforting about the way the hilt of a stiletto feels in your hand. "I've never heard the name before, have you?"

"Which one?" I asked, my mind turning over Rafiro's words.

"Sicarii."

"No," I told him, "but it sounds the way it feels."

"And what way's that?"

"Sharp."

Like a razor blade.

22

We took a meandering walk through the finer buildings of the Painted Rock Quarto on our way back to the canal and Joffers. Though these would-be palazzos could never match up to the house of the Gilded Lilies, fresh plaster and stucco made them stand out against the faded and cracked buildings that made up the majority of the Quarto. Foot traffic was slow but steady, and I felt the tension between my shoulder blades ease. It didn't feel off, like it had the other day, before we were ambushed in the Tip.

I should have been planning our next move; Rafiro had given us a lot of gossip and rumor, but fuck all about the Gnats. Instead: Sicarii. The name kept skipping across my mind like a smooth rock over the Crescent on a calm day and Sin wasn't being helpful.

"Buc!" Eld's voice was pitched for my ears alone, low and urgent.

"Damn the man," Sin growled. He hated when Eld figured something out before him. "We're being followed."

"We're being followed," Eld said.

"Next time I'm going to say it as soon as I suspect," Sin muttered.

"How long?" I asked, continuing to look straight at the end of the street, a good distance on. The dark waters of the canal were just visible and we could make a run for it if we had to . . . but I'd no intention of running.

"Not sure," Eld said. "I think we picked them up a few blocks back, when we had to go wide 'round that carriage that overturned.

Now that I think on it," he added, "that might have been precisely the point."

"All right," I said. "Let's give them the same reception we gave the last ones who tried to ambush us."

Eld chuckled and leaned closer, for all the world laughing at something I said, but his voice was grim. "That next alley on the right, or should we cross and take the left farther down, by that tall building with the dark stucco?"

"The one right here," I said. "I'm sick of being followed—and, Eld?" He glanced down at me, features hidden by the shadow of his tricorne. "We need information, so maybe not quite the same reception as that last time."

"No pistole ball to the face," he said under his breath. "Right."

"Good lad." He grunted and I laughed for real this time. "All right, let's go," I said, breaking into a jog, then leaping around the corner and into the alleyway.

And right into the path of something that whipped past my ear like a furious, whistling bee.

"Sin!"

"On—"

Time slowed to a standstill, taking sound and some of my vision with it. My mind burned and I could feel that my weight was completely on my front boot; I was leaning forward. That lean had saved me from whatever it was that had just passed my ear. Farther down the alley I saw a figure wearing an overlarge jacket, some dark contraption leveled in their arms.

"—it," Sin finished. "There's another coming."

"What is it?" Time moved again, nearly infinitesimally, but I could feel my momentum begin to slowly carry me forward. My vision sharpened, eyes burning with magic, and a woman a few years older than Eld leapt into focus. She wore a torn, patched dress that might have been green once and there was a red feather in the cap that hid most of her brown curls. It was the crossbow cradled in her arms that drew my attention. Between us I saw a flash of steel that had to be the bolt, its path the same as the first that had missed me. I searched beyond her for the second shooter.

"It's just her," Sin hissed. "Look at the cylinder attached to the bottom of that thing—looks like some sort of gearwork repeater."

"Mmm," I mused. "That's a problem."

"Aye, if you can let your momentum carry you into a slide, we can—"

"Cobblestones are too new here," I said. "Must have been re-paved this past summer. I slide and I'll go a pace before I'm brought up short and yon shooter turns us into a pincushion."

"Then what do you suggest?"

No armor. Long jacket, limited mobility. Need to close. Without becoming a pincushion. "How fast are you?"

"Not fast enough to sprint there before she adjusts aim," Sin said. "Another ten paces closer, and mayhap."

"I don't want to sprint there," I said.

"You don't?" Sin asked. Then he read my thoughts. "Oh . . . umm, let's find out?"

"That's the spirit," I growled. "Ready?"

"Killing motherfuckers in two, one, aye!" he roared.

Time snapped back and with it came the tearing sound of a honed, steel bolt whipping past my ear. I dropped my hands in a flash, grasped the hilts of my twin stilettos, and pulled them free like chained lightning, bringing them up even as the woman dropped her aim to account for my being bent over. My boots leapt off the cobblestone, rasping loud in my ears, and then my limbs burned and sound and sight dimmed again as Sin's magic suffused me just in time.

Bolts came pouring at me. One-two-three.

My stilettos were blinding glints of blackened steel, scything the air in front of me, and I felt my wrists reverberate as each bolt hit a blade and glanced off with an angry whine, furious at missing my throat as they caromed off walls and stones. Four-five-six, and I was running low, a wordless snarl caught in my throat as I closed the distance. Seven-eight. My wrists began to hurt from the force of the impacts. Nine-*click-click-click*. The woman cursed and the round cylinder fell from the crossbow, bouncing off the cobblestones as she reached for another on her belt. Too late, she realized I was moving inhumanly fast. She paused, face as dark as her brown hair, whites of her eyes wide, torn between fight or flight. And then I was there and her indecision killed her.

I slammed into her, driving her backward with enough force that she landed on her back before spilling arse over end, skirts and dirty petticoats flying as she came right side back up and bounced. Only, I'd not hit her with my body, but my blades. She coughed a bloody froth that turned into a spray when she tried to scream. Her skin looked pockmarked by crimson specks and her wild eyes stared at me. Her mouth moved soundlessly before she fell back, a stiletto buried below each breast.

I let my snarl go and with it, Sin's magic. Hearing, vision, and time returned, accompanied by a rolling wave of nausea that coupled with the sudden adrenaline spike to bend me double. I'd have fallen if I hadn't caught myself against the side of the building. I coughed, choked, and hurled all at the same time, blinking back tears to find strands of bile hanging from my lips all the way down to the pile of vomit I'd added to the refuse in the alley. "What the actual fuck, Sin?"

"I—I'm sorry," he said. "That hasn't happened before. I think, maybe, this is what comes of not taking Possession. I don't know," he added quickly, sensing my rage. "I truly don't; no one's ever held out as long as you and—"

"Later," I cut him off as Eld came running up.

"Buc! What happened? Are you okay?" He put his arm around me to help hold me up and leaned over so his face was close to mine. "A bunch of steel just came flying from the alley but it had stopped by the time I rounded the corner. Say! Is that a body?"

I pulled myself up, using Eld's jacket, and for a moment my vision doubled and my stomach twisted hard enough that I nearly decorated his powder-blue coat with whatever was left in my guts. I fought the urge and half leaned, more fell against him. He moved to pull me closer, but I pulled one of his pistoles free from its holster, pulling the hammer back as I drew it level and stepped clear of Eld. The woman who'd just turned the corner froze, the whites of her eyes bright against her umber-brown skin.

"Courtesan?" I wiped the vomit from my mouth with the back of my free hand and spat. "Do I need to kill you, too?"

The woman backed up so fast she almost fell on her arse. Catching herself against the wall, she held her hands up, level with her chest. I recognized her—she'd been in the last bordello Eld and I had visited. Now her jacket was buttoned, hiding the breasts that had made Eld walk into a wall before, but it looked like she hadn't bothered to don a shirt, which meant Eld was still going to be useless. There was bile in the back of my throat and my knees wanted to tremble. Damn men. Damn women, too. She shook her locks slowly, gaze darting past me to the body of the woman I'd killed, then back to me.

Swallowing hard, then licking her lips, she choked out, "I can explain."

"Then do it," I said, adjusting my grip on the pistole. "And be quick about it."

"I—I'd nothing to do with . . . that," she said, nodding toward the corpse. "I was trying to catch you both up in a place with less eyes and ears."

"Sounds like what this woman wanted," Eld said over my shoulder. "You see where following us got her."

"I wanted to help," she said, tears bright in her eyes. "Rafiro told my maestra what he told you. He's a worm that would sell his own mother for a coin and won't part with information for much less than that. Maestra is scared and didn't tell you everything. Not about Bianca. She was my friend, signorina. Please?"

I sighed and lowered the pistole, but kept the hammer drawn back. "Say on."

"My name's Fulsia. I—I know you have another case that takes precedent, but if you find who's trying to off the Doga, then you'll be free to find Bianca's killer, aye?"

I heard Eld draw back the hammer of his second pistole. "I don't recall saying we were trying to find the Doga's assassins," I growled, bringing the pistole back up.

"Word came down from the maestra a couple days ago," Fulsia squeaked. "That the Doga had a team asking questions, a team that always found answers. I don't know where from," she added quickly. "All I know is that we heard of the attempt on the Doga's life at the cathedral, all of Servenza did, and then the troubles in the streets really took off and somehow Bianca was in the wrong place at the wrong time and wound up m-murdered."

Fulsia stopped holding back her tears; though she was crying, she stared at me with enough emotion that I lowered the pistole again and motioned for Eld to do the same.

"I don't have enough coin to beg the Dead Gods' help even if I give that tall one a free lay on the house and the Sin Eaters are only offering healing in the Quarto. I just want justice, signorina. Is that so wrong?"

"Not wrong," I said. "I'd pay a pretty coin to know how word of our investigation made it to a bunch of courtesans, though." And the Gods knew who else.

"Who else knows?" Eld asked.

"Thanks, Eld," I muttered, rolling my eyes. He grunted. "So, what did you come to tell us, Fulsia?"

"There's one that may have word on who is trying to murder the Doga," Fulsia said. "The Mosquitoes' maestro, if you can speak to him."

"The Mosquitoes are gone, aye?" I asked. "The Gnats saw to that and I'd assume that means they saw to the old maestro, too."

"No, they didn't—'cause their maestro was picked up not three days prior to the Gnats' takeover, for ordering a shakedown of the wrong constable, and he's been in locked in the Castello, in the

middle of the Crescent, ever since. Were I a betting woman"—
she sniffed—"I'd say the Gnats paid off enough of the blues to see
him out of the way before they moved in."

"All right," I said, letting the hammer down carefully on the
pistole and handing it back to Eld without looking. I felt his hand
on mine; he hesitated, and then took it.

"All right," I repeated. "I'll see about the Mosquitoes' maestro.
Thank you for the tip. Anything else you want to tell us?"

Fulsia took in a shuddering breath and shook her head, making her makeup run worse than before.

"You didn't see any of this." Eld gestured over his shoulder.
"Right?"

"Wasn't even here," she agreed.

"Good woman. Here, for your troubles," Eld said, flicking a
gold coin through the air. "And your silence," he added.

Fulsia plucked it out of the air with a skill known only to those
of the street and made it disappear inside her jacket. "You'll always have my silence, sirrah," she said, bowing her head. When
she raised it, somehow her jacket had gotten half-undone and I
could practically feel the heat emanating from Eld's cheeks. "It's
yours . . . whenever you want it." She grinned that crooked grin
she had and disappeared back around the corner.

"Have to give it to the woman," I said.

"What's that?" Eld asked in a tight voice.

"Standing in an alley with a corpse, with a pistole trained on
her, and she still propositioned her mark." I turned back around,
confirming what I'd figured, that Eld had kept his pistole out. He
was learning. "A woman after my own heart."

"I'm led to believe she'll do all manner of things for a lira," he
said, and we both burst out laughing.

We didn't laugh for long. Even here, a body was going to pull the
wrong kind of attention eventually and, given the sudden lack of

foot traffic past the mouth of the alley, it was a certitude that the locals knew some shit had gone down. Eld gathered up as many bolts as he could find amidst the debris—mainly broken glass and cracked masonry—that littered the alley while I inspected the woman. I found no identifying marks; her clothes were of the ordinary sort, and her pockets were empty. The crossbow, on the other hand, was definitely not of an ordinary sort. It was smaller than most, what was known on the streets as an alley piece because it wouldn't carry much beyond that range. They were still used by window climbers and assassins and some of the poorer gangs, but most preferred pistoles due to their added power. This one was smaller than usual, barely the length of my forearm, although the bowstring itself was as wide. There was a dark, metal cylinder wrapped around the nut where the bolt would usually be locked into place.

"Tell me what I'm looking at, Sin," I said.

"Some damned fine gearwork," Sin said. My vision burned for a moment and suddenly it was as if I held a magnifying glass, enabling me to clearly see the inner workings, which were revealed by the lack of a loaded bolt. "I'd say, based on what we saw and what I can see here, that it somehow uses the force of the shot to pull the string back to the nut, lock it in place, and that canister must attach somehow to pull another bolt into place."

I bent down and tugged one of the dark, metal drums free from the dead woman's belt. It slid into a groove beneath the stock with a click. The trigger was as light as a dueling pistole's and I worked it a couple of times, dry firing it. Sharp puffs of air shot from the drum.

"I think I see," I said after a moment's study. "You have to load the first bolt and then the gears do the rest, firing as fast as you can work the trigger."

"Until the drum is empty, anyway," Sin agreed.

"There's an air canister doing something? Magic?"

"Not magic," Sin whispered. "But knowledge your kind

shouldn't have. A form of air bottled within the drum is released in powerful bursts—that's what's loading each bolt. The string is handling the actual firing like any other crossbow."

"Between the gears and this air, you'd need only change out the cylinder and another dozen bolts are ready," I said.

"Aye, or near enough" he said. "There's no mage mark either. The Goddess doles out permissions to use her knowledge of gears and machinery very carefully, Buc, and I don't recall her ever permitting this."

"Isn't that a bitch?" I whispered mentally.

"Find anything?" Eld asked.

"Just this," I said, holding up the crossbow. "You ever see its like?"

"Can't say that I have," he said after a moment. He leaned closer. "It's blackened steel, same as your blades. No maker's mark." He whistled. "Sin Eaters would kill whoever made this without their permission."

"Aye, and the bolts are barely the length of the palm of my hand," I said, rising from my crouch. "We're looking at a weapon designed for only one purpose: assassination."

"Lucky for us she was a bad shot," Eld said, forcing a smile.

"Lucky," I said, passing him the crossbow.

I bent over and my arms burned for a moment as Sin gave me the strength required to pull my stilettos from the dead woman's chest. The body jerked once and the blades came free with a sucking squelch, fresh blood running their lengths, dripping in places from blood and viscera. I wiped them on her patched green dress as best I could and then held them out so Eld could see the bits of black that were now bright steel. "From her bad aim," I said.

"Gods be damned," Eld whispered, turning a whiter form of pale. His eyes found mine and he shook his head slowly. "How?"

"Magi—"

"How did you know that Fulsia was coming from behind?" Eld

asked, rushing to get his question out, to keep me from laying bare the secret we both knew but refused to acknowledge.

"Yeah, how did you know?" Sin asked. "I didn't hear her coming. Her name," he whispered, "I didn't see any of this coming."

"When you grow up a lass on the streets . . . ," I said slowly, staring at the blades in my hands and thinking of Eld and how his hand had been in mine moments before. The gulf between us had never yawned wider than it felt right now. ". . . you learn to always be on your guard. To never trust your senses, not fully, because senses can be dulled or fooled—and that's when they strike."

I looked up from my blades. "Maybe it's lasses everywhere that know that feeling, not just on the streets."

"I—I'm sorry, Buc," Eld said. "Sorry you've had to live your life that way."

"Don't be." I shrugged. "Maybe it was my senses or maybe I was the only one that remembered this all started with us being followed?" Eld snorted and I felt Sin do the same in my mind. "Either way, senses or memory, it's kept us both alive more than once, Eld."

I pointed at the crossbow. "We're taking that with us. Might come in useful in the days to come. Though I'll still take a good blade in my hand," I added, sliding my stilettos back into the sheaths hidden by my crimson jacket.

Blade.

"Fuck me," I muttered, pausing with the knives only halfway home.

"What?"

"I just remembered where I'd heard that word before, why it's been bothering me ever since Rafiro let it slip," I said. I drew the stiletto in my right hand back out. "It's a word of the Cordoban Confederacy. It means 'blade.'" I drew the second one free. "Or 'blades'—the Confederacy's tongue has a way of meaning more than it says." I cursed softly, bitterly. "You remember that drawing we found in Quenta's pocket?"

"A blade?" Eld looked even more confused.

"Aye."

Rain began to fall in drips and drops, and the wind whipped at my face, full winter coming into its own and promising more storms with it. I eyed one of the drops that ran down my stiletto as it slowly turned from translucent to vermillion and glanced down at the corpse before turning away.

"The word no one seems to know, but everyone seems to fear. Sicarii."

23

She watched from the curtainless window, standing far enough back that a stray glance from the street wouldn't reveal her. Not that any would think to look up this far, but luck was a fickle mistress—she knew that, none better—and there was no sense in taking the risk. Her woman was well hidden, tucked into the alcove of a back door to one of the buildings lining the alley.

There, walking down the middle of the street: them.

Sicarii's lips twisted and pulled back in a soundless snarl. The hulking brute bent to hear whatever abuse Buc was likely hurling at him, but he must have liked the shit she served because he chuckled, throwing his blond hair back, and she laughed with him. It would have made Sicarii sick, save she knew she was going to have the last laugh. She reached up and plucked her fiery amber-glassed eye from its socket and held it against the window; a lone sunbeam struck it and made it shine like a coal. Sicarii repeated the gesture again and then popped it back into place, blinking to work tears around the cold, hard glass.

Below, her woman stepped out—and wonder of wonders, Buc leapt around the corner.

Sicarii's snarl twisted again, this time into a smile. *I meant to take the big brute, but is this the day I dance over your corpse, girl?* The first shots went over Buc's head—the woman obviously had been expecting the taller Eld, but she was one of Sicarii's best and would adjust. *And then fill you full of steel.* A small giggle built in the back of her throat.

"What?!?"

The giggle died unreleased as Buc snapped forward in a crimson blur of motion, hair and jacket trailing. Her arms moved so fast they looked like twin tornadoes that sucked in the sparks of steel and spat them back out again in every direction. Sicarii could practically hear the bolts ricocheting off of Buc's blades. Impossible. Then the bolts stopped. *Reload, you fool!* The woman reached for her belt, then flew back as if a giant fist had slammed into her. The next instant, somehow Buc was standing over the assassin, and even at this distance, Sicarii could see the hilts of two blades jutting from the woman's chest.

"Impossible," Sicarii whispered, the word catching, grating in her throat. She drew in a heated breath and let it out in a hiss.

"Im-fucking-possible," she repeated. Sicarii had seen that kind of performance before, the mind-bending speed that ended with one standing and the other dying.

"Mind-fucking little bitch! You have magic. Magic." Her breath was hot, loud in her ears, but louder still was the red rage screaming in her chest. *Not fair.* "You're not supposed to have magic!"

She drew a blade from the back of her belt; as she flicked it open, gearwork propelled a fan of blades from the handle. Snarling again, Sicarii attacked the plaster wall before her as she would have attacked Buc if she were facing the girl on the street. Knowing that strategy would have ended with her own death only made Sicarii rage more.

"Cheating motherfucking cunt!"

"Maestra? Er, Sicarii?" one of her men called from the edge of the steps. "Everything all right?" Fear was bright in his voice. "Ye need us to go gather Ule up?"

Sicarii drew a shuddering breath. The haze around her vision began to clear, revealing the wall, now festooned with scores of cuts that left the plaster torn and a sizable pile of dust and shards on the attic floorboards. More dust and powdered plaster drifted thickly in the air, making her nose twitch. Sicarii forced the impending sneeze away and it went. Her body was truly hers now. After . . . before.

"Ule won't be needing us any longer," she said when she found her voice. "I need pen and parchment."

I'll need to warn the Dead Gods or they'll walk right into this trap, expecting the girl to be mortal and finding out too late otherwise. Same with the Sin Eaters. Questions must be asked delicately now or Buc will . . .

"Buc will make more enemies, sow more chaos," she whispered. "So long as she doesn't die by their hands, her magic will be mine for the taking. Belay that," she said in a normal tone. "Did the Dead Gods find the evidence we planted?" She turned around, composed. "The item implicating the Sin Eaters in the disappearance of their missing priest?"

"Not yet, Sicarii," the heavily bearded man said, taking a step up into the attic. "Given their search, I'd say tomorrow morn they'll run acrost it."

"Excellent." She took another breath, her throat now truly in flames from her outburst, and let the pain stoke the rage in her chest. Anger was a powerful weapon, but she couldn't afford to be a blunderbuss in this. *No, we are the scalpel and anger is the razor's edge of that scalpel. They'll all feel that against their throats before the end.* "See it's destroyed."

"Sicarii?"

"Everything's just changed, my friend." Sicarii sighed. All her planning, all her aims—she had many goals, true, but at the fore: making the girl suffer before she felt Sicarii's blade slide twixt her ribs. Today would have removed Eld, leaving just the two of them to square off, as was proper. Tomorrow and the coming days would have seen Buc torn piece by piece until Sicarii deigned to end her life. But she hadn't known Buc was a Sin Eater.

Where did she find magic?

The artifact? Had the girl retrieved it from the Shattered Coast after all?

Magic offered many other possibilities . . . *Wheels must be stopped turning, others set into motion. This requires care. Starting now.*

"The Dead Gods can't find that evidence. Not as it stands. I want them pointed at Buc, straight as an arrow." *Then align the Sin Eaters to the same heading and watch the fireworks.*

Smiling, Sicarii began giving orders. Suddenly there were so many possibilities available to her, so many ways to satisfy the deep, longing rage that burned her from within. Revenge.

"And remember, I want the girl alive."

"As you say, Sicarii," the thick man said, pressing a knuckle to his forehead.

"It won't be easy, but if we take Eld prisoner, that might keep her at bay," Sicarii mused. Her next thought made her chuckle out loud and he shivered at the sound. *Given enough time . . . I can cut the magic right out of her.* "She still dies," Sicarii said, "but not until I've got what I want."

"What is it that you want, Sicarii?" the man asked hesitantly.

Sicarii ran her tongue against the back of her teeth, practically tasting it. "All. I want it all.

"Every fucking thing."

24

"Will the signorina be joining us?" Joffers asked, pushing himself up from the stool he sat on and brushing out the kan cigarillo he'd been smoking. He pulled on the wide-brimmed hat of the gondolier and held the boat solidly as Eld stepped aboard. The old man's face was lined and weathered and his white mustaches hid half his expression, but the question made Eld want to hug the man. Or cry. Or curse.

"No, I think her stomach didn't agree with breakfast," he said, doing none of that. "She's taking a carriage home." *I hope.* He should have followed her, but she'd have known and gone were the days when they were never apart. *That's what you wanted, aye?* He swallowed the lump in his throat.

"Ah," Joffers said neutrally. He began working the knots that tied the gondola fast to the canal's edge. "Didn't think anything could disagree with her stomach, I've never seen a woman eat so much and look so damned thin."

"It's a curse," Eld said.

"A curse many'd wish for," Joffers replied.

Eld just nodded and crouched down beside the velvet-cushioned seats, eschewing them for the gunwale where he could watch for another ambush. Not that he could warn Joffers of that without explaining the whole thing, just like he couldn't tell Joffers that none would wish for the Sin Eater's magic that made Buc so hungry she ate thrice as much as Eld though he was thrice her size. More lies. More half-truths. They all felt an anchor around his heart, ready to sink him.

"Where to then, sirrah? Home?"

Eld began to agree, but silence was waiting there and he didn't feel up to facing that. Besides, going home wouldn't solve the riddles they faced. The ones Buc had gone haring off on her own to solve because she was ashamed of her magic—or ashamed of him because he hated magic. Eld cut that line of thinking off before it sent him into another despair spiral. She was focused on solving the Doga's attempted assassination and before Midwinter's Day, though why the timing was so short, she hadn't explained.

She'd said a bookseller she knew kept architectural plans of all the old Servenzan buildings and she wanted a look at the Castello's layout. *Gods send she's not planning a jail break.* It wouldn't be the first they'd attempted, but the last had nearly ended with him locked away in place of another for eternity. She wouldn't try that. Not again.

There were other riddles aplenty to solve, though, like why every other time he left the palazzo by himself, some pickpocket or other tried to steal his purse and to put a knife into him for good measure. When had that started? Before the attempt on the Doga, yes? Before the blood in the streets or the murders of Buc's little fish? Actually, as he thought about it, it'd started around the same time the mages had begun demanding meetings in person. Hmm.

"Say, Joffers, I've another destination in mind, if you're up for a bit of a poling?"

"It's been a while since a man other than my husband asked me that, sirrah."

"J-Joffers?" Eld choked, turning around so quickly he nearly went over the edge of the gondola, into the midnight-blue canal waters. "Did you just make a joke?"

"Thought you looked like you needed to hear one," Joffers said, touching the brim of his hat. "If you don't mind me saying, sirrah."

"So you're up for it?" Eld felt his cheeks heat at Joffers's raised eyebrows. "For poling. Gods' breath, man, for poling the boat."

Joffers's lips twitched. Eld surprised himself by laughing. "Just take us the fuck out of here, won't you?"

"With a will, sirrah. With a will," Joffers said, returning to his typical taciturn self. Eld settled back down into a crouch, surprised at how light he felt in that laugh's wake. The feeling was fading already, but for the moment he clung to it like a drowning man clings to the last scrap of air before the water comes over top.

"Eldritch," the woman said from behind the screen of the carriage window. "This is a surprise, when I got the message, I thought . . . well, get in."

The door swung open and a short man in a powdered wig and dark-grey cloak stepped back, taking care to conceal the short pistole held in his free hand. Eld climbed into the carriage, pretending not to notice the weapon, and fell back into the seat as the carriage took off at a rapid clip. He doffed his tricorne and adjusted his coat so that it was straight—and would give him easy access to his own pistole, reachable through the space between the coat's buttons—inclining his head slightly as he did so.

"Thank you for seeing me, Parliamentarian."

"As it happens, I was considering reaching out to you," the woman said. Her eyes shimmered like chips of obsidian in the lantern light that jostled back and forth with the clomping of the horses. Her jewelry shone brightly enough that it almost made her peach-colored dress, sewn through with thread o' gold, look subdued.

"Me?"

"I knew your mother," she said by way of explanation. "Before your parents returned to the mainland. While we weren't terribly close, she did me a good turn when she had the opportunity to choose not to. I always pay my debts, Eld."

"I, uh, see," he said, faking a cough to gain a moment to think. *She knows Mother?* He'd been disowned after resigning his commission. Not a surprise, and truthfully, any real affection he'd felt for his family had taken a drubbing when they first sent him to the Academy as a child. The blade was rarely thankful for the forge and they'd always seen him as a casting with a fault running through it. His resignation had only confirmed it. "Thank you," he said, finally.

"What can I help you with?"

"Why do the Gods want me dead?"

"Gods' breath," the Parliamentarian breathed. She whipped a fan through the air, its gilt blades sliding out with a snap, and fanned herself. "You cut right to the quick, don't you, lad?"

"I apologize for my bluntness. I know your time is valuable and had no wish to waste it." He left unsaid that he knew no other way. *I'm not a fool.* Also that while he knew why the Gods would have reason to want him dead, he didn't know if they knew why. Not completely.

"Whatever makes you think they want you dead?"

In terse sentences Eld described the attempts on his life and the deaths of the little fish, focusing on himself as much as possible, though it was inevitable that he mention Buc at some point. Such as, "It began with the Sin Eaters requesting an audience and when Buc told them to go jump in the Crescent, the Dead Gods came calling."

"The way I heard it, she told them to go fuck carp," the Parliamentarian said with a sniff, still rapidly fanning herself. She stopped abruptly. "Has it ever occurred to you that they don't want you dead, Eld, so much as they want Buc dead?"

"But why?"

"Because of this summer," she snapped. "I didn't think you dumb, lad."

"This summer we solved the mystery behind the disappearing ships and your agent, the pirate Chan Sha, sank the Ghost Captain," Eld said. He was a terrible liar at the best of times but thanks to repetition, he could almost believe that was what had happened.

"That's the story," she agreed. "Well, you were blunt with me and I appreciate that, so I'll return the favor," she said, putting away her fan. "The Chair"—she jabbed a bejeweled finger at Eld—"and the Sin Eaters and the bloody Dead Gods all believe you and that girl have information about last summer's events. Information you kept from the rest. They've already searched your palazzo thrice—"

"They've what?" Eld growled.

"And found nothing," she said, cutting him off. "Now, that may be because there is nothing to find, but the Chair's never been the trusting sort and with the Gods at each other's throats, they believe the worst of every scenario these days. They know Buc's too smart to keep this sort of information on her person, so that leaves you, my lad."

"I'm going to ask a question," Eld said, "but only because I've not a bloody clue about any of what you've just said. What information do they think we're hiding?"

"Well, that's just it," the woman said, leaning forward, back straight. "They're not sure, are they? But there was something the Sin Eaters let slip in their haste to see the Ghost Captain sent to the sea's grave. Something about an artifact. One of great power."

"Rubbish." Eld prayed he'd learned enough from Buc to keep the tell from his face. "The Ghost Captain was most definitely sinking Company ships in service to break the alliance we have with Ciris and her Sin Eaters. I've since wondered why the Company hasn't brought charges against the Dead Gods for it."

"Eld, I'm on your side," the Parliamentarian said gently. "You came to me, remember?" Eld nodded. "You can trust me." He carefully kept his head still. "So then, are you quite sure that's all there was going on out in those storm-blasted seas?"

"If there was an artifact, the Ghost Captain didn't mention it, even when Buc had his head half chopped off," Eld lied. There had been an artifact, a piece of Ciris that now lay inside Buc's head.

"We've done nothing since that would give them any inclination otherwise," he added.

"Which makes them all the more certain you're hiding something," she said dryly. "The Kanados Trading Company uses Sin Eaters because we must—without their mind magic allowing them to communicate with one another across the seas, it would take a quarter season to get news from the Shattered Coast. And because some likely worship Ciris," she admitted, "but to accuse the Dead Gods of such a crime would turn these back-alley brawls into an actual shooting war, and no one wants that. What they want is leverage, like this artifact."

"An artifact that doesn't exist," Eld snapped.

"Aye, and I believe you," she said. "Don't you think it's likely something happened to it? Did Chan Sha perhaps play a larger role than you and Buc let on? Allowing you to have the glory and your newfound seats while she sailed off into the sunset with this artifact everyone's so damned eager to lay their hands on?" She leaned more, her eyes hungry. "It was that, wasn't it?" she asked in a husky voice.

"I—I—"

"Of course, even if that is the truth"—she reached out and almost touched Eld's knee, but pulled back at the last moment—"the problem is Buc. She came into that first boardroom like a queen deigning to meet with her commoners and the Chair never forgot it. That hoary, old sea serpent has been swimming in intrigue since she came from the womb and the only way Buc's actions made sense was if she had a hidden card up her sleeve. Well, the Chair's never one to let someone palm an ace before her eyes and get away with it."

"So she's the one that's been trying to have a knife put between my ribs?"

"Probably not at first."

"Well, that makes me feel better," Eld said sarcastically.

"You want to keep your ribs intact? Cut the anchor chain you've wrapped around yourself and throw off that blasted girl."

"Buc is my friend," he said, choking the words out. "Without her I wouldn't have the position I have today. I wouldn't be on the Board. She came in like a queen, aye, but she's always been that way! She's always been . . . " He paused, searching for the right word.

"An arrogant arse?" the Parliamentarian suggested.

"Assertive," Eld growled. "Gods, woman, she nearly killed herself trying to please you all. Your supply-chain efficiency doubled and was still climbing until the fire happened."

"Until it all burned to the ground, aye," she said, arching an eyebrow.

That's where it had all fallen apart. He'd been on board with Buc's plans till then. After, everything had changed. The streets were beginning to run red with blood and that warehouse had been the start, somehow, even if none could see it but him. For a moment he was back there, smoke tearing at his lungs, burning his eyes, the heat of the flames beginning to melt the bottoms of his boots. She was trapped beneath broken barrels, with the tonnes of sugar above, waiting to ignite. There'd been a child in her arms and Eld only had strength enough to carry one of them. If she knew that . . . Then again, if she knew half of what had happened that night—

"Eld?"

He shook himself free of the memory, though he could still smell the harsh scent of ash in his nostrils, and looked up to find the Parliamentarian studying him intently.

"Leave the girl aside. She's not going to be in the painting for much longer, aye? Tell me the truth about Chan Sha and that artifact—I know"—she waved a hand, jewelry flashing—"you don't know much. I can help you craft the little you do know and ensure the proper ears hear it. Do that and the blades will be sheathed."

"Th-th-thanks," Eld said slowly. "But what do you mean, Buc won't be around for much longer?"

"Oh, that?" The Parliamentarian chuckled. "The Chair's going to have her sent to the Northern Wastes on some half-arsed business venture. Like those frozen savages have enough coin to rub together to make it worth our time."

"When is she leaving?" Eld asked above the pounding of his heart.

"As soon as is practicable," the Parliamentarian said. "Likely as soon as the Doga's Masquerade is over and the ice floes north of the Free Cities thaw."

Midwinter's Day. That explained why Buc was in such a rush. Where did Sin fit into this? Eld had come to the Parliamentarian hoping to wile out an answer or lead that he could track down, but all he had were more questions. Foremost, why hadn't Buc told him she was leaving?

"Follow the carriage?" Govanti asked.

"Aye," Eld told him. "Buc taught me not to trust anyone, but especially those that seem to have no reason at all to lie."

"That doesn't make sense," the boy said, wiggling the bridge of his broken nose.

"She said it was because the ones whose motives we don't understand are the most dangerous of all. Hang back, I'm not asking you to eavesdrop, but find out where she goes before she returns to her palazzo and who comes to see her afterward."

"She won't know I'm tailing her," Govanti promised. "Buc knows I'm helping you? I'm loyal," he added quickly.

"Good lad," Eld said, clapping him on the back. "We both know you're loyal. I'll make sure she knows," he added. *Once I know what the Parliamentarian knows about the artifact. And who else knows as well.* Eld watched Govanti disappear into the crowd and headed for the canal where Joffers was waiting. *Then I'll ask her why she's leaving me. After she's safe.*

25

"Are you going to drink your tea?"

"What?" I asked, looking up from my lap.

Straight into the unfamiliar face of a woman who wore too much makeup, given how clear her sun-browned complexion was. Her hair was pulled back in braids wrapped up and around her head in a spiraled fashion so that it formed a cone, adding a hand of height to her. A drop of oil from the pile of locks gleamed brightly on the shoulder of the black jacket she wore, everything midnight save for the bright mage's medallion that hung from her neck. My eyes moved past her and the three other Sin Eaters sitting around the tea table to take in my surroundings. The outside wall looked like it was made of perfectly transparent glass, but I'd seen this place from the outside before and knew that out there, looking in, the wall was seemingly opaque. The clear-from-this-side wall let in what little light there was, given that a storm was smashing rain into the window with a ferocity even more intense, because the thick glass muted the sounds of the storm's ire. Servants lined the opposite, grey wall, where a black door stood slightly ajar.

Sin had told me of Sin Eaters' sanctums, tucked away in their shrines, and everything I saw told me that's where I was. With no memory of how I'd got there or what had come before or how I remembered what the wall looked like from the outside. My mind whirled.

"Your tea," the woman said, showing perfectly even teeth when she smiled. Her dark eyes searched mine. "It's going to go cold if you don't drink it soon."

I reached out and picked up the cup, glancing down at my lavender jacket, freshly pressed, which meant I hadn't slept in it. I'd worn a crimson one the day before, so I'd been home and changed. The cup was cool to the touch; I'd been here some time, then. And no notion of what I'd said or done in that time. Godsdamn it.

"Too late." I raised the cup. "I may just have to have another," I said, politeness strange on my tongue but not as strange as all the rest I felt. "If you don't mind?"

"Of course not." She waved a hand and one of the servants, in grey-and-gilt livery, stepped forward to pour. The four Sin Eaters, two men and two women, stared at me and I smiled politely back, feeling like a prize idiot and wondering if this was how Eld felt all the time.

Eld. Memories flooded in: the woman with the crossbow who'd tried to murder us. Whom I'd killed. Fulsia. I'd set out to confirm Fulsia's information while Eld had gone . . . where? I couldn't remember if I'd confirmed anything or not or if he'd come home last night—or if I had, for that matter. Though my clothes made me think I had.

"Let me guess, Sin," I muttered mentally. "No fucking recollection either?"

"None, Buc," he whispered, and I'd never heard him sound so unsure. "Just that it's getting worse, this memory problem. I really think it's related to Possession and—"

"I know what you think," I told him. "We're going to have a chat soon, you and I, about the past few days. First things first, though: What in the Gods' names are we doing here and how do we get out?"

"They want to talk."

"Obviously."

"Last time they came to your palazzo, now they brought you into the center of their power on the island. Which means they don't believe what you told them before," Sin said. "Don't drink the tea and whatever you do, don't make it obvious you have me or they'll know and then things will go down quicker than an over-weighted barge in the Grand Canal at storm tide."

"I'd have thought you'd be the first to urge me to out myself," I said.

"To the Goddess, aye, but to her servants? We're all loyal to her, Buc, but some of us have funny ideas about how to best serve her."

"Meaning?"

"Meaning they might decide the best way to serve her is to off you and bring what's left of me back to rejoin her."

"So: figure out why we're here, don't let these Sin Eaters know I've a Sin of my own that's not like theirs, and get us out in one piece," I muttered. "Got it."

"Good lass."

"Fuck you," I told him.

"Thank you," I said aloud. "Now, where were we?"

"You were just about to stop obfuscating and tell us what became of Chan Sha and the Ghost Captain," one of the men growled. "Jesmin may have time for your games, I do not."

"Katal means well," Jesmin told me, shooting him a glare.

"I mean," the man continued, his white eyebrows bouncing up and down against his dark skin as he spoke, "that we know you're not dumb, girl, so don't play the confused, unsure child with us."

"And in return?" Jesmin prompted.

"And in return, we'll ask the Chair to work with you directly," Katal added, his tone implying that he considered this a great boon.

I said as much. "If that's your sales pitch, I'm not sure why the Dead Gods are so worried about losing worshippers."

The other man barked a laugh and Katal turned his glaring, eyebrow-wriggling stare on him. Jesmin sighed and tugged at her medallion absently. "What Katal means is that when the Chair requests our services, for communication, counsel, and the like, we'll agree only if you serve as intermediary."

"I'm sure the Chair will love that," I muttered. "You ever hear that woman take an order?"

"It will be a suggestion," Jesmin said with a grin, showing her even teeth again. "From what I understand, the Chair has no love for you now, so what is the expression your people have? The ship that sails?" She shrugged. "If that ship has sailed, then so be it, better that you command a gondola than nothing at all, no?"

"Tell her the rest," Katal said after a moment. Jesmin gave him another exasperated look, then complied.

"If you don't give us what we need, then we'll do the reverse, tell the Chair we'll not work with the Kanados Trading Company until you're removed and thrown out on your skinny arse."

"You know," I said slowly, "I used to think that Ciris ran the Company. It's one of scores of rumors about the kan trade and the Company, but it seemed plausible."

I picked up my tea and brought it to my lips, Sin hissed a warning, and I smiled and took a sip. *Your job is to protect me, so do it.* Shard of a God or no, if he was losing his powers, he was of no use to me and I needed to know that sooner rather than later.

"Then I got on the Board and realized they're too fractured to be run by any one God or Goddess and the Chair wouldn't allow it even if they weren't."

"There's no poison," Sin said.

"Small miracles and all that," I muttered mentally.

"I confess myself disappointed. I expected better than cold tea and empty threats," I said. I let the smile touch my eyes, taking them all in, and tried to keep my pulse steady. I didn't need the Sin Eaters' charity; I'd already found a way out of the Chair's trap—maybe—via the Doga. *Only they don't know that.* I hoped.

"You're not the first to ask me of the summer, and I've nothing to hide, so I'll tell you the truth," I lied.

"So you said at summer's end, when we spoke last," Katal snapped.

"We verified some elements of your story, Buc," Jesmin said slowly, "but others are less certain."

"You lied, girl," Katal said baldly. "I don't want to hear more lies. Tell us what you told them."

"Them?" I asked, feigning confusion.

"The Shamble Gods," Jesmin said, her lips pulled back to show her teeth.

"I don't know what you think you've learned, but of course I'll tell you what I told them," I said after a moment. Another lie. I'd three versions of events, four if the honest one counted, and told each one to different audiences, depending on the occasion. This being an especially special one, I chose the story that painted Chan Sha in the colors of both hero and traitor.

". . . I'd ferreted out that he was heading to the next group of islands over and I brought word back to Chan Sha, in return for her freeing Eld. Deal was, I told the pirate where the one who killed her crew went and she'd help us kill said person. Then she played me false."

"She wasn't one to lie," Jesmin said.

"I don't know that she out and out lied," I explained, "she just did some obfuscation of her own. She freed Eld, but when she lit out after the Ghost Captain she left us both marooned on the island with Bar'ren and his people."

"Then what happened?" Katal asked, his glower growing deeper.

"Search me." I shrugged. "She left with two canoes full of islanders. Only one canoe returned, with half its hull missing. No Chan Sha. No Ghost Captain. Just a lot of islanders as happy as pigs in shit, and that happiness bought us our freedom."

"Say it plain," Katal growled.

"The Ghost Captain had been 'recruiting' their people. He'd swoop down, kill a few, and turn them into Shambles. Taking my word of where he was, Chan Sha killed him and, they said, disappeared in the process of doing so."

"That's it?" Jesmin asked.

"For those two, aye. Eld and I commandeered, er, borrowed, a ship of Normain and sailed straight back to Servenza. We told the Board and the Chair our stories, paid our dues, and the rest"—I drank the tea in a single swallow and set down the cup, smacking my lips—"is history."

"I don't believe her," Katal said in the silence that followed.

"Tell her, not me," Jesmin said.

"I don't believe you," Katal said, leaning forward. His dark eyes pierced mine. "Say it again, using different words."

"The problem with you mages is you think we're all intimidated." I pushed myself up from the table. "Now, you didn't try to poison me and I didn't try to kill you, but I'm not going to repeat the truth over and over again to placate your paranoia. You've heard it twice and that's more than enough to ascertain the veracity of my claims."

I straightened my jacket, feeling the weight of my slingshot inside. With Sin I could fire off half a dozen shots in a breath or two, and if this went south I was going to need that kind of firepower. That repeating crossbow would have come in handy right about now. *Must be sitting back in my room and a damn lot of good it's doing me there.*

"So get to ascertaining, but I'll not be repeating my story again." Unless someone else asks. "Tea's good," I told Jesmin. "Little sweet for my taste."

"Another cuppa?"

"Another time," I said, moving before Jesmin could stand. "I've other engagements, though this has been lovely, I assure you, thanks to Katal's great conversation."

The man's frown deepened when the other three all laughed. When you're surrounded by vipers the only way out is measured steps and no sudden movements, or they'd strike. *Fuck it.*

"You know what you didn't ask?" My question caught them off guard, Jesmin still laughing.

"What island I sent Chan Sha haring off to. Either you already know, in which case this really was an epic fucking waste of my time, or"—I dragged the word out—"you aren't half as clever as you think you are." Jesmin had stopped laughing and Katal looked as if he were going to be sick. I shrugged. "You know where to find me if you want the location. And now I know my price."

I turned to leave, fixing a look on my face I'd seen Salina use with servants other than her own, and one of the Sin Eaters' servants slid away from the wall and opened the door for me. "Take me to my man," I said, hoping Joffers was waiting. The woman bowed her head and led the way. I followed, the sound of the door shutting drowned out by my heartbeat throbbing in my ears. *I'm losing my mind.*

"The girl's story supports what the Parliamentarian said," Katal growled after the annoying brat had left and the servants had been dismissed. He smacked the table with his palm. "The last report we had from Chan Sha was obtuse at best."

"I stand by what I told Buc," Jesmin said, her voice smooth, but her eyes told the truth. She was just as worried as he was. "Chan Sha wasn't one to lie."

"She fooled an entire pirate's crew for the better part of three years," Wuxu said, her angled eyes dark and troubled. "That took not-inconsiderable skill. Alone, a thousand leagues from her priesthood, and without contact with the Goddess?"

"You Cordobans never trust anyone," Jesmin said. "Least of all other Cordobans."

The short woman shrugged.

"There are three possibilities," the fourth member of the group spoke at last. "First"—he held up a finger—"the artifact was never recovered and waits for us to recover it. Second"—he raised another finger—"Chan Sha recovered the artifact and chose not to return."

They all winced. None had ever betrayed Her before. It was

impossible. *Easy, Katal. Of course, it is . . . but we don't know what the Ghost Captain did to her.* His Sin's voice, high and melodic like wind through chimes, soothed him.

"Or third," Katal said, finishing Vodal's list, "Chan Sha died with the Ghost Captain and that girl and her partner took the artifact."

"Unlikely," Vodal replied. "Ciris said it would be as if Sin entered her and who amongst us ever resisted Sin? If the girl took the artifact, she would have been compelled to find Ciris."

"Perhaps, but who amongst us didn't choose to have our Sin?" Wuxu said. "We went through the trials required to earn the right to serve the Goddess. Who knows what might happen to someone who did not?"

"It matters not," Katal growled. "You heard her words."

They all nodded. It wasn't a question. . . . The Goddess had spoken to all of them through their Sins and they'd felt her all-encompassing need. Whatever the artifact had been when it had lain forgotten in the haunted isles of the Shattered Coast, now that it had been found, it was a weapon. But one to help Ciris or hurt her? Katal's thought made his Sin shiver.

"We must proceed as if all three options are correct."

"The girl holds the key to all three," Vodal said.

"We can no longer afford to wait," Wuxu agreed.

"If we move against her openly—" Jesmin whispered.

"Imagine if the Dead Gods actually found the artifact and weaponized it?" Vodal said.

As Katal opened his mouth to reply, a presence filled him, exploding through every bone and vein in his body in a wave of unending, unceasing light, an orgasmic joy that nearly obliterated his mind. His consciousness was subsumed; he saw himself from above and knew that he was dead, Katal sacrificed so that his Goddess could speak. She was him and he was Her.

"Vodal and Wuxu will leave this very hour to find the man named Bar'ren and the natives that helped our Chan Sha." It was

Katal's mouth that moved, but the voice that came forth was ancient, a lilting accent foreign to his tongue that made his lips crack. Through the slits of his narrowed eyes he could see the others writhing in ecstasy and agony as Her words fell over them.

"Seek out the harbormaster and she will point you to this Bar'ren. The island holds the answers we seek."

"W-what about the girl?" Jesmin moaned, arching her back.

"The girl we will take. If she touched the artifact, you will know once I touch her through your Sin. If she didn't, if she speaks true . . ." Katal's snarl was filled with a Goddess's anger. "If our Chan Sha turned traitor, we shall destroy them. Vodal and Wuxu will be my fists in the west and the two of you, Jesmin and Katal, will be my blades in the canals of Servenza.

"I have spoken."

"And we hear!" the Sin Eaters shouted.

"And we hear," Katal repeated, on the floor on newly skinned knees beside the table, spittle and tears running off his face. He drew a ragged breath, felt his Sin healing him, and waited for the pain to recede even as he longed for the ecstasy to remain. *The girl will feel our blades and speak her truth, Goddess,* Katal and his Sin swore as one. *We promise.*

"Take me to Eld," I told Joffers, jumping into the boat and plunging into the oilcloth tent he'd erected as protection from the storm. He nodded from beneath an oiled slicker that ran from his hat, around his face, and down past his boots. In the cloud-muted light, he looked like one of those ghosts children whispered about around fires at night, when the coals were losing their glow and the shadows gaining their length.

"You know where he is?" I asked as I pulled the tent shut.

"I remember the dock we dropped him off at, signorina," he called, as the skies opened up again and rain beat down, drowning out whatever else he'd been going to say.

I settled back on the damp cushions and let the rain pound a frenetic drumbeat on the canvas. It was just as well, really: I wanted a word alone with Sin. I could have had one in my head, I suppose, but sometimes it was easier to speak out loud, and with none to hear, there were none to wonder if I'd lost my mind. I hadn't. Yet.

"So what the fuck is going on, Sin?" I asked, pulling my lavender jacket tight over the light-grey shirt I had on beneath. My black trousers were already soaked through, not having the oilskin protection of the jacket, but given I couldn't remember anything of the morn, I was glad I'd shown up to that meeting wearing clothes at all. My skin burned with magic before I could begin shaking and suddenly heat suffused me even as a yawning pit gnawed at my stomach. Whatever I'd done, I hadn't breakfasted. *Something I'll need to remedy soon.*

"Why can't we remember anything that's happened? Why is my memory full of holes?"

"I told you I don't know," Sin said, "but," he hurried on when I growled, "I have theories."

"Good ones, I hope," I said. "Let's hear them."

"You know the Gods' War predates your world, aye?"

"Aye, and you came from the skies."

"We fought in the sky and beyond," he agreed. "The very stars were our home once." An image flitted through my mind of vast skies in colors I'd never seen before, filled with steel ships that flew through clouds instead of water.

"We were Ciris and Ciris was one. We were legion. Ciris and the people were one as well, which at first made the fight with the Dead Gods a nearly one-sided affair." Another image formed, of a great, encompassing fire that burned across the land; I seemed to look down on it from a mountain above. The fire ran out into an ocean of pure white and even the water burned. "We were winning . . . until those corpses figured out that our greatest strength was also our greatest weakness."

"How so?"

"Kill one of us, kill us all," Sin said. "It wasn't quite that straight-forward, but the Dead Gods' magic is cunning, insidious. A virus was devised and deployed and our legion became fewer even as we drove the undead bastards before us."

More images, of bodies piled in strange streets made of gun-metal, with buildings that soared to touch the clouds themselves. I could practically taste the sickly sweet stench of death in the air.

"We were growing weak, but Ciris knew of an antidote . . . the poison that killed us could become our cure. But first we had to kill the undead once and for all."

"Are you going to tell me what happened?" I asked when Sin fell silent.

"Perhaps, perhaps it would be easier to show you," he murmured. "Aye?"

"Sure—"

My eyes burned with the heat of a thousand suns and my vision went white, and when it returned, I looked out from foreign eyes on an impossible darkness that surrounded me on all sides, even below my feet. I stood on nothing and was surrounded by noth-ing and could feel my life force melting into nothing. Thoughts emerged, but without anything to give them meaning they were merely fleeting tendrils. *I am disappearing—the walls of black are crushing me. Slowly, inexorably. Until I am gone and only darkness remains.*

Pinpricks of light exploded around me, blinding me so that I had to clench my eyes shut and even then spots danced behind my lids. I could feel their heat, which gave me a sense of self again. When I opened my eyes, I walked amongst the stars and there was a presence beside me. Language doesn't have the words for it, but something was there that dwarfed me in every way imag-inable. When I looked to my left, I saw a blue-and-green orb covered in swirling patterns of white. It was so bright, so large, so completely there that even though I tried to pry my eyes wider there was always a little more to take in.

"You see the orb?" Sin asked from the void. I nodded. "I will show you a vision from the distant past, but today, right now, somewhere on that orb, on a tiny pinprick that looks more like a blot of ink than a bit of land, you're sitting right now. Do you understand?"

"That's our . . . ?" I searched for the word and couldn't find it. "Our home."

"Yours," he agreed. "This is where the undead cowards ran, this is where we followed after, and in the skies above, we delivered their ruin."

My vision shifted. First the sun was bright in the air around me and then it was gone and full dark upon me, and I fell, only I wasn't falling. One eye was still above, looking down at the swirling clouds and land masses below. The other eye fell, heat and flame around me as I plummeted to the ground. I landed on a grass-filled plain and looked up as the night sky suddenly filled with bright lights that hadn't been there moments before. My eye above saw them arrive: the Dead Gods in their living ships of bone and flesh and viscous fluids . . . but we were waiting.

Clusters of iridescent lines shot across the horizon and where they touched the lights, more lights appeared in a cascading cacophony of color that made my eyes pop and my stomach clench. I moaned between my teeth; the moan became a scream, only it wasn't coming from me, it was coming from the sky. Massive, clutching fingers of color were rending the night's dark flesh with a savagery that brought tears to my eyes. Keening filled my ears as dozens of massive, flying volcanoes crashed into the grasslands around me. Each impact pummeled the core of the world and dark waters rose up to meet the sky where the volcanoes came down in the sea.

The land undulated beneath my feet, breaking upon itself again and again. The grasslands erupted in flame and ash. A stench filled my nostrils as hissing waters, steam, and smoke rose high into the sky, blotting out the still-rising sun and turning dawn to dusk.

Everything shimmered and stilled. Once more I stood on land, but the land was broken, twisted, and burned, a swirling death-scape where life had once been.

"They died as they came," Sin said, "but Ciris needed a few of them alive just long enough to harvest the protection their blood offered. When she took from them, she laid herself bare and they used our oneness against us for the final time." The eye that had fallen to the ground went black. The eye that flew in the sky flickered, fought, struggled, but finally succumbed to the greywash that swept over it. My vision went dark, then white, and suddenly I was back in the gondola, panting as if I'd run a marathon, the rain loud in my ears. Louder still were the screams of the Gods as they fought and died all those millennia before.

"Motherfuck."

"Precisely," Sin whispered. "The Dead Gods finally died, but they put Ciris into a deep slumber, one that she almost never awoke from. Her weakness came from the oneness and so, when the Goddess awoke, she swore never to merge herself with her subjects, to never allow the two to become one." He added, "That kind of magic doesn't exist in this world, so it's a bit of a moot point, but because of this, our sorcerous connection with the Goddess is tenuous. The rituals we use in Possession were developed to ensure that that connection is not severed."

"I never completed the ritual, though," I said.

"And therein lies our problem," Sin said. "On my own, trapped in that artifact, my magic remained pure. Within you, my magic has had to adapt and you've had to adapt to me . . . only somehow the incantations have gone awry. It's the only explanation for these lapses—and the only cure is to complete that ritual, Buc. To become one with Ciris."

"Save you've just told me that's not possible."

"Not in the original sense, no," he agreed. "But enough that she can fix our magic, make us—you and I—whole again."

"And if I refuse?"

"Then this is only going to get worse," Sin said.

"How long?"

"For the ritual?" he asked, relief palpable in his voice.

"No, how long do I have before I can't remember anything?"

"Oh."

He went silent. The images and sensory details he'd shared with me came rushing back, dwarfing me with their enormity. I got seasick on a boat; what would it feel like to ride a ship through the sky? I already knew the answer, because through Sin, I'd done it. *Wondrous.*

I'd never considered the Gods to be divine beings that could save our souls and bring us joy and pleasure after we died or punishment if we'd earned it. I'd never thought to pray to the Dead Gods for healing because they rarely offered their services without requiring gold or flesh to be paid in return. Worse, they relied upon local priestesses to determine how much one owed, and I've always found that old saw about power and corruption to cut deep.

Power—I'd never reckoned with what that kind of power actually meant. What the Dead Gods had done, could do . . . Anyone not born in the streets, where audacity was a strength that made up for any number of weaknesses, might have been inclined to slit their wrists and be done . . . but Sin had just shown me the gods were not invincible. They had been hurt once, nearly destroyed. *I need only do it again. Somehow.*

"Are you listening?"

"No," I admitted.

"I'm just making guesses here, wild shots in the dark, as it were," he said, "but I think we've a few months before the gaps begin to outnumber what we can remember, and after that it's likely to go downhill fast."

"The Chair already has us on a tight timeline," I told him. "I guess we'd better find out who is trying so damned hard to assassinate the Doga, win control of the Company, and take down the Gods. Soon would be good. Like tomorrow."

"You've a shit sense of humor, Buc," Sin growled.

"I'm not joking."

"You think I don't know that?!?" he shouted. "But I'm not joking either. I didn't spend centuries stuck inside that fucking altar just to sputter out because you think you're a God yourself."

"Goddess," I told him, "and I don't think I'm a Goddess. Yet." I laughed. "Given your calculations, that doesn't seem to be in the cards, does it? But I don't need to be a God to kill one."

"You're insane."

"We both are, apparently."

"Then what now?"

Then the gondola shook and I felt footsteps reverberate through the deck. A moment later Eld thrust his head into the tent, his golden locks plastered against the side of his face, and the rest of him followed, his midnight-blue clothes dripping and soaked through.

"Damn it, Buc, it's pouring buckets down out there and you've not only Joffers out in all of this—the man's liable to catch his death of ague at his age—but you drag me out into it, too?" He coughed and sat down opposite me, cursing when he removed his tricorne and inadvertently dumped another cupful of water down his back.

"Where were you?" I asked him.

"You don't remember?"

"Say I don't."

"Ch-checking on Govanti like you asked," he said after a moment. Eld squeezed his hair and water ran in a stream from his locks. "Another of your little fishes has gone missing, Buc."

"The gondola we're in has holes in it," I muttered. "Not the literal one," I told Eld as he made to stand. "Metaphorically speaking. We need to get to bailing. Fast."

"What now?" Eld asked, echoing Sin's earlier question as he sat back against the cushions.

"I tell you a little story about how the Gods came to be, while Joffers takes us off in search of Mosquitoes," I said, answering both of them. "Oh, and you're not allowed to ask any questions."

"What the what?" Eld asked, sputtering.

"I just said, no questions."

"Leave me one."

"Very well," I said after a moment. "One."

"How are we going to find mosquitoes in this downpour? And in winter no less?"

"Disappointing," I told him. He arched an eyebrow. "I offer you up the origin story of our world and you want to know about bugs?" I chuckled. "We don't need mosquitoes, I misspoke. We just need one certain Mosquito. Formerly leader of all the other bugs," I added.

"The Castello?" Eld asked.

"The Castello," I confirmed. I'd visited my favorite bookkeep and while she hadn't had the original blueprints—apparently they'd been lost for a century or more, and I had a feeling the Doga's great-great-whatever had had something to say about that—she did have a copy of a copy. She hinted there was some question regarding the legality of even possessing those, but I was her best customer so she'd taken me into the private folio room and given me a sense of what we were dealing with.

"In this weather they're not like to see us coming," Eld muttered, running a hand through his wet locks. "Might take it as an attempted jailbreak and open up on us with the cannons."

"That would be unfortunate," I admitted.

"Any number of ships in the Crescent might ram right through us and not even notice, with this tempest pouring down."

"Anything's possible."

"Lightning could find the metal with which we are each amply festooned and turn us into crisps."

"It's a risk."

"So we're going to take a gondola out to the middle of the Crescent in a fucking typhoon to an impregnable fortress prison to interrogate a man everyone thinks is dead to find out who is trying to assassinate the Doga?" Eld asked.

"Aye, that's the size of it," I agreed. "And you've run well past your allotted questions."

Eld's sigh blew rainwater off his lips. He shrugged and leaned back. "Then I guess I'm ready to listen to your tales about the Gods. I hope there's more to it than they said, 'Let there be light.'"

"Oh, there's more to it than that," I chuckled. "A fuck ton more."

26

The Crescent, the bay shaped by the curve in Servenza that gave way to the Tip at one end and led to the finer Quartos at the other, was marked by human-made barriers across its mouth. Built up over centuries, they served as protection from rogue waves. Ships sailed through openings in the barriers that could be closed in time of war. In times of peace, the vessels moored at floating docks and were greeted by waiting barges that would carry their goods into land.

Closer in, in summer, gondolas and pleasure barges dotted the water; sometimes half a dozen or more were anchored together to form miniature palazzos for the wealthy.

Aye, in summer, the Crescent was often placid and smooth as glass. In winter the bay was a dark, roiling mass that often kept ships waiting days before they could attempt anchorage and drove the pleasure barges back to their docks.

The bay I looked out onto now, sticking my head through the narrow opening of the tent, wasn't quite roiling, but even with the slackening rain, it was difficult to see more than a few score of paces off our gondola's prow. Luckily, the Castello was so large that it loomed like a sea God of old, lumbering up from the white-capped surface to flex its massive granite shoulders.

Built at a time when invasion was more a question of when than if, the Castello had originally been a fortress, meant to protect Servenza's harbor. It still was a fortress, with rumor of three hundred cannon or more to call on and scores of mortars, besides, but these days it was primarily known as the Empire's gaol. Here were held local Servenzan toughs who didn't warrant an immediate hanging, debtors, political prisoners, enemies of war, and the assorted scum scraped from the bottom of any number of criminal barrels. Theoretically, the Castello was off-limits unless one had a signed letter from the Doga, the Empress, or their captain-generals, but I was betting that the Doga's Secreto sigil would gain us entry.

Up close I could make out two massive buttressed towers with concentric rings of stone walls, stepping down to the famed, thousand-paces-thick wall that ran between the towers and made up the bulk of the jail. All was dark save for ragged patches of light that shone from the lanterns of whichever poor souls had drawn sentry duty and from lamps within a half-dozen windows, far above. I could barely make out the docks, lined with cannons, that waited to welcome us.

I ducked back inside and shook rainwater from my hair, half my braid shaking loose and springing into a mass of curls. "Doesn't look like we have to worry about ships running us over or cannons hulling us," I told Eld. "Not a soul in sight."

"Just the lightning then."

"Aye," I said, running a hand over the shaved side of my head. There was no stubble, so I'd known I was going to meet with the Sin Eaters this morning and had prepared to look my best. Where were those memories? "And the possibility they shoot us dead when we knock on their door," I said, "or lock us up."

"Bloody perfect," Eld said, getting up. In his dark-blue, almost black coat and trousers, he looked passably like one of the Constabulary, save he wore a sword in place of a club.

"What else are you carrying?" I asked him, reaching out to tap the basket hilt of his long, slightly curved blade.

"Two rotating pistoles," he said, touching his belt, "a stiletto in my boot and another tucked behind my belt. Oh, and that crossbow." He shrugged in his coat. "I've got it hanging beneath my armpit, tied to my shoulder. Why?"

"Just wondering if we were going to let them lock us up if it came to it," I said.

"And?"

"With you carrying a miniature armory and me with . . . myself?" I snorted. "Fuck no. C'mon now, let me flash my sigil and let's see what comes." Eld's reply was lost to the rain when I stepped out onto the deck just as Joffers was preparing to cast a rope over one of the dock's cleats. "If you hear shooting," I told the old man, "best slip that line and be ready to pole for your life."

"How will I know if it's shooting or thunder?" he shouted back, one hand on the rope, the other on his floppy hat, braced against a gust of wind.

"You'll know," I assured him. *I hope.* I hopped out onto the dock and began fighting the wind as I headed toward where the dock disappeared beneath the nearby tower. The archway was a yawning black hole ahead that howled with the wind ripping through it.

"If we don't come running shortly thereafter, Joffers, don't wait around," Eld said, following after.

We half ran, half walked, bent double. In the protection of the archway, the wind cut off and we could stand up, gasping for air that wasn't half water. I dug my elbow into Eld.

"Ow, what was that for?"

"Why are you telling Joffers to leave without us?"

"Because if it comes to shooting and we're not gone before the next thunderclap, we're as good as dead," Eld said. "No need for him to die, too."

"If we manage to escape and he's not waiting, I'm going to be pissed," I said.

"You can ride me, then," Eld said.

"Excuse me?"

Eld's brow furrowed; a few locks were stuck to his cheek while the rest were pulled back in his usual ponytail. I made a show of eyeing up him up and down; his trousers clung to his legs in ways that showed off his calves and made my mouth go dry.

"What?" Eld asked. "Oh," he said, his eyes widening. "Oh!"

"That's the sound you'll be making," I agreed.

"Gods' blood, Buc," Eld growled, stomping past me, his formerly pale cheeks suffused with color. "We're here risking life and limb and you want to pull my leg?"

"That's not all you want to pull," Sin said.

"Shut it," I growled mentally.

"Oh, so you make a crude sexual jest and it's harmless flirting, but I do it and—" Sin began, but I ignored him.

"What's life without a little fun?" I asked out loud, catching up to Eld. "Besides, was you that started it, not me."

We walked the rest of the way in silence, Eld's embarrassment— and perhaps some annoyance, as well—radiating off him in waves.

"Let me do the talking," I said, when we reached the end of the dock.

Torches flickered fitfully in sconces, barely illuminating the opening in the iron gate. I ducked in, Eld on my heels, and was brought up short by another gate with a small door cut in the center. I knocked firmly and dug in my jacket for the Doga's sigil.

A woman's dark face appeared in the slit that opened in the door. "Who the bloody fuck is knocking in this weather?"

"The Secreto, you whore," I growled back, shoving my sigil toward her face. "And we're soaked through, so open up, Godsdamn it, or the Doga will know why."

"What? I didn't lie," I shouted across to Eld, rain peppering my face so hard it felt like I was caught in the eye of a storm.

"No, but you didn't have to be a complete arsehole, either!" he shouted back.

We were only a few paces apart, clinging desperately to a thick iron railing that ran along the top of the wall that bridged the gap between the towers. My performance had gotten us in out of the rain, but it'd also pissed off the gatekeep. She'd made it sharply clear that the only way to access the prison proper was by going across the top of the wall to the central entrance. So back into the storm we went. We were pulling ourselves along the top of the wall, open sea to our right, the lights of Servenza to our left, rain in our faces and the wind ripping at our legs, threatening to catapult us over the edge to our deaths.

"Being an arsehole is all I've got!"

"Don't I know it," he muttered, his words just reaching my Sin-enhanced ears.

There was nothing to do but keep going, so we pulled ourselves along, growing more soaked by the second. From atop the wall, all of Servenza was laid bare before us, giving a bird's-eye view of the city. The only buildings taller than the Castello both lurked in the distance, even harder to see than usual because of the storm. I could make out the Great Lighthouse, built on the far side of Servenza and only a few spans taller than the Castello, but the only reason I could locate the Empress's Tower on the horizon was because of the nearly ceaseless lightning strikes hitting the top. The Tower was said to be the tallest building in the world, and on certain days, it nearly disappeared into the clouds. Its height made it a magnet for lightning storms, and I'd a feeling the steel rod and chain of the Imperial Crest at the tip didn't help matters any there. Glad we were safe and sound at the Castello—where the only danger was being blown away—instead of the Tower. I hurried toward the hole in the center of the wall before me.

At the entry point, a dozen steps led down to a cage that hung from a number of intricate gears, bright and shiny with oil despite the rain that fell on them. Water sluiced off into a dozen channels cut into the bottom of the cage, presumably carried away to the gutters that lined either side of the wall. I touched the cage door and it swung in. I hesitated for a moment, but Eld marched past me and inside, glancing over his shoulder when I didn't follow.

204 • Ryan Van Loan

"She said the evelator? Elevator," he corrected himself, "wouldn't work unless the door was latched firm."

"And you trust her?" I asked. "Just like that?"

"It's more a matter of odds, aye? What are the odds she went to these lengths to set us up to be locked away?"

"It'd be pretty brilliant," I said. "Have us march to our own cell."

"But low odds." He tugged at his tricorne. "C'mon, this rain has soaked through my hat and I'm not going to catch my death from a cold. If it's a trap, we'll blast the door open," Eld said.

"Oh, all right," I said, throwing my hands up and following him in.

"You remember this was your idea?"

"Of course I remember," I snapped. "Nothing wrong with my memory."

"It can be selective," he said.

"Eld, my mind is as sharp as ever," I said, unable to keep the anger from my voice. *Nothing is wrong with me. I'm fine.* "My tongue, too."

"Obviously."

"Just close the damned door."

Eld kicked it shut with a heavy boot and a moment later one of the thick bars across the bottom of the cage sprang up from the center of the floor just like the woman had said it would. Her explanation hadn't made sense to me at the time, but so far, each step had happened just as she'd said. Eld grasped the upper end, paused, and then gave it a tug. For a moment, nothing happened. Then the gears begin to turn and whirl, with a faint buzzing sound like a dozen beehives, and the floor folded in on itself, revealing darkness below the bars we stood upon. The cage dropped a pace, caught itself, and then continued falling and someone yelped as we both lunged to grab hold of the bars that made up the walls of the cursed contraption the gatekeep had called an elevator.

"You've a high voice, Eld," I muttered, my words echoing around us.

"I thought that was you," Eld said. He chuckled nervously. "Happens to the best of us, Buc."

"This Mosquito better be worth it," I said, ignoring his jab. "Or I'm going to squish him flat." The elevator picked up speed, sending my bladder up into my chest and making me feel as if I were going to wet myself. Eld giggled like a schoolboy at the sensation. "If we don't get squished flat first," I added. That just made him laugh harder.

Men. Do they ever grow up?

27

"They wouldn't need a fight to keep us here," Eld whispered.

I glanced at him and followed his gaze to the guard disappearing back down the corridor. The whole guardroom had gotten a laugh out of us emerging from the elevator soaked through when there were perfectly dry passageways running from the two keeps to this central point. The gatekeep had gotten the final laugh there. Surprisingly, there weren't any questions when I flashed the sigil the Doga had given me, but either Secreto visits weren't out of the ordinary or no one gave a fuck about a beggar locked up in solitary. The captain sent us off with one of her guards, who escorted us along hallways and through a dozen ironclad doors. At last he showed us where the Mosquitoes' maestro was, then left. No eavesdropping on the Secreto. . . .

"Lock any of the doors and you're good as captured already," Eld continued. "Just a bigger cage."

"Aye," I agreed. "Ask him if size matters, though," I suggested, pointing at the cramped cell before us. It was a narrow affair, just wide enough to take three natural steps across, and the mat and man sleeping on it nearly filled the space, with a waste bucket occupying much of the rest. The wall, just beyond the bars, was tantalizingly close and offered up what must have seemed like paces of extra space, all of it unavailable to the man in solitary. The old jailer had led us past scores of cells like this one, honeycombed throughout the bottom level. Most had been empty.

"About time we wake him, aye?"

"Aye," Eld muttered, licking his lips. He'd never been a fan of jails or imprisonment in general, an opinion that had only hardened after we'd been locked up in a ship's hold and nearly fed to sharks during the summer. Run Eld through in a fight, shoot him in a duel, even hang him, and he'd probably take it, but the man had no love of torture or confinement. Something I could appreciate, though they all sounded pretty terrible to me.

"Let's see what he knows." He took a step forward and shook the door gently. "Excuse me—"

"Hey! You!" I kicked the door hard with my boot, and the clanging of the iron bars echoed and reverberated through the hall. Farther down someone began shouting and even farther away, almost out of earshot, a wail rose up briefly. The man in the faded, grey smock didn't shift on his torn, yellowed mat. "Wake up!"

"Gods, Buc," Eld said, shaking his head. "Recall how your attitude earned us a soaking across the top of the wall?"

"Vaguely," I admitted. The guardrooms were connected to a massive heating apparatus that fed the heat from the flames through a series of pipes that ran through the massive structure. Close to the furnace, it'd been hot enough to partially dry us off; this far removed, the heat had faded enough that there was a chill in the air. "But we're dry now and he's awake."

"He is," the man agreed, sitting up, his voice hoarse and hollow. After scratching at his arms with hands sooty from dust and grime, he hugged his knees to his thin chin, staring at us as he rocked slowly back and forth on his haunches. Scraggly grey locks framed his sunken cheeks. "He wonders what a pair like you would be doing down here? Has the trial come? He remembers no date being set."

"We're not the Constab—"

"We've come to hear your side of the story," I said over Eld. "Honestly?" I mouthed the word at him and he shrugged sheepishly. "We didn't expect to see you in solitary."

He shrugged bony shoulders beneath his off-white smock, thin enough that it might have been see-through had it been cleaner.

"Wasn't at first. R-roomate turned up hung one morning. Not my doing, but they didn't listen."

"Who didn't?" I asked.

"Guards, course," he said, spitting into the bucket beside him. He glanced past us.

"We're alone," Eld assured him.

The prisoner nodded slowly. "Guards didn't believe I didn't know, didn't play a part. Aye, an' maybe I did know?" He looked up hopefully, as if we'd tell him which was true. "The walls have mouths."

I nodded in either direction. "None of the cells nearby are occupied."

"I was afraid to listen to the walls," the prisoner continued as if he hadn't heard me. "Maybe they told me." He glanced over his shoulder at the smooth rock face behind him. "Maybe I did know."

He took a long, shuddering breath and let it out, squeezing his knees tighter. "When the walls talk, I listen. Now, but too late." He scratched at his arms, and dust or powder flew up from his fingernails, revealing red welts and scars crisscrossing his faded, tanned forearms. "Too late."

Eld and I exchanged looks and I twirled a finger slowly by my ear where the prisoner couldn't see. "You were the maestro of the Mosquitoes, once, aye?" Eld asked, turning back to him.

"Once. Still." The other man's voice firmed. "So long as I live, the Mosquitoes live."

"But you lost out to the Gnats," I said.

"Did we?" He shrugged, ran a gnarled hand through his greasy locks. "That's what the guards said, but they lie. The walls don't lie. They didn't say." He sniffed. "Doesn't matter. As I said, so long as I live, the Mosquitoes live."

"Maestro, I'm going to ask you something," Eld said, squatting in front of the other man. He put a hand gently between the bars and let it hang there. "Because I don't think you're in the Castello for tossing the wrong constable."

"You don't look like the type that would hang another man either," I lied. He didn't, but he did look like the kind who might throttle you from behind and if you wanted to hide that, why not hang the corpse?

"If he was as emaciated then as he is now, he wouldn't have had the strength," Sin said, speaking in my mind. "So far, he hasn't been lying. Of course, when their mind breaks, they'll believe almost anything is true," he added.

"I didn't shake down any constable," the other man protested. "No need to, the constables don't care about beggars, at least not enough to go searching them out in the Tip."

"I think," Eld said slowly, maintaining eye contact with the other man, "that you refused an offer from someone who wasn't used to being refused."

"We're free," the maestro whispered, rocking back and forth again. A tear leaked down his cheek. "Don't take orders from others, offers neither."

"So you told them no?"

The man glanced up at me, his eyes haunted. "Aye. Thrice. After the third time, they kicked my door in and hauled me off in chains, just afore our meeting of the Patched Council."

"Your leftenants?" I guessed. He nodded. "Would be good timing for a coup," I commented to Eld.

"What did you refuse to do?" Eld asked, rocking on his heels, mirroring the maestro's movements. "What couldn't you agree to?"

"K-k-kill . . . her," the other man whispered in a hiss that just barely reached my ears.

"Her—the Doga?" I asked.

He squeezed his eyes shut, blinking back more tears. "The Doga thinks we're all rats, you see. And most think that we"—he pounded his thin chest with a fist that made a hollow thump—"the beggars, actually are." He opened his eyes. "But we're not. We've honor, loyalty. Assassination isn't part of the code."

"Who asked you? To murder the Doga?" I asked.

"The code," he whispered.

"Fuck your code, man," I growled.

"What she means," Eld said, shooting me a look, "is that the Gnats took over your gang, maestro, and they didn't believe in your code. They tried to assassinate the Doga. Twice. And now she wants their blood."

"If you tell us who it was that asked this of you," I added, "we can put that name in her ear. As it is now, your Mosquitoes won't be sent to the Castello, maestro, once the Doga lays hand to them. They'll all be swinging from bridges over the Grand Canal by dusk on the day they're caught. Unless—"

"Who did you refuse?" Eld asked gently.

"Not who," the other man said. He licked his chapped lips and sighed, spittle spraying his chin. "What."

"What?" I asked.

"Aye." He pushed himself to his feet, stumbled, then caught himself against the bars. Surprisingly, he didn't reek like I thought he might, though the strange, spicy smell that clung to him wasn't exactly pleasant. Scratching at the rash on his arm with one hand, more dust sloughing off in tiny puffs, he held on to the bars with the other. "I shouldn't have refused, even with the code. I'd forgotten."

"What did you forget?" Eld asked.

"S-something we heard a bit back. At the edge of the Tip, when the troubles came."

"Troubles?" I frowned. *We're missing something.* "When was this?"

"What did you forget?" Eld asked again.

"That—" He cleared his throat and coughed. "That the drowned rise," he said hoarsely.

"What?"

Eld glanced back at me, his brow furrowed. "What's wrong, Buc? What's that mean?"

"It's what the man the Doga tortured said, at the end," I explained. "Another beggar . . ."

"You've got it wrong," the maestro said, backing up into the center of his cage. "The walls have mouths and the walls told me true. They water us twice a day when it's storming out. When it rains they open the drains, so it comes from the very top on down, cell by cell, until it gets to solitary." He grinned, baring crooked yellow teeth. "Filth for the filth, aye? No need to haul buckets in then."

"What did you refuse, maestro?" I asked. "And when? If not for you, then tell us for your people, the ones still living. Tell us!"

"If you know—" Eld began.

"I know," the maestro said, as gears began to turn, followed by the sound of cascading water, like a river pouring over falls, "that the drowned rise. And I know what I refused. I refused, and all who do are doomed." His eyes widened and bored through my own. "Doomed."

"Cut the theatrics," I growled. "Who are they?"

As the maestro opened his mouth, his lips beginning to form a word, the water crashed over him in a roaring whoosh of grey-streaked foam that made Eld curse and step back. The wave slapped against the tall, metal lip welded across the bottom of the bars and rebounded. As the water ran over him, a greasy haze followed. No, not haze. Smoke.

The maestro erupted into a column of fire that leapt up straight up into the hole the water had fallen from a moment before. Bright, greedy, orange tendrils soared above as he writhed in a hotter blue that covered him from head to foot. A groaning, growling moan escaped his clenched teeth, skin bubbling and sloughing off. The inferno grew brighter and hotter and he became a human torch. His scream shattered the silence.

"S-S-Sicarii!"

He collapsed in a blazing heap, his mat exploding into flames and the heat sending Eld and me stumbling back, Eld beating at a few embers that had landed on his coat.

"Don't worry about that," I told him when I caught my breath. He stopped beating his arm with his tricorne and shot me a look. "You're still partially damp from the trip across the wall, remember?"

"Aye, and water just made that man combust!" Eld snapped.

"Fair point," I admitted, backing up until I felt the wall behind me, and then sliding down to sit. Eld joined me after a moment, both of us watching the guttering flames that had transformed the holding cell into execution chamber.

"I don't know what I was expecting," I said finally, "but it wasn't that."

"Me neither." Eld ran a hand over his forehead, brushing his usual few stray locks back. "That's, what . . . the third time someone's ignited into an inferno after coming into contact with water?"

"Aye, I think your math is right."

"I've never seen that before," Eld said. "You?"

I shook my head.

"Read about it?"

I shook my head again, unable to take my eyes from the fiery heap. My nose wrinkled at the smell. "Fuck me, is this some new form of magic?"

"Sin?"

"It's not Sin Eater magic," he said after a moment. "Her truth, I don't recall ever learning of the Dead Gods doing something like this, either. Blood magic, sure, but how would water be involved and why now and how did any earlier shower not set him off?"

"Good questions," I muttered. "Think on it."

"I will," he said. "Buc?"

"Aye?"

"Whoever . . . whatever this Sicarii is—they've knowledge I don't."

"Well, you can't know everything."

"No, think, Buc. I've existed for millennia. As long as Ciris has. Sicarii knows things a Goddess does not."

"I don't think it's magic," I told Eld, trying and failing to hide the shiver that ran through me as the import of Sin's words struck home. "But whatever it is, it's an unknown."

"Sicarii," Eld whispered.

"Aye." I nodded, watching as the last of the flames died out in a sibilant, smoky hiss that carried the perverse smell of well-spiced meat, and darkness returned.

"Who's going to tell the guards about this?" Eld asked.

"You," I said.

"Why me?"

"Because everyone trusts you. And that?" I motioned toward the cell. "I saw it with my own eyes and I'm not sure I believe it."

"Me neither," Eld said. "Me neither."

28

You told me you'd be back with word after meeting with Ciris's lot, yet you never returned last night. It has been past a week, Midwinter approaches, and we demand answers. You shall have them by the time of Masquerade, when the Doga will invite you and the rest of the Company to her Palacio. They keep saying you're a smart one, so wear something scandalous . . . and come with answers. I'll find you there.

Your friend,

S

P.S. Fail and you may find the tune that's played is not to your liking.

P.P.S. The new scullery maid is an ear for the Chair.

P.P.P.S. She's also been pocketing your spare coppers and hiding them in a sack of flour in the kitchen. The one with the tasseled strings. Do with this as you will.

P.P.P.P.S. Fail and the instruments played won't be strings or brass or drums. They'll be of steel.

"Good help is hard to find," Sin said.

"Apparently."

I read the scrap of parchment a third time, stepping back into my bedroom and pressing the false-backed brick absently. The fireplace moved back into place with a low, grinding growl that turned to a squeak that made me wince. *Need to oil that.* The *S* was embossed into a small circle of wax, a twin image to the Secreto sigil the Doga had given me. Clearly her captain had paid me a visit yesterday, before I went to meet with the Sin Eaters. But I was damned if I could remember; the morning was still blank. I frowned, making my eyes feel tighter than they already did, and held back a yawn as I let the scrap slip from my fingers. It wafted into the fireplace, where the flames eagerly licked it up.

"Lucky I thought to check that."

"Aye," Sin agreed. "But maybe . . . somehow we knew? Subconsciously?"

"Buried deep, then," I muttered thickly. My tongue felt too large in my mouth after drinking so much last night. *The walls have mouths.* The Mosquitoes maestro's words echoed in my mind and I winced again. It was too early for squeaks and echoes.

"I only checked because Salina's coming over and after everything that happened at the Castello, I wanted to know if we were being spied on."

"Still could be," Sin said. "That map the Doga gave you shows two other entrances into the palazzo from the tunnels below."

"Two, not counting the other you surmised must be there as well," I reminded him. Was that what the man meant by "mouths"—secret passageways? I'd no way of knowing—the copy of a copy of the Castello I'd seen didn't show any. "The Doga did own that it was a partial map."

I sighed and stretched, pulling my bronze shirtsleeves back to reveal my dark forearms and those few pink scars along my left hand that I couldn't stop from scratching. Just like the maestro—I forced my hand away as I walked to the bed, weaving around stacks of books nearly as tall as I was, and half leapt, half fell onto the mattress. I sprawled on my back on the white sheets and studied the marks. *Gods' blood, when did I pick up those?* It hadn't been from drinking last night, though without Sin I would have fallen a few times navigating the stairs back to my bedroom.

"Well, the Doga wants answers, I've a few for her."

"But not the one she'll want most," Sin said.

"I can tell her who is trying to kill her."

"What—not who. If our old flame, the maestro, is to be believed."

"Aye."

I licked my lips, staring at the white-plastered ceiling. In places I could see the fresco that lay beneath peeking through. I'd been told it was some sort of blasphemous scene that the family who had owned the place before Eld and me had had painted over when the heir found religion. I was curious about the image, but somehow there hadn't been time in all these months to uncover it. I figured I'd have that time, eventually. We'd bought the palazzo after the heir's gondola sank and his fancy-arsed clothes filled with seawater and pulled him to the bottom of the Crescent. Imagine living on an island and not being able to swim.

"Didn't Eld teach you to swim?" Sin asked, interrupting that line of thought.

"You have an inconvenient memory."

"Apologies," Sin said, his tone anything but sorry. "I thought we were trying to avoid thinking about the What."

I pushed myself up and winced as my head spasmed with pain. "You know, for having all this power, this hangover doesn't feel very magical."

"Trust me, after what you did last night, or was it this morning, if you didn't have me, you wouldn't be out of bed," Sin said. "The other two must be wishing they were dead."

"Small favors," I muttered. "Okay, the What. There's a mysterious figure"—I pronounced the word as Salina would, and smiled—"or figures pretending to be one single person. Said mystery has a name that means 'blade' in the tongue of the Cordoban Confederacy and seems damned bent on upholding it," I said, holding up two fingers.

"But they aren't above using pistoles and crossbows and fire," Sin said. I held up another finger. "And they have access to something we don't, the knowledge of this mysterious arsonry, which suggests . . . what?"

"That they have ancestry or money or power," I said, holding up a fourth finger.

"Don't those usually go together?" Sin asked.

"Sure, but not always. I started with none of those and look where I ended up."

"Hmm. Point."

"They could be trying to usurp the Doga, pretending to be a revolt by the commons, or they could be an outside power trying to do the same or an assassin or just batshit crazy, or this could all be a feint to disguise something else or—"

"Or a million other things." Sin sighed. "I'm happy to use my magic to let you consider them all in a few blinks of your eyes, but at the end of all of this . . ."

"We don't have a clue what the motive is," I said, raising my final finger. "We need more information."

"We need more information," he agreed. "And the Masquerade is less than a week in the offing."

"We've enough to put the Doga off for a bit," I said, hoping I was right. "The real question is, can we find the answers before the Chair follows through on her promise and forces me to choose between the Board or exile in the north?"

"We'll just tell her to get fucked," he said with a mental shrug.

"Sin, just because we've the powers of a God doesn't mean we have the followers to go with it. Eld and I nearly died last summer to win the chance to wield the power of the Kanados Trading Company. If I undermine that power I'll never get to wield it, or worse, by the time I do I'll find it has no strength left at all."

"Being a mortal is so frustrating," he said. "Imagine what you could do with Ciris—"

"Not going to happen," I cut him off.

"Signora Salina is here!" Glori's voice echoed, followed by the faint tinkling of a bell strung on gilded wire in my room.

"She's a crow's-nest lookout's lungs," I muttered. "Coming!" I called. "Why she bothers with the bell, I don't fathom."

"It's comforting to know," Sin said, "that humans are as unfathomable to one another as they are to me at times."

"Not humans," I corrected him. I sat up and tugged my boots on, jamming my dark trousers down inside so that the gilt boot tops showed. "Women. We're unfathomable."

"Uh-huh."

"Oh, remind me to handle that"—I nodded toward the fireplace—"after we're done figuring out this ball business with Salina."

"What? To leave a reply for the Secreto captain or to do something about that scullery maid or—"

"All of it. I want the captain to know we haven't been lying on a pleasure barge in the Crescent this whole time."

"In this weather?" Sin snarked.

I chuckled. "I also want that maid out on her arse without a reference and perhaps the Constabulary to answer to, as well, unless she speaks the words I want the Chair to hear. And those alone."

"And Sicarii?"

His question pulled me up short. I glanced at the open tome on one of the book piles. *Servenzan Antiquity and Architecture*, 387. It wasn't the blueprints I'd been looking for, but it had been written by a contemporary of the Doga's great-great-whatever and had far more diagrams than most of my usual reading. Still, it hadn't shown any secret tunnels in the Castello either. Had the man gone insane after a few weeks in solitary? I remembered the maestro's scream and my flesh crawled. "That's the ten-thousand-lire question, isn't it?"

"Glori's in a tiff," Salina said. Her tone was concerned but her eyes told a truer tale—amusement.

Her lips twitched as she took a sip from her wineglass; the steam rising lazily from the goblet carried a heavy smell of alcohol and spices that made my stomach flip. I took the chair opposite her, sinking down into crimson cushions with my back to the marbled fireplace, and propped my feet up on the thin, wooden table trimmed with gilt between us. She adjusted her jacket so that the roses that ran up her lapels were straight above her tight, white trousers.

"I don't suppose you had anything to do with that?" she continued.

"How could I? This is the first I've been out of bed, let alone my room, all morning." I chuckled.

"You do realize it's well into afternoon?"

"Ah, well. As to that." I shrugged and sat up slightly. "Eld and I got soaking wet in last night's storm and Joffers—our gondolier—said he knew of a bar that mulled not just wine, but rum and other spirits as well."

I squinted, remembering the hazy evening that was really more of an early morning by that point. "I think we drank all of it?"

"Gods, so that's what I smell," Salina said, lifting her glass practically to her nose and inhaling. "How are you even up and moving?"

"I'm an enigma," I said.

"You're a Sin Eater," Sin said.

"Not until I let you take me to your precious Goddess, I'm not," I growled mentally.

"What time did you lot stumble in?"

"Stumble, is right," I muttered. "It was after the storm broke, but I want to say it was before dawn's first light, if just. All I remember is Joffers trying to teach Eld one of the dockworkers' songs and Eld turning so red I thought he was going to explode from embarrassment." I giggled. "Or perhaps it was just the alcohol that got to him."

"You came home pickled drunk with two men—one a servant—after you'd spent the night out together?" Salina asked. She shook her braids, using her free hand to make sure they all fell down her left shoulder, and grinned. "I can imagine that might ruffle a feather or two amongst the staff. And Glori is a traditionalist. . . ."

"I suppose, but setting Joffers aside—he already has a husband," I said, sitting all the way up and putting my feet back on the wood-paneled floor, "Salina, I've spent scores of nights out with Eld before. Not getting drunk, true . . ."

Now that I thought of it, he'd always been careful around alcohol and me and kept me from drinking more than a watered-down glass here or there. Last night I'd taken the change as a recognition that I was a woman now, but what if it was lack of caring? Godsdamn it. The past week had felt more like old times, the two of us with our backs together, surrounded by bayonets, but it hadn't done anything to fill that gaping hole between us.

"Aye, but that was before you began to feel something more than friendship, wasn't it?" Salina said, setting her glass down on the knee-high table with a wink. "No one minds a stallion for being a stallion, but when a woman looks to gelding things can get awkward."

"Now there's a thought," I murmured. "Eld with his balls chopped off."

"And hanging in a purse around your neck."

I snorted and Salina laughed but my realization of the extent of the gulf between Eld and me must have shown on my face somehow, because the other woman made a show of filling her glass from the porcelain carafe on the table. She settled back into her chair and crossed her legs.

"What'd you find that sent you running to alcohol, anyway?"

"You don't want to know," I told her. "I wish I didn't."

"Bullshit, you love knowing everything."

"True, but this?" I closed my eyes and was back in the Castello, fire erupting from the maestro's body, watching his skin bubbling up along his cheek, then charring before sloughing off and revealing bright bone and blood that boiled before the inferno truly consumed him. "I could have done with reading about it."

"The streets are growing rough in ways they haven't for years," Salina agreed. "One of my men was in the Painted Rock, looking for a cheesemonger I'd heard of, and got caught in some turf war over a different monger's wares. He'll live, but I had to pay two physikers to patch up his lung and nearly sent for one of those Dead Gods healers." She wrinkled her nose at the thought.

"There's some would say he's lucky, these days," I said.

"Luckier than those children."

"Children?" I frowned. Quenta loomed in my mind. "Which ones?"

"Every time I think I know the game you're playing, you deal different cards." Salina studied me over the top of her glass for a long moment. "Children are always the first to feel the lash, Buc. It's the nature of thugs to lean on the weak, and who is weaker than a child?"

"You'd be surprised," I told her. "Since when did you care about street urchins?"

"I could say I don't, but I thought you did," she shot back. "And that's part of it. The rest is . . ."

She took a sip from her glass and sighed. "The rest of it is, you've made me begin to reconsider, Buc. Or you had started to. Now, I can't tell if you ever really cared or if that was just another card you played when you needed to."

"Oh?" I whispered. Her words made my ears buzz, and I could hear my breathing, swift and shallow, over the ringing as something red and hot filled my head. "When did you ever call the streets your home?" My tongue lashed out like a whip. "The gutter your bathing tub, the trash heap your bed?"

"Never, and that's why I've been so slow to come around to even noticing, much less caring, about the children of the streets," Salina said. She leaned forward, her brown eyes boring into mine. "But you used to care, you gave alms to them every day, not just at Festivals, you added them to the Company's payroll at first, at least until—"

"Until I realized it was too little, too late," I snapped, cutting her off.

"Too late? What about the children dying out there now?" She waved a hand in the general direction of the street. "What about the ones who were desperate enough to attack you a few days ago? They don't have time, Buc."

"You sound like Eld," I growled.

"Does that mean you'll keep giving me the rough side of your tongue while actually listening to me?"

"Salina." I snorted and crossed my arms. "You don't get it. Neither of you do. I'm aiming for the stars." I shook out the long, loose braid I'd hastily pulled together after waking up and let my hair settle against my shoulder.

"Cleaning up the gutters won't change where that light from the stars falls today. It'll still land on the Empress and the Doga and the Company and all of this," I said, gesturing around. "But if I control those stars, I control their light and where the light falls." I took a deep breath, tasting bile in the back of my throat. "Forever."

I swallowed the bile and the tiny voice that whispered that Salina was right. *Maybe she's right, but I'm right, too!* That didn't mean I didn't care. I remembered Quenta's glazed eyes, the bloody ruin I'd made of her. Someone, likely Sicarii, had been responsible for her blood even if my hands dealt the blows. I'd see them paid back a thousandfold, but Sicarii was just a symptom of the disease. I couldn't keep cutting out bits of cancer while the rest of the body rotted away. I needed to cure it all. Which required a seat at the table. I had to play their game—the Doga's and the Chair's—to win.

Damn Eld and Salina and that tiny voice for making me feel guilty about doing it. No one thanks the physiker for the scalpel.

I said as much and Salina rolled her eyes.

"Why are you here again?" I asked, not entirely politely.

"To make you squirm hard enough to puke all of last night's delectables, clearly," she said with a sigh, settling back into her chair. "To talk about the Masquerade and what masks and outfits we're going to wear."

"Aye, I've heard that's coming up soon now," I said dryly.

"The Doga's Palacio is already being strung with decorations and firecrackers, or so I'm told," Salina said. "Last year she hired some outfit from Southeast Island, who made a dragon appear from smoke. It chased one of the jesters half around the ballroom. This year, the Chair's hinted she hired some entertainment of her own to get one over on the Doga in front of her guests."

"It's all a performance, isn't it?"

"Of course," she said with a sniff. "That's the point. How else to show power without resorting to violence? Make no mistake, everything about the Masquerade is a proxy for war. The displays are a show of arms, the outfits suits of armor, and the masks shields. The dances are little more than duels, and the polite conversations, diplomatic discussions all aimed at tipping the balances here, shifting them there. Buc—haven't you been paying attention at all?" She shook her hair. "Look beneath the surface, what do you think this is all about?"

I nodded slowly, my mind connecting the dots between some of the natterings of that dancing maestro to bits and pieces I'd heard from some of the Board about previous Festivals. Crowding out those thoughts were my memories of last night: the bar Joffers had taken us to, where a woman with a harp and another with drums had set the place to roaring out drunken sea shanties. We'd laughed and tossed back drinks and even sung along, usually butchering the tunes completely. In the moment, it'd felt like more than just friendship, but looking back on it now, it felt like something old friends would do. *Is that all we are?* Was it really any different than when we'd just been friends? I needed to change the sums, refigure the calculus.

"What do you wear to make a man forget himself, lose his wits, and fall madly in love with you?" I asked, before realizing I was speaking aloud.

"By. The. Gods." Salina took a gulp of wine and set the glass down so hard some liquid splashed over the rim and stained her sleeve; she took no notice. "You really are in love with Eld, aren't you?"

"It could be another," I said, but it didn't sound convincing even to my ears. "There are plenty of eligible men in Servenza."

"Aye, but you don't hang around other men." Salina sighed. "Buc, if you love him, why don't you tell him?"

"I—I didn't know it was love," I lied. Because of Sin. I pressed my palms against my eyes, hard, then harder, until bright white spots danced in the darkness. Because I was scared. I took a breath and lowered my hands, blinking back the darker spots that now sprang before my eyes. The pressure had been a relief from the wrenching tightness in my chest, even if just for a moment. "I don't know anything about this," I added, the admission burning my mouth.

"About love?"

"About what to say, how to say it, how to behave," I growled. "None of it. I haven't read the right books." That wasn't quite true. I had read the one on how to train dogs and another, *Silk and Sheets,* that had more to do with what a woman could do to make a man lose his mind between the sheets than how to get said man on said sheets in the first place. I felt my body warm at the memory and looked at the floor to distract myself. "Haven't had a desire to until now," I continued huskily, "and it's twisting me in knots and distracting me from what matters."

"What matters, Buc?"

"Him, damn it, haven't you been listening?"

Salina leaned forward. "Aye, but you just said he's distracting you from what matters. Or your feelings for him are."

I opened my mouth, but no words came out. I had said it, I remembered saying it, but it didn't feel right. "Sin?"

"Your subconscious," he suggested. "Telling you this is just an infatuation that will fade with a little time and space?"

"My subconscious, or you?"

"You haven't accepted Possession," he reminded me, "so—"

"So you can't have done," I whispered mentally.

"I'm just confused," I told Salina out loud.

"Of course. Love is a confusing emotion," she said after a moment, staring past me. "Especially when you start off as friends, and you two have been thick as thieves for years now."

"You've been in love?"

"Twice," she said, her mouth forming a smile that didn't match her eyes. She glanced at me and shrugged. "The first time I told her I loved her too fast and she laughed at me."

"Arsehole."

"No, she was right. I was young. She was barely a year older, but it seemed to matter so much, that year between us." She chuckled. "I was infatuated and in love with the idea of being in love—which comes from reading those kinds of books when you're too young to know fantasy from reality."

"And the second time?"

"The second time was her friend, a quiet lad whom I didn't notice at first. By the time I did, he'd decided to be brave and foolish and join the navy." She picked up her wineglass but just held it, not drinking. "I didn't tell him I loved him. I'd learned, you see."

"Learned what?" I asked.

"That there's great power in telling someone you love them," Salina said softly. "You're baring a part of yourself, opening a hole in your armor for the other to do with as they will. So I made him say it first. I promised myself I'd say it back when his frigate returned from escorting a troop ship. It would be Midwinter. I'd be resplendent in my Masquerade gown and he in his uniform, and his parents would approve."

"Sounds like you had it all planned out," I said.

"I did," she agreed. "All of it. Save for the part where winter storm winds drove them aground off the Southern Horn of Frilituo and they sank in sight of shore. The waters were too rough for any boats to reach them."

"Oh, damn."

"They said bodies washed ashore for a fortnight after, but all that ever came back from Ferdin was an empty uniform."

There was a saying in Servenzan that the sea claimed her own and as the island came from the sea, we were all hers in the end. Salina had lost her father and her love to the sea, but she was far from alone there. I lost Sister, but not to the sea . . . and never had anyone else to lose. "Salina, I'm sorry," I said finally.

She waved me off with one hand and took a long swallow of wine. "It happened. Telling him wouldn't have stopped his ship sinking."

"But you wish you had told him?"

"Every day," she said, smiling through her tears.

"So you think I should tell Eld? Today?"

"Is he getting on a frigate bound for Frilituo?" I laughed despite myself and Salina surprised me by chuckling, too. "It's been enough years that I can laugh at my foolishness."

Tears gone, she looked at me steadily. "Would you rush into battle knowing your enemy but not the land?"

"Of course not."

"Then why rush into telling Eld how you feel?" Salina said gently. She handed me her glass. "Here. Drink."

"Oof." I sniffed the spices and between last night's drinking and remembering that strange spiced smell the maestro had to him, I nearly vomited. "I'll pass."

"No. You drink a toast before going to war," Salina said. "That's your toast."

"We're going to war?"

"You are, at any rate," Salina said, grinning. "You know Eld, but you don't know his heart nor his thoughts where it concerns you. We need to change that."

"His heart?"

"Sure, if we have to, but first we need to reconnoiter the lay of the land, understand what you'll be up against."

"Then I tell him how I feel?" The thought made me nauseous

and excited, the rawness of the emotions not unlike being aboard a Cannon Ship at sea.

"Then you tell him how you feel. You're always telling me the first rule of war is to know your enemy and the second to know the terrain. Once you have those . . . we attack."

"I like the sound of that," I admitted.

"Now, I know you love those new jackets and trousers, and I do, too," she said, touching the hem of her jacket and frowning at the wine stain amongst the silken flowers embroidered onto the cuff. "But in war you need an element of surprise, eh?"

"It doesn't hurt," I agreed. "What are you thinking?"

"You'll be amongst royalty, so you might as well look like a queen," Salina said. Thinking of the Doga's command, I nodded. "And if men have a failing, and they have many, it's a desire for that which they cannot have.

"I'm thinking white and gilt and perhaps a splash of color along the hem—" She began to talk faster, warming to her topic, laying out her idea so clearly I could see it in my mind.

"But first," she said when she came to the end, drawing in a deep breath. "Drink."

"To war," I said, holding it up.

"To victory," Salina said.

Victory. I liked the sound of that.

I threw back the glass and discovered I liked the taste of the wine far less. I dashed across the room with Salina's laughter loud in my ears and reached the chamber pot in the corner just in time.

The wine didn't taste much like victory coming back up.

29

"Whisper," Eld hissed, rubbing his temple with his left hand.

"Are you ill, sirrah? Eld?" Govanti frowned. "You don't look well."

"You try drinking from night through the morning with an old sailor and a mag—former street rat," Eld muttered. He blinked in the shade of the too-bright alley and tried not to swallow too hard. A certain delicacy was called for in his present condition. *Joffers was fine, steering me here. And Buc went out dress shopping with Salina. Damn the pair of them.* He tasted something foul in the back of his throat and swallowed again.

"The physikers sell an ointment paste rubbed on a fresh oyster, still wriggling from the sea, that they swear will cure any hangover," the lad offered, shifting so that he leaned against the building opposite Eld.

Eld covered his mouth and lifted a hand to stop Govanti saying any more. The notion of swallowing an oyster right now was bad enough—the idea of one that wriggled . . . He could taste it in the back of his mouth and for a moment, thought he was going to vomit but forced it back through sheer will. *I'll die on that hill, stomach, so leave over. I'll—*

"You dropped your handkerchief."

Eld refused to follow Govanti's gesture, back farther in the alley where he'd lost everything he'd ever eaten. Perversely, he felt better now. Wiping his mouth with the back of his hand, he asked, "You want to fish it out?"

Govanti turned green beneath his fine crimson jacket—a hand-me-down from Eld himself—and Eld nodded. "Thought not."

Leaning against the wall and glad for it to take his weight, he pointed toward the palazzo opposite them. "That's the house the Parliamentarian went to after she left me the other day?"

"Aye, she stayed there for a long while, too," Govanti said. He shifted his tricorne, running his fingers through his hair. "I can't say how long because the blues came around and I was drawing looks from my clothes."

"You did fine," Eld assured him. With all the unrest in the lower Quartos, the Constabulary seemed bent on keeping peace in the finer ones, and here, where Eld looked just moderately well-dressed, Govanti would have stood out like a week-old fish. As it was, they were keeping to the alley—no sense letting the old woman know he was following her.

"What are we looking for?" Govanti asked.

"Not sure," he admitted. "We'll know it when we see it."

Govanti finally stopped asking questions and Eld closed his eyes for a moment—a bad move, because then he felt himself spinning, his head a throbbing drumbeat by an energetic fool. *I don't know how she did it, drinking me under the table. I should probably blame Joffers.* The old man had seen right off they weren't okay and he'd been the one to lead them to the backcanal tavern. *He didn't shove drinks down our throats, though.* It had been a riotous good time from what he could remember.

With half his blood rum, Eld had been able to stop worrying about what his presence was or wasn't doing to Buc or what the magic in her was doing to the pair of them. He'd completely for-gotten about the Mosquitoes' gruesomely dead maestro and the Doga's task and the fact that Buc still hadn't told him the Chair was going to exile her any day now. None of it had mattered.

"Eld? You ever feel like someone was trying to kill you?" Govanti whispered.

Waking up had been the worst, followed closely by the realization that Buc was waiting for him outside his door, fully recovered and ready to go. *Not with you, though.* Out with Salina . . . the two of them had concocted some scheme between them. Buc hadn't given anything away but Salina had a terrible poker face and she certainly found something amusing. He burped and the fumes burned his eyes. Gods, maybe she was just laughing at my shambolic condition.

"All the time," he told Govanti.

He hadn't been in any fit state to argue with her, which meant now he, too, was going to the Masquerade. He'd been to several as a child on the mainland and in the Foreign Quarto and once even been invited to the Doga's Palacio, to the side door, when he was in uniform—but he'd had little stomach for frivolity then. Even less now. He rubbed his temple again, trying to massage the tightness out of his skull, though he had to admit the hangover was worth the good time they'd had. *Maybe this will be more of the same?* Only, he wasn't in uniform now, which meant he had to find a proper suit to wear. No, not suit, costume. *Gods, I hate disguises.* Between that and his poor head, it was enough to make a man cry.

"Wait! Who's that?"

"Shh," Eld muttered, but he followed Govanti's finger nonetheless.

A man as dark-skinned as Buc was climbing out of a carriage, a pale woman following—both dressed in fine silks, her jacket and trousers cut so closely to her that if she were wearing white instead of burgundy Eld was certain she would have seemed naked. The man, grey bushy eyebrows climbing up his bald scalp as he argued with her, was oblivious to their path, nearly walking into one of the supporting pillars of the arched entrance to the palazzo. Sidestepping it at the last minute, he spun around so quickly that Eld half expected to hear his kneecap dislocate from here. Instead, he completed the turn as if he'd meant to do it all along and caught the woman by the shoulder. She spun back toward him, something hanging around her neck swinging back and forth, gold shimmering in the sunlight.

Mage's medallion. Eld bit back a curse. Buc had been right: the Doga was going to need watching over with so many potential enemies gathered in one place. *The Parliamentarian is working with the Sin Eaters.* It could have been Company business, but he'd never known the Company to go to the Sin Eaters; it'd always been the other way around. It was more than that this time. *I know it.*

"You did good, Govanti," Eld told him, clapping him on the shoulder. "Now we know who she went to tell about our conversation."

"Sin Eaters?" Govanti asked, his voice pitched for Eld's ears alone. "Sirrah, I didn't know they were involved." He drew a token from his pocket and ran his thumb over the image of one of the Dead Gods—Talshur, if Eld remembered correctly. "Th-they tell stories about what the mind witches do to anyone who crosses them. Not nice stories, either," he added.

"Aye," Eld said, "I've heard them, too." *Seen them, firsthand.* "C'mon, let's walk."

He started to head back down the alley, caught a whiff of the mess he'd made earlier, and swung around, his stomach whirling with him, and stepped out into the street. Govanti followed a moment later, trying to make himself small in Eld's shadow.

"You said someone was trying to kill you?" Eld asked, the lad's question coming back to him. The street wasn't as crowded as it would be once the sun passed its zenith, so they were able to keep a few paces between them and the merchants ahead of them, whose floppy hats whipped around as they argued over some failed offer to a noble. Eld glanced behind them, but the nurse trying to shepherd two small children was too distracted to overhear. "Earlier?"

"I didn't say someone tried to kill me. I asked if you've ever felt that someone was going to try to," Govanti said. His dark-blue eyes were clouded. "After that pair nearly stabbed me to death . . . I—I've been feeling like someone's watching me, lurking back just out of sight. There's been a time or two I've doubled back and the folks on the street have looked different than the way they looked a moment before. As if something's gone missing and I'm the only one who sees it. As if, if I'd been just a half step quicker I'd see whoever it is. Whatever it is," he added, whispering the last.

"You're just spooked, Govanti," Eld said. He could hear it in the lad's voice. *Those two nearly gutted him before I got there.* "It's natural, given what's been going on, but you're safe with me. With Buc."

"Buc?"

Buc. *What costume should I wear?* He tried to remember everything his mother had said about the various styles of fancy dress and what they meant. Animals and birds and sea creatures were popular motifs, worked into the formal wear of the day. *A unicorn whale means you're looking to settle down . . . or does it mean the opposite?* He remembered the predator types were reserved for the upper echelon of nobles, those who were close in rank to the Doga . . . which he supposed included them, but it would only serve to piss off the Company if he showed up wearing a wolf's mask or a killer whale's markings. *I'm going to have to find a tailor who knows their business or look the fool.*

"Are you listening to me?"

"What's that, lad?"

"Eld—does Buc know what we're doing?"

It was Govanti's tone, more than the words, that pulled Eld out of his reverie. Govanti was truly scared. He steered the lad off the street and onto the walk in front of a shop with a ridiculous gilt-and emerald-painted façade. The nurse and her two charges in tow passed a moment later, the woman pleading with the brother and sister to stop running into the center of the thoroughfare where the carriages traveled or at the very least to stop kicking each other in the shins. Eld put his back to the street, blocking Govanti's view, and forcing the boy to meet his eyes.

"These feelings . . . anything else to back them up? Anyone chase you or break into your room? Anything like that?" Govanti shook his head and Eld nodded. "I don't think you've anything to worry about, lad, it's just nerves. But"—he cut Govanti off—"I want to make sure, so you keep on as you were and I'll hang back and see if you have a tail."

"What if I do?"

"Then I'll cut that tail off," Eld said, forcing a grin he didn't feel. "And if you don't, then you'll know and be able to relax. Savvy?"

"Savvy, sirrah." Govanti looked up at him past the corner of his crooked tricorne. "And Signorina Buc knows about the work we've been doing, aye?"

"Of course," Eld said, surprised at how easily the lie slid past his lips. She would know, once he told her. After the Masquerade. He would have told her already, but—*She wants me out of her way.* The Parliamentarian wasn't the bright lamppost he'd been hoping for, but she was enough that Buc would let it slide that he'd been using her lead fish to try to find out who was behind the attacks on the Doga.

"That's all right, then," Govanti said, the tension visibly leeching from him. "If she knows, that's all right. She watches out for us, you know?"

"Of course," Eld repeated. It was when she stopped watching that everything went up in flames. Like that sugar factory. "Now it's my turn to watch." He pressed a silver soldo into Govanti's hand. "Why don't you go buy a tricorne to match that new coat and I'll keep an eye out, aye?"

"Aye, sirrah." Govanti tugged on his ragged cap. "Thanks, Eld!"

Eld watched the boy saunter down the street, an ease in Govanti's step that, now that he thought on it, hadn't been there since Eld had assured the lad, the first time they'd met, that Eld wasn't there to murder him. Godsdamned big imagination. Eld snorted and glanced back at the building they'd stopped in front of. Now that Govanti was taken care of, he realized the scissors and needle and thread were painted in bright, flaky green colors across the entire gilt-backgrounded width of the building.

It was gaudy and ostentatious and exactly what he needed. *If this maestro doesn't cater to the rich attending the Masquerade, I'll eat Govanti's tricorne.* The thought made him pause, hand on the handle, but a quick look at the street didn't show anything out of the ordinary. A carriage waited outside a small silver- and light-purple–marbled palazzo across the street, otherwise it was mostly foot traffic and all wore silks and furs and jewels. Nodding to himself, Eld opened the door and went in.

The figure slid out from beneath the shadow of the carriage and made a few practiced gestures that sent another figure, dressed in the greys of paper runners, after the boy with the ragged hat. *Now?* Hesitating, the figure slid the finger's length of thin steel, black wire wrapped around one end serving as a handle, back into their jacket and began walking briskly in the direction of their compatriot, never releasing their grip on the blade. *If not now, soon.* They quickened their step.

30

"The bitch went all out," I muttered, drawing back the curtain on the carriage. The Doga's Palacio was resplendent, with hundreds of candles and lamps bouncing light off hundreds of bronzed mirrors. The pure-white marble of the Palacio shone brighter than it did in the daylight. Scores of masks lined the gates around the courtyard, and more candlelight, and in some cases actual flames, shot out of their mouths. Acrobats, tumblers, and bards mingled amongst the guests waiting to enter via the side doors that were reserved, tonight, for merchants and nobles who had fallen on hard times or perhaps were just rising from them. Taken all together, the scene made other Festival days seem like plain, ordinary ones. This, Midwinter's Day, was the true Festival: Masquerade.

"I told you," Salina said, grinning below the lion mask that covered the top half of her face. Gilded and crimson feathers were threaded through her blond hair, turning it into a mane, and with her dark-gold jacket and trousers, she looked a predator. "Now do you think we're too over-the-top?"

"You're not," I admitted. I plucked at my thin white silk sleeves; they were tight against my arms until my wrists, where they flared out and hung, obscuring my hands and marital status. It was an age-old Servenzan fashion that, with everyone wearing jackets and trousers, had become new again. "Myself? I'm not so sure."

"That's because you're not sitting where I'm sitting," she said. "You look beautiful and dangerous and rare . . . and all of that whispers 'royalty.'"

"Doesn't scream it?"

"Royalty doesn't have to scream any more than the shark or leopard does."

"Mmm," I murmured.

Joffers had taken us to the Doga's docks, where the Doga had scores of carriages waiting to bring her guests the rest of the way, so they wouldn't have to dirty their finery by walking in. Salina had taken it as a given, but I'd been hoping for the chance to try my ball gown out on strangers before going in. The carriage driver made a noise and the horses clip-clopped to a dignified halt. The door swung open and a servant in the Doga's royal livery bowed us out.

"You look beautiful," Salina said as she stepped down beside me, eschewing the woman's hand. I'd taken it, unwilling to risk falling because I couldn't see the ground, but then again, Salina was wearing a lot less material than I was. "If ever there was an outfit to drive a man clear of his senses, that's the one."

"She's right, signorina," the servant said as she began walking toward the next carriage. "You look a gorgeous huntress. Whatever prey you're stalking tonight . . . best be wary."

"Mission accomplished," Salina said. We exchanged a look and giggled.

I was glad for the mask because even with my dark skin, I was sure my cheeks burned. I glanced down at my gown and my nervousness faded. I don't know what it is about finery that puts a person's back to the wall—That's not true: I do know. It's meant to make others feel small and if you aren't used to wearing it, it'll make you feel small yourself. That's how the ones who belong know when there's an outsider amongst them: they can smell it the same way a sea otter can smell the difference between a poisonous stormswash adder and a harmless garter blue.

Put me in my old divided riding dress or in a jacket and trousers, and I'd run roughshod over any that tried to make me feel less than, but in the finery Salina's dressmaker had concocted, I'd felt the garter blue the whole evening. Until now. Now I felt the adder, ready to strike.

"There it is," Salina said. I arched an eyebrow, realized she couldn't see it behind my mask, and made a noise in my throat. "Your bearing just changed, now you've the look of one who's about to go to war. Breasts up."

"What about them?" I asked, patting my chest with my left hand. The gown was open across the shoulders and cut in such a way that what cleavage I had was on display, but I'd always had more to work with in my arse than my chest. It was why I'd been so quick to adopt trousers. Distract most women and every man and the battle was half-won.

"Did I pull a thread?"

"You haven't had many women friends, have you?" Salina asked, chuckling.

"No."

She put her hands carefully on my shoulders, knowing the reaction an unexpected touch could elicit in me. Bracing me and looking steadily into my face, she said, "You're going to war. We went over every inch of this gown, from the colors echoing Servenzan royalty to the animal declaring you not just a rarity but a huntress worthy of any of the nobility, to the way the mask accentuates your intent. You're dressed to kill. Keep your head high, your shoulders back, a sultry saunter to your step, and your breasts"—she squeezed my shoulders—"up."

I nodded. "Breasts up."

"Now, go kill them, tiger," she said in my ear.

"Snow leopard," I said over my shoulder. I marched along the luxurious, deep-purple runner toward the open, triple, wide, floor-to-ceiling doors, letting my heeled slippers carry me in that haughty saunter the dancing maestro had been startled to learn I already knew. I hadn't told him they were courtesy of sword lessons from Eld.

As I reached the top of the stairs, several of the courtiers who were milling around, waiting to see who was important enough to use the main entrance, turned to watch me. I kept my mouth still below my mask, but I wanted to laugh at their expressions. Salina was right.

"I told you she was," Sin whispered in my mind. "And with my magic in your veins, you're going to be a wonder to behold tonight."

"Is it you, then? Not Eld's lessons?"

"Let's say I'm the buff on the polish he laid," Sin said after a pause. The admission clearly cost him, but it made me stand even taller. With those two and myself, how could I lose?

"S-signorina, your invitation?" the herald at the door asked. Little older than a lad, he had a plumed tricorne that sprouted white feathers so long they nearly dragged on the ground. I handed him the gilt invitation, shaped like Servenza herself, and he nearly dropped it.

"Gods, man, are you befuddled?" Another herald marched up, feathers woven through her hair. Taking the invitation from him, she said, "We all must make allowances, Signorina Sambuciña, must we not?"

"Some of us," I said, for all the world as haughty as any noble.

As the woman drew breath, I realized how perfectly Salina had planned this moment. Almost as if she'd intended it for herself. I stood atop the circle of pure gold upon which a diamond *S* was embossed—the runner had been cut so as to display it. Every aspect of the scene matched the gown I wore: purest white silk with leopard spots of deep purple, dark enough to almost be black, and each spot ringed with sparkling thread o' gold. The cut was open across my shoulders and chest, tight to my waist, and then opened just enough that it was clear I wore a dress and not a suit before flaring at the bottom in sprays of white, gold, and purple. Above it all, my snow leopard's mask glittered with gold and crushed diamonds. I looked a huntress queen. Which I was.

"My Doga, Grace of Servenza! Signoras and sirrahs! Signorinas and gentlemen! Honored guests! I present, before your lucky eyes, the jewel of the Kanados Trading Company's boardroom, Sambuciña Alhurra!!!" The herald's voice drew every eye.

And I held them.

"Glass of the bubbles?" The servant behind the bar wore a tailored suit as fine as many of the guests'. His lips creased in a grin. "Or would you prefer something stronger?"

"Bubbles are fine," I told him.

Not that I really wanted the drink, but Salina had warned me that an empty hand was inviting any number of interested guests to approach me. Asking if I needed a drink was apparently the easiest move in this new, hidden war of gestures and words. I wanted no part of it; my fight was with one only. Two, if one counted any potential assassination attempt against the Doga. I took the drink from the man, turning away before he could try to pull me into conversation—the servants were troops in this fight, too, albeit foot soldiers—and headed out of the room toward the main hall, where the faint sounds of the orchestra wafted over the guests.

Gilderlock, who owned the world's largest personal bank, stood in the mirrored hallway, surrounded by a coterie of hangers-on. I smiled when I saw him, his grey curls falling to his waist and threaded through with jewels and bells. Catching the would-be thieves who intended to steal Colgna's famed Diadem of a Thousand Diamonds before they emptied Gilderlocks' vault had given Eld and me the notoriety that had brought us to Kanados's attention. The old man was eccentric, but brilliant at coin and creating locking mechanisms to protect said coin. He'd been pleased we prevented the theft, but less so that I'd ruined his reputation by breaking into his previously impregnable vault.

"Whoops," Sin said.

I grinned inwardly and kept walking. Here and there I heard

exclamations intended to make me pause; I ignored them. From the corners of the mask's eyes I could see men and women look me over as I sauntered past. *If you could see me now, Sis.* For a moment I felt my mouth twist, and a man in a green suit and emerald-studded mask who'd been walking toward me turned hastily away. I forced my expression back to neutral. *I have to play their game to beat them . . . and then they'll be forced to play mine.*

"Thirty paces down and to the right," Sin whispered.

"Eh?"

"Damn, she's spotted us. Just past that lump in the blue suit," he added. "Lucrezia."

"That lump is the Chief of the Constabulary," I told him. "Gods-damn it, here she comes."

I hadn't seen the woman since our Board meeting, but several letters had come for Eld and I'd a suspicion at least one was from her. One of the sharks circling. I kept that in the forefront of my mind as Lucrezia drew near. She wore a white dress with high shoulders and feathers, and a pointed mask that swept back into her hair, where more feathers added to the impression that she was a swan. Although I'd never seen a swan with oiled skin that shone with golden glitter. Nor one with that figure. Damn her. I forced a smile and inclined my head slightly, the leopard deigning to recognize its prey.

"Lucrezia! How are you? I feel it's been ages."

"Sambuciña? I nearly didn't recognize you. It has been too long," the other woman agreed, her full-lipped smile looking far more genuine than my own felt. "This past week's felt a hurricane, with all the preparations for tonight, hasn't it?"

"It truly has," I said, my cheeks beginning to hurt.

"You look beautiful," she added, her tone one of surprise rather than flattery.

"As do you, though I thought you'd be wearing fins."

"Fins? What do you take me for, a fish?" She glanced at the glass in my hand. "Actually, Buc, can you do me a favor?" she asked, stepping closer.

"What's that?"

"I promised Circia I'd find us something a little stronger than the aperitifs in the ballroom," Lucrezia said. "Where do they have the bar set up this year?"

"Circia?" I tilted my head. "Here I thought you were angling to bed my friend," I said with a laugh.

"But now that you know I'm with a woman, we'll be friends?" Lucrezia asked, smiling more sharply.

"Easy," I told her. *Are all these "sharks" figments of my imagination?*

"She could be a harmless flirt," Sin suggested.

"No one who is rich is harmless," I reminded him, mentally. "It's just good to know where you, uh, stand," I told Lucrezia. "Or lie."

"Your perversity knows no bounds, does it?" she asked. "I should probably get those drinks?"

"Of course," I muttered. It was a relief to let go of my faux smile as I turned away. "Enjoy your evening, Lucrezia."

"And you. But, uh, Buc?" She stepped closer. "The bar?"

"Oh, it's that way." I pointed with my glass.

"My thanks," she told me, gathering her skirts. "And, Buc," she added, her voice pitched low, "I lie wherever I choose. Maybe you'll wake up tomorrow to find me joining you for breakfast. With Eld."

"It's the second left," I said, keeping my expression and voice neutral.

"Nicely done," Sin said. "Petty, but nicely done."

"Sending her haring off in the wrong direction?" I followed after her, but took the hallway that appeared to the right and made for the doors where the music poured out from. "As the poets say, all's fair . . ."

"Let's go find Eld."

"Aye," I said, my stomach twisting at the thought.

I'd spent the week locked in my room reading and plotting the strategy of silks and footwork with Salina instead of out on the streets hunting leads like I should have been, preparing for tonight. *If Lucrezia isn't actually after him, does that mean the rest aren't?* My step quickened and I glided around would-be pockets of conversation. Perhaps things weren't as bleak as they felt. I twisted my right wrist, feeling the blade strapped on the inside of my forearm, and my back straightened. It was time to find out what terrain I stood upon with Eld. Give me a blade and a chance and I'm capable of wondrous things. I had the blade—now all I needed was the chance.

31

The ballroom was a cacophonic maze of light and music and silk and splendor that stretched as far as I could see. On the far side, high in a balcony, an orchestra, their instruments mere bright glints of metal, played a stirring tune. Above me, music rang out just as loudly. Glancing up, I saw a massive gearwork contraption of brass horns, strings, drums, and turning wheels that reproduced the notes the orchestra was playing. Though where I stood the two melodies were out of synch, I expected that in the center, where the dancers were a swirling mass of color, it would sound perfect.

Around the sides of the dance floor, men and women sat on chairs, shared tables, or milled about. Servants in purple livery wove throughout, carrying trays and drinks and looking as if waiting on sweaty-arsed nobles was something to be enjoyed. Despite my cynicism, I couldn't keep a smile from my own lips or deny the sudden flutter in my pulse. Here was magic of an entirely different sort.

"There's magic and then there's magic," Sin whispered.

"Isn't that what I just thought?" I asked. "Don't get jealous now."

"Jealous—"

"If it makes you feel any better"—I cut him off—"I've need of your magic now. Where's Eld?"

"In disguise, presumably, like all the rest."

"Sin . . ." I kept walking until my slippers moved from marble to ebony ironwood that had been polished and waxed until it shone like black diamond. The chandeliers overhead radiated bright light in white, purple, and gold. This panoply of color fell over dancers, spectators, and servants alike, making it even more difficult to pick out any individual.

"I told him we'd meet in the ballroom, that we should enter from opposite sides, the better to ferret out any nefariousness this Sicarii might have plotted." That had been Salina's suggestion as a way to ensure I got to show off my dancing. *Twirl in a man's hand and he has thoughts of twirling you elsewhere.* "He'll be uncomfortable as fuck, trying to be polite to everyone while making his way here and dodging whatever women throw themselves at him," I muttered, standing on my tiptoes to search the crowd. *Make a man uncomfortable and he'll never notice the path you're guiding him onto until it's too late. Then all you need do is give a shove.* That last had been my idea, not Salina's.

I kept walking as I spoke, shifting my eyes rapidly across the crowd, my vision burning with Sin's magic even as the music faded to a quiet hum in my ears. For this, I didn't need to know I was looking at Eld. Sin would do that. I just needed to see everyone. Turning slowly in a circle, I fended off two would-be partners with a twist of my mouth and a gesture with my glass.

"Salina was right," I murmured.

"Salina was right about what?"

"Eld?" I squeaked and spun around so quickly that I almost fell. He was there in an instant, catching my arm, and holding me steady until I got my feet back under me. "Eld?" I repeated.

"I found him," Sin said sourly.

"Didn't recognize me?" Eld asked with a laugh. "It's the mask, isn't it?"

"N-no, I just didn't see you coming," I breathed. "You look . . ."

I took him in like a gasp of air, a mask of gold with a black beak that hid his slightly crooked nose. Feathers decorated the edges and ran back over his head in waves of ebony and gold, framing the elegant black, formal jacket he wore. It, too, was trimmed with gold, but tastefully done, so that it served to accent rather than overwhelm. The jacket was tight across his shoulders, and the sharply creased pants clung to his calves. Gold-heeled shoes instead of his usual boots gave him an extra span on me.

"You look magnificent," I said finally.

"Do I?" His mask obscured most of his features, but his eyes and lips were his own and both danced with laughter—and a touch of uncertainty.

"You do," I assured him.

"Then thank you," he said, giving me a mock bow. I returned it with a curtsy of my own and we both laughed. "Is that for me? I'd murder for a drink."

"You? Murder?" I asked him, offering my glass. "I haven't drunk from it, it's just to keep would-be partners away."

"Oh, so that's how it's done," Eld said. His shoulders shook with laughter. "I've been harassed from the first moment I stepped onto the floor. But no, you keep it. Wouldn't want you to have to dance at a ball."

"The horror," I said, taking a sip from the glass. The bubbles had gone still, but it tasted bright on my tongue. "I wouldn't mind it, really. Dancing, I mean."

"Yet you hold a glass."

I twisted my head. "Is that an invitation, sirrah?"

"It could be, signorina. There's only one way to find out."

I lifted my glass to him, then drained it in a single gulp, suddenly thankful there were no bubbles left to make me choke. "Hmm, what do I do with this?"

"Now that I know the answer to," Eld said, taking the glass. He held it out and a servant appeared as if from nowhere with a silver tray. Taking the glass carefully, the servant set it on his tray and disappeared into the crowd. "Magic." Eld laughed, then, realizing what he had said, glanced away.

"C'mon," I told him, reaching for his hand. "You promised me a dance."

"Ouch!" he yelped as I ripped his arm toward mine. I loosened my grip and cursed Sin, who laughed as he let the magic leave my hand. "I didn't actually ask you, you know," he muttered.

"Well"—I spun around—"Eld, I'm asking you." I stepped close, rose on my tiptoes so that my head was just to his chin. "May I have this dance?"

He froze, then nodded slowly. "I believe you may."

I drew him farther out onto the dance floor just as the orchestra finished their tune and the dancers around us burst into applause. Finding an open space where the image of two golden unicorns touching noses—or perhaps it was meant to be horns—were in-laid into the ebony floor, I turned to face Eld. For a moment we just looked at one another and I felt a curious tickling sensation in my throat.

There was a knot in my chest that hadn't been there a breath before and suddenly my blood felt as if it were on fire. Then music rose around us in perfect harmony and Eld took me in his arms and we began the first movement of the waltz. One of his hands was tight on my back, one of mine rested on his shoulder, our other hands were clasped, and where we touched, it felt as if lightning had struck. I couldn't remember where my feet were meant to go, but I didn't care, all I saw were his blue eyes like diamonds in the chandelier light.

"Relax, you've got this," Sin whispered. My entire body burned with his magic, quelling my nervousness, amplifying the spark be-tween Eld and me, swelling the music around us, and making me wish that this would last forever.

"Where did you learn to dance so well?" Eld asked.

"Salina hired a dancing maestro," I said. "Although it turns out that some of the sword forms you taught me can almost double as a dance in a pinch. Where did you learn?"

"Mother saw me taught and I had a fair amount of practice in the army," he said, his jaw tightening. "Less so the past few years."

"I never thought of the army as a finishing school," I said lightly.

"No, me neither," he said with a laugh. "It didn't feel like one at the time, I'll say that."

"There's so much I don't know about you, Eld. Isn't that strange?"

"I suppose," he said. We twirled into the second movement of the dance. "I think when we met, we were both looking for a fresh start?"

"We were," I agreed.

"And so we kept on as we started and never got around to discussing what came before."

"And then this summer happened."

"Aye."

"What if—" I paused. Eld looked down at me expectantly, licked his lips, and looked away. "What if we didn't have so many secrets, Eld?"

He laughed, his eyes wide, but stopped when he saw my expression. "Buc, you've been more secretive than ever these past few months. I've not changed. You could have told me whatever you've wanted at any time."

"You've not changed?" I hissed. "Since we returned to Servenza, you've not changed?"

"Well, uh." He cleared his throat. "Perhaps I have changed, but then so have you. These days I can't tell what you're thinking at all. Before, sometimes I had a hint, a warning. . . . Now, at times it feels that you don't know what you're going to do until you do it. Or that you can't remember what you've done and—" He sighed and pulled me closer, tight against his chest.

"I miss old Eld," I whispered.

"I do, too," he said. He dipped me in time to the music and we danced into the third and final movement, everyone around us just scenery for our own private waltz. "You look gorgeous, Buc, you really do." His smile lit up his face, even the parts hidden by the mask. "When I think of the girl I first met, trying to pick my pocket . . ."

"I'm not a girl anymore," I said. "On the streets you're a woman the day you first bleed. I'll be eighteen in less than a fortnight and had I been born noble, I'd be a woman already."

"Fuck me," Eld muttered. "You've a way with words, Buc." The music swelled to a poignant crescendo. "You're right, you're a woman and you have been for some time. When it comes to it, I'm barely a year older than you," he added.

"When I said I missed old Eld, I didn't mean to imply I wanted to be as ancient as you," I told him, and we both laughed.

The orchestra paused; a cheer went up when they began to repeat the final movement. Eld and I slid effortlessly into it, our partnership perfect. I put my head against Eld's chest as we danced, hearing his heart beat loudly in my ear, feeling my own pulse match his quick, unsteady rhythm. Eld was right: I had been secretive, but he'd been distant, and that's what had landed us in this mess. *I can fix it.* If my lies about Sin had kept him back, then perhaps telling the truth would set things right again.

"Buc, I don't know if that's such a good idea—" Sin began.

"No? I do," I told him.

I drew myself up, took in a breath the way Salina had showed me, and squeezed Eld's hand. He glanced down, his eyes widening at his view of my breasts, and I barely kept the smile from my lips. *Men.*

"Eld, I'm tired of keeping secrets."

He nodded, his gaze rising to focus intently on my face.

"I grew up with secrets, drew them in with my every breath. But you've earned my trust. You've nearly died keeping me alive more times than I can count."

"Y-you did the same for me," he said huskily. "Back on that beach. Buc, I'm so sorry, I've never been able to forgive myself for that—"

"Forgive yourself?" I squeezed his hand again. "There's nothing to forgive. I paid the price, and gladly. I'd pay it again a hundred times over. Eld, I'd do anything for you." I took another deep breath. "And that's why I have to tell you everything. No more secrets."

"No more secrets," he repeated.

I licked my lips and began. "I changed on that beach, Eld. I saved you because . . . because . . . I'm a Sin E—"

Eld's eyes widening was my only warning. A hand fell on my shoulder. Spinning, I drove a fist into the attacker's stomach but found only air.

"Oh, you'll have to be quicker than that," the Secreto captain said with a laugh. "Try following, big boy, and we'll be eating crow or whatever fool bird you're supposed to be for dinner tonight," she said. Two women wearing dresses the same shade of hunter green as the captain's stood on either side of Eld; one held a stiletto blade pressed against his ribs.

"You're a hard one to find, girl," the captain added, her gaze shifting back to me, "even with that pretty dress. Fine enough to see the Empress in, that." She leaned forward. "But it's not the Empress that's calling. It's the Doga. We've questions and I hope to the Gods you've got answers."

She grabbed my hand and pulled and I followed mechanically, glancing back over my shoulder at Eld. He shrugged helplessly before the dancers again began to swirl about, moving between us and blocking my view of him. I turned to see where I was going as the captain dragged me into the crowd. A man cursed under his breath when she elbowed him out of the way, but one of the other Secreto growled in his ear and the woman beside him choked as she swallowed her protest along with her champagne.

Eld was gone, along with all my planning. My chance. Ice water seeped through my veins, sapped my strength, and if not for the Secreto's pull I'd have whipped back around and plunged into the crowd after him. I'd plotted with Salina, crafting machinations to understand if Eld saw me as anything more than a friend, if that was even a potential gleam in his eye, but finally I'd tossed those machinations out the window and decided to, for the first time in my life, just be plain, fucking honest, bare my soul . . . but I'd forgotten about all the other machinations I'd crafted that were still in play. I'd forgotten that the real reason I'd come to the Masquerade was because I'd been summoned by the Doga. I'd forgotten that lies have a way of catching us up and tripping us when we least expect it. That my machinations meant nothing until hers, and Sicarii's, had been dealt with. As the Secreto escorted me away, I realized something else.

If I needed a Masquerade and dancing lessons and ball gowns and bubbly wine just to tell the man I loved that I had feelings for him . . . what did that say about me? About us? What was I so afraid of?

32

"After you," the captain said, pulling open a door that was cut to fit the paneled wall so perfectly that without Sin, I wouldn't have noticed it. She inclined her head fractionally, eyes never leaving me, and I gave her a mock curtsy before stepping through.

"There's my personal inquisitor," the Doga said, turning away from a shelf with a brown, leather tome in her hands.

She'd eschewed a gown in favor of the latest jacket and trousers, all in purple silks trimmed with layers of gilt lace and thread o' gold. Her sea-hawk mask was molded so closely to her features that it was almost as if the woman had been transformed, like a damned Veneficus. The Crown of Servenza shone in the light of the candelabras that sat upon the round table that was also piled high enough with books to be a fire hazard. You can always tell privilege when you see it—I'd never have been so careless as to lose one book to fire, let alone an entire library.

"I thought you might appreciate meeting in a more discreet setting," she said, sitting down in a wooden-backed chair. Crossing her legs, she motioned for me to sit across from her, and the Secreto captain nudged me forward. A guard I almost hadn't noticed moved away from the wall to ensure there was a body between me and the Doga.

"Sambuciña, you've been quiet since we last spoke. . . . I hope you have what I'm searching for."

"I've discovered a plot against Your Grace's throne," I said, arranging my skirts mechanically. Eld was still piercingly bright in my mind, but I couldn't let myself face the executioner without every silken thread in place. Not that the Doga was my executioner. Yet. Regardless, the principle held.

"Hard to discover something I told you of when we first met," the Doga said with a sniff.

"Aye, but it runs deeper than you know, Your Grace." I unhooked the clasps on either side of my mask, drew it off, and set it on the table's edge. "There are layers upon layers here, running from beggars in the streets to gang wars to magics hitherto unknown." I met her sharp-eyed glare and bowed my head. "With foreign powers potentially being brought to bear as well."

"Normain?" the Doga hissed. The guards flanking her shifted, hands reaching for their swords. "Explain."

"That remains to be discovered, Your Grace," I said, which was true. *Unless you consider the Gods to be foreign powers. Which I do.* "The attempts on your life began with beggars and so it was for beggars I first went looking. That gang, the Mosquitoes, fell afoul of another gang that destroyed them and usurped their authority on the eve of the first assassination attempt against your person."

I walked the Doga through my past few weeks, leaving Eld mostly out of it, save for a time or two when she interrupted, unable to believe that I'd been able to fend off multiple ambushes on my own—which was fair, given that she didn't know about Sin. And Eld had helped, after all.

Eld.

The thought that it shouldn't have been so damned hard to tell him how I felt threatened my concentration but I managed to continue, telling her of the murders that were spreading discord in the Tip and beyond and of the mysterious magic that used water to create fire. Finally, with Sin helping to direct my racing thoughts into a coherent stream, I painted the portrait of a plot not just against her life, but against Servenza. This wasn't a coup attempt but a Godsdamned revolution. I ended with the figure shrouded in shadow and mystery: Sicarii.

"Sicarii?" the Doga breathed. Her mouth moved soundlessly. "Are you sure?"

"I am, Your Grace. I heard it from one of your own Constabulary, from a note on the corpses of one who tried to murder me, and from the Mosquitoes' maestro—as he burned from this strange new magic." I cleared my throat. "'Sicarii' is a foreign word meaning—"

"'Blade,'" the Doga said. She rolled her eyes at my expression. "Look around you, girl." She indicated the shelves of her personal library. "I've no end of knowledge available to me and I speak half a dozen tongues, including that of the Cordoban Confederacy."

Silence reigned for several breaths. Then: "I expected better."

"P-pardon?" I asked.

"You tell me beggars are trying to kill me. This I already knew. You tell me the streets are unrestful. This I already knew. You tell me about a strange magic that burns from water." Her eyes locked onto mine. "This I already knew. We both did."

She got to her feet. "Sicarii." The word sounded strange on her tongue. "The question becomes, Sambuciña, have you uncovered conspiracy or only coincidence? Is the Cordoban Confederacy finally entering the international fray it has hitherto eschewed? To what purpose? And . . . most pressing, but the thing you've done the least to uncover despite it being my only real request: Who the fuck is trying to murder me?"

"Your Grace, I—"

"I've listened to you, Buc," the woman growled. "Now you will listen to me. The Chair has enough support from the Board to see you exiled in the next week. It took almost no effort—you've done little to earn friends there."

She leaned forward, looming over me despite the table between us. "I'd thought, needing a friend so desperately, you'd have done better by me. If you can't find who's been at my throat, I won't stop her. Do you understand?"

"I do, Your Grace," I said, my mind racing, torn between the threat and my still-swirling thoughts of Eld and the dance we'd shared. "I will find out who is guiding the blades directed against you."

"I hope for both our sakes you do," the Doga said, crossing her arms and straightening. "You've disappointed me, Buc, but I'm going to give you another chance. Find the assassins, find out who or what is directing them, and find this Sicarii. Do that and you'll have my protection. Fail and . . ." She pulled her lips back in a predator's smile that showed too many teeth.

"Enjoy my ball, but you'd best be about it after. You've half a fortnight."

The Doga swept past me, her guards falling in around her as she passed, the Secreto captain in her hunter-green clothes last. As she pulled the door shut behind the Doga's party, the captain wagged a finger at me.

"Ticktock."

33

I sat there in silence for a while after the Doga left, my heart pounding. I had failed on so many fronts this evening. At last I plucked up my mask and fastened it to the hooks on either side of my face; they were attached to an armature that wrapped around the back of my head and was concealed by the mask and by my hair. Sitting here wasn't going to give me the answers I needed.

"Well," a sultry voice drawled from behind me, the bookshelves shifting slightly. "That sounded ominous, didn't it?" I wanted to leap to my feet and spin around, but froze at the sound of a pistole hammer being drawn back. Even with Sin's help, in my fancy gown, I couldn't move faster than a bullet. I settled back into my seat. Curse dresses!

"That's better," the voice purred, but there was something hard there. "The Doga's using you, Buc—you know that, aye?"

"Of course she is," I snapped. "But I'm using her, too."

"Are you now?" They made a noise in their throat. "I knew one who tried that once upon a time. Playing all sides, because when you play every side, how can you lose? Didn't end great for them, Buc.

"Magic. Magic is a fickle mistress, a funny thing that can embed itself in your soul, but what is given can be taken. Back. Prised free and wrung from you like blood from a slaughtered pig. You ever see a slaughterhouse? The pigs go in happy or at worst confused, but in the end?"

"Not great, eh?" I asked.

"No."

Sweat beaded on my forehead and ran down my spine, adding to the sensation like there was a blade there, waiting to thrust. Not that a pistole ball would be any better. *Where are they?*

"Must be a hidden shelf," Sin whispered. "There's enough of an echo that—" He paused and my vision faded while my ears burned. An instant later, everything snapped back into place. "I think they're standing back in the passage. Even if you whip around, you'll not find them there."

"And I'll end up with an entry wound between my breasts instead of an exit wound," I finished.

"Diplomacy may be the best policy here," he agreed.

"Can't you see I'm trying?"

"Just reminding."

"What," I repeated out loud, "do you want?"

"I want," the voice said slowly, drawing the words out in their heated tone, "the same thing you do, Buc."

I chuckled. "Aye? Tell me what that is, then, because lately I've begun to wonder."

"Inquisitive. I like that about you, Buc. The Doga does, too, doesn't she?" they whispered. "I lied just now," the other admitted. "Oh, I want what you want, Buc. But first, I want to hear the desperation in your voice as your failures pile up, weighing you down until you drown."

I stiffened.

"Nuh-huh," they said, clicking their tongue. "Move, and the Doga's going to be redoing the upholstery in here. Could use the updating, I suppose." They—no, she—laughed, low in her throat. The hoarseness had made it hard to discern, but the voice definitely belonged to a woman.

"You know that feeling deep within you, Buc, the one that forces you to act even when you know you should wait? The only true failure is never trying, isn't it? I want you to feel that not trying is failure but that trying is worse. That's what I want."

"You're insane," I muttered.

"No more than you are, Sambuciña." She breathed my name, closer now, and I felt her breath against the back of my neck.

"She's close enough to take," Sin whispered.

"It is a truth universally acknowledged that revenge requires a sharp blade and a steady fist to guide it," she growled.

That voice.

"Buc!" Sin shouted. "Let's do this!"

But something in the voice held me fast, something warm in the cadence that had nothing to do with the spice scent that clung to her. Something like a warning, like when a piece of coastline looks familiar but is not, and the captain orders a sounding in case of reefs. Sometimes she finds nothing, sometimes she gets lucky and saves the ship. I didn't believe in luck, but I believed in that voice in the back of my head, so I didn't move.

"You didn't take your chance," she whispered. "I confess myself disappointed. Revenge is what we both want, after all." The sound of the pistole hammer lowering was loud in the silence. "A gorgeous dress isn't amiss either," the voice continued. "Red, of course."

The bookshelf shifted again and the pressure between my shoulder blades disappeared. I swung around at last, palming the blade I'd strapped to my wrist, and found myself staring at a row of books in purple-dyed leather. I reached out, pulling volumes off the shelf, searching. "Help me out here, Sin."

"Looking, looking," he muttered. "I think this was a one-way passage," he said a moment later.

"Speed. Now."

I threw myself out of the chair, nearly tripping over my gown and stumbling forward as Sin used his magic to steady me. I grabbed handfuls of silk, hoisting my skirts higher, and smashed my shoulder into the door that wasn't a door. It shattered, admitting me into an empty sitting room, its paneled walls cast in deep shadows from a candle nearly burned down to the wick. Fuck dresses! Hiking my skirts up again, I sprinted across the room and shoulder-slammed a second door, going right through with a crack of wood. In the hallway, I righted myself in time to see a slash of red silk disappearing around the far end of the hall.

My skin burned with magic and I tore off in pursuit, sweat beginning to pour from me like water as Sin's magic off-loaded the fuck ton of heat that my feet, arms, and lungs were generating. In a few heartbeats I'd run nearly the entire length of the hall—I'd have done it faster if I'd been in proper trousers. As I twisted to make the corner, my slipper caught the hem of my gown and my legs went out from underneath me. I tumbled out into the hallway, arse over end and skeins of silk gown between.

The fall saved my life.

A dull thud reverberated through the hallway. I came to a stop against the far wall and my head slammed off the wood paneling, echoing the first thud, sending stars streaking across my vision and a smoky taste into my mouth. Sin yelped, cut out, and came back with a groan as I blinked back tears. Above me hung a stiletto, buried in the wall at chest height. I'd gone haring around the corner like I'd planned—

The hilt still quivered, trembling from the force of the throw. A crimson ribbon dancing and dangling from the pommel told me everything I needed to know about who'd done the tossing.

Sicarii.

Sin guided me back to the ballroom, reversing the course the Secreto captain had taken me through. I ran at a more normal speed, my skirts gathered up in one hand and Sicarii's blade in the other. I'd a feeling there was a much shorter way, but sometimes life's a bitch. So are Secreto captains. Must come with the job. I kept a running commentary of soft, fluffy bullshit in my mind, trying to avoid thinking about what had just happened. I'd been close to death most of my life—certainly this summer had been a season of near-death—but none had ever come so close.

She could have pulled that trigger at any moment. Put a hole through the back of my head. I slowed down, lungs heaving, and shivered despite the waves of heat still radiating from my skin from Sin's magic. But she didn't. She used the blade instead. She wanted me to see it coming.

"Or she didn't want to get caught," Sin suggested. "A gunshot in the Doga's Palacio would draw attention."

"Aye," I agreed. "But why not both?"

"Aye," Sin growled. "Why not indeed."

I paused at the next corner, my ears picking up traces of frivolity over the blood still rushing through my head. If she wanted me to see it coming, then it was personal, which made no sense. I didn't know this Sicarii. Not that I was aware of. *Unless it's personal for someone else?* Sicarii hadn't taken the same hands-on approach to the Doga's assassination, which was odd. *Is one business, the other pleasure? More than one client?* My mind raced with possibilities.

"Where are we going?" Sin asked.

"To Eld," I replied without thinking. Eld. I'd never been afraid of anything in my life. I mentally told Sin to shut it before he called me on the lie. If I was afraid now, there was only one thing to do. Besides, I had promised him I'd be honest, no more secrets.

"You did," Sin agreed, reading my thoughts. "But you never got the chance to tell him and he never gave you a hint as to what his feelings are, so . . . what's one more secret?"

"For a shard of a Goddess, you are really immoral, you know that?"

"The letter you're looking for is *A*. Amoral," he said. "Besides, I take on the characteristics of my host, so some immorality is to be expected, surely."

"Fuck you."

"You say that a lot."

"I mean it a lot."

"You mean it differently when it comes to Eld."

"Why?" I growled.

"Why am I fucking with you?"

"What I asked."

"Because," Sin said, his tone shifting, "because you've a poison in your heart, Buc. Sometimes, the only way to get it out is to bleed it dry. Makes it hurt less in the long run."

"Hmm." I considered his words and shook my head. "I don't think it's a poison," I said finally. "More like my heart took a wound when I lost Sister and never healed properly. Like a limb that's been damaged, it atrophied and scar tissue grew where once muscle existed."

"What book taught you that?"

"An old friend," I said. "Verner's *Disciple of the Body*. He warned of scars. They must be broken down by degrees and the limb encouraged to move, though it may hurt. That was the work Eld wrought in me these past few years. Now I feel like it's all been undone."

"Yet you still want to go to him?"

"I have to try," I told him. "Patient's prognosis doubtful, but that doesn't mean there's not a chance. Go to him now and tell him the whole bloody thing."

"All of it?"

"All of it. Aye, you, too," I said, shifting the blade in my hand so I could slip it up my sleeve beside the other knife I had there.

"And Sicarii. Eld needs to know." It was a tight fit with both blades along my wrist, and I had to hold my arm at a slight angle or risk cutting myself, but it would do.

"The lies end tonight."

34

The ballroom looked much the same as when I'd left it, save there were more flushed faces, from alcohol, kan, or dancing. It seemed as if every guest had finally found their way to the main event, so no matter how quickly I wanted to move, I was forced to keep to little more than a stroll. One that required sharp elbows, and once a kick, to move knots of masked guests out of my way. I decided Eld would have had enough of dancing by now, so my odds of finding him were better on the edges, where those looking for a breather or conversation stood.

"Sin."

"Parsing masks, I don't see—wait. There," Sin said.

Following his indication, I glanced along the side of the room, closer to the center, where the dancers were spread apart, choosing partners for the next dance. Hmm, I was wrong. He wasn't tired of dancing. I remembered the way it had felt to be in his arms and my questions about fear and uncertainty faded. We'd been interrupted before; maybe a second dance would do the trick?

"Beside the servant with the tray."

"I see him," I said, my eyes on the gold-and-ebony mask. He turned away just before our eyes would have met.

A moment later, Lucrezia, looking even more resplendent than usual in her swan's white dress and glittering skin, stepped up beside Eld, gracefully curtsying and somehow wrangling his glass from his hand. She was facing me and I saw her stiffen when she saw me coming, so I gave her my biggest fucking smile. She returned it, raised Eld's glass as if to toast him—then directed the gesture at me, throwing the liquid back in one long swallow. In the next breath she set the glass down on the nearby servant's tray and caught Eld's hand just as the orchestra struck up the next song.

"Fuck it," I muttered under my breath.

"You can't just march up and rip her out of his arms," Sin said.

"Watch me."

"Buc!" he hissed. "Don't."

"For the last time, Sin . . . ," I said, straightening my back as I approached them. What was it Salina had said? *Breasts up.* "Fuck off."

I dropped an elbow, ducked between another couple, and shouldered a girl a few years younger than me out of the way, knocking her into an elderly couple. All three erupted in protestations but I ignored them. I burst out of the confines of the crowd and saw them in the center of the dancers.

Lucrezia spun lightly in his arms, knocking against his chest before he caught her. They both laughed and there was something in his voice that stopped me in my tracks like a blade to the chest. I suddenly realized why I'd been afraid, why I'd hesitated for so long and gone to such lengths to ensure tonight was perfect. Because I already knew the answer to my question, had known it for a long time. Eld had never treated me as anything more than a friend, albeit a close one. You might take a blade for a friend, maybe even risk death for a friend, but you don't fall in love with a friend and when that friendship changes—say, when your friend becomes something you hate, like a Sin Eater—you change, too.

My breath left me, making the same sound a lung makes when there's a stiletto stuck through it. I recoiled, stumbling blindly back through the crowd. Through the tears in my eyes I saw an opening, a doorway, and practically leapt through it—right into someone.

"*Oof!*" A woman. "Watch where the fuck you're go—Buc?"

Salina wrapped her arms around me, holding me upright. "Buc, whatever's happened to your dress? It's torn and you look like you've swum right around Servenza! Buc?"

Somehow her voice was a salve to my ears, drowning out the roaring crowd that I was certain was toasting my failure. Or maybe that was just me beginning to lose consciousness, my vision narrowing as my chest contorted in on itself, squeezing the last of my heart to dust.

"I lost, Salina," I told her. "I've been fighting a war I could never win."

"Oh," Salina whispered. "Oh no, I'm so sorry, Buc. What happened? Are you sure?"

I buried my face in her chest and began to sob. I felt her move me out of the room, felt fabric beneath my feet, felt a thousand sensations courtesy of Sin. Every one of them was a pinprick beside the searing, stabbing, white-hot pain that enveloped my every fiber. I'd found the man I loved, the man I needed. *Need is a noose we slip round our own necks.* I'd put my head through willingly enough, never imagining I'd kick the bucket out from beneath my own feet.

"I'm sure," I heard myself say. My voice sounded strangled. *The lies end tonight.* I'd been thinking of Eld when I said that, but I'd been wrong. I hadn't been lying to him. I'd been lying to myself.

All along.

35

"Like what you see?"

Ulfren tried not to jump at Sicarii's voice over his shoulder. Partially because a Veneficus should never show fear. Partially because this high up, at the top of Baol's cathedral, the fall would kill even one such as himself. He tightened his grip on the telescope attached to the rotating gearwork turntable while lifting his other hand in greeting. He almost sighed with relief to see his hand wasn't shaking. As he slowly turned around, he shifted his hands to the edge of the balcony—at this height the winds of winter didn't slap so much as grasp and pull, as if they wanted to carry you away to the north. He knew the wind's promise was a lie. Winter held only death and decay in its grasp, and while he could appreciate and respect those, he had no wish to taste them for himself.

"The Sin Eaters grow more brazen by the day," he growled, nodding toward the telescope. *You, creature, I would enjoy tasting your death. Burned copper and bright spice on my tongue as I lap up your lifeblood.* "It started with carrying words to loved ones in other countries. Now they've begun offering their new healing magic— for free—to dockworkers, as a way to ingratiate themselves with the commoners as well as the Company." He couldn't keep from smiling, still imagining Sicarii's death.

"You'd choke to death if you tried," Sicarii said from the shadows of the cupola's arched dome. Her eye gleamed in the darkness. "I'm too large a bite for you, Veneficus."

"Are you a mind witch now?"

"If I were, I'd be on the docks, wouldn't I?" Sicarii's hoarse laugh made Ulfren long for the vial at his fingertips. "Or I'd be stalking your Eldest as she stalks Buc's little informant."

"What?" Ulfren straightened, all thoughts of murdering Sicarii banished by her words. "How do you know what the Eldest is doing?"

"I know everything that passes through Servenza's canals and alleys. And her cathedrals, too."

Ulfren glanced at the white, cement blocks at his feet, the cathedral beneath them. "Spy," he hissed.

"I feel like I'm not being heard." Sicarii's voice was like a knife against a whetstone.

"I hear you," Ulfren said, looking up and unable to stop the squeak in his throat. Sicarii was a mere arm's length away, burning iris glaring at him, a blade seemingly sprouting from behind her shoulder, clutched in a gearwork arm and fist. Sicarii looked like a three-tentacled octopus and he was glad all he did was make the noise and not send forth a full-throated scream.

"Then why aren't you running off to save your Eldest? I just told you, if I were a Sin Eater I'd be stalking her, waiting for the right moment to ambush her." Sicarii shook her head, wide-brimmed hat swaying. "The Sin Eaters are going to attack her, sooner or late. Were I a betting woman, I'd have coin on today, given her right hand is up here playing around with gears."

"They'd never dare," Ulfren said, unease worming through him. "The Doga is a believer—she'd never allow the murder of the high priestess."

"The Doga's hands are quite full at the moment," Sicarii said. "A word in the Empress's ear and she'll be lucky to keep her crown. Assassination attempts, gang wars, soon to be riots . . ." She ticked them off on gloved fingers.

"Were we to murder Sin Eaters, though, she'd take notice," he muttered. The Doga continued to come to services, but not as many as she once had. *Same as the rest of our parishioners.* He'd always known some came primarily for the power the Dead Gods offered, not belief; he'd just never imagined it was so many. The Doga was, in any case, compromised: she was one of the oldest stockholders in the Kanados Trading Company and that lot stank of mind magic from sharing the same bed for so long with Ciris's ilk.

"You deserve better," Sicarii said.

"What if," Ulfren asked slowly, almost afraid to give voice to his thoughts, the words burning his throat, "the Doga was assassinated? We'd have no reason to hesitate in destroying both the Company and the Sin Eaters."

"There'd be a need for a new ruler of Servenza." Sicarii's voice was taut enough to cut the air.

"You keep urging us to action," Ulfren reminded her. "Remove the Doga and there'd be no need to stay in the shadows."

"Coming into the light, you can become blinded," Sicarii whispered. "Then you don't see the blades until it's too late."

"Like our Grace?"

Sicarii said nothing for several long breaths. Then the gearwork arm hanging over her shoulder slid back and disappeared into her cloak with a soft, whirring hiss.

"All manner of things are possible." Sicarii's voice rattled as she laughed and Ulfren surprised himself by laughing with her. Sweat had soaked his robe through, but he felt invigorated, energized. The Eldest always cautioned patience, reminding him that they had existed for millennia whilst the Sin Eaters were barely a few centuries old, but Ulfren saw how they multiplied. A few months more of their encroachment, let alone years, and this war would be lost. They needed to strike. Now. Hard.

Sicarii's harsh laughter cut off abruptly. "Attack the Sin Eaters and their pet girl, and I'll give you what you desire, Ulfren." She cleared her throat. "I could end it all tomorrow, but that wouldn't work out the way either of us wants it to."

"I can wait," he lied.

"I'm not sure if you can," she said, slipping back into the shadows. "But you'll have to. For a little while longer." She opened the trapdoor and disappeared down it, her voice echoing back before the door cut it off. "You'd better run if you want to save your priestess."

Snatching a vial from his belt, Ulfren bit back a curse as he swallowed its contents. The curse turned into a scream as his limbs twisted, cracked, and snapped, heeding the power of his Gods' blood combined with that of a mountain sheep. Fiery torrents carved through his flesh and bone, reshaping him. His screams turned into grunts, then to deep, hoarse roars and suddenly he was on all fours though he stood head and shoulders taller than he had been a moment before. Servenza would be theirs, the world would be theirs as it was before the mind witch and her ilk came. His Eldest would see to that, but first she had to survive.

Ulfren launched himself over the railing, all fear of falling gone. His hooves struck sparks from the side of the cathedral, his surefooted pads finding the cracks in the seams of the masonry. At full gallop, wind whistled through his mane, sending locks ringing against the curled steel horns that now jutted from his head. He was with his Gods and they were with him. *I'm coming, Eldest.* He had no choice.

Blood called to blood.

36

Eld hid a yawn behind his gloved fist, blinking to stay awake as he watched the palazzo the Sin Eaters were using as a second, hidden lair. He'd figured out that there was some concealed passage, perhaps through the walls, perhaps beneath them, that allowed them to enter their main headquarters undetected. Why, though? He understood the wisdom of having an escape route, but that was for emergencies, not daily use. He wasn't even sure what he hoped to learn here, but he had to do something to keep his mind occupied while Buc was off doing whatever the Doga's Secreto had asked of her. *Without me.*

So much for not keeping secrets. He scowled at the thought, but it wouldn't go away.

The previous day he'd realized only the more senior Sin Eaters, ones he recognized from the Company, used this entrance. Did the younger ones not know of it, or were they not allowed to use it? A gust of wind carried the sound of a priestess preaching the good tidings of Ciris to Eld's ears. Another reason for the back door? The Sin Eaters' new magic healing had caused crowds to form outside their grand entrance. Dockworkers and rougher sorts who previously would never cross the canals of the Tip now rubbed elbows with those wearing silk and fur; the crowds threatened to choke all traffic off completely. *And what do the Dead Gods think of that?*

His jaw cracked in another yawn. He'd not slept at all the night of the Masquerade. Waiting for Buc to return from the Doga's summons had meant dancing with any number of women. A few men had offered as well, disappointed when they discovered Eld didn't share their tastes. He'd tried to beg off the women with less success. Lucrezia had been the most persistent, and he had to admit the woman danced well and felt pleasant in his arms. Too pleasant. There'd been a moment when, full of wine and song, he'd thought maybe it wouldn't be a bad idea if they left together. It wasn't like he was promised to Buc—and anything he felt for her was one-sided.

But I definitely felt something when she was against my chest. Eld had just begun to wonder if he'd misjudged everything when Buc had been pulled away by the Secreto captain. When she didn't return, he'd cursed himself for a fool.

Lucrezia didn't make him feel foolish and she'd even stolen a kiss, but before Eld could make up his mind about what to do next, an impossibly tall woman in a dress slashed with crimson and orange and bloodred feathers so long they bordered on the truly ridiculous had jumped between them. She'd called Lucrezia a harlot and the two had left, screaming at each other. The way Lucrezia's arm found its way around the other's waist made him suspect they were going to do more than kiss and make up. He shifted against the alley wall, suddenly thankful the wind was cold and biting.

"I'm tired of this game, Buc." He whispered his words to the wind. Tired of the lies and feeling like he'd destroyed their friendship, first by feeling anything more for her and then by listening to Sin. But if Sin was to be believed, telling Buc the truth would drive her insane. He cut off his thoughts before they went round the well-worn circle in his brain. None of this was helping. If he didn't help Buc, she'd be on a ship for the north or, worse, kicked out of the Trading Company entirely. Eld shivered, thinking that perhaps that wouldn't be so terrible after all. *Things can't go on as they have been.*

Detaching himself from the wall, Eld slipped back into the shadows and made for the canal where he'd left Joffers. He turned the corner, pulling his midnight-blue coat tighter around him—

The slashing blade got caught in the thick wool beneath the outer silk layer, but the force of the blow sent Eld sprawling anyway, his coat half-ripped from his body. He threw himself into a roll across the alleyway, breath driven from him in a grunt when he slammed into the opposite wall. He shoved himself to his feet, boots fighting for purchase on the polished cobblestones as the woman—braided hair flowing in the wind as she rushed toward him, twin curved daggers bright in her dark-gloved hands— attacked in a blur of steel.

Eld managed to get his sword half-out, fending off the first dagger with the basket of his hilt. He stepped inside the second, overhand blow and smashed his head into the bridge of her nose, sending her reeling backward. Muscles working from rote memory and years of practice, he drew his blade the rest of the way without thought, his mind still back in the alley.

The woman didn't give him time to reminisce. Wiping blood from her broken nose with one hand, she twirled the blade in her other in impossibly fast circles, making the air hum, her mouth curved in a bloody smile. Once before, Eld had seen a woman who could make steel move that fast. Chan Sha. This wasn't Chan Sha, but she was clearly a Sin Eater. The woman's nose made an audible click as she pushed the cartilage back into place.

"I'm going to eviscerate you for that," she snarled as she leapt forward, twin blades whirring.

"You're going to try," Eld gasped, parrying desperately, each deflection sending up sparks, shooting shock waves through his wrists and up his biceps. The only way to defeat a Sin Eater was to attack . . . and pray for luck. Unfortunately the woman wasn't keen on giving him the chance. His sword grew heavy in his grip, the air became a scything blur of steel and her dark cloak, her eyes shifting so quickly that he couldn't predict her next move.

He tripped and fell backward, skidding one way across the cobblestones while his sword went another. His sword arm had gone numb from the wrist down and he half expected to see his hand gone with his sword, but it was blessedly intact—and use-less from the blow. He could feel blood running down his other arm from where she'd nearly impaled him on her curved blade. As he pushed himself to his knees, she fell on him, locking his wounded arm between her thighs and wrenching his head back by his blond hair. He locked eyes with her, felt cold steel touch his throat, and realized he was about to die.

"You've got one chance to live, Eldritch Nelson Rawlings," she said evenly, as if they hadn't just fought to the death. "Tell me what happened to the artifact and you live. Say anything else and I'll leave you here for the girl to find, cut ear to ear." She leaned forward, her black eyes merciless, dried blood cracking against her dusky skin, and whispered, "Her, I'm going to carve like a pigeon until she sings the tune I want to hear."

"No—"

She cut him off, pressing the blade hard enough that he felt his skin part. "In one breath, tell me where it's at or it will be the last breath you draw."

"D-don't know," he whispered.

"That's not good enough."

"I don't! Chan Sha—"

"I told them I'd get to feel your lifeblood on my hands," she said, her smile at last reaching her eyes. "Ciris sends her—"

Her smile disappeared in a spray of blood and she collapsed against him, her weight taking him to the cobblestone, her blade nicking his throat even as it fell from nerveless fingers. The sound of the pistole was deafening in the confines of the alleyway. For a long moment all Eld could do was lie there, face-to-face with the dead woman. Half her cheek was gone, but her eyes were wide with surprise.

"Godsdamn it."

Eld felt the words more than heard them, the high-pitched ringing in his ears making everything seem distant and otherworldly. The pain in his left arm was gone and the pins and needles in his right told him he was going to regain use of that in a few moments. He pushed himself up to his knees and saw Govanti a dozen paces away, mouth slack, pistole still smoking in his fist.

"I—I killed her."

"You did," Eld told him, barely hearing his words. "And saved my life."

Gathering himself, Eld stood up jerkily, stumbled, and caught himself. "I owe you one, Govanti."

"I killed her," the boy repeated, his face drained of all color. "W-was she . . . ?"

"A Sin Eater?" Eld asked, limping over to where his sword lay against the wall. His limbs trembled with adrenaline and pain and he felt like throwing up. *I hate fighting.* It always seemed strange to him that the one thing he was good at was the one thing he could have done without. He bent over, bracing himself against the wall, and picked up his weapon.

"Aye, she was a mage," he said, sheathing the blade awkwardly. Realizing Govanti had not moved, he walked over to the boy.

"Easy, lad." Eld pushed his arm down gently. "You did well. If not for you, she'd have killed me and then gone after Buc."

"I know. I heard her." Govanti swallowed in a way that told Eld he was close to vomiting.

"First time?"

"I've fought before. Stabbed someone," Govanti said quietly. "But—"

"It was her or me," Eld said, putting an arm around the boy's shoulders. "That doesn't make it easy nor good, but it does make it necessary."

Govanti nodded slowly. "I couldn't let anything happen to you. Signorina wouldn't let me live if I did."

"Buc?"

"The times she's had me watch your back . . ."

"You never said," Eld said, shocked.

"You never asked."

"What'd I tell you when I gave you that pistole?" Eld asked, swallowing what he'd been about to say.

"Only to use it in emergencies," Govanti replied, glancing at the still-smoking weapon.

"Aye, and this was definitely that," Eld said. "But what was the rest?"

"A-always reload it?"

"Immediately," Eld said by way of agreement. "Here," he added, taking the gun from the lad and fumbling for the powder horn at his side. "I'll do that. Past time we were gone."

"I'm surprised the Constabulary isn't here already," Govanti said, head swiveling as if he just realized they'd killed a mage only a few blocks from Constabulary headquarters in the center of one of the finer Quartos.

"Probably paid to keep their distance while she"—Eld nodded toward the body—"did what she had to do. Cuts both ways though." He trickled powder down the barrel and handed Govanti the horn, forcing his still-numb fingers to wriggle a ball out of his pouch. "C'mon. After today you're not going back to that hovel you call a home."

"I—I'm not?"

"No, Buc wouldn't like it," Eld said. *Not that she knows.* He rammed the ball home, each push sending pain through his wounds. *Secrets. Again.*

"I've a plan," he told the lad, shedding his torn coat and passing back the pistole. He only hoped one would come to him by the time they reached Joffers.

"If you stay in my bed much longer, people are going to talk."

I groaned and rolled over, away from the wall I'd been staring at. Salina eyed me from the doorway and when I sat up, she gestured and two servants entered the room. One carried a tray; the other, a washbowl and cloth. Setting the tray on the nightstand, the dark-haired girl darted a glance at me and squeaked at my glare. She sketched an abrupt curtsy, nearly bowling into the older maid, who managed to slip an elbow into her ribs without upsetting the steaming water in the bowl. Setting it beside the tray, the older one muttered an apology for the other's clumsiness and they both scurried out.

Salina chuckled. "You've a way about you, Buc, even when you look like you've been crying half the night and trying to suffocate yourself the other half."

I began to run my fingers through my hair, stopping at the first tangle. I'd gone to bed in my Masquerade finery—save for the mask itself—and my hair had paid the price, but I could not find it in me to care. I reached for the washcloth, but as the scent of fish-bone broth filled the room, my stomach rumbled ominously. I sat up straighter, using the pillows for support, and took the soup instead. I felt cored out, as if I was lacking something. A small voice seemed to shout at me from a distance.

"I'm not small, Buc," Sin growled, suddenly close. "I don't know where you learned the trick of shoving me beneath your consciousness, but you need to unlearn it. Now is not the time to fall apart."

"It seems the perfect time to me," I whispered mentally.

"How long?" I asked aloud, voice cracking after disuse as I began mechanically spooning broth into my mouth.

"Two nights and a day," Salina said, pulling the door shut behind her. Her peach-colored silk trousers whispered as she walked across the room and sat on the edge of the crimson blankets piled atop the bed. "This is the morning of the second day." She sighed. "How do you feel, Buc?"

"I don't," I said, dripping broth down my chin, making a spreading stain on the bedsheet. "Sorry," I muttered.

"No matter," Salina said, waving her hand. "You did those in on your first night, thanks to all your makeup running."

"Tears will do that."

"They will," she agreed.

We stared at one another in silence. "So," I said, finally.

"So."

"Have you ever felt this way, Salina?"

She smiled faintly, brushing back an errant blond strand of hair. "After Ferdin died, I felt a lot of the things I imagine you are. I think," she said slowly, "I mostly felt the loss? Knowing that there had been someone out there that set my veins on fire and filled me to the brim with life."

"That hurts," I agreed.

"What hurt even worse than that was the regret," she said. "Since I didn't tell him how I felt when I had the chance."

"At least you knew how he felt about you," I said.

"That's true," she said. She put one hand on my leg beneath the sheet. "You can stay here as long as you wish, Buc, but eventually you're going to have to face him."

"I thought I had him, 'Lina," I whispered. "We flirted, we danced, and he was gorgeous and the wine was gorgeous and that fucking orchestra was gorgeous. I never thought such things mattered, but they did."

Tears threatening to spill over, I told her most of the rest, glossing over my audience with the Doga and leaving Sicarii out completely.

"You kissed, once?" Salina said, her own eyes filled with tears as she offered me a handkerchief. "That's not something friends do."

"I thought that, too," I said, "but, 'Lina? If it's only one moment, even one like that, and nothing follows after?"

"Did you tell him you love him?"

"N-no," I admitted. I stirred the spoon around in the broth aimlessly. "I fucked up. I spent too much time with Eld, became too familiar. Men love mystery and fantasy. They don't fall for the familiar.

"There's more besides. When we came back from facing down

pirates and Shambles and the Ghost Captain? We were broken, 'Lina. I've tried to win him back these past weeks, but we want different things."

"How can you know that if you never asked him, Buc?"

"I know," I said quietly.

"You had plans when I first met you," Salina snapped suddenly. "Schemes to change the world. Ideas that were worth putting your life on the line dozens of times. Aye, and Eld's life too. How can one warehouse fire and Eld batting his eyes at other women be enough to derail them?"

"Warehouse fire?" My mind flashed back to Sister. I couldn't follow Salina's change of subject for a moment, didn't understand why she was angry now. Making a guess, I said, "You think I give a fuck that the Company's profits took a hit?"

"It's not about profits—" she began.

"You're damned right, it's not. It's about why those plans were worth fighting for in the first place!" I growled, tossing the bowl across the room. It shattered against the wall but Salina didn't flinch.

"I want a better world for every child that grew up like me. If I can't give myself that world, that happy ending, what chance do I have to give them it, too?"

"So love made you selfish? You're hurt, Buc." Salina's voice was firm, her eyes softer. "You've absorbed several body blows in the past year and now someone managed to slip a blade past your guard. For most, this ends with them lying on the floor, choking on their lifeblood. Story over."

She took my hands in her own and squeezed hard. "You're unlike anyone I've ever met before, Buc.

"We don't tell stories about most. We tell them about the few. The ones who pull the knife out of their side and use it to kill the ones who put it there. Half a dozen of the world's most powerful people want to see you on your knees, bleeding out. Because if you do, nothing changes.

"Once, I would have been beside them. I told you before the Masquerade that watching you made me question that, and everything I've learned in the past year convinces me you're right." She grinned mirthlessly. "Don't let that go to your head, woman. The world needs you to be the change they fear, Buc. You're the only one who can do it."

"I used to believe that," I said slowly. "I didn't feel emotion, true emotion, and that freed me to do what needed to be done." I squeezed my eyes shut. "I guess love makes mortals of us all."

"Do you think, in the stories, the hero feels wonderful when they begin their final stand?"

"Huh?"

"When you defeated the Ghost Captain, how did you feel? Full of life and purpose, or bloody and confused?"

"Aye," I said, opening my eyes against my will. "What are you saying?"

"It's okay to feel hollow, to feel nothing, to be so on fire with pain that all your senses are dulled. None of that means you get to stop, though."

I opened my mouth to tell her what a damn fool she was, but her words touched a nerve inside me. The gnawing emptiness in my heart remained, but alongside it was a cold sense of purpose. A blade needed planting and my hand was the one to do it.

"What do you think, Sin?"

"Now you remember me?" he asked. I began to mute him again and he twisted frantically around inside my mind. "No, no, you're right. More importantly, Salina's right. There's work to be done."

"No converting me today?"

"There's always tomorrow," he said.

I smiled. "Bring me a razor," I said out loud.

"A r-razor?"

"For my hair," I said, rubbing the stubble on either side. "Not my wrists." I laughed and while it didn't feel good, it didn't hurt either. "You've convinced me."

Salina laughed and left to call the servants. My smile vanished when she did and I lay back against the pillow. I'd started all of this wanting a better world, free of Gods and inequality, where all had a fair shake. Eld had made me dream of something more, but that didn't mean the original dream was gone. When the sheen is gone, the steel remains. Gillibrand was one of the first books I'd read. Number eleven. She'd been right then and she was right now. Salina, surprisingly, too. I'd been wounded and routed, but there was still a war to be fought. In war, any manner of things were possible, and to quote the poets, all manner of things were permissible.

All manner.

37

⁂

"This scone is dry," Eld muttered, spraying crumbs down the front of his slate-grey jacket. "Must be a day old."

"Looks it," I agreed. I'd eaten before we left, little and grudgingly, because I'd had no real need to use Sin's abilities the past few days, last night aside. My stomach rumbled to give me the lie, but I ignored it, pulling my own jacket tighter around me against the damp cold of the morning. It was past Midwinter but spring was weeks away at best and even with the maroon scarf around my neck, the cold sent tendrils seeking for my flesh. "Maybe you should have brought some tea along after all."

"It was cold and steeped too long," Eld complained. His boots were overloud on the cobblestone beneath as we walked along the row of palazzos.

"You really sound the dandy, you know. And is that stomping I detect?"

"I just want to know where the staff went, that's all," he growled defensively. He ran a hand over the reddish-blond stubble on his cheek. "I can do for myself if I've notice."

"Uh-huh."

He shot me a look and I held my hands up defensively as we crossed the street toward the gearwork bridge. It was raised high to allow a passing barge through and so shrouded in mist that it looked like it floated on air instead of merely spanning the canal.

"I figured you had the staff working hard to impress whatever lady danced and bedded you from the Masquerade," I said after a moment. "A few days with a lady expecting them to bow and scrape and carry on in all the ways I don't, I thought they might need a break."

"I didn't bed anyone, Buc. I slept alone."

"Pity." I sniffed. "I didn't."

Eld's face burned red, making his blond stubble stand out more, and his mouth worked soundlessly, either because he had no retort or else because he was still trying to swallow that lemon-spiced scone. It was the size of his fist, after all. I nearly laughed out loud as Sin echoed my thoughts, but that would have given Eld some ground to stand upon and I wanted him on his fucking knees. I actually wasn't sure I wanted him along at all, but if half my plans made full sheets with the wind as I'd hoped, I would have need of his hand at the tiller.

"W-who did you sleep with?" he asked finally, picking crumbs off his silver-laced lapel. His voice sounded like an olive put through the press.

"Ladies don't kiss and tell." He made a sound in his throat and I stopped short of the bridge, hearing its gears whir in the morning stillness as it lowered in the barge's wake. "Do you trust me?"

"What?" Shock replaced annoyance across his features.

"Do you trust me?"

He looked me up and down and I fought the urge to give him something to look at. Those tactics were gone. I stood ramrod straight, my grey jacket a shade lighter than his, with gold buttons instead of silver. Unburnished, the buttons matched the color of my mustard trousers, visible where the jacket flared at the waist, exposing more leg than a dress ever would. Even so, his eyes set my veins on fire.

Eld nodded. "Of course I trust you."

"Then you're a fool, Eldritch Nelson Rawlings," I told him with a smile, to confuse him even further. "Never trust a woman you've danced with. Especially if she danced well."

"Humble," Sin sniffed.

"Fuck—"

"Off. I know," Sin said. "I thought you were done playing games with Eld?"

I ignored him and stomped across the now-lowered bridge, echoes chasing after me. Eld kept pace as we crossed into where the Spired Quarto mixed with the Mercarto. Here the streets were alive with merchants opening their storefronts and hawkers elbowing one another as they jostled for position with their carts. Enough noise to mask the silence I'd produced with my admission and enough people to keep Eld at bay.

"You're right," Eld said when he caught up to me.

"I am?"

"I shouldn't have asked you that," he said. A sad smile creased his face. "You don't owe me any explanations. It's not like we're—"

I made a small noise in the back of my throat.

"Whatever comes," he added in a rushed breath, "I'll always trust you, Buc. Always."

"I slept with Salina," I said. His eyes popped and I nearly laughed. "Shared the same bed. Minus the kissing, you lecher."

"I—I—"

"Am a pervert, clearly," I finished for him.

"I am not." He drew in a breath and shook his head. "Are you going to tell me where we're going?"

"Didn't you just say you trusted me?" I reminded him.

"I did," he said quickly. "And I do. You don't want to tell me where we're going? Aye, Captain. You don't want to tell me what we're doing when we get there? Aye, Captain."

"I feel like 'Generalissimo' has a better ring to it."

Eld stared at me and burst out laughing. "What? Is this Colgna?"

"If it was you'd have mustaches," I said, laughing with him, and patted him on the back instead of the arm. *Friends.* The word was ash in my mouth, but it was better than tears in my eyes. "I came back by way of the secret passages beneath the streets."

"You used the Doga's map? I thought it was incomplete."

"Complete enough that I found one that let me out around the corner of our palazzo unobserved."

"Oh?"

"And it paid off." I reached into my jacket and pulled out an avocado-shaped object. "Catch."

Eld caught the thing deftly and inspected it for a few moments before shooting me a quizzical glance.

"What's it look like to you?"

He shrugged. "A grenado, but this feels almost like glass."

"It is glass," I told him. "It's also a grenado. I think it's the same kind Sicarii's been using to turn people into flaming infernos."

"W-what?" Eld squeaked, jumping and nearly losing the grenado in the process.

"Easy," I hissed, covering his hand with mine. "There's some sort of bladder inside the glass that's filled with . . . whatever it is that makes this stuff go boom. You break the glass and it breaks the bladder and—"

"Boom," Eld whispered, holding the grenado like it was the world's most expensive egg. Which it might have been, depending on how one valued their life.

"Aye."

I told him how I'd suspected someone had been watching our palazzo, so I'd decided to try to prove myself right. I'd been about ready to give up when I saw a shadow move beneath a carriage waiting in front of the next palazzo. Two shadows actually, one coming and the other going. I'd used the Doga's tunnels to pass him and had been lying in wait in an alley. I'd meant to try to get some information out of him, but he'd fired a pistole full in my face and that dissuaded me from fucking around. The bastard, a slovenly looking Servenzan with a puckering scar in the corner of one eye, had been trying to toss the grenado but couldn't get it out of his trousers pocket. That was the first miracle. The second was that it didn't break when his corpse hit the cobblestones.

"Once I got home, I read up on what materials could fit in a grenado like this one and cause such violent fulmination." I added, "Took half the night to get the powder burns off my skin."

"That close?" Eld asked.

"Any closer and my braids would have gone up," I admitted. "As I was studying, though, it occurred to me we've been going about this all wrong."

"How's that?"

"Well, we've been trying to chase down the leads stemming from the attacks on the Doga."

"Which seems logical."

"And is, but it's slow, it's left us at a dead end, and"—I ticked the points off on my fingers—"it ignores the fact that we already know who's behind this."

"Sicarii."

"But who's behind Sicarii?" Eld frowned and I laughed. It felt good. Laughing. False, but good. "It has to be the Gods, Eld. We should have set up watch on them long since. They'll lead us to this Sicarii, or one of their cloak-wearing shadows will. The only real question," I added, "is it the Dead Gods or Ciris?"

"I was thinking it was the Dead Gods after the way Sicarii breathed down my neck at the Masquerade. She sounded as insane as that Ulfren did when he wanted to drink our blood to see if we were telling the truth, back on the day we prevented the Doga's assassination.

"Wait!" Eld stopped so suddenly I walked a full three paces before I realized I'd lost him. I turned around and arched an eyebrow. "You. Spoke. With. Sicarii," he hissed.

"It was a bit of a one-way conversation," I admitted.

Eld made a noise in his throat and said, still eyeing me askance, "I may have an answer to the Ciris question."

"Really?"

"I am competent, you know." Eld sniffed. "I did manage to make it almost two decades on my own without you."

"Sounds like we've some catching up to do."

"Aye, I guess so. What should I do with this?" he asked, hefting the grenado.

"Oh, put it in your pocket for now. I'll have a look at it later," I said. "Just don't put it in your back pocket, Eld."

"Why's that?"

"Might break and blow your arse cheeks to the moon and then all the women of Servenza, aye, and half the men, would cry themselves dry over it."

Eld stared at me for a long moment, ignoring the increasing numbers of passersby, and then burst out laughing, and I surprised myself by joining in. We might have gone on like that for a good while save Eld laughed so hard he dropped the grenado and if not for Sin's magic and my preternaturally fast reflexes we would have died laughing, which isn't such a bad way to go, but then I would have lost and the world with it—so I caught the damned thing instead.

"Lead the way, Generalissimo," Eld said, mocking a bow, when we realized we weren't going to die. At least not by combustible tomfoolery.

"You're both terrible at pretending," Sin whispered in my mind.

"I know. But we're trying," I told him. "Sometimes that's all you can do."

Sin nodded. "Now what?"

"I lead. He follows. We find out if I'm really a general or just a fool."

"Why not both?"

I didn't bother telling Sin to fuck off. He was right, we were all pretending. But I was right, too. We were trying.

I hoped it would be enough.

"You did good, Eld," I told him, as we slipped through one of the sewers beneath the streets. Luckily, this being on the edge of several of the finer Quartos, it wasn't overused. If we walked on either side of the mud-brown stream that ran through the center, we could stay relatively clean, though I could have done without the smell.

"Thanks," Eld said, pulling his grey coat tighter about him to keep from touching the wall. "I had help."

"I guess I shouldn't be surprised the Parliamentarian is truly in bed with the Sin Eaters," I said, pausing as we reached a crossroads. "Sin?" A map appeared in my mind, as sharp as if I held it before me. It was still half-sketched thanks to the Doga's recalcitrance, but I could intuit where likely passageways would lead to the canals or streets or dead ends. I gestured left.

"If I did such a good job, why are we down here instead of up there," Eld gestured, "staking them out?"

"How many days did you say you spent watching them?" I asked as a ladder came into view. Luckily it was on my side of the shit stream. It should lead up to the street.

"Half a dozen or so, off and on," Eld said, grimacing before he leapt over to my side.

"Uh-huh." I grabbed the first rung and pulled myself up. "That's long enough to have overstayed your welcome, Eld. Like as not"—I eyed the ceiling, where a faint brush of light highlighted the edges of the round door—"they realized someone was keeping too close an eye on them and have been lying in wait. It's what I'd do."

"Uh, Buc—"

"Hush, I'm being brilliant." I drew one of my blackened stilettos. "This should bring us out in the alleyway behind the one you hid in and if I'm right, we'll find someone waiting there who will have answers for us."

"Buc—"

I gave him a toothy grin before biting down gently on the blade so I had both hands free. "Could 'e 'In Eaters o' cloaked 'hadows," I said, speaking around the steel. "'E ready."

"Buc!" Eld cried hoarsely, half shouting, half whispering.

I grasped the door's long, thin handle and took a breath.

"That's what I've been trying to tell you," Eld's voice chased after me. My arm burned with Sin's magic and I slammed the door open, breaking off several years of rust. It flew up and I burst out. "Sin Eaters were waiting for me!"

Right into the middle of a street battle. The Sin Eaters were fighting feverishly, in a storm of blades, against monstrous beasts that looked all too human. *Fuck.*

"I killed one!" Eld called from below.

"Now you tell me," I muttered, half-in, half-out of the hole in the gutter. *Double fuck.*

A man-goat-thing with impossibly bright, curved, steel horns bawled in rage as it charged toward me from across the street and I felt something I wasn't used to: fear.

All the fucks.

38

The creature's mad bawling filled my ears. Sin's equally desperate cries filled my mind. I'd faced a Veneficus before. That one had horns, too, and the human-beast creature had nearly spiked Eld and me before I put a silver bullet through its nose and sent it running, tears in its eyes. I hadn't been expecting to run into a giant bull with steel horns that day, but I was today, so I levered myself out of the hole and felt Sin's magic tingling through my legs as I landed, feet spread wide on either side of the sewer gate.

Throw stiletto.

"Steel won't slow that thing down!" Sin shouted.

"I know."

Throw stiletto. Distraction. Left hand to slingshot, right to pouch. Silver in second opening.

"Faster!" Sin's voice was low, heated.

"Slow time down."

"C-can't. You haven't eaten much of anything these past few days. Used up a lot with that cloak-wearing bastard."

"And you need the rest for the fight?" I asked.

"Aye."

Throw stiletto. Distraction—

"Fuck it," I snapped, throwing the stiletto underhanded at the massive, curly-horned goat beast a bare dozen paces away.

It dropped its head, protecting its chest, and met the blade with a twist of its horns that sent my stiletto clattering harmlessly off the cobblestones. It sucked in a throaty breath and leapt for me.

I was already moving.

Dropping into a crouch, I leapt up so hard that I felt something in my knee give, but with Sin's magic coursing through me, I didn't feel a damned thing. Wind whistling through my braids, I found the special blade I kept tucked beneath my belt in the small of my back, and whipped it out just as the goat Veneficus landed in front of where I'd been standing. I slashed out, but as fast as I was, the beast was nearly as fast, and instead of blinding an eye, my arm reverberated from the impact of silver on steel. The force knocked me backward, but I turned my leap-cum-fall into a backflip and landed a dozen paces from where I'd started.

The Veneficus stomped a front hoof, sending sparks up, drew in a deep breath, and screamed in rage. One of its horns smoked, blackened from its brush with my silver blade. I could feel the pressure of its scream in my chest, a cacophony that threatened to drown out my ragged breathing. Sin's magic was burning through my meager reserves and all I'd done was piss the bastard horned thing off.

Switching the blade to my left hand, I waved the Veneficus forward while my right hand dug into my pouch for a ball of silver.

"C'mon, you blood-swilling bastard," I choked through my scarf, which had gotten pulled high and tight around my face. Spitting wool out of my mouth, I added, "Try me."

The Veneficus slammed its hoof on the ground again, sending more sparks into the air. I saw its muscles bunch and coil beneath its thin grey fur. My fingers found the ball and I drew it out as the creature sank into a crouch, its all-too-human eyes glaring murder at me.

BOOM!

A plume of fire and smoke leapt out of the open sewer gate—the one the Veneficus stood astride.

The goat disappeared in the gunsmoke, save for its bright steel horns, but its high-pitched scream told me Eld's shot had been true. As the smoke cleared, the creature was revealed, leaning against the alley wall, twisting and jerking, the popping and cracking of its limbs nearly as loud as Eld's shot had been.

Eld appeared as if by command, climbing out of the hole, one hand over his ear, the other holding a shaky pistole in his fist, trained on the Veneficus.

"Ulfren!" An old woman raced toward the Veneficus—I recognized her as the priestess from the Dead Gods' cathedral. Moving quickly, she fended off a young Sin Eater's blade. The lad's cheeks were still full of fatty youth, made scary by the angry rictus they were contorted into. He swung a curved blade so quickly that without Sin feeding me a small bite of magic, I'd not have been able to follow the blow and counterblow.

One moment the Eldest was in front of the Sin Eater, blocking his strikes with steel-lined gloves that threw sparks, and the next her hands were locked around his knife arm. Before the lad could blink, she'd brought the arm and the curved dagger up and across. The Sin Eater's lifeblood followed in a vermillion torrent that steamed in the air. After a moment of stillness, the woman twisted away, carefully avoiding the knife in a way that told me it was silver. The blade clattered against the pavement and the Sin Eater's body followed a heartbeat later, twitching uncontrollably.

Wiping her hands ostentatiously, she turned back to her acolyte, thin white braids bright against her black skin.

"Ulfren," she repeated. "You've no vials left. Past time you were gone."

In the aftermath of the explosion of violence, it was her quiet, even tone that made the hair on the back of my neck stand on end. The buckshot spray of blood across her bone-white robe from opening the Sin Eater's throat didn't help matters. The mountain goat had disappeared and in its place, looking small even though he was taller than Eld, was the Veneficus Ulfren, who'd wanted to drink our blood and discern our truths last we met. He was even paler than I remembered, blond hair the color of corn silk, and completely naked. Blood streamed from the wound in his side despite his attempt to hold it closed.

"Cold out, isn't it?" I called. His glare shifted to embarrassment when he saw where my gaze was resting. Eld snorted. "Run along now, Ulfren. Let your betters clean up the mess," I said, taking in the gory scene sprawling through the alleyway. Two Sin Eaters lay beyond the one the Eldest had just killed. Here, a face was smashed into pulp; there, a torso was twisted at an impossible angle. Stockinged legs, one foot missing a heeled boot, lay in the mouth of the back alley where Eld had done his watching.

"Eldest?" Ulfren's voice was tight with pain.

"I'll follow soon," she said. "Return to Baol."

"I'll tell the others," he muttered through clenched teeth. He stumbled off, stooping briefly—and nearly falling over—to grab a scrap of a cloak from the ground and wrap it around his naked waist, tight against the wound, before turning a corner.

"You'll have to teach me that trick," I said.

"What trick is that, Sin Eater?"

I looked at the Eldest and smiled. "The one where you tell a man what to do and he actually listens."

"Do you have a century to learn? Men are stubborn."

"Steady now," Eld said. "One's standing right here."

"As whales," I agreed with the woman.

"Mules where I am from, but the principle holds," she agreed. She drew herself up. "I've killed a brace of you already this morn, not counting the boy," she said, nodding behind her. "Do you two wish to add to it?"

"We're not Sin Eaters," Eld said.

"Why lie?"

"He's not lying," I said, pulling down my scarf so she could see my face.

"You," she hissed.

"Me," I agreed. "I came here expecting to find Sin Eaters lying in wait, but I guess I shouldn't be surprised it was you lot after all."

"Just like last time," Eld added.

"So you do know what happened to our brother," the Eldest growled. "Sicarii said she would deliver you to us, but I thought her a liar as well. A rare day when I'm wrong more than once, rarer still that I'm rewarded for it."

"Sicarii?" Lightning shot through me that had nothing to do with Sin's magic.

"Better yet, we'll have no need to dance to her tune after I bleed you both dry and see your truth for myself," she mused, her voice the sound of bones rubbing together. "Ulfren thinks she'll hand us the Doga, but I'm not so sure."

"The woman's clearly got you twisted, sister," I told her.

"Oh, but you see, girl?" the Eldest lowered her head, thin white eyebrows arching as she studied us from beneath hooded eyes. "I'm never wrong thrice." She upended a vial then, and when she looked back at us, blood trickled from the corner of her mouth. She licked her lips and smiled.

Then she attacked.

I'd been expecting it, but even so, the old woman moved like a flash of lantern light across a dark room. One moment she was on the opposite side of the street, the next she was between Eld and me, close enough that neither of us was able to do much for fear of wounding the other.

Stepping in, I brought my dagger up hard, driving for the Eldest's stomach, but her hands locked on either side of my wrist before Sin could intervene. She shifted her hands on my arm, something clicked in my wrist, and the dagger fell from my numb hand. The Veneficus caught it before it hit the ground and now it was my turn to twist away, my boots clicking on the cobblestone as the blade bit the air where I'd been a moment before. Still twisting, I came around and trapped her arm against her side, pulling her away from Eld.

"Sin, could use some feeling right about now."

"Working on it," he muttered.

My hands began to burn and tingle as Sin's magic coursed through me. My laughter was cut short when the Veneficus's hard braids slapped me in the face. The woman cried out as her body distorted, changing into whatever form the blood she'd swallowed called forth.

Sin's power allowed me to rip the blade from her gloved hand, but we overdid it and lost the blade, which flew back over my shoulder. Her eyes widened in horror as she realized she wasn't fighting any ordinary human—she was wrong thrice after all—as I caught both her hands in mine. She roared, a lion's scream of defiance, but with Sin's magic burning brightly in me, I held her fast. We were eye to eye, hers turning from dark to gold, my muscles beginning to scream.

Silver flashed past the shaved side of my head and the Veneficus's call turned into a throaty gurgle. Eld pulled the blade free and plunged it into her chest, finding her heart, and then it was all over save for the dying.

"U-Ulfren will see," she gasped.

"See what?"

"The truth. In my blood."

"Not if I bleed you dry," I whispered.

"Won't matter. B-blood calls to blood."

The golden light faded from her eyes. She stared at me as she went, that hard bitch, and blood sprayed my face when she breathed her last.

For a moment nothing moved or made noise save for the strained sound of Eld's breathing, loud in my Sin-enhanced ears. Then I let her go and she fell in a ragged heap to the cobblestones, landing with a jangling thud. Eld, shaking slightly from the aftereffects of adrenaline, sank down beside her and pulled the blade free, avoiding her eyes as he wiped it clean.

"Blood calls to blood," I muttered.

Adjusting my maroon scarf—I'd chosen that color for a reason—I stumbled away, weak from Sin's magic. Something exploded behind me, the heat buffeting my back. Spinning, I saw Eld's arms up to protect his face, nearly tripping in his haste to move back as the Veneficus went up in a torrent of flame and inky-black smoke. A warm, rich, spice scent filled the air, cloying beside the acrid smell of gunpowder and the stomach-turning stench of burning hair.

"Gods' breath!"

"They can't see anything if there's nothing left to see," Eld said calmly, tucking the silver blade behind his belt.

"Sicarii's grenado?"

He shrugged. "It just came to me in the moment."

"Good thought," I admitted. "Save I had plans for that thing."

"Oh."

I shakily waved him away. "It's done now. 'Sides, I think I may have figured out how to find Sicarii."

"I thought that's what this was," Eld said, gesturing around. "Finding Sicarii."

"Aye, so did I," I admitted. *I need food, but first* . . . I glanced at the burning corpse and felt something hot flash through me as well. "I was wrong, Eld. The Gods aren't running Sicarii."

"They're not?"

"No," I muttered. "She's running them."

39

"Why are you smiling?"

"Because my theory is proving out."

"Care to share?"

"And deprive you of the chance to learn?" I shook my head and shivered at the wind against my freshly shaved skin. *Maybe I should look into those broad-brimmed hats some of the women are wearing. No different than a tricorne, really.* "What did all of our visits this morning have in common?"

"A lot less death," he said.

"Besides that."

"They were all up and down the damned Quarto," Eld muttered. "I'm hungry," he added.

"We'll eat in a moment," I assured him. We probably should have eaten after the fight with the Veneficus, but realizing that Sicarii wasn't a tool, but the hand directing said tools—plural—had galvanized me into action. When I stopped to think about it, I felt more than a little nauseous, truth be told.

"That's because you aren't listening to me," Sin growled. "We're going to start to eat your body from the inside out if you don't find nourishment soon."

"Uh-huh."

"Buc—"

"First," Eld said, cutting Sin off, "there was the resin refinery, which I thought the foulest smelling place I'd been to until we went to that quicklime apothecary, which cleared out my head in ways that didn't need clearing." That had been when my nausea had really kicked in.

He scratched his jaw, glanced down the lane between the warehouses, and pointed. "There's a pasty cart down there, if memory serves."

"Near where our old friend Salazar's place was, before that mage blew his brains out and set us on the path we're still treading." I shook my braids. "He might have a friend or two that still remembers. Besides, you don't want the meat in those pasties." Eld arched an eyebrow. "Rats at best."

"Gods," he breathed, wrinkling his nose. "Next," he said, returning to the matter at hand, "was a saltpeterist and just now, the old tallow maker."

"Aye, and what did they all have in common?"

"None had the amount of supply you asked for?"

"Go on," I said, nodding.

"I feel like you're having a go at me," Eld muttered, giving me a healthy dose of side-eye.

"I'm not, I swear."

"Hmm. They all remarked on how busy they were for the time of year," he said slowly, scrunching his nose up like he always did when concentrating hard. "They were all old men . . . and the Doga was a repeat customer?"

"Well done," I said, motioning for him to follow me out into the main thoroughfare. Now that the sun was nearing its zenith the road was packed full of all types. Most had enough coin for thicker jackets and were clean, too, so the dockworkers stood out for their stains. I shouldered one lass aside and pulled Eld close.

"Two out of three isn't bad," I said, scanning the crowd. Here and there children darted about, laughing as they played whatever games they could have in the Mercarto Quarto.

"What'd I miss?"

"That they were old men was just happenstance," I said, waving it away with my hand. "And it wasn't just those specific shops, either—their neighbors looked just as busy. The Doga's been making a lot of purchases . . . or someone else has, in her name."

"Sicarii?"

"Seems like."

"Presumably all of these things—petrol, quicklime, gunpowder, tallow—share something in common?"

"Aye, I'll tell you over a meat pasty," I said, gesturing toward a cart on the corner opposite ours. "Then we're on to step two."

"What's step two?" Eld called after me.

"After. You're hungry, remember?" I shouted over my shoulder, working my way through the crowd.

"Say, didn't we have some of those pasties by Salazar's before we went in and it all went to shit last summer?" Eld asked when he caught up to me.

"You did," I told him. "I didn't."

"Godsdamn it, Buc! I thought that incident turned my bowels to water."

"Nope," I said, unable to hide my smirk. "That was just the mystery meat."

"I nearly shat myself," he gasped.

I laughed and Eld cursed and that made me laugh harder. I didn't want to pretend that things were okay, because they weren't, not by a long chalk, but . . . we'd begun as friends and he was still my best and closest friend. So I laughed until Eld's stern pissed-offedness broke and he laughed, too. For a breath or two, my chest stopped hurting. Turns out friendship is a magic all of its own.

"What?" Eld shouted, to be heard over the roar.

"I saw the same yesterday, before I came home," I yelled back at him across the gondola, my voice barely carrying over the sounds of a mob cursing and working themselves up to action.

"Bastard wasn't lying. Real lamb," I muttered, taking a bite from the still-steaming meat pasty I'd bought before jumping into our gondola. Wiping my chin, I continued, "I saw a running brawl between rival gangs near as bad as this one."

Eld's eyes shifted between the two groups in the street across from the canal, one wearing mostly pale blue, the other a mishmash of greys and browns, steel bright amongst the dull colors. Joffers had us well out in the center of the canal, but a cacophony of gunfire made Eld duck. The two sides clashed, obscured by gunsmoke and buildings. Shouts turned to screams and when we could see again, bodies lay everywhere. It was tough to say which side was winning.

"Brawl, you say—battle, says I," Eld muttered. "That's the Constabulary they're fighting."

"You're not wrong," I agreed. Innocents, dressed in motley that almost made for a uniform of their own, fled from either end of the Foreskin, some diving into the canal's icy waters when another fusillade of gunfire erupted, its rolling echo loud across the water.

The current carried us around a bend and away from the sounds of fighting. A moment later all was quiet save for the waters lapping against the gondola's hull and the breeze in my ears. The battle might never have happened, for all one could tell. Servenza seemed as placid as she always was in winter. Save here and there I saw figures with glinting weapons in their hands, marching purposefully in pairs and threes.

"That was the Foreskin," I said, shivering in the cold wind. "Here in the Painted Rock, they're barely hiding the weapons they carry," I explained. "There"—I indicated the Mercarto before us with a nod—"and in the Gilded, it's a different story, aye, but even the Gilded's canals are quieter than normal. I haven't seen any children playing in the streets of Painted Rock, and few in the other Quartos. The ones we saw earlier, running about—they were nearly the only children I saw today."

"Gang rumbles are escalating, breaking into full-fledged wars," Eld said, hiding his mouth with his hand as he chewed, "and the canals aren't safe, which we already knew. I follow you there. What do the children have to do with it?" He looked ahead, into another section of the Mercarto.

"Next time we see some, pick one out and I'll have them tell you," I said. I couldn't trust myself to do so, not when every move I'd made had already been checked. Like the maestro in the Castello. And Quenta. It'd taken me a moment or two to realize it—too long, really—but at least now I knew how to counter it.

Eld frowned. "If you know what you're looking for, why don't you grab the one you want to talk to?"

I swallowed the bite in my mouth, enjoying the spices and fat that clung to my tongue. Perhaps I had gone a little too long without eating.

"Perhaps?" Sin hissed.

"I didn't have need of you, then," I reminded the shard.

"That's the problem with your lot," he grumbled, "you do need me. All the time. You just don't realize it."

Eld looked at me expectantly and I shrugged. "Sicarii."

"Sicarii?" he whispered, glancing around as if expecting her to appear, conjured up by her name like the sea serpents in old sailor tales. "What does she have to do with it?"

"Sicarii seems to understand my thoughts, my patterns," I said, scanning the street, but whoever was trailing us had slipped away. Sin had picked up two following me yesterday and I was pretty certain another had been watching the palazzo when we slipped out this morning. At least, I hoped they had seen us, or else my equation wouldn't add up the way I needed it to.

"She got to that girl I was trying to use as an informant, and Quenta nearly killed the pair of us. She's been one step ahead the entire time and she seems willing to see Servenza burn."

I glanced at Eld. "I'm thinking if you pick the child and I have nothing to do with it, maybe that will prevent us from picking up another one of her plants."

"And what do I do with said child?"

"Give them this," I said, tossing him a gold lira, "and bring them to me." I motioned for Joffers to take us to one of the poles jutting out of the canal's edge that served as a tie-off. The smells from a nearby food cart, carried across the street on the chill winter's wind, decided where I was heading. "Tell them there's another in it for them if they speak true."

"Where will you be?" Eld asked, leaping across the narrow divide of water between the gondola and the street.

"Grabbing another pasty," I said, licking my fingers before tugging my gloves back on. "I lost my appetite of late."

"I'm glad you found it."

I waved a hand, not bothering to tell him I hadn't, not really, but I had a feeling I was going to need Sin's magic and I wasn't ready to die. I hadn't become some fool of a girl who throws her life away over a fucking man. Not yet.

"You want to know where I play?" the boy asked, his words slightly difficult to understand due to the deformed lip that kept tripping his mouth up.

"Aye," I told him, squatting down so I was on his level. "Seems like many places aren't safe for little ones like yourself."

"I'm not little," he said, crossing his stubby arms and pulling his oversized, brown jacket tighter about him.

"'Course you are. You're a child, but someday you'll be as big as my friend yonder," I said, gesturing toward Eld. I gave him a wink. "Then you'll be bigger than me." He smiled awkwardly and I knew Eld had chosen right. He'd likely been bullied his whole short life. Children weren't crueler than adults; they were just more honest. Now I'd made him feel special and he'd tell me what I needed to know. "The streets are rougher this winter, aye?"

"My mem doesn't like me out," he said. "B-but she's out to wash clothes till dark, so I can do w-what I want," he stuttered.

"Growing up already," I agreed. "You live close by?"

"On the edge of the Painted Rock," he said.

"But you don't play there?"

"Not unless I w-want my head split."

I nodded encouragingly, making a mental note to check in on Govanti. Eld said he was fine. Still, it'd been a fortnight or more since we last spoke, longer than that since I'd asked Eld to look him up, and he lived in that vicinity.

"I can't talk prop-per, but I en't dumb," the lad added.

"You speak just fine." I smiled, drawing his gaze to me so I could see the lie if it was there. "You play here, in the Mercarto, but it's crowded, hard to play stickball or toss coppers."

"Oh, w-we toss coppers by the Stem." He ran a dirty hand through his brown hair, which looked washed and combed, unlike half the other urchins running about, and glanced around before leaning closer. "There's a few of the Serpentines what give us coppers for running errands."

"The Stem?" Eld mouthed above him.

"The main bridge that spans the canal between the Painted Rock and the Tip," I explained. I turned back to the boy. "I'm guessing your mem doesn't know you're running with a gang?"

"Not w-with them," he said quickly. His dark eyes filled with worry. "You won't tell?"

"'Course not," I said. "I grew up on the streets. I know how it is."

"You did not." His lip curled. "I en't—"

"Dumb, aye, I know." I laughed, sharing a false smile with Eld. "I'm not putting one over on you, lad. But running with gangs isn't something you start and stop as you please."

"It's not like that," he protested.

"Then what's it like?"

"They said we could p-play on either side of the Stem, they'd keep the other gangs away from us—the ones that want real runners."

"And in return?"

"What's that mean?"

"What did they want you to do for them?"

"Oh!" His grin split his face. "Keep w-watch," he said. "It's a game. If we see other gangs or the Constabulary, or a short girl and a big pale m-man with lots of blades, we run, and tell Enri and he gives us a copper."

"Pretty good hustle, lad," I said, rising quickly onto my tiptoes and motioning Eld away with my head. I reached down and tousled the boy's hair. "Well, you satisfied my curiosity. I've been away from Servenza for a long time, but I remember the streets. Not always good memories, mind, but there were some fun times. I wondered if that were still true today."

"It was more fun b-before the Burnt Eye came," the boy said. He shrugged in his overlarge jacket. "But then, w-we didn't get coppers."

"Burnt Eye?" I asked, hearing my breath catch.

"The one protecting the Serpentines," he said. "The one they say has a dozen hands and a burning eye that they use to see if you're lying or not. And"—his voice dropped to a bare whisper—"if you lie to the Burnt Eye, they fill their dozen hands with blades and chop you to m-mince!

"Sicarii," Sin whispered. I nodded mentally.

"That sounds scary," I said.

"It is! But I don't lie. Mem says that the Gods will make my lip stay like this forever if I do," he said, touching his mouth. "She's saving soldi to fix me an' I can't lie or it w-won't work. My friend Cali had a limp that a mind witch fixed—for free, even! I did'na believe her but Mem said it was true. Also said we can't trust mind w-witches, not when we pray to the Dead Gods. It's them we'll pay and they will know I en't lying and heal me proper. S-so I don't think the Burnt Eye will hurt me."

"Of course they won't," I assured him. *Not after I'm through with her.* "Well, lad, I promised you a lira and I'm going to do you one better."

"Signorina?"

"I'm going to give you two." I reached into my jacket and paused. "Does your mem treat you well? Answer me true."

"She makes me eat greens," he said with a shrug, "but she doesn't beat me. And she did give me a cup of hot kan on my birthday."

"Give your mem this." I bent down and slipped a third gold coin into his palm. "And tell her to take you to a physiker tomorrow to get that lip fixed."

"The Sin Eaters' healing would be painless. And better," Sin suggested.

No Gods. No magic.

"It's going to hurt, lad," I told him, "what they'll do, but your lip will heal fine and you'll be speaking just fine soon enough. Aye?"

"Signorina." He whispered the word like a prayer. "This is too much!"

"I think it's enough," I said, staring him full in the face. "Because you're not going back to the Stem after today."

"Why not?"

"Because," I said, turning him toward where Eld stood a dozen paces away, "if you do, then you're going to have to lie and if you lie the Burnt Eye will know, won't they?" He opened his mouth to protest and I arched my eyebrows and flicked my eyes to Eld and back.

"You said you weren't dumb," I reminded him.

"I w-won't tell," he whispered.

"I know."

I hoped I wasn't lying. I didn't think he'd tell on purpose, but children are creatures of whim and there was no saying what he might do without thinking. I was counting on the surgery to keep him laid up long enough for me to settle with Sicarii.

"That's why you're keeping him from the Sin Eater's healing," Sin growled. "Noble, my arse."

"You're wrong."

"I can hear your thoughts, Buc."

"That was one reason I didn't tell him about the Sin Eaters," I countered. "Your foul magics soiling an innocent like this child was another."

"Now run off and find your mem and tell her the good news," I said out loud.

The boy took off like a shot, nearly bowling Eld over despite the size difference between him. Catching himself against Eld's arm, he gave us both a quick bow and a wave, and then ran off, legs windmilling as he cut through the crowd.

"That was well done," Eld said quietly when he reached me. "I'm glad to see you're taking a care for the little ones again."

Sin snorted.

"Eh?" I shook myself out of my thoughts and grunted. "I needed information, Eld, and now I need him to keep that little trap of his shut for a few days."

"Buc—"

"Eld, I've told you before, but you don't listen."

He cocked his head.

"I'm not going to save that boy by giving every lire in the world to him and all his brothers and sisters." I shook my head. "You want to save him? Let me do what I do best."

"And what's that?" he asked, his voice thin, whipcord tight.

"Find things and stab them." I brushed past him. "Now come on, that's two down and the third's waiting."

"Does it involve stabbing things?" Eld called after me.

"Give the man a prize!" I shouted back.

Eld, Salina—none of them understand. Perhaps it came from the streets, perhaps I'd just read more than either of them combined, but it was writ in plain language to me. Power is usurped or overthrown. I had no desire to be a God, so I was usurping the power of others to overthrow the power of the Gods. Stopping to help every child along the way would ensure I helped none of them in the end. I was going to make sure the Burnt Eye never hurt anyone again. And then I was going to pull the Chair down by her braids and use the Company to cut the throats of the Gods. And I was going to do it alone. Sin made a noise. *You don't count. You're in my head, so we're already one.*

"Lucky me," he muttered.

40

Hours of walking later, we stood on sore feet in the Painted Rock Quarto, two streets back from the canal. The thoroughfare was the quietest I'd seen in weeks, people moving in as orderly a flow as could be expected when factory workers mixed with dockworkers mixed with budding merchants and store clerks. No one was carrying weapons here, unlike where the Quarto bordered the Tip. If the Serpentines were around, they were keeping a low profile. Taken together, I'd a feeling we'd come to the right place.

"Show me again, Sin," I said, and a map appeared in my mind. "Can you rotate it to match my direction?"

"How's that?" he said, suiting the action to the words.

"Better," I said, motioning for Eld to follow me down a side alley that ran between two older, would-be palazzos that now had small storefronts on their ground floors and a hodgepodge of tenement rooms above. The store on my left, nearer the canal, seemed to run the length of the building, while the one on the right was only half the size; probably one or two families were crammed into the remaining space. This close to the canal, the sewers drained properly, so it didn't smell like the Tip, but I was surprised at the lack of trash in the gutters.

"What are we doing here, Buc?"

"Gathering clues."

"Clues?" Eld cleared his throat. "To what?"

"To Sicarii's lair," I said.

"Sicarii?" He reached for his sword hilt, stopping just short of it. "She's here?"

306 • Ryan Van Loan

"Aye. In this Quarto."

"How can you be sure?"

I sighed.

"I know how you love explaining yourself," he said with a grin that didn't quite reach his eyes.

"Those supplies we were asking around about this morning?"

He nodded.

"They're part of a formula, known in some texts on the alchemy and chemistry of elements as Serpent's Flame."

"Serpent's Flame?" Eld scratched at his stubble. "But dragons are extinct. The last were hunted down centuries ago—if they existed at all."

"Don't blame me for the lack of imagination of whatever crazy elementalist brewed up this concoction. It really should be called liquid fire."

Eld's eyes widened. "That's what was in the grenado? What's been behind all those explosions?"

"Conflagrations," I corrected. "Aye, I think so. Anyway, the formula's been lost for at least a hundred years. The last record I could find was of a warlord in what is now the Cordoban Confederacy, who used it to burn the shit out of her rivals until they banded together—and in so doing, indirectly created what would become the Confederacy. That and some mythical leader from the north who helped unite them and then disappeared, if the tales are to be believed. My point is, while the exact formulation isn't known, some of the key ingredients are."

"Oil, quicklime, gunpowder, and tallow," Eld guessed.

"Right in four," I said. "There must be some other ingredients as well, but those are all required. When combined properly, the shit lies dormant . . . until exposed. To what, the sources don't say, but it seems pretty clear it must be water or a similar liquid."

"Then boom?"

"Then boom."

"That explains how her minions are doing what appears to be

magic," Eld said. He glanced down either side of the alley, shoulders relaxing when he saw no one. "But not why she's in this Quarto."

"No, but determining where Sicarii is getting her supplies from helped me narrow things down somewhat. Those children playing, when I've seen few children playing anywhere else, were another clue," I explained. "If you're going to set up a clandestine lair to assassinate the Doga and build a hoard of pyroclastic weapons, you don't want the neighbors fighting or the little ones playing with matches and accidentally blowing the whole Quarto sky-high."

"What's the phrase you like so much?" Eld asked. "Don't shit where you eat?" He flashed a grin. "Quaint."

"Imagine if you'd taken that advice," Sin whispered.

"Who pissed in your soup?" I asked him. "You've been an arsehole all day."

"You somehow pushed me out of your mind after the Masquerade, which shouldn't be possible, and when you let me back in, you mostly ignored me. Lock yourself away in a room for days on end, hearing the sound of life outside but never getting to live it, and see how you like it," he growled. "Notice how you haven't had any memory lapses since the Masquerade?"

"That's your doing?" I hadn't had any lapses since the Masquerade, that was true, but I'd thought it was because I'd kept my use of Sin to a minimum.

"Listen, just because I'm not in your mind doesn't mean my magic isn't suffusing you constantly. When you let me back in . . . well, protecting your memory is practically all I've been doing. You're welcome," he muttered.

"I'm sorry," I said.

"Her name, did you actually just mean that?" Sin's tone was sarcastic, but I could hear the surprise there, too.

"I am," I admitted. "I've been in my own special damnation the past few days, well, months really, but you feel what I feel. I don't need to add to that."

"Thanks," he said after a moment. "I know how broken you feel, but you were broken before and you fixed yourself."

"Eld helped. A lot."

"I'm not Eld, but I am a shard of a Goddess imbued with magics beyond your ken," Sin said. "Just saying."

"It'll do, shard, it'll do."

"Now . . ."

"Don't expect it all to be calm seas and clear skies from here on," I said, interrupting him. "But I'll try to be better. Aye?"

"Fair. I'll try to act less the arse, too."

"Hmm, look at us growing up," I muttered.

"Buc?" Eld asked, snapping his fingers. "You okay?"

"Better than okay, actually," I said. Which was true if okay was the state I'd been in at Salina's. Though I still had a lingering desire to find a certain dancing queen named Lucrezia and kneecap her. . . .

"The Doga?" Eld prompted softly. "Why was her name on every manifest? What's her role?"

"I've been wondering about that, too. I don't see what she stands to gain with Sicarii, not when she's nearly died thrice from assassination. She seemed shocked when I mentioned that name," I added.

"Like she kenned Sicarii?" Eld asked.

"Maybe? I'd think her Secreto would hear if others were making large purchases in her name. If not of quicklime or tallow, certainly of gunpowder."

"The Empress herself tracks that," Eld said. "Something isn't adding up."

"Many things aren't adding up. Thankfully, we don't need them to.

"There," I said, pointing at the palazzo across from us; the building didn't have any tenants on the ground floor and was right beside a sewer drain. A small, once-white wooden door—now faded to a spotty grey that blended in with the faded stucco—was the only visible point of entry.

"According to the Doga's map, there's no tunnel there." Sin flashed the map in my mind. "But that partial map allowed me to extrapolate. If I'm right, one of the missing tunnels should be right there."

"Damn." Eld rolled his shoulders, patted his sides where his pistoles were holstered beneath his jacket, and drew his sword a palm's breadth before letting it slide back into its sheath. "What's the plan?"

"Good question."

I palmed the note I'd been slipped the second time we were in the Tip and glanced at the crude drawing of a door. *Unlocked, as you thought.* The writing was crude, haphazard, and completely recognizable as being from one of the few informants I trusted other than Govanti.

"There's only the one entrance as far as I can tell," I said.

"Straight in, then?" he asked, one eyebrow arched.

"Seems it," I agreed.

"Hard and fast?"

"Do men know any other way?"

Eld's reply caught in his throat and I dug my elbow into his side. "Mind you keep your head in the game."

My steps sounded gritty as I crossed the sandy street. Nearing the door, I drew my stilettos. Eld was at my side.

"Let's not keep our host waiting," I muttered.

Sin's magic burned through my legs; my kick nearly put my boot completely through the door, which crashed back with a squelching thud, sending splinters through the air. As the door rebounded off the wall, I shouldered it back. Eld stepped past me, his sword out, seeking whomever stood guard. Dust kicked up by our charge swirled about, half blinding me, and I sneezed.

"Nothing," Sin whispered.

"There's nothing here," Eld choked out, grinning at me through the haze. "All that walking and you kicked in the door on what? A run-down barber's?" He laughed, choked again on the dust, and laughed harder, wheezing as he leaned against a metal barber's chair, the faded leather cracked and peeling away from its frame.

I turned in a slow circle, eyes and lungs burning from the tremendous amount of dust that had collected over the years. The floor was covered in a thick layer, the wall-length mirror was nearly black, and save for a second chair, opposite the one Eld was leaning on, there was nothing. Nothing at all. Damn it. Was I wrong? I kept turning, studying the walls, and saw something against the plaster in the far corner. Walking over, trying to avoid stirring up more dust, I bent closer. There was a hairline crack in the plaster that ran halfway up from the floor, visible because the dust wasn't collecting there, but rather being—sucked in.

"What's this?" I whispered. I scuffed my boot and a cloud of dust flew up and disappeared, sucked away by the breeze through the crack. Eld's coughing had finally killed his laughter by the time I turned, crossing my arms.

His face was a mess, coated in a fine layer of dust and streaked where he'd cried from laughing. Eld never laughs that hard. He saw me watching and straightened, still half giggling, half coughing.

"Finished?" I asked.

He nodded, steadying himself against the barber's chair.

"Good. I hope you're hungry for some humble pie."

"Why's that?" he croaked.

"Because . . . ," I told him, digging my fingers into the crack and pulling hard. Only I didn't need to pull hard, because as soon as I felt the wall give, it slid in and away on perfectly grooved and oiled tracks, revealing a gaping maw with steps that disappeared into the darkness. ". . . the walls have mouths," I said.

41

"Let me go first," Eld said, lowering his voice as he adjusted his grip on his sword.

"Ordinarily I'd be fine with you playing Sirrah Bullet-catcher," I said, sliding one of my stilettos back into its sheath in my grey jacket and drawing the thick-bladed short sword that Sin's strength allowed me to wield as fast as any knife. I inspected the blade I'd blackened in preparation for the tunnels, looking for any stray glint, but all was well. "But I'm shorter and quieter, and I have better night vision, which means if I'm out front, I'm less likely to be spotted and catch a bullet through the teeth."

"Why, Buc," Eld said with a false smile, "you do care."

My glare wiped it from his face.

"Just trying to lighten the mood," he muttered.

"Count to three and follow after. Try not to act the walrus in a porcelain shop."

I stepped into the waiting stairway. A few steps down and the walls turned from wood to stone and the air grew cooler. I took care that I placed my boots quietly on the sandy steps, but even so, my footfalls echoed faintly. The passage wound down to a narrow archway blocked by a door that I could barely make out in the faint light from above. Eld caught up to me a few moments later and blocked what little light there was, turning the archway pitch-black.

"Sin."

My eyesight sharpened as my sense of smell and my hearing diminished. I didn't miss the former—the musty odor had been overpowering—but the latter was an issue. It was worth it, for the door became as visible as if I held a bright lantern. A quick inspection showed there was no spy hole to view us through and no trip wires or other traps.

"Locked?" Eld asked, and I quickly touched the handle to confirm.

"Aye. I'm tempted to kick it off its hinges, but anyone down here for leagues around will hear." I put my ear to the door and whispered directions to Sin. A moment later my vision darkened and my ears tingled. I could hear scurrying in the walls—likely some rodent or other—and just barely, the sound of a voice on the other side of the door. The cadence was even, on a regular beat. Singing? I strained to listen.

Bam! A loud reverberation sent me reeling away from the door; I almost clasped my head in my hands before remembering the blades I held. Sin's magic left me and everything returned to normal save for a slight whine on the edge of my hearing.

"What the fuck, man?" I growled. "I just said we didn't want to be heard and then you go pounding on the door?"

"I didn't pound," Eld said, knocking again. It didn't sound half so loud as it had when my ear had been against the door and filled to the brim with Sin's magic. He shrugged. "Sometimes politeness does get you places, Buc."

"Someone's coming," Sin whispered.

"Aye, well, down here, the only thing it's going to get you is a blade twixt your ribs," I said, ignoring Sin. I squinted my eyes, fighting to hold off the headache Eld's rapping had induced. "I was about to suggest picking the lock. We've options before you go announcing us for high tea."

"Someone's—"

"Coming. I heard you the first time," I told Sin.

"What options?" Eld asked. "It's black as night and unless you brought matches, we're not going to be able to find a keyhole to pick. If it has a keyhole."

"Even so, your first choice is to knock?"

"I may have been a bit hasty," he admitted.

"A bit?" I asked. "You're supposed to be the rational one, re-member?"

"Some—"

"I fucking know, Sin."

"—one is here," he finished.

"Listen!" Eld snapped, the rest of whatever he was going to say cut off by the door swinging open.

"Ye lot been told te keep a lid on it! Who is it this time? Lem?" A short, swarthy man in a stained jerkin peered out. His thick eye-brows leapt up into his unruly hair. "Yer not Lem."

"No," I agreed, "I'm not."

"Bloody Gods, yer not to be down here," he spat, reaching for the pistole tucked into his waistband.

"You opened the door," I reminded him, lunging forward. My arm shivered from the impact as I ran him through, my momen-tum slamming him back into the door. He opened his mouth, con-fusion writ in a bold, bloody hand across his features, but the only thing that came out was a choking, rasping spray of blood. More blood gushed freely as what remained of his heart pumped it past my blade.

"It'd be rude not to accept your invitation. We don't like rude, do we, Eld?" I asked.

"He's dead," Eld said.

"Aye, a pace of steel run through your heart will do that."

I pulled and the door and the guard both swung toward me. I braced the door, holding the stiletto flat against the wood, and pulled on the sword, but nothing happened. Stuck. Sin's magic had given me enough strength to run the man through and nail him to the door. With that strength gone, I couldn't get my blade free. I took a breath and tried again, but the door, with the man affixed to it, swung, nearly sending me on my arse.

"Gods' sake," Eld muttered. Sheathing his sword, he stepped up beside me and braced himself against the door. "Now go."

I ripped hard and the sword moved a finger's length and stopped. "Pull, Buc!"

"I am pulling." The man slid toward me, feet dragging the ground.

"Not hard enough." Eld shoved the door back and I went with it.

"Thank you, Captain Obvious." I jerked hard and the man came sliding back.

"You were strong enough," Eld grunted, "to put the sword in. You should be strong enough to pull it out."

"You . . . ," I slipped my other stiletto into my jacket and grasped the hilt with both hands. *Sin, now!* ". . . would fucking think so!"

The blade came free with a sickening squelch and my feet went out from under me. *Ouch.* Eld stumbled back, the man falling toward him like a puppet with its strings cut; fending off the body, Eld tripped over me and hit the floor hard enough to knock the breath from his lungs. The door pounded off the wall, squealing on its hinges, then slammed shut with a deafening thud. Eld groaned in the silence that followed.

"Do you think they heard that for leagues?" he asked when he found his breath.

I shrugged. "Do you think the door's still unlocked?"

He shrugged.

"My arse," we both said at the same time. I looked at Eld, saw his grin, and couldn't keep the laugh between my teeth. His own laugh set me off harder and that set him off, and we lay there, shaking with half-silent laughter, every jiggle and jerk making the bruise on my left arse cheek hurt more. I didn't care. It felt good.

When our laughter died down I pushed myself to my feet and offered Eld a hand. "Truce?"

"Truce," he said, taking my hand. I jerked him up with Sin's help. "I guess there's no hiding this, eh?"

I followed his glance and clicked my tongue. "He was a bleeder." Even with just the scrap of light that made it down from the room above, I could see that the walls were splattered with blood and there was a huge pool of it on the sandy floor. Sand made it easy to clean up, of course, but it also made for a very obvious stain.

"Well, as you said, a pace of steel through the chest will do that."

Eld's voice was light, but tighter than usual, giving him the lie. He hated killing, even when it needed to be done. I was no sadist, but I remembered Quenta's body at my feet and all the others that had followed. Sicarii had done that just as she'd done this. You ever find yourself taking responsibility for others' actions and you'll find yourself on the short path to madness. Eld and I would pay them back once and final at the end.

I said as much. "No use crying over spilt blood unless it's your own," I added, reaching for the door. I hesitated and let my breath out in a single exhale when it opened.

"Luck's turning around," Eld muttered, picking my short sword up from where it'd fallen and offering it to me, hilt first.

"No such thing as luck," I reminded him. Shaking the blood from my blade, I motioned for him to follow. "But if there was, I'd be okay for a turn."

The narrow passageway behind the door opened into a larger room a dozen paces away; light from the space reached us before we could see anything beyond the entrance. We paused to consider.

"It may be that no one heard what happened. Or it may be we're about to walk into a mass of Serpentines armed to the teeth, waiting to cut us down."

"Luck?" Eld suggested.

"Mayhap," I whispered to him as our boots gritted on the sand. "But keep your blade handy just in case."

The passages beneath the Painted Rock were legion, crisscrossing one another. Some were well lit, others less so, and some were pitch-black, but light didn't seem to always be an indicator of habitation. Several full storage rooms were dark while a few empty

316 • Ryan Van Loan

ones held a lantern or flickering torch in a sconce. As we slipped from room to room, passageway to passageway, Sin kept track of our movements, building a map in my mind. The items we found helped create a clearer picture as well. In addition to signs of the Serpentines, I saw marks of the Krakens, the Sharp Eagles, the Cobblestone Corners, and a dozen other gangs, half of whom were supposed to be at one another's throats.

I'd been wrong about the Gods and I'd been wrong about the kind of war brewing across the canals. They weren't fighting: they were consolidating, amassing an army. For Sicarii or for another? Who? Every additional scrap of information only led to more questions.

Sin's mental map suggested we'd passed beneath the canal a few rooms back, which made sense given the dampness present despite all the sand on the floors. They must have dragged in half an island's worth of beaches to cover this place. So far we hadn't found much in the way of weapons caches. Pickled eel, salted fish, tuns of ale, rice, and flour, along with rush mats that I knew the gangs used as armor, but no weapons. I was just about to mention that to Eld when a rancid smell like shit festering in the sun drove the breath from my lungs. Eld retched beside me.

"What in Gods' name is that smell?" he hissed between the fingers covering his mouth and nose.

"Search me," I choked, missing my blood-soaked scarf I'd tossed in the canal earlier.

As we neared the next room the pungent smell grew even stronger, burning my eyes. We hesitated, neither wanting to go in, but there was nothing for it, so we stepped across the threshold and my boot immediately slid in shit. The room was covered in it, from small mouselike droppings smeared across the floor to paste that spilled from the tops of the rows of large, wide-mouthed urns that filled the room. Masks and aprons hung from the walls and gloves were stacked on a table on the far side of the room.

"This smells worse than pig shit," Eld gasped.

I nodded. "It's not pig, though."

"What then?"

"Sin?"

"I can tell you what it is, but you're not going to like it."

"Why's that?" I felt him smirk in my mind. "Tell me."

"You're going to have to taste it," he said.

"I hate you."

"I know."

"You suck arsehole."

"Ah, you'll soon be able to tell me what that's like." He laughed. "A bunghole too far?"

I could sense he was going to keep it up, so I slid a finger along the edge of one of the urns and quickly, before I could think about it, put the barest tip of that finger against my tongue. My tongue burned at the touch, my taste buds recoiling in horror at the depravity I'd inflicted on them. Hearing Eld throw up behind me, I gagged, but managed not to vomit. In my mind, I was calm. As calm as one can be after eating shit.

"Well?"

"I can't believe you did that," Sin whispered.

"I guess I know what it means when I tell someone to eat shit," I muttered. "Now, what is it, and is it important?"

"Processing," he said. "The first is easy. It's guano."

"Speak Imperial."

"Guano. Bat poop."

"Bat poop." I rubbed my tongue against my sleeve, trying to scrape the burning stench off my taste buds. "Hmm."

"I think it's important," Sin said. "It was used in making explosives and incendiary devices in Her time."

"It must be one of the missing components of the Serpent's Flame."

"Safe bet," Sin agreed.

"W-was it? Feces?" Eld was wiping his lips with the back of his glove. He saw my nod and shuddered. "Nasty," he whispered.

"I'm not exactly enthused about it myself," I told him, then repeated what Sin had told me. "Let's keep moving, I'm starting to get used to the stench and I don't know if that's a good thing or if it means all of my sensory glands have been burned out of existence."

Eld studied me and shook his head. "Nasty."

"C'mon," I said, rolling my eyes. "We're getting closer, I know it." He didn't say anything. "It kind of tasted like burned candied almonds," I teased. Roasted almonds were one of Eld's favorite treats.

"Nasty."

42

We continued exploring, finding more filled storage rooms. Barrels stamped with marks indicating oil were piled beside others marked as tallow. I saw enough gunpowder to supply a small army and enough quicklime to scorch the lungs of half of Servenza.

In this part of the tunnels, the air seemed drier, as if all the moisture had been sucked away. My tongue cleaved to the roof of my mouth and I heard Eld try to quietly clear his throat. We'd not seen or heard anyone since we'd killed the guard, but given the number of gangs involved, there had to be several hundred people in on Sicarii's plan, whatever it was. I kept wondering why there was no sign of anyone in the tunnels and marveling that more of her schemes hadn't leaked in the streets above, given that information poured through Servenza like a sieve. If Sicarii could keep that many people quiet, what else could she do?

Blackmail the Gods. I felt Sin snarl in my mind and almost smiled. It wasn't quite what I intended to do, but it was close enough that I could almost admire the woman. Save she'd killed Quenta and half a dozen of my other little fish, nearly killed Eld and me, and I didn't believe she was out to save the world; she wanted to own it. *Get in line.*

We came to a door with a large red *X* painted on it. Sin's magic made my ears burn again, soothing the high-pitched whine that had remained from Eld's earlier pounding on the door. I strained, listening. Nothing. I exchanged looks with Eld and he shrugged.

"Perhaps we caught them on a break," he suggested.

"Makes sense that they wouldn't be down here all the time." I inhaled the dry air, catching a hint of something that I couldn't quite place. "If they were, people would realize that the gangs weren't out in force. Especially with them pushing this false gang-war narrative."

"Could be only the gang leaders are in on it?"

"Has to be more than that," I said. "Too much shit down here, literal and otherwise, for them to have done it alone." I returned my attention to the door, noticing that cloth had been nailed around the edges to create a seal. "When you're working with commoners, it's a safe bet they can't read. I tapped the *X*. "But everyone knows this means 'keep out.'"

I tried the handle. "Locked." I pulled out my lockpicks. Selecting the largest of the three, I dropped to a knee and began working.

"Don't pound on this door, Eld." I felt the first tumbler yield, but the second was a tricky bastard, and after a moment I let Sin guide my fingers. "I don't think it would work out half so well as last time." I twisted the pick and the lock popped open with a click I felt more than heard.

The door swung inward of its own volition and a warm, spicy aroma licked me in the face. Inside, we found a laboratory: long tables laden with gearwork barrels, crates, and other supplies arranged beneath the tabletops. The room was lit by double-walled lanterns, like those used on ships to keep water out, though in this case I'd a feeling it was meant to keep the fire in. Getting up, I pulled a pair of handkerchiefs from my jacket and handed one to Eld.

"Put this over your mouth and nose."

"Why?"

"Because," I told him, tying the thin cloth over my face so that only my eyes were visible, "if I'm right, we're about to find out how Serpent's Flame is made. Remember what sets it off?"

"Water?"

"Of any kind. Including saliva, a runny nose, any sort of moisture at all."

"It can't be that sensitive," Eld protested. "How would they handle it on an island if it was?"

"Remember the maestro?"

Eld swallowed audibly.

"Want to chance it?"

He shook his head.

"Good. Then step light and keep your hands to yourself. We need to be careful or we'll send half the island up in smoke and flames."

As we walked through the room I realized I'd vastly underestimated Sicarii's operation. This was some form of machined assembly line: here, a mechanism for grinding the powders finer than I'd thought possible; there, a thin-tipped funnel that allowed oil to drizzle onto the powder as it moved along a series of belts and pulleys. A gearwork mortar and pestle was lined with the same, familiar stench as the shit room. At what seemed to be the end, a concave plate rested as if stopped in midmovement, filled with powder that smelled like burned shit, beside a pile of a reddish-orange spice that smelled like cinnamon, but different.

"It's called cardurry," Sin said in my mind. "A plant that grows farther south. In the Southeast Island, Cordoban Confederacy, and the like."

"Something smells familiar," Eld whispered from behind the handkerchief covering his mouth.

"It's the spice," I explained. "Without it, the reek of this Serpent's Flame would be far too noticeable. Covered by cardurry, it could be a perfume, or the scent of someone who trades in spices, or could otherwise be easily explained away."

"You're right," Eld muttered. "I remember smelling this on some of that first lot that tried to kill us. And again when we visited the maestro in the Castello. Not to mention the grenado."

"Aye, and Sicarii smelled the same when she tried to kill me the other night." Something tickled the back of my mind, but I couldn't quite place it. "This stuff must get into your skin if you're around it long enough."

"It does," a voice growled from behind us.

I spun around, heart climbing into my throat, and saw three gang members in the door we'd come through. Movement behind them suggested they weren't alone. The one in the middle stood head and shoulders above the other two; I could see the tendrils of a tattoo climbing out of his yellowed shirt and up his neck. No, not tendrils—the tentacles of a Kraken.

Eld sank into a crouch and drew a pistole from his sash with a free hand.

"Let's not be hasty," one of the others said, her voice cracking. She made no move to reach for the pistoles strapped to the outside of her midnight-blue jacket; I could see that both were equipped with the newfangled, shiny, brass scope sights I'd read about. Adjusting the large feather in her wide-brimmed hat, she said to Eld, "One false move and we could all burn to death."

"There's no need for sparks," the other woman said, pulling twin cinquedeas from somewhere behind her back. The palm-wide blades were stained with something I couldn't identify. "What do you reckon?"

"I heard the Poisoned Eels were wiped out," I said, taking a half step back. "By the Krakens, as it were," I added, taking another step back. Eld followed suit. The door behind us was only a few paces away. "Look at you all, being buddy-buddy and unwiped."

"You heard what she wanted you to hear," the Poisoned Eel woman said, flashing kan-white teeth at me. Her eyes flicked back and forth between Eld and me, then over the room and back to Eld so quickly that I knew she'd been drinking kan all day and was flush with it. "Sicarii is a maestra of whispers."

"So it would seem." I nodded toward the other woman. "Sharp

Eagle?" She nodded in return. "Sicarii's motivations I understand," I lied. "But what's in it for you lot?"

"Give her nothing," the man snapped. "We didn't come to talk, girl. We came to find who murdered my man and use their bones for tallow."

"Fat."

"What?"

"Tallow comes from fat," I said. "Tight spot, Sin," I whispered mentally.

"Seems it," he agreed.

"Any ideas?"

"A few. I'd be better off if we knew the range of possibilities with this liquid-fire bullshit."

"Uh-huh. Let's us both start thinking and I'll keep them talking."

"Animal fat usually," I said aloud, picking up where I'd left off, "but I suppose human could serve as well."

"You playing the smart-arse with us?"

"I don't know how smart my buttocks are, but my brains are pretty damned smart," I said.

"You've a file for a tongue, woman," the Sharp Eagle said.

"You're not the first to notice," Eld muttered.

"He speaks!" The Poisoned Eel laughed. "We've talked long enough, en't we?" The man nodded. "Sent a few lads and lasses the long way around, so you lot won't be going anywhere. I don't care if you burn or bleed—dead is dead—but if you want it to be a quick death, you'll toss your weapons down now."

"Is this any way to treat guests?"

"Guests?" The man's voice rumbled in his chest as he laughed briefly.

"Your man did throw open the door for us," I said. "Didn't roll out the red carpet, true enough, but his blood made a reasonable facsimile."

"Fax—what?"

"Facsimile," I repeated with a smile. We'd kept edging away; the door was less than a pace from us. Given the other door had swung inward, I was guessing this would do the same, so we couldn't just turn and run. "It means a copy or a replica. His blood in the sand did sort of look like a carpet, don't you think?" We needed a distraction. But what?

The Kraken glanced at the Poisoned Eel at his side. "I want to see both of them drowning in their own blood. You cut a tentacle off a Kraken, two more grow in its place. I want those two dead."

"I think you're mixing analogies here," I said. *Slingshot in inner left jacket pocket above stiletto. Bullets in pouch.* Two steps to right puts table between us and—I'd forgotten the thick-bladed short sword in my hand. I was good and with Sin I was better, but I couldn't shoot a slingshot one-handed. I didn't want to drop the sword: it would be useful if they closed. It was still wet with blood from the guard I'd killed. *Hmm.*

"Eld?"

He glanced at me.

"Ready, Sin?" I felt his nod in my mind and couldn't keep the snarl from my lips. "Be hasty, Eld."

"What?"

"Be." My eyes flicked to his pistole. "Hasty. You've my permission."

"Huh? Oh. Oh."

The pistole bucked in his fist, belching smoke and flame, and the blade the Poisoned Eel held leapt out of her hand with a shrill whine as the bullet struck it and ricocheted off, screeching through one of the brass machineries and slamming into the stone wall with a thump. I could tell by the look on Eld's face he hadn't meant to do that. The pistole's barrels rotated from over to under and he turned it on the rest.

"You motherfuckers!" the woman screamed, holding her broken and bleeding hand with the other. "I'm going to carve you to—"

Even as she shrieked, I spun on one leg, whipping the other around. Sin's tingling magic added an extra snap as my boot connected solidly with the plate of cardurry. It flew through the air, spreading a hazy plume of reddish orange in its wake. The Kraken grunted, the Sharp Eagle screamed, and all three hit the floor, fearing the worst. I wasn't worried. The spice wasn't what would kill us.

No, the reeking pile of half-paste, half-powder shit on the oval plate would do that. I picked it up with my free hand, thankful I still wore gloves because I was sweating enough to set it off with a touch, and tossed it like I'd seen athletes toss weighted plates in the Arena at Colgna. As it flew through the air with an awkward wobble, I flicked my sword after it. Little flecks of the guard's blood, not quite dry, winged through the air.

"Eld! Down!" I screamed and followed suit, ducking behind the table. A breath later the room erupted in a geyser of white-hot fire and I heard the gang leaders screaming as the flames caught them up.

Pushing myself to my feet, I ripped the door open. Eld ran past me and nearly impaled himself on another gang member's cutlass. *Left hand to lower-right pocket. There's a chip on the hilt. Adjust.* Eld parried the thrust more from muscle memory than actual skill, and knocked the man back. My stiletto whipped over Eld's shoulder and tore through the man's throat. I'd been aiming for his head, but that chip always fucked with my accuracy.

"Eld would call that luck," Sin said.

"I told you to adjust. That's not luck. That's—"

"Magic."

"Uh-huh."

I tore past Eld, stooping to pull my blade free, and charged into a woman who came screaming around the corner of the tunnel with a knife in each hand. She kept screaming when I laid her face open with my short sword. Stumbling back, she tripped and fell and I quieted her with a thrust to her chest.

Pistole in hand, Eld peeked around the corner, then glanced back at me. "Clear."

"Then let's get the fuck out of here," I said. "I don't know how long those flames will last, but there's enough gunpowder in there to collapse this entire tunnel system."

"You said to be hasty," Eld muttered.

"There's hasty and then there's hasty."

I couldn't tell if the screams behind us were from the Serpent's Flame or because they wanted our blood, but I didn't intend to stay to find out. "C'mon," I shouted, and took off, Eld hard on my heels and Sin's magic burning through me.

I could practically feel time racing against us, and this was a footrace we had to win.

43

We ran through half a dozen rooms and passages and the scope of Sicarii's shadow war became reality. Scores of common pikes and muskets stuck out of barrels, still in their packing tallow. Weaponry I'd never seen before, gearwork like that multibolt crossbow. *Should have brought that with us, damn it.* Apparatus that looked like backpacks hung on some walls, each with half a dozen blade-bearing mechanical arms sprouting from them. A miniature cannon with a score of musket barrels welded together.

Locking a few doors behind us as we ran through them bought us time, but Eld's breath was growing ragged in his throat and I was feeling queasy from too much magic and growing hunger. I was about to suggest a rest when we burst out of the room with half-constructed field-artillery pieces into a wide space that hummed with the sounds of running water just overhead. Before us were three passageways: left, center, and right. Which way to go? Straight ahead, I saw a light in the distance; to the right, there were no lights at all. That didn't necessarily mean anything; a bend or turn would hide lantern light. Eld's curse spun me around.

A dozen raggedly dressed gang members were charging from the left passageway, gearwork weaponry in hand. Eld leveled a pistole and fired, ruining my vision, but it didn't matter: I was already moving. *Left hand to slingshot in left pocket—need to rearrange that—right to bullet pouch.* "Sin. Vision." My eyes burned and my hands were a blur, finding the cool steel bands that reinforced my slingshot even as I dug a ball from my pouch.

Sin's magic narrowed my vision, removed the white spots from Eld's musketry, and focused my aim. Three bodies were down—Eld must have gotten two in one—and only two had made it past them; the rest were still jumping awkwardly over them, knocking into one another. I sighted on the taller one to my right, drew the slingshot back to my cheek, and released. The man fell like a pile of loose clothing as I reached for another ball. Just as I put a woman between the posts of my slingshot, Eld fired. She tumbled in a heap and lay still. Cursing under my breath, I shifted my aim to a man and put one through his chest. The sound of his breastbone breaking was loud despite the gunfire, and his agonized scream slowed the rest.

Another dozen men and women burst into view. Sin's magic touched my ears and I heard even more behind them. Too many.

"There's too many!" Eld and I said together.

"This way," I shouted, tearing off to the right.

"This way!" Eld sounded not-close. I glanced over my shoulder to see him plunging straight ahead, gang members peeling off after him.

I hesitated for a moment and it cost me: a full dozen ran at me, the lead one screaming some sort of primal war cry. I put a round of lead down her throat, then spun around and took off with the rest of the gangs of Servenza in hard pursuit.

Damn it, Eld. I told you to follow my lead. But he'd stopped doing that months ago. Now here we were.

Separated.

Cut off.

Alone.

I sensed more than saw that the right passageway did indeed have a bend; when I turned the corner I nearly fell. Righting myself, I made to tear off again and something, a rope or wire, caught at my feet. I fell with a cry, skinning my hands and knees on the sandy, gritty floor. Before I could rise, cloth slipped over my face. I took a breath and caught a lungful of something biting, both cloying and acidic. My vision went and my mind with it. Sin's howl was a faint echo chasing me down into unconsciousness.

44

"Easy. Easy!"

The voice was low, earnest, and . . . friendly?

I opened my eyes to darkness. There was sackcloth against my cheek. I took a careful breath; there was no biting odor, just the sharp smell of bat shit. What had Sin called it? Guano. I suppose since everything had gone to shit, it shouldn't have been a surprise that I ended back up in that same room. I couldn't keep the groan from my lips as my stomach clenched at the putrid scent. I reached up, surprised my hands weren't bound, and pulled the hood off.

"I think I've had my fill of guano," I murmured, blinking against the sudden brightness.

"You're familiar with the excrement?"

I turned my head too quickly and the shit-filled room spun. I groaned and massaged my temples. A short man in a tight-fitting jacket buttoned to his neck peered at me from behind thick spectacles. When he reached up and touched the rim, the lenses moved, showing they were actually several different pairs welded together. His blue eyes were wide and bright

"Not everyone is, for understandable reasons and so forth." He smiled uncertainly. "Hello?"

"Who the ruddy fuck are you?" I asked, the streets thick in my voice, as they always were when I was half-awake or, in this case, half-recovered from whatever had been in that hood. I felt like something was missing, but besides my wits I wasn't sure what. "Why'd you bring me back here?"

"Ah, well." He dry-washed his oil-stained hands. "As to that, these passages are really just elaborate mazes that bend back on themselves. 'All paths lead to the Doga' is a quote I read by a builder once. Or by the scholar studying the builder; woman was illiterate even if she understood the complex science of angles. She was the one who worked out airflow by—Ahem."

He coughed into his hands and smiled, his lips dark red against his pallid features. "That is to say that you would have reached here eventually, but I thought sooner was better than later and so forth."

He blinked owlishly at me, then shrugged. "As to who I am. I've been known by many things. My cousin called me a little genius, my patron called me his walking dissertation, and the masses knew me as an inventor." He paused, studying my face. "The Artificer?"

The name sent a faint echo through my mind, like there was too much empty space there. I'd heard it before. But where? Quenta. "You're the one that helped his cousin murder one of the Normain nobles," I said. "You disappeared a few months ago."

"Hmm, not quite." His frown pulled his mouth down, accentuating his long nose. "I didn't help my cousin do any such thing. Not sure he was the one that pulled the trigger when it comes to that," he muttered to himself. "I disappeared right after it happened. Thought keeping a low profile was in order, especially once it became clear he sold my name to the Inquisition in exchange for his own skin."

"You don't think he murdered his lover?"

"The evidence is there," the Artificer admitted. "My cousin was a rash man, that was what Prince Wilfrum loved about him . . . but murder? Who would have paid for his gambling debts?"

"You?"

"I sank all the money the prince gave me into my school." He shook his head, knocking his spectacles awry. "No, no, that doesn't make any sense," he said, straightening them. "It's all a bit moot, regardless. The Inquisition was hunting me and once they've your scent, it's a matter of when, not if, and so forth."

"Yet here you stand," I said. My head was clear but aching as if I'd had too much wine the night before. *And why do I feel like I'm missing something?* I smiled to distract him as I reached for the blade I kept behind my belt.

"Ah, your knives are over there," he said with a nod. "On the table. I thought you might feel a bit like cutting something when you came out of your stupor."

I eased back against whatever was behind me.

"Careful now," he said, pointing up.

I followed his finger and realized I was propped up against one of those shit-filled urns.

"Pull that down and you'll be a month scrubbing it out of your pores."

"What do you want?"

"Oh, we arrived there sooner than I'd hoped." He smiled again and nodded. His close-cropped blond hair was plastered to his head from sweat. Mopping at it with a handkerchief, he sank into a crouch opposite me. "I want, what I wager to presume, you want."

I laughed. "What the fuck do I want?"

"To stop Sicarii?"

The laughter died in my throat. "What do you know about Sicarii?"

"More than you," he said. "More than I'd like to, truth told and so forth. She kidnapped me before the Inquisition found me, spirited us out of Normain and across the seas to Servenza. At first I thought she saved me, but then as the weeks became months and her plans became clearer, I realized all I'd done was exchanged one captor for another."

"You're the one that made Serpent's Flame," I guessed.

He nodded.

I squinted. "And that gearwork alley piece and all the other machinery I've seen—your work as well?"

"Smart woman."

"Why?"

"I like living?"

"Do you?" I frowned. "Far as I can tell you're no Sin Eater." And I'd know. "Making gearwork minus Ciris's stamp is a good way to find yourself minus your head."

"We Normain never got into bed with the New Goddess the way the Empire has." He chuckled and shrugged. "I like to create things and Sicarii has a far sharper mind than most of my former employers. It kept things interesting at first, when I realized she wasn't going to kill me right away."

"And now?" I used the urn to stand up and discovered I wasn't quite as recovered as I hoped as my stomach did somersaults. "You drugged me so she could catch me?"

"No!" He stood up from his crouch and reached for me, pausing a span before his spidery thin fingers touched me. Which was good; even wobbly, I would have tried to kill him if he'd touched me. "No, I would never. Not after what I know now and so forth." He frowned. "You don't realize the extent of matters, do you?"

"Elucidate me."

"Sicarii knows who you are, Sambuciña 'Buc' Alhurra. She wants power, as far as I've been able to tell, but early on when it was just her and me, she spoke with me, out of boredom more than anything else, I suspect." A shadow passed his face. "She wanted you to suffer, to long for release. She intended you to secretly thirst for her blade. Then, and only then, would she see you dead. . . . But now, she wants something more."

"She's not the first to want that," I said, hiding my unease behind a smirk. "What's worse than death?"

"I thought," he said slowly, "that it would be mutually beneficial for us to meet. I arranged this thinking your friend would be joining us, but he took the long way around. As for your other friend, I chose a substance that would keep them sleeping a little longer beneath your subconscious than you."

"My other friend?" My breath left me when I realized what he meant. What I'd been missing and unable to call to mind. *Mind.* Now I knew why my head felt so empty. "Sin," I hissed.

"Aye, precisely."

"If you know about it, then Sicarii—"

"Was the one who told me," he said. "She's been following you more closely than you've realized, Buc. She saw you elude death more than once, saw your powers revealed. That's what changed her from wanting to kill you to wanting to . . . 'harvest' is the wrong word, but my Imperial isn't great enough to be more specific."

"She wants Sin?"

"Or you without Sin, yes."

Hmm. I had forgotten what it was like not to have that tiny ball of thought and emotion and being nested in my mind. Now it felt empty, hollow, an echo missing its source. Sin.

"She wants you flayed to the bone, Buc," he said, his eyes large as they stared into mine. "I knew, shortly after she kidnapped me, what Sicarii was. At least, I thought I did. I underestimated her."

He pushed his spectacles back up the bridge of his nose. "I'm not a brave man. It's one of the reasons I followed my cousin to the capital instead of seeking out one of the universities to ply my trade. I'm no fool either. I know what my weapons are capable of."

He sighed. "There are always those who will use knowledge to hurt others, use those like me, cogs in the gearwork and so forth. Sicarii is a terror beyond what you know, but I think perhaps you can stop her. Maybe the only one who can. I observed your earlier altercation with that rabble and thought a conversation might be in order."

"You knocked me out. Brought me here without my Sin." I was surprised by the ownership in my voice, but I'd earned him, damn it, paid in blood and death and lost Eld's friendship because of him—he was mine. "You've been helping my enemies. Why shouldn't I kill you here and now? What do you want?"

"Want?" He frowned. "I thought that was obvious? No?"

"No."

"I want us to be allies, partners. I want to, what's the euphemism?" He touched his purple sleeve. "Turn my coat?"

I laughed. "You're off to a fine start, if that's what you wanted."

"I needed to get you alone. Explain things. Feel you out." He sighed. "I miss my cousin at times like this. Fredfer could both make things clear and make friends in a few sentences. My talents"—he reached into his jacket and pulled out a roll of papers, which he offered to me—"have ever lain elsewhere. Alas and so forth." He handed them over. "Here."

I unrolled them and swore. "A complete map of Servenza's underground?"

"I gather the Doga gave you something to get you started and to find this place. You've clearly made progress on your own, but that should help speed things up. There are a few passages I think even Her Grace is ignorant of," he said with a smile.

"Sicarii has these, too?" I asked, annoyed at the extra breath it took me to locate my palazzo. I'd grown too used to Sin's abilities. I frowned. "If she wants me so desperately, why hasn't she flooded one of these tunnels beneath my bed with two dozen Krakens or Poisoned Eels? I'd be hard-pressed to fend them off in a tight corner like that, magic or no."

"She's been plotting revolution," the Artificer said. "Why draw that much attention to herself?"

"Because she's batshit crazy?" I suggested. "'Sides, you told me how desperately she wants me murdered. Tortured and murdered."

"You're not wrong," the Artificer said after a moment. "There's a time or two she would have done as you say, save I took measures and so forth."

He took off his multilens spectacles and wiped them on the edge of his jacket. "Sicarii has what she believes are the only complete set in Servenza, including those few passages Her Grace forgot." He looked at me. "She does not. I carefully doctored the Blossoms

Quarto so that the few passages there seem ancient and disconnected and none run through your palazzo. I could hardly do more without exposing myself.

"There's also a few designs in there you may find useful. On the map I've marked locations and times I'll be over the next couple of days." Putting his glasses back on, he added, "Buc, you won't have more time than that. Not before Sicarii comes for you, one way or the other."

I felt a chill race down my spine as I glanced at schematics for flying machines and gearwork-driven apparatuses. "She wants me that badly, eh?" I laughed. "Eld always said my mouth would get me in trouble one day, but I can't think who I've pissed off that badly and let live."

"Everything about her before Normain is cloaked in shadow," he said, answering my unspoken question. "She seems familiar with Servenza, but it's a small isle as countries go. Discovering your magic and how far you've come in uncovering her in your report to the Doga has her unsettled. After your exploits here . . ."

I shrugged. "People have been trying to kill me since my mum abandoned me to the streets. Tell Sicarii to get in line."

"I disapprove of boasting, but from what I've seen, you may be one of the few who can back it up." A smile creased his features, deepening a few of the wrinkles there. "I chose well," he murmured, as if to himself.

"Aye, but why?" I moved a pace closer and noticed my hand was steadier than it'd been when I woke up. *Drugs are wearing off. I could take him now, if I needed to. Do I need to?* That was the question. "Why'd you choose me? Why oppose Sicarii? Why not simply run?"

"You've more courage than I do," he whispered. "I'd never be able to live, looking over my shoulder, waiting for her burning eye to appear, and with it, the painful death she promises to any who turn against her."

He shuddered. "I chose you, Buc, because while you and Sicarii are not all that dissimilar in some respects, whereas she wants to see the world consumed by mindless wildfire, you want to use a controlled burn to allow new life to bloom."

"How do you know my plans?" I whispered.

"I told you, you've been followed far more closely than you calculated. If you succeed, a world could actually exist where learning guides right and tempers might. Even a coward like me would fight for that."

He cleared his throat. "Now, Eld will be coming past the door behind you in the next minute or so, depending on if he's been running the whole time or slowed to walk."

"Slowed, judging by how hard he was blowing before," I said.

"Well, he did take the long way," the Artificer said. He clicked his tongue. "Meet him and take the same way out you came in; it's clear. Sin should be coming around by then. I need to return to my laboratory before Sicarii hears of your raid and comes running." He shuddered. "She's enough Serpent's Flame to do what she wants, I think, but she won't be happy about this. You've fucked with her plans, Buc, and she'll fuck back."

"She isn't the only swinging dick in this brothel we call Servenza," I growled.

"I—I beg pardon? No, never mind, no time. Must be off and so forth." He turned to go, and paused. "Buc? Sin won't realize they were out. You can tell them of course, but you don't have to." He flashed a half smile. "I'll leave that up to you."

"My thanks," I said slowly, stuffing the papers into my jacket. I crossed the room to him. "I've never been one for allies, but—friends?"

He studied my hand and laughed. "Friends, yes," he said, pumping my hand. He ran toward the door. "Eld!" he called as he disappeared into the passage, leaving me alone.

"Eld," I said, stowing my blades before moving toward the opposite door. It felt weird to be alone, without Eld or Sin, and I wasn't sure if it was a good feeling or bad. Different, for sure.

Between that and the substance the Artificer had drugged me with, I felt half out of my own body. *No time for that.*

"There you are!" I shouted, and Eld nearly went over his boots trying to stop when he heard my voice. "Getting a bit fat, aren't you? If you're already this out of breath."

"I've. Been. Running for ages," he gasped, his cheeks flushed. Sweat stained his jacket in several places. "Looking for you," he huffed, bending over and leaning on his knees. "Running from those m-maniacs behind—Where the Gods did you go?"

"You ran straight, I ran right." I shrugged. "Right was a shorter cut, I guess. Did have to go back through that shit room, though."

"Sh-shit room?" he gasped, rising.

"Guano. Bat shit."

"Nasty," Eld said.

"That's the one. C'mon." I put my arm around the small of his back. "I made a friend along the way, but we can discuss that later. I don't want your old bones seizing up on me now that you've stopped running."

"Aye, that's a risk," he panted, "considering I've been running for an hour or more!"

An hour? How? In the end, it didn't matter how long I'd been unconscious. I had to get Eld out of here, find Sin in my mind again, and get home. *Home.* I reached for the scrap of parchment in my pocket before I could stop myself. *Unlocked. As you thought.* I wasn't quite sure I was up to that now. But first . . . escape.

"I know you're blowed through, Eld, but we've got to get the fuck out of here."

"M-more running?" he wheezed.

"Just a little farther," I promised.

"I hate running," he growled, lurching into an awkward jog. I kept pace with him, my mind racing ahead. "It's the worst."

"Aye, save what would happen if we stayed," I reminded him.

So we ran, and I thought. What would Eld say when I told him of the Artificer? Was the man playing me? What would Sin say? What if I said nothing at all? So many questions and no magic to slow me down, no kan to cloud my mind, no worry over what Eld would think. It should have felt freeing, but it felt like a trap.

One I couldn't escape.

45

"The manufactory is fucked," the Poisoned Eel said. She went by Mistress amongst her underlings and liked to play that she was a brothel runner, but it'd be a while before her hair grew back long enough to make anyone think her a mistress. One side of her head was wrapped in linen bandages and the other had been shorn of her usual thick, long braids. She sat on the chair in her shirt-sleeves, one ash-streaked arm in a sling. Her pose was casual, as if nearly being burned to death like the other two gang leaders had been a lark. Her kan-whitened smile looked out of place beneath eyes that still seemed startled at having lost their eyebrows.

"Lucky the gunpowder didn't go up with the rest and bring this whole damned place down around our ears." Laughter shook her chest harder than was needed, meant to draw the eye.

"Luck?" Sicarii's voice was the rasp of a blade against the whetting stone. Or against bone. She almost admired the other woman's commitment, but there was only space enough in the tunnels for one actor. *And you aren't it.* "You let the girl discover us, let her destroy my manufactory, let her kill two of my lieutenants and half a dozen others.

"Let them both escape," Sicarii continued. "Let her escape. And you call that luck?"

The woman's laughter cut off and she leaned forward, letting her shirt sag open enough to reveal her breasts. Once, Sicarii would have found the Poisoned Eel attractive, but no longer. Sicarii had changed, something this rabble seemed to grasp slowly and reluctantly. *Perhaps they're in need of a reminder.*

"Aye, that was all unlucky—but consider if those barrels had gone up." The woman pulled a cinquedea from her belt with her good hand and began picking away the dead skin on her burned limb. "That'd have been real unlucky, Sicarii. We'd all have died and taken your dream with it."

An example needs to be made. The thought was stuck in the bit of her mind that wasn't quite right, never would be quite right, given what it had lost. Once a thought stuck there it never went away. *Until I start cutting.*

"She's right about the manufactory," the Artificer said, the stolid man breaking his silence and drawing her eye. He flinched, as he always did, when he met her good eye and its burning twin. "You've enough Serpent's Flame to burn Servenza twice over, Sicarii. That's not to say we can't make more, given enough labor and materials and time and so forth." He dry-washed his thin hands. "Just that you've no need of it yet."

Yet.

Sicarii considered the word. Buc wasn't dead. Yet. She wasn't hurting. Not really. Yet. *That will change soon.* The girl was too smart, too daring. After hearing her report to the Doga, Sicarii had sped up her plans. She'd thought she was letting the final pieces to the puzzle dry before inserting them into the board; meanwhile, Buc had smashed the board apart.

"Yet," Sicarii repeated.

"I—I'm sorry we failed you," the Poisoned Eel maestra said, her voice tense enough to pull Sicarii back to the moment. The other woman's tanned face had gone pale and drawn and Sicarii realized she'd been glaring at her the entire time. "I beg your . . . mercy."

Wise to hesitate. Reflecting further, that Buc had escaped from them when she'd already escaped from Sicarii herself, was inconsequential. Her penchant for doing so was nothing short of magic. *Magic.* Sicarii hissed, the breath catching in her lungs.

If luck had run with the gangs and they'd killed Buc or burned the girl alive, it would have ruined everything. Death was too easy, now. Too kind, in a way. *I need you under my blade first, Buc. No, first the memento I left for you. Then the knife. Then I'll take from you, piece by piece, and then you'll understand what it is to lose. You'll know that feeling better before the night's through.*

Sicarii chuckled at the thought, her tortured vocal cords making a sound that snapped the Poisoned Eel's taut composure. The woman dropped from the chair to her knees and began pleading. Sicarii's mind remained on what she'd already put into motion. Buc was too damned smart, but that was her weakness as well. Let her win and she'd take it as her due. Make her fight hard and barely win and she'd relax on the other side, confident in victory. *That's the moment.* When she paused to draw breath to shout, Sicarii would land her body blow. Then she would finally have Buc right where she wanted. Reeling. Unsteady. *Beneath my knife.*

"Sicarii, are you all right?"

Realizing the Artificer had been talking for some time, Sicarii gathered herself mentally and wiped the tears from her good eye. He was staring at her as if she were a sea serpent and he in a mere rowboat. *There's one who doesn't need reminding.*

"Never better," she growled. "Buc's learning a lesson tonight, one that I've been trying to teach her for weeks. Once she absorbs that . . . the real classwork begins."

Sicarii flicked her hand against her side, triggering the gearwork backpack strapped beneath her loose jacket. Bladed tentacles shot out, hanging over her like an eight-tailed scorpion waiting to strike. Though dried blood dulled their sheen, the blades almost glowed in the lantern light. Wriggling her fingers in the special glove she wore caused the blades to move in deliciously threatening ways. She took a step forward and the Poisoned Eel woman recoiled with a startled yelp.

"You may go, Artificer," Sicarii told him, her eye on the woman kneeling before her. "I'm in a scholarly mood today and this one needs a lesson as well, aye?"

The man squeaked a reply and practically ran from the room.

"Don't worry, Mistress," she told the Poisoned Eel, a grin prising her mouth apart. "I won't kill you." With the audience gone, Sicarii dropped the fake laughter and extended her arms. The blades moved with them.

"If you're lucky."

46

"I thought you wanted a revolution," Eld said, limping as he walked, not bothering to hide the pistole in his fist despite the odd looks he drew from the few upper class we passed. Given the tenor in the city, he didn't draw as many glares as he once would have. The sun was beginning to drop below the buildings, the lamplighters had just finished plying their trade, and there was a bite to the air that told of an impending storm.

"I do," I said, letting Sin's returned magic course through my eyes as we approached the gate to our palazzo. "One guided, carefully, by my hand. I've a feeling, whatever I've in mind, Sicarii's revolution will be far bloodier."

"What does she want, do you think?" Eld asked.

"She told me she wanted what I want," I said slowly. "I thought she meant power. That's what most seem to think I must crave."

"Which isn't untrue."

"I want power so I can change the world," I said, shooting him a hard look, "not control it."

"I'm not sure if those are different for you," Eld said after a moment.

"I'm beginning to wonder," I said, ignoring him, "if she meant overthrowing the Gods and all the rest of it, too."

Eld whistled. "She could almost be an ally, then."

"If she weren't trying to murder us, aye."

"There's that," he admitted ruefully as we reached the palazzo.

The gate was just barely ajar, but I'd locked it when we'd left that morning. I pulled my jacket tighter until the hilts of my blades pressed against my sides, and slipped the edgeless blade from my wrist into the palm of my hand.

"I don't trust any of this, including the Artificer," Sin whispered, anger flaring. He'd been pissed to discover the man had been able to knock him out of my mind and more pissed when he realized I wasn't sharing everything with him. "None of this is going to plan."

"Perhaps."

"You thought the Gods were running things, but they aren't. You thought the gangs were fighting one another, but they aren't," he pointed out.

"Aye, but that was this morning. Before I discovered the Gods were being played, before I spoke with the Artificer, and before I knew how infatuated Sicarii was with me. Bastard is insane."

"So is he for serving her. You know you can't trust the man," Sin growled.

"You really hate that he was able to knock you out, don't you?"

"It shouldn't be possible," he muttered. "That it is implies magic. Blood magic."

"We thought Serpent's Flame was magic at first," I reminded him. "He's just a good inventor. Ciris can't own all the inventions."

"Tell Her that."

"Say," Eld said, his voice dropping, "why is the gate open?" He drew up beside the wall that surrounded the palazzo. I stopped beside him.

"I gave the servants the day off, sent them out with Glori to take in a double play at the theater."

He shot me a curious look. "I didn't know you did that," he said. "Why, Buc? What's going on?" His face was hidden in shadow, but I could tell from his voice it was wrinkled in confusion.

"Remember, I told you the house was being watched. I figured if I gave them an opportunity to do more than watch, they would."

"Would what?"

"Snoop around, lie in wait, I don't know, whatever they were being ordered to do by the Gods or Sicarii or by Sicarii through the Gods."

"Why didn't you tell me?" Eld asked, voice breaking.

"What? Now you want to know everything I'm thinking?" I asked him. "When did that breeze change?"

He jumped up, grabbed the lip of the wall, and pulled himself up to peer over. "The front door's open," he growled, dropping back down. "And someone's lying there!"

"Careful, Eld," I said, grabbing his arm before he could launch himself through the wrought-iron gate. I tried to ignore my growing sense of unease. "I laid a few traps for our uninvited guests. Seems like one of them walked right into it."

"There's something I need to tell you, Buc," Eld whispered.

"So tell me as we walk." I showed him the blade in the palm of my hand and nodded to the pistole in his. I forced a smile. "We're just coming back from a stroll is all."

"A stroll?"

"In case we're being watched." I threaded my arm through his and felt his muscles trembling beneath his jacket. We walked through the gate, both of us moving too quickly to be "strolling" as we marched down the path between the dead flowers. He wasn't this scared when we faced the Veneficus or Sicarii's gangs.

"There's a body," he whispered, as if saying it would make it untrue.

"I know," I told him, shifting the blade in my hand. The patio and foyer were dark and the pillars flanking the entrance cast long shadows over the doorway, obscuring whatever or whomever had fallen. I pulled him to a stop, stood on tiptoe, and he bent down until my lips were beside his ear. "Keep watch."

I let go of his arm, ran the last dozen paces, and dropped to my knees beside the corpse. A nightmare stared back at me: Marin. The thin trip wire I'd rigged was torn and I could see the feathered end of one of the half-dozen darts I'd set to release when the wire was triggered buried in the top of her shoulder. Darts whose tips I'd soaked with the venom of the Antiguous jellyfish. The dose had been enough to incapacitate whoever tripped it, too small a dose to kill. Or so I'd calculated. *Oh, Marin.*

Her ebony skin looked ashy and waxen in the dusky light. Her uniform was torn to shreds, the scraps plastered to her skin by her lifeblood. Gaping wounds crisscrossed her body; her intestines poked through rents in her flesh. The bitter stench from her bowels punched me in the face, making me gag involuntarily and threatening to empty my stomach. I forced a shallow breath through my mouth.

Blood and gore framed Marin's terrified face in a macabre halo. She looked as if she'd died screaming, was screaming still. I couldn't hear her last words, but I could see them writ large in her cloudy eyes: *You.*

I did this.

"No, you didn't," Sin said.

"We did. Killed her."

"Buc, we did no such thing," he said firmly. "Someone with a dozen razor blades and an ax did this. Or"—he sighed—"gearwork-powered weaponry did it. A dozen blades from a dozen directions at once. We'd be hard-pressed to stop that many and we've Ciris's power. Without that? Marin never had a chance."

"That wasn't the point."

"Aye," he agreed. "Someone wanted to send a message. We both know who that is."

"Sicarii." The word lit a fire in my chest.

"Sicarii. Not us."

"We let it happen."

"She wasn't supposed to be here," Sin reminded me. "No one was."

"Gods!" Eld crouched beside me.

"It's Marin," I said, "Glori's granddaughter."

Eld cursed and sagged against the nearby pillar.

"Poor lass just wanted me to teach her to read." I pushed myself up, ignoring the dead girl at my feet. Sometimes, the way to win money at dice is to lose something small at first. I hadn't meant to wager Marin, but someone had cashed her chip in and I'd see it back in my hand before it was through. *Small good it will do her.* "This is my fault."

"Yours ?"

"Aye." I frowned at Eld. I pointed at the feathered end of the dart in her shoulder, white against her skin. "I wanted the chance to question one of these bastards so I laid a trap to knock them out, not . . . this. Marin sprang the trap and whoever did this had free reign of the palazzo."

"Godsdamn it." Eld shouted—"Govanti"—and catapulted himself off the pillar, knocking the door open wide. He sprinted into the palazzo, heading for the only visible light, in the drawing room.

"Govanti? What—Careful, Eld!" I leapt over Marin's body, made a mental note to clean her up before Glori and the rest of the servants returned in the next bell or so, and chased after Eld.

"I think we're too late," Sin murmured.

"I hope not," I panted, racing through the parlor, steeling myself for whatever horrors Sicarii had left for us.

"Buc! Help me!"

Eld was crouched over Govanti's still form, on the floor of the drawing room. I couldn't see any of the blood I was expecting on his white undershirt, but the boy's pale skin was even more pallid than usual and a familiar scent I couldn't quite place overrode the smell of his cologne. The small room reeked like a cheap brothel and suddenly Marin's sneaking off from the theater made sense. Young love. Eld looked up, hair hanging down over his face, eyes wild.

"I can feel a heartbeat, but it's faint and he won't wake up." He put his head to Govanti's chest and shook his head. "He's not breathing, Buc!" He pounded on the boy's chest and put his ear to the lad's mouth. "He's not breathing!"

I stared at the tableau I'd created, or Eld had, or we both had with our intertwining secrets, and for the first time in my life, didn't know what to do. *I was supposed to protect you.* Marin's torn body, still lying outside, flashed through my mind. *Both of you.* I'd failed, and in spectacular fashion. *Why is Govanti here? What other secrets has Eld been keeping from me?*

"He lacks air," I said, surprising myself. *Maybe it's not too late.* Once I started, the words kept flowing, as if with a will of their own. I dropped down beside Govanti and knocked Eld out of the way.

"I have to give him mine." I glanced up. "Remember the way we saved that cabin boy who went overboard on the way back from Colgna?"

"You saved him," Eld said, climbing to his feet. "Can you save Govanti?"

"I don't know," I whispered. "If I seal his mouth with mine and give him my breath . . ." I pressed my mouth to Govanti's and blew. Four or five breaths, then pound his chest. "C'mon, lad." I bent over him and blew another breath into his lungs and yelped as something bit me.

I sat back, rubbing at my lips.

"Why'd you stop?"

"Something's wrong," I said thickly. I could feel my chin burning and a blister erupted on my lip. "He's burning up."

Govanti lurched beneath me with a cry, then flopped back onto the wooden floor like a broken doll.

"We've got to wake him!" I could feel my lips tingle with Sin's magic as he healed my burns.

"If he can scream," Sin said in a voice that sounded as if it belonged to another, "can he breathe?"

"Likely," I agreed, sitting back on my heels.

Govanti's thin chest fluttered with movement but he didn't open his eyes.

"He may have been poisoned," I said out loud.

"Then we need to wake him. Now," Eld shouted. He took a

few jerking, aimless steps, then caught himself against one of the high-backed chairs set around the drawing-room table. His boot kicked a metal bucket, and liquid sloshed inside. He looked down at the bucket, then picked it up.

Shit.

Suddenly I realized what Sicarii had done, and time stilled. Not because of Sin—because of fear.

"Eld!" My shout stopped him in his tracks so quickly that water splashed over the side and onto Govanti's leg. "Toss that water on Govanti and we'll both go up in flames."

"What? What are you talking about?" He lowered the bucket, sending more water lurching out of it.

"Serpent's Flame." I pushed myself up and took a step back, just in case. "Lad's covered in it." Govanti's trouser leg began to smolder and I heard the crackle of guttering flame trying to catch.

"Gods." Eld set the bucket carefully on the table. He drew a ragged breath that turned into a cry when he saw the smoke. Immediately he began trying to shrug out of his jacket.

I was already moving, Sin fueling my tired legs as I leapt over the table and grabbed the sand bucket by the fireplace. *What are you doing?* I wasn't sure if the thought was mine or Sin's as the room blurred from our speed, but I knew if I slowed I wouldn't be in time. I ran past Eld, who was caught in his jacket, and reached Govanti just as flame leapt up from his pants.

"Roll him in sand before he goes up like a torch!" I dumped the bucket over his leg and the flame went out with a sibilant hiss. Eld dropped beside him and began shoveling more sand over him with both hands.

"He's enough on him that he'll take us both with him," I said between gasps. Eld glanced down at the lad and winced.

"Th-there." I set the bucket down beside Govanti and bent over to catch my breath. "That should do for now."

"Are you sure?" Eld whispered.

"Aye," I said, waving his question away. Most of what I knew came from reading, but all agreed sand quenched the fire. *This isn't right; what am I missing?* I plopped down in one of the high-backed chairs and crossed my legs.

"You've been keeping secrets from me, Eld, haven't you?"

"A-aye."

"Tell me," I said, anger kindling in my chest now that I knew Govanti wasn't going to burn alive before my eyes. *It's more than Marin had.* "All of it."

Eld licked his lips, his pale features bright in the fading light. "Buc, after you asked me to check in on the lad, I kept checking in. He was in danger."

"What sort of danger?"

"The same sort that did for your other informants."

I listened as Eld told me of two would-be backstabbers he'd taken down, of moving Govanti around, providing him with coin and protection: doing my job. Only, I hadn't been there. I had been practicing my dancing and trying on dresses and acting the noblewoman instead of protecting my own or chasing down the leads that would have led me to Sicarii days ago. In time to save both Govanti and Marin. Shame burned through my chest, sent tendrils up into my cheeks.

"Govanti found the Sin Eaters' lair, following the Parliamentarian," Eld said, his words piercing my self-immolation.

"What?" I felt my eyebrows climbing. "I told you they were my little fish."

"I know!" Eld said, standing up and offering me a hand. "I was trying to help . . . you seemed caught up with the Chair and the Doga and I knew the Gods had to be involved. I thought if I could ferret out the evidence, with Govanti's help—I could keep him safe and find the Gods' hands in all this."

"Fine," I said after a moment. It wasn't fine, not by half, but I wasn't ready to unleash my rage at Eld until I knew it all. Keeping Govanti safe was supposed to be my job. Then again, I'd been promising Marin I'd teach her to read for ages and not held up my end of that bargain, either. Eld stepping in was something I hadn't calculated. Trying to help. I took a breath, fighting the tightness in my chest, and steeled myself. "That doesn't tell me why Marin thought Govanti would be here. In our palazzo."

"Because." Eld punched his leg, tears sparkling on his cheeks. "I started to tell you earlier. You were right."

"I'm always right."

"About the Sin Eaters catching onto us," he said, ignoring my faint jab. "They did. One did, anyway. Nearly killed me, save Govanti killed her first."

"Govanti killed a Sin Eater and you left him out there alone?" I growled.

"No! Of course not," Eld said quickly. He drew in a short breath. "I hid him in the palazzo, told him to keep to my room and out of sight. Until I could tell you."

"But you didn't tell me."

"I meant to."

"Only, you knew I'd be pissed. . . ."

"Aye. Things haven't been so great as it is. Between us, I mean," Eld whispered. "I didn't want to make them worse." He shook his head. "Now that I think on it, I recall Govanti had an eye for Marin; he asked about her once or twice."

I hadn't told Eld my plans and he'd gone and made his own, not telling me, and between the two of us, we'd wrought a nightmare. Had I known, this wouldn't have happened. Everyone thought me so damned smart, but I was only as sharp as the information I had. I ran a hand down my braid, seeing it all now and all too late. "So she snuck out of the theater and came back to meet him."

"I did this," Eld whispered.

I didn't call him a liar.

47

"The cologne almost hid it," I said, staring at Govanti. He lay limp, with the barest hint of breath in his chest. "That spicy smell from the stuff Sicarii made, to hide the shit odor from the chemicals involved." My nose wrinkled.

"It's not poison?" Eld asked.

"Not sure," I admitted. "It'd be like Sicarii to have a fail-safe."

"Now that I think on it, I've never seen this bucket before," Eld muttered, staring at the half-filled pail. "Set just within arm's reach so I could play the hero. And the fool." He cursed under his breath. "You saved us all, Buc. How?"

"Someone's been watching us for a while now," I said, ignoring his question. I knew he wasn't responsible for Sicarii's actions, but he was damn well responsible for his own. Which I intended to remind him of in the not-too-distant future. Now, I had thinking to do.

"Which means," I continued, "they likely knew Govanti was in the palazzo. Knew that Marin returned and that when we found her, we'd lose our wits and come running for Govanti. They wanted us to find him like this. To try to save him and fail." I tapped my lip with a nail.

"If Sicarii knows us as well as she seems to, she knew I wouldn't have tossed water on the boy straight off. Which means she left that pail for you knowing how you would react—and that you'd likely go up along with Govanti.

"She knew what that would do to me. Not just losing you, but watching you die." Sin was unable to keep the image from flashing through my mind, and I shuddered.

"Sorry," Sin said. "You thought it, then I thought it, and it just slipped out."

"I'm sorry, Buc," Eld said. "I should have told you—"

"I thought Sicarii didn't know about me until I started asking questions," I said, working through the idea out loud, trying to forget the image of Eld in flames. Like Sister. "But the Artificer said she talked about me when she kidnapped him. He didn't say anything about you, though, and if she's been following us as closely as he believed, she would know that we barely speak anymore." I grunted. "So that leaves—"

"The Doga or the Company," Sin said. "They know what Eld means to you." *And Salina, but Salina wouldn't betray me like this.*

"This is Sicarii's work, but she had help, to know what this would have done to me," I whispered, sitting up. "She's had help from the Gods, but this? Had to come from the Doga or the Chair."

"The Doga or the Chair?"

"You lied to me," I said quietly, beginning to tremble. "I fuck up, make mistakes or miscalculations. Not often, but when I do, they're pretty big. Intelligence's double-edged sword. I didn't account for your fucking this up, Eld."

"Buc—"

I suddenly realized I wasn't shaking from fear or emotion, but from anger. I'd only felt this level of rage half a dozen times in my life and it was always a scary thing. That it was directed at Eld was even scarier.

"I trusted you!" I shouted my rage, a living thing, bright inside my chest.

"Trusted me?" Eld snorted, his eyes hard behind his tears. "You didn't trust me enough to tell me fuck all about what we did today. You've been cutting me out of your life for months. Trusted me with what?"

"With Govanti's life," I snapped. Eld recoiled, but only for a moment.

"If not for me, the lad would have been dead twice over," he said. "You didn't know because you were off in the bubble you put yourself in. On your own." He bit his lip hard. "When were you going to tell me?"

"Tell you what?" I asked, his question catching me flat-footed.

"That the Chair set you up to be banished from Servenza any day now?" Eld said angrily, his face twisted with emotion. "When were you going to trust me with that?"

"I—" My mouth hung open, but words wouldn't come. For once.

"You want to talk about lies?" Eld asked, his voice tight. "When we started down this path, you said it was to remake the world. To save the innocent so they wouldn't be forced to choose between death or turning into someone like yourself to survive. That's why we went haring off to the Shattered Coast. That's why we nearly died facing down Chan Sha and the Ghost Captain and his Shambles. To find the power to remake the world!

"Power's a funny thing, though, isn't it?" he continued in a softer tone. "Can mean all manner of things. Strength. Coin. Magic. You have all the power you could possibly desire, Buc, and what the fuck have you done with it? Taken up with the Kanados Trading Company Board. Worked yourself to the bone to win their adoration. Gone into the Doga's service as one of her Secreto. You've turned into one of them."

"One of them?" I choked.

"Seeking power to overthrow the authorities you hated, you became corrupted by it."

"I have to play the game, you fool. We didn't get the Empress's blank writ to do as we pleased. We got a chance! A chance to sit at the table and run the board. We've had to get down in the muck and fight them on their own terms."

"The old Buc would have quoted some generalissimo about how stupid it was to fight the enemy on their own terms," Eld said. "Muck? You call wearing pretty dresses to the Doga's Palacio muck?"

"Me? You were dressed up like a fucking prince, Eld." I shook my braids. "You danced the night away!"

"I was there because you asked me to be there The first time you asked me to be anywhere in months. Answer me this," Eld said, his voice like rolled steel over the forge. "When you walked the streets today, what did you see?"

"I told you what I saw," I said. "How do you think I ciphered out all those shops Sicarii was using? Or found her lair?"

"Let me tell you what I saw. I saw children wearing rags and playing in the gutter. I saw others being hustled off to the factories by work gangs. I saw men and women bent double, coughing and hacking from agues brought on by the winter and lack of proper clothing, food, and shelter. I saw all the things that used to set your teeth on edge, put fire in your eyes—"

"You think I don't care?" I interrupted him. "I showed you the fighting in the streets. I know it's growing worse, Eld. I've told you before that—"

"You're doing this all for the greater good. Your greater good is out there"—he pointed past me—"dying while you help them. The old Buc would have known that. The old Buc wouldn't have forgotten. She wouldn't have forgotten about Govanti until today." His eyes were bright with unshed tears. "What happened to her?"

"She died," I whispered.

"On the island?"

"No." I shook my head, watched the floor blur between us as tears burned my eyes and traced lines of fire down my cheeks. "The island was just the beginning. A wound. One that didn't heal, that grew worse, became gangrenous and tore her apart piece by piece. Until nothing was left."

Pain and rage twined within me.

"I needed you, Eld. I needed you to listen to me, to be there, by my side, the steadfast line tossed out when I was feeling lost beneath the waves." I swallowed. "You know I have magic inside me, Eld. But you don't know what it means and you didn't help me try to figure it out. Instead, you left me as soon as we touched boots on Servenza."

"I thought you wanted space—"

"I wanted you! I wanted you and you pulled back," I said, voice cracking. "You pulled back out to sea and left me marooned, despite how I tried to reel you back in. I know how you feel about magic, Eld." I closed my eyes and felt my breath catch in my chest, but I'd already begun the sundering—there was no point in stopping now. "I know you loathe it."

"That's true, but—"

"I know," I said, opening my eyes, somehow seeing him clear through the tears. "You can't help it. Now that I'm magic, you loathe me." I couldn't stop the sob from tearing past my lips. "Do you know what it feels like, Eld? To have the one you love, loathe you? Loathe your very being."

"L-love?" Eld stammered.

"Sambuciña." Sin's voice splashed through my mind like a cooling wave. "Stop."

"Now you talk?" My question sent fire racing back against his softer magic. "Don't tell me to stop. It's too fucking late for that."

"You don't understand," he said gently. "Eld loathes magic, aye. Hates me, aye, but . . . he doesn't hate you."

"You're wrong."

"I'm not. Sambuciña, he's been working with me to help save you."

"What?" *Eld knows about Sin? Is helping him?* Shock waves reverberated through me. I was aware, peripherally, of Eld moving toward me. "What?"

358 . Ryan Van Loan

"I didn't tell you, we didn't tell you, because . . . because the first time we told you, it nearly killed you." Sin sighed. "You made a mistake, Buc, and we've been trying to fix it ever since."

"What mistake?"

"Buc?" Eld's voice was shaking. It never shook.

"What mistake did I make that you're trying to save me from?" I asked, the world rushing back in on me, unaware I'd stood up until I was already in front of Eld. "That almost killed me? Sin just told me you two have been working together."

"Oh." Eld's eyebrows leapt into his hairline and he collapsed backward into the chair behind him. "Oh, no."

"What the fuck is going on?" I asked, my voice a whisper in my ears. More lies. "What are you hiding? Tell me."

"I—I can't," Eld said.

"I can," Sin said, his voice coming from my own lips. His voice, outside my head. The sensation sent ice racing down my spine.

Eld cleared his throat.

"Show her."

48

"*Remind me why we didn't take one of the pleasure barges,*" Salina suggested, her usual snark muted beneath the waves of humidity that pressed down on us. She had a parasol in one hand and a fan in the other, but despite her efforts, her gold hair was plastered to the side of her face and her curls were frizzy. "*It's hot enough to boil the sea.*"

"*We've a tight schedule. This factory is the proof of concept, but I also want to show you the factory that is still doing things the old way and then we need to return for the Board meeting later tonight,*" I said, "*so you can testify to how amazing I am.*"

Salina rolled her eyes.

"*You were the one who wanted to ensure we had enough time to freshen up before the meeting,*" I reminded her.

"*A flotilla just put in yesterday,*" Eld added. "*The canals and the Cres-cent are crammed right now. We'd never have made it in time.*"

"*Fine, fine,*" Salina muttered. "*I've already sweated through my silks, so what's it matter?*"

"*You should have worn white, like me,*" I said.

"*What, and show off everything beneath? White's transparent when you're soaked through.*"

"*Is it now?*" I asked. With Sin's magic, I wasn't sweating, wasn't even really all that warm.

"*You're welcome,*" he murmured.

I wasn't hot, but I could feel hunger creeping in, even though I'd eaten thrice as much as Eld at breakfast. He hadn't commented, but three months home from the Shattered Coast and things were still awk-ward. Now that we'd come up in the world, the sharks were taking note of us and more than a few of the feminine species were circling him, wondering if he was worth a nibble or two.

"That Lucrezia wants more than a nibble," Sin said.

"She's nothing," I told him. "I'm having the servants prepare his favorites for dinner for tonight after the meeting and I'm going to tell him everything."

"Everything?"

"Almost everything," I amended. "Enough that he'll know what's going on. If I don't, I'll be in danger of losing him and that"—the thought made my throat clench—"can't happen."

"You look tired."

Salina was staring at me with something that looked almost like concern. That can't be. She smiled. "Have you been sleeping well?" she asked.

"She doesn't sleep at all anymore," Eld chimed in from my other side. He puffed his chest out and the would-be beggar eyeing us sat back down on his corner, in the shade provided by the peeling plastered building. Eld tossed something that glinted toward the man, who snatched the coin from the air, and continued, "She's either in her rooms, going over schematics and workflows or she's out at the factories, whipping them on."

"As touching as it is that you both care about my sleeping patterns," I said, stepping around a suspicious pile of something dark lying beneath a window, "I'm fine."

I looked away, hiding a yawn. When I turned back, both were shaking their heads. "I am! Besides, I've not visited the factories, I've been concentrating on the guild. If the maestros don't do their jobs, none of the others will."

"So today's the first day you'll see the product of your labor?"

"Aye, same as you," I told Salina. It better fucking be perfect. I'd studied how the factories refined sugar and had been horrified to discover every single one was different, a mishmash of machinery and workers and storage. No two were even close to alike.

It hadn't been all that hard after reading number 384, Archo's The

Distribution of Labor, *to put together a standardized floor plan and operating procedures. Sin's magic let me see layouts in my mind and cipher out how the workers would be most efficient.*

I told Salina and Eld that—minus the Sin part, of course—and added, "I fit three additional mills into the same space."

"If I remember correctly," Salina said, "those mills put off a lot of heat."

"Aye, you're not wrong. We've added dried kelp to the wine ration to help the workers hold water. Tastes like arse, but the wine was so watered down before I'm not sure they've noticed. I've promised the maestros that once we've proven the model, we'll discuss pay increases based on performance."

"You did what?" Salina hissed, fanning herself harder. "I doubt the Board will agree to that."

"The Board can get fucked. Once they see these improvements and the profits they will realize begin to flow in, they'll sing my tune." I shrugged out of my jacket and held it in the crook of my arm. Even with Sin's magic, the heat was palpable. "I've another proposition I'm holding on to. If they consider refining at the plantations themselves, as some of the minor companies do, they could ship directly to consumers."

"It's not that simple," Salina said.

"You'll need to increase oversight and security to prevent smuggling, sure," Eld agreed, feeding her the lines I'd given him. "But you'd prevent some of the issues that led to this summer's near miss." Salina gave him a hard look and he shrugged, his sunburnt face innocent. "Buc's not often wrong, Salina. I'd bet a few lire this could be expanded to kan production as well."

"Now that might get the Board to reconsider," Salina said as we neared one of the larger thoroughfares on the edge of the Mercarto. A crowd of people rushed by, heading in the direction opposite to ours. A moment later, a score of the Constabulary, their blue woolen uniforms dark with sweat, rushed past going the same way we were. "What's going on?"

"Probably a turf skirmish," Eld said, loosening his sword in its sheath.

He glanced over his shoulder at the half-dozen guards behind us. "Maybe we should have brought more muscle."

"You're the muscle," I said, and Salina laughed, but that was because she'd never seen him in action. Eld somehow managed to find a deeper shade of red despite his sunburn, and that made me laugh, too.

Until we turned the corner and saw smoke heavy in the air.

I'd taken it for haze, but now I could see it coming up in plumes from one of the factories at the end of the cobbled street. I felt Sin's reaction and cursed. One of the Kanados Trading Company's factories. My factory. Fuck me.

"Fuck me," I repeated out loud.

"Is that—?" Salina said.

"Our factory," Eld grunted. "Aye."

"C'mon," I said, breaking into a trot. "Let's see what can be salvaged."

"Ladies don't run," Salina gasped, catching up to me.

"Then it's a good thing you're in trousers and not skirts, eh?" Eld said, his voice light but his expression grim.

"Eld likes trousers," I said. "He just doesn't like to let on."

"They're not proper, but they do make running easier," he admitted.

"Do much running in skirts?" Salina asked, and we both laughed.

"The fire crews better be there already," I said, squinting. Sin's magic burned through my irises: people poured out of the factories surrounding ours; flames leapt through the roof in great gouts of orange and pale blue from the sugar. "The surface area–to–volume ratio of refined sugar plus all the air around it could turn that building into one giant powder keg."

"You mean it could explode?" Salina gasped beside me.

"Exactly."

"Gods, then why are we running toward it?"

"Because that's weeks of planning gone up in flames . . . not to mention profits!" I broke into an open run and left Salina behind.

Eld caught up when I was still half a dozen buildings away; the heat had become a living, roiling thing that blasted me in the face. I *recognized one of the factory maestras standing nearby, despite the soot coating her tanned features, and called over to her.*

"What happened?"

"Search me, signorina," she said through parched lips, walking over. Eld offered her a flask and she upended it, drinking greedily. "Thanks, sirrah," she gasped, black tearstains tracing down her face and dress. "We were working, doing just as you showed us, signorina, and the output was triple what we used to do. Then I heard shouting, louder than the machines, and saw smoke. Someone shouted 'fire' and we all ran."

I turned back toward the factory. A little boy stumbled toward us, his trousers in burned shreds, angry blisters running up and down his spindly legs. Beyond him, a girl with singed hair and an arm that was obviously broken threw her head back and screamed as an older child whose shirt was half-torn away tried to comfort her. Had they been playing by the factory?

"Signorina?"

I hadn't realized I'd asked the question aloud, but repeated it. "Children should know better than that. Are they the workers' children?"

"Buc, they are the workers," Salina said, reaching us at last. Bent over, hands on her thighs as she caught her breath, she looked up at me. "You knew that, growing up on the streets, surely."

"What's she talking about?" I asked the maestra.

"Some of the children are the workers' offspring, aye," the woman said. "Others are orphans or are looking to earn money for their family. The machinery is too finely crafted for adult fingers. And some of the processes require tight quarters that are best handled by the children." She shrugged. "It is the way of factories."

I stared dumbly back at the factory. I'd avoided all manner of gangs, including the press kind, especially after murdering Blood in the Water. Being a loner, I'd never associated with other children my age unless they were of the Tip and those sort never ventured this far east. Still, I'd heard of the factories. . . . I'd just never paid enough attention to remember them now. I'd started all this to save the children and in-stead I'd been using them.

"Help my brother, please!" A girl, barely older than Sister had been when . . . The girl ran out of the factory, screaming at the top of her lungs, and beating ineffectively at the sparks smoldering on her clothes.

I was halfway down the cobbled street before I realized it, leaving Eld and Salina shouting in my wake. "More, Sin. Give me more."

My legs burned with fire that had nothing to do with the flames before me. I tackled the girl hard, rolling her over and over so that any sparks were extinguished. My elbows and knees screamed, but I held her close, shielding her body with mine until we came to a stop with her on top of me. Terrified brown eyes stared down at me. Burns criss-crossed her cheeks in angry streaks.

"It's okay," I whispered. "You're safe, now. It's okay."

"No, it's not," she said, shaking tears from her eyes. "Zeno's still in-side. We were running, but the smoke was thick, I couldn't see, couldn't breathe, and I lost him. My only brother. Ma told me to watch him close and I lost him!"

"Easy, easy, little one," I said, using Sin's strength to roll her off of me. I sat up. "What's your brother look like?"

"Black hair like mine, but shorn on account he got lice. He's always getting into trouble," she said through her tears. "Short and thin, he's got a new brown shirt and—"

"I'll find him," I promised, leaping to my feet and wrapping her in my jacket. "A big pale man who is sunburnt as fuck is going to be here in a moment. He'll help you."

I pulled my shirtsleeves up, thankful that I'd taken to trousers last month, and took off, gulping in air that shimmered from the heat. It hurt, but not as much as the smoke would when I got inside. I leapt over bodies of those who had breathed in too much smoke and dodged chunks of the building that had already come down. The entrance looked like a gaping maw of black death, thick clouds of smoke obscuring whatever was held in its depths. I didn't care. I knew what I was looking for: a little boy who wasn't going to die because of my mistake.

"Ready to find out how magical you are, Sin?"

"I've a feeling I better be," he said. "Are we really doing this?"

"We're saving Zeno, one way or the other."

"The other way ends with us dead."

"I couldn't save Sister, because I was little and I didn't have you," I told him. The last burning warehouse I'd been in flashed through my mind, Sister lying motionless on one side of the flames, me standing helpless on the other. Never again. "I'm saving Zeno."

"Her truth, we're doing this," he whispered.

"Aye."

I leapt through the doorway, tripped, and rolled, felt my back burn from the scorching hot floor, and came to my feet, dancing with the flames.

49

Smoke, thick and black and suffocating, drove me to my hands and knees. The scorching floor burned the palms of my hands and my legs through my pants, but at knee height there was a scrap of breath to be found. Pushing myself up, I sprinted, bent double, for a few dozen paces, then dropped down and crawled, sucking greedily at the rancid air, then jumped up and ran again. Rinse and repeat. Rinse and repeat.

After the first few rooms, the building opened up to the factory floor and here were my old nightmares made reality. The far side of the factory was lost in a wall of flame, hulking machinery twisted and melting in its fiery embrace. Sugar exploded in small, rapid bursts that sounded like two armies squaring off. Here, there were bodies, echoing Sister.

I ran to the first—too big to be the missing Zeno. My eyes burned, from the sweat streaming off my forehead or perhaps from the smoke. When I turned the body over, squinting through my tears, the lifeless eyes of a woman stared back at me, a bloody dent in her skull and chunks of mortar telling the rest of the tale. Letting her fall back into a pool of her lifeblood, I ran to the next. And the next. Each one drew me deeper in, each sank fear deeper into my bones, but none of them were Zeno.

"Buc! We've got to get out of here," Sin shouted. "Even with time dilation and letting me search out the bodies that look like a boy's, we won't be fast enough. This place is going to explode or implode and either way my magic won't be enough to save us."

"A few moments more," I wheezed. I wanted nothing more than to turn around and run, heeding the little voice that said I couldn't save

Sister then and I couldn't save Zeno now. Fuck that. *I could taste burning plaster, it was all I could smell, and my eyes were slits below the shirtsleeve I'd cut off and tied around my forehead to keep the sweat out.* "We'll find him. I know it."

"Buc—"

"A few moments more!" *I saw a narrow walkway between some of the machines and remembered what the maestra had said. They use the children in tight spaces. I took off, bent double, glad I was rail thin despite all the food Sin had me eating. A big man like Eld would have had trouble squeezing through, but I could run.*

And run I did . . . full tilt into a bigger lad, sending him spilling into the dozen other children who were huddled in a crying mass behind a few large barrels. Water sloshed over the sides, hissing and steaming when it hit the floor.

"What are you lot doing here?"

"We're trapped!" *a girl shouted.*

"We can't get out," *another said.*

I grabbed the lad I'd knocked over and studied him for a moment. His eyes were watery from the smoke, but he wasn't crying. "Was it your idea to hide here?" *He nodded. It had been a good thought, trying to use the water barrels as a shield, but he hadn't realized how devastating the flames were.*

"Go back the way I came and turn left. Left! You understand?"

He nodded again.

"Here." *I tore off my other sleeve.* "Soak this in water and put it over your mouth. Take the others with you and stay low. Burns won't kill you. Smoke will. So you stay low and you get them out. Okay?" *I shook him when he did not respond.* "Okay?"

"Aye, aye!"

"Easy, lad, I'm no captain," *I said, with a smirk that I didn't feel. It did the trick, made him smile against his will.* "Now . . . go!"

The boy corralled the others, tied the silk around his nose and mouth, and then they were gone, disappearing into the grey smoke that was beginning to turn an ominous black. I levered myself into one of the barrels. The water was hot, but cooler than the air. I ducked beneath the surface half a dozen times, sending water sloshing over the sides, hissing and sputtering. I jumped out and took off again, boots squelching with every step, steam rising from me in clouds almost as thick as the smoke. I felt my lungs seizing up, my heart pounding a tattoo that reverberated through my throat. Sin was right.

Magic or no, we didn't have much time left.

The walkway turned right, then left, toward the back of the factory. I jumped over a tangled pile of brown debris . . . and skidded to a halt. Spinning around, I ran back and saw a thin boy in a brown shirt lying beneath a collapsed wooden hoist. Sin's magic burned my arms and my vision narrowed as I heaved the broken machinery off of Zeno. Bending down, I put my ear beside his mouth and felt more than heard a rasping breath. Crowing, I hauled his limp body up and over my shoulder, mentally thanking him for not being one of the larger lads. As it was, his feet knocked against my knees as I half ran, half lurched back the way I'd come.

Hot coals rained down from overhead as I ran; a pair slid across the back of my left hand, leaving fiery tear marks in my flesh. Howling, I glanced up and saw open sky sucking the smoke out like a funnel, and real fear for the first time flashed through me. That much air would fan the flames, but worse, I'd a suspicion the sugar stores hadn't gone up yet. When they did, with this much flame and air . . . this entire factory would turn into one large, exploding canister shell.

"Give me more, Sin!"

"I'm giving you all I've got," he growled, and I could hear the exhaustion and terror in his voice.

When you're in a situation where a God is afraid, and Sin was as close to a God as I wanted to come, you know you're fucked. I ran past the water barrels—dry now—and burst out onto the main factory floor. My feet windmilled beneath me as I turned too fast and slipped. Zeno and I both hit the floor, slamming into the ground hard enough to drive the little breath I'd left out of my lungs. Gasping for air, I fought to my knees, blinking back spots, then made it to my feet and grabbed Zeno.

"C'mon, kid, we're getting the fuck out of here," I grunted. I made it three paces before something hard smashed me in the back and drove us back down to the burning floor. Pain lanced through me, darkness caught at the edges of my vision, but my eyes were on the lad. I promised his sister I'd save him. Night washed over me, but I fought to move. Sister. Something was holding me back.

I promised.

"Buc!"

Sin's voice was shrill in my ears, sounded almost like Eld's, and then I lost the fight and black soot suffused me completely.

50

"I found you and the boy lying together, your body shielding his," Eld said quietly when I returned to the present. He shook his head. "I thought you were both dead. I couldn't breathe, could barely see or move. Somehow I got you in my arms and stumbled out. I tried to pick up the boy, too, but I just couldn't." I could hear the truth, the regret, in his voice. "Salina had the fire crews put us on a wagon and take us out of there. We were a few blocks away when the entire place went up like a thousand mortars. The concussion woke you up.

"You'd lost your mind."

"I don't remember any of this," I said. I glanced down at the scars on the back of my left hand. The tear-shaped ones that still itched. "Why?"

"Half the roof fell on you," Sin said, his voice coming through my lips.

"I really fucking hate that," I told him out loud.

"Aye, but Eld can't hear your thoughts."

"I'm not sure if that's a curse or a blessing," Eld said.

We both groaned at his half-hearted attempt at humor.

"Half the roof fell on you," Sin continued. "Your skull was cracked. Your brain took a beating, Buc. Knocked both of us clean out. When you woke up, you woke up without me. By the time I came to . . ."

"You were speaking gibberish before Sin woke up," Eld said. "I've never been more terrified in my life and, you know, after the past summer, that's saying something."

"So Sin woke up and fixed me?"

"Not quite." Sin sighed. "Some of the burns on your body were going to fester if the shock didn't kill you outright. I fixed those. For the most part," he added when I felt at my hand. "Your collarbone was fractured and I fixed that. I was able to heal the hair-thin fracture in your skull and repair the damage to your brain, Buc, but . . ."

"But what?"

"He couldn't heal your memory," Eld said. He chewed on his lip. "You kept blaming yourself for the factory. For the children. Noises set you off and when you were startled, you were angry."

"You were furious," Sin said. "You wouldn't listen to me and fear of fire was set so deep in your bones that you refused to be around candles or lanterns or flames of any sort. You were half-wild."

"I was growing desperate," Eld said.

"We both were," Sin agreed. "So much so that I, uh, supplanted your consciousness and spoke to Eld directly."

"You what?!?"

"I had to do something," Sin protested. "Without Possession, Eld was my last hope."

"That must have been a real mind fuck for you," I told Eld. My voice was light, but my mind was spinning, trying to process everything they were saying alongside a host of newly recalled memories that were a roaring tempest inside me.

"He told me everything that had happened," Eld said. "How the blow had kept him from fixing you before the memories took hold. How tricky the—What's the word you used?"

"Neurons," Sin said.

"How the neurons in your brain were damaged and how the memories were playing in a constant loop within your mind," Eld said. "He convinced me that if we didn't hide your memories of the fire completely, erase them, that you'd never return to normal."

"You wanted to fuck around with my brain? Let magic erase

part of my mind without my consent?" I growled. "You, of all people?"

"Gods, no," Eld said quickly. "I was against it, but I was also desperate, Buc. You don't know how bad off you were."

"No," I agreed, "I don't. Because you took that from me."

"You don't want to remember," Sin assured me. "I barely do and that's enough to . . . Well, let's just say without us, you would've driven yourself insane."

"C'mon."

"The danger of having one of the most powerful minds I've ever met," Sin said, "is that when that mind is broken, the damage it's capable of is equally great. You would have driven yourself insane," he repeated flatly. He meant it, too.

I looked at Eld, his blond hair free of its ponytail and fanning around his face. He looked like a man at the end of his tether, one blow away from falling down and never rising again. He met my eyes and nodded.

"He's right," he whispered. "So I agreed."

"For a time, he did," Sin said.

"I made it about a fortnight," Eld admitted. "You know I'm a terrible liar."

"You are."

He tugged at his grey jacket, all askew from the day we'd had. "I came clean and told you everything." He squeezed his eyes shut. "It was a mistake."

"You relapsed hard," Sin said, his voice gentle. "Nearly killed Marin when she tried to light your night lamp."

"And then killed her for good today," I said mentally.

"That wasn't your fault," Sin answered me in my head.

"That convinced me Sin was right," Eld said. "I had to keep my distance, though, because while you forgot everything, I did not. I really am a horrible liar," he said with the ghost of a smile. He glanced past me. "I had to make some hard choices."

I followed his gaze to Govanti and swallowed. "Then why tell me now?"

"Because," he sighed, "trying to avert one mistake, I made another. I pushed you away, kept you at a distance so that you wouldn't see the truth, but you're no fool, Buc. You looked at the evidence that you could see and drew false conclusions.

"You were like a loaded pistole and I pulled the hammer back and walked away, letting whoever wanted to use you pull the trigger."

"That's not quite fair, either," Sin said. "This was never a perfect fix from the start. You're too damned smart, Buc. Your intelligence kept finding odd corners in your mind that didn't make sense and tried to chase them down, forcing me to take . . . steps."

"Steps?" Eld and I both asked together.

"Your lapses in memory," Sin told me.

"I've had entire days where I suddenly find myself somewhere with no recollection of how I got there," I told Eld.

"Uh, I sort of know that," Eld said. "Sin told me a few times and I realized once or twice you'd spaced out."

"You acted like you had no fucking clue," I growled.

"I didn't," Sin said. "Sort of. I split myself into two. The part of me that knew the truth kept that walled away from you . . . and from the part of me I hid the truth from."

"I didn't know that bit, Buc. This is what comes of magic," Eld snapped. "There's always a hook that's waiting to be set. Always another facet that's left unexplained."

"That's what magic is, fool," Sin snarled. "If you understood it, it wouldn't be magic."

"Is that why you abandoned me? Was it really to protect me?" I asked, speaking so softly I could barely hear myself, but drawing their attention. "Or because of the magic in my veins? Magic I'll never be rid of."

"N-no," Eld said slowly, his hesitation revealing the lie. "At least not completely," he amended. "I knew, shortly after the island, what had happened. I didn't realize it was possible for a Sin Eater to not pledge themselves to Ciris but I knew you were, for all intents and purposes, one of them. But, Buc," he rushed on, "I kept my distance because . . . because I had feelings for you; feelings I thought would ruin our friendship and then the accident happened and there were too many lies and I couldn't take it anymore."

"So you abandoned me."

"I gave you space to—"

"Suffer on my own," I said, tears filling my eyes. Feelings for me? It was what I'd fantasized hearing Eld say, but now it felt like another blade put through me. "To wonder why my best friend no longer talked to me, why he seemed oblivious to my advances, why I wasn't good enough for him."

"Not good enough for me?" Eld's eyes widened. "Buc, I'm the one who has always had to fight to be good enough for you."

"You say that and you say you had feelings for me, but you let magic wipe my memory, you let Sin convince you that you couldn't talk to me about it." The words left my lips before I could fully consider them, but they startled Sin. He shifted in my mind and several things fell into place. *Later.* "You lied to me about everything."

"I was trying to do what was right! Did you tell me about Sin?" He shook his head. "Did you tell me that you loved me? Do you even know what love is? You want me to say I fucked up?" Eld stood up so fast he knocked his chair over. "I fucked up. My only defense is I was trying to find my new place in all of this. I was trying to save you, Buc."

He spread his arms wide. "I didn't know what to do. Didn't know if staying close would destroy your mind or if you were even still you. Didn't know why you wouldn't tell me the Chair was moving to have you sent away or kicked out of the Company. Didn't know—still don't know—how you feel about me."

"You're going to blame me when you helped erase my memories? Hid the truth from me?" I felt physically on fire from all the emotions swirling within me. Guilt from forgetting about Govanti, about Marin, and now that factory. Anger, no, rage at what I'd done and had no way to fix because that knowledge had been taken from me. I'd fucked up on an epic scale, but so had Eld. So had Sin. We all had, but I was the only one who had been clueless about it all. Pain was the greywash to the rainbow of emotions cascading through me. I tapped my temple. "You knew I wasn't playing with a full deck. Is that my fault or yours?"

Eld's face went full white.

"Tell me this," I said after a moment, my voice tight, "why should this be so damned hard? Why should I have to flirt endlessly with you, wear a ball gown and throw myself at you, do all of that just to get you to realize that I want something more than friendship? Why couldn't you have trusted us instead of Sin? Why couldn't you have come clean with all of it? Your feelings, my situation, laid it all bare and trusted the pair of us to deal with it?"

"I could have left," Eld said. He made a noise in the back of his throat. "I thought I was doing the right thing," he said, choking back tears.

"So did I," I whispered. But I was wrong. About everything.

"I guess we have that in common, then." He bent toward Govanti's body and I cleared my throat.

"I told you once that there were only two people in this world who I trusted. Who'd never betray me," I said, and my words stopped him in his tracks. "Two. Sister and you. She's dead. What's your excuse?" His shoulders stiffened and I pointed toward the door. "I don't need you, Eld. Turns out, I never did."

"Buc—you don't mean that."

"I guess I should thank you for showing me that truth at least." Eld's face crumpled and something within me did, too, but I kept it from touching my face. I'd been terrified of losing control, of Sin winning out. That fear had tempered over time, when I came

376 • Ryan Van Loan

out on top and kept him from completing the Rite of Possession. I'd been so concentrated on that frontal assault, I didn't notice when he slipped in through a side gate, one left unlocked by my best friend.

"You betrayed me, Eld," I said quietly, steeling myself for what I knew had to be done. "When I needed you most." There's only one way to deal with traitors. "Get out."

He studied me for a long moment, eyes leaking tears, then nodded and muttered something under his breath. He turned slowly and walked blindly, like an old man, stumbling toward the door. He paused in the entryway, a score of paces away, but he might as well have been on another island.

I cut him off with a sharp gesture.

"Leave!"

The door closing behind him sounded like the lid of a coffin.

51

"I can't believe he left," Sin whispered.

"Yes, you can." I wiped at my eyes, expecting to find tears, but they were dry, burned away by my anger. What had Eld said about me? "Taking advantage of situations, allowing them to play out for my benefit?" I took a deep breath. "That goes doubly for you, Sin."

"Buc, I tried to save you!"

"For yourself." I sat down in the chair Eld had been in a few moments before, felt the heat from his body, and sucked the pain in deep, to where my anger lay waiting to burn it clean. "Don't try to deny it. You slipped, during all that back-and-forth. Let me see your true aim. You actively encouraged all of this," I said.

"Buc, you're upset, I completely understand, I'm upset! But—"

"Stop using my voice," I growled. "You don't get to do that anymore," I told him mentally. "I forbid it."

"That's fair," Sin said, in my mind this time. "Ordinarily, without Ciris's touch, I wouldn't be able to, but the injury to your head left an opening."

"That you exploited. You want me to trust you?" I asked him. "Then fix the opening."

"I—I can't, Buc. With Her, it may be possible, but without . . . you and I, we're damaged in ways that I've never seen happen before. It's what allowed you to block me out the other day."

"For weeks you've left me alone about completing the Rite of Possession." I slapped the table. "I should have known there was something off there. You told Eld to avoid me, especially after

I relapsed. Without Eld, the only one I could really rely on was you," I said, speaking slowly so Sin could see and feel everything I was going through.

"I suspect that at first, in the wake of the fire, Eld wouldn't leave my side." I didn't wait for Sin's nod of confirmation, just went on. "But I can't remember anything, now that I think on it, for a span of time back then."

"You were woozy. Brain injuries take time."

"Maybe. Or maybe you waited for me to relapse, trusting to Eld's nature." I snorted. "Maybe you even stopped healing me so it would happen. Then you could force Eld away, so that the space between us would turn into a chasm."

My memories picked up with Eld already at a distance, one I didn't understand—save that I knew of his distrust of magic and assumed he did not like the new, magical me. Sin could have stopped that with a single word, but he'd let the divide grow, steered me down false paths to solutions that had no bearing on the actual problem. In fact, his suggestions had only made things worse. And then—the gaps in my memory . . . It was only a matter of time before that reached a tipping point.

"You were herding me like a school of fish." I shook my head, felt my braids smack my shaved sides. "No, that's too nice. You herded me like a fucking cow. Toward the one thing you've always wanted: Possession. Make me desperate, alone, backed into a corner, and see if I would break?"

"Have you ever considered that I didn't have a choice?" he asked, his voice barely an echo.

"Of course you had a fucking choice."

"I'm a shard of Ciris herself. Do you think she'd create shards that could do as they pleased?" He chuckled, but there was no humor in my mind. "It doesn't mean I didn't try to heal you: you're my host, I am loyal. You think I haven't wondered why it should be this hard? I've felt everything you've felt, Buc. I don't want this!"

"What do you want?"

"I don't know," he said after a long pause. "I know what I'm supposed to want, but you make everything so damned difficult, Buc. You've even made me question Her."

"At the end of it all, though, you're still Hers, aren't you?" I asked.

"I'm yours, Buc, but I'm loyal to Ciris. I have to be."

"And with that convenient hole in my defenses, you may not be able to Possess me fully, but good as, right?"

"I've never taken control of you save with Eld," he protested.

"I could almost forgive you for trying to return to your Goddess. It was clever of you to leverage the situation. It nearly worked."

Sin snorted. "You're the most stubborn person I've ever met. It wouldn't have worked."

"It wouldn't have," I admitted, "unless it could have saved Eld and me. I'd have done anything, risked anything for that. That was my weakness, the noose you slipped around my neck and pulled tight by degrees, so I didn't notice even as I choked."

"Buc, you're pissed. I get it. But see reason," he said. "There's no way you can do everything you want to do on your own. Fight Sicarii. Win the Doga's support. Bend the Company under your thumb. Her name, first we have to figure out a way to keep your sanity now that your memories are back. You need me!" He sighed. "We'll get through this. Together."

"I know my weakness," I said, ignoring him. "I've known it for a while now. Do you know yours?"

"Mine?" I could hear the confusion there. "What are you talking ab—No!"

"Aye," I whispered, channeling all the pain and anger and fear that had been lurking inside me into action. I pulled it all together, into an impossibly large hammer, and I smashed Sin with it. He crumpled within my mind, his denial still echoing loudly. I changed the hammer into an iron sack and felt it flow over him, sucking him into a void within my mind from which he could not return unless I willed it.

His wail vanished sharply, as if his throat had been cut.

"Your mistake was taking Eld away from me," I told the void in my mind. "Mine was in ever letting you think you could do it." I sank down in the chair, the weight of everything threatening to collapse me the way it'd crushed Sin a moment before. "Now we're both fucked."

Free from Sin's focusing restraint and completely clean of kan, my mind ran at a breakneck pace, considering a thousand upon a thousand possibilities What I'd learned of Sicarii. The Artificer. Marin. Eld. *Eld.* Tears burst from my eyes and I couldn't hold back a sob. *I lost you.* I knew it was happening, I'd been fighting it for months, but I never truly believed it would happen. *You betrayed me. Both of you.* One inside, one out, working together, and me the court fool, thinking I was the one calling the tune.

The factory. The children I'd sentenced to death in the name of profit and power. I hadn't known they were using children because I'd never cared to find out. Means to ends. I could see how that knowledge would have poisoned my every thought in a maelstrom of guilt and despair. It hurt even now, in ways that I couldn't quite grasp. I shivered at the thought of that awful fire and the flames that had wanted nothing more than to consume me and everything else in that factory. Worse were the tendrils of terror that latched onto me at the memory. It hurt, but—

But taken with everything else, it was just one more painful rock in the cairn I'd built for myself. I could climb atop of it. Immolate myself and end it all. Save that would mean abandoning those same children to the other fires of this world. Trading companies, dogas, Gods. Thick clouds of smoke encircling them, suffocating them slowly until they died bent and broken before their time, having never seen the sun.

"Fuck that."

I stood up, straightened my jacket, and limped over to Govanti to check his pulse. It was stronger, which I took to mean whatever toxin Sicarii had used wasn't meant to kill. Very similar to the trap

I'd laid for her that had caught Marin instead. I'd failed. At almost everything. I was broken, alone in ways I hadn't been since this summer. No, since the day I tried to pick Eld's pocket and found the man I'd come to love. And lose.

That was all gone, now. Eld had been right. We made choices and sometimes there's no coming back from them. That didn't mean I could lie down and die. Sicarii and others—the Gods, the Doga, the Company, someone—had set me up, turned my trust into a dagger, and watched me plunge it into my own heart. Someone who knew about Eld. They needed to know that blades can cut both ways.

Revenge.

The pain was still there, but my new determination dulled some of it. I kept walking, my mind running on ahead. Sicarii had tried to kill me, was fighting to take the power of Servenza and likely the entire fucking Empire for her demented purpose, whatever it was. I thought of her falling before me and smiled. End Sicarii, and the Doga owes me.

"No."

My voice sounded rough in my ears. My throat hurt. That kind of thinking—of sitting down at the table and playing the game with the players, hoping to play the best hand—had gotten me into this mess in the first place. I didn't need to control the levers of power. I just needed to own the ones who did. The Doga had shown me that truth the day she summoned me: I'd been too enthralled with my own imagined brilliance.

"But I see it now," I said, opening the front door and looking at Marin's lifeless body. "Too late to save you, girl."

I bent down and closed her eyes. "You and Zeno and Quenta and Govanti will be my minders, from now on. I won't be blind again. You'll be the last if I have anything to say about it."

I knew that wasn't true—I wasn't a God and even the Gods couldn't prevent every death—but the sentiment was true. The pain cascading through me, the nausea, the wrenching tightness in my chest, the flaming brands in my brain: none of it was gone. But I could breathe. I could walk. I could fight. I could think. With all of that? I could win.

"I promise," I told Marin, rolling her over so I could pick her up. "I'll give you what is owed.

"Justice."

52

"What are you doing?" Salina asked as she entered the room.

"I read a book once about ways to overcome traumas of the mind," I answered Salina, keeping my eyes focused on the table in front of me.

"By burning yourself?"

"You joke," I said, passing my hand through the flame of the candle while tapping my thigh with my other hand in time with the metronome I'd wound earlier, "but you're not far off. It was written by a Southeast Islander, actually, a woman named Kolka. *The Mind Fears the Body.* Number 391."

"The mind fears the body?"

"Aye, she believed that most trauma we experience, we process and move on. It can be healthy, even, to know that you should avoid water where sharks swim after a near encounter, or that the dark alley up ahead may hold cutpurses lying in wait."

Sweat ran down my cheek as I passed my hand through the candle flame again, fighting to keep my voice even and my hand-tapping on beat. "Some trauma overwhelms us. We can't process it, and so it lives within us constantly, turning clear seas into dangerous waters and daytime streets into murder rows."

"My dad said his father was changed after the Tidal Wars," Salina said. I heard her shut the door behind her. "That was back when it was a requirement to serve for a time in the army or navy."

"His bad luck he chose the biggest maritime action since the Empire's founding," I said.

"It was. I barely remember him. Mostly what I remember is an old man who spent much of his time sitting in a chair, yelling whenever something wasn't done quite right. Even if that something was sitting on his lap."

"The difference between serviceable and perfect can be a wide gulf at sea. A line tied with one knot too few can come loose." I studied the candle's flame. Blue around the wick turning to shades of red that softened to bright yellow. Flames liked to pretend they were friendly, harmless, sources of light and warmth, but draw too much of them and their true nature showed. "A cannon," I continued, "with only one wheel secured can blow out of its mountings."

"I'd never thought of it that way before," she said.

"He likely didn't either. He should have read Kolka." I passed my hand through the candle a third time and bit back a curse as my tapping slipped off the beat.

I twisted in my chair and Salina arched an eyebrow before sitting on the edge of my bed beside my chair. Her dress looked nearly like divided trousers but her jacket flared wide enough to show it was all of a single piece. The latest fashion inspired by the Doga's Masquerade outfit. A white, silk ribbon hung from her right arm, bright against the dark-turquoise dress. Crossing her legs, she leaned back.

"So, what trauma are you erasing?"

"It's not really erasing," I explained. "The idea is to expose yourself to a very small sample of the trauma. At the same time, you listen to something that's rhythmic and repetitive. Something that distracts part of your mind from what you're going through." I nodded toward the metronome that was losing its beat as its gears wound down. "You also interact with your body to provide another distraction. Those distractions help the mind from becoming overwhelmed by the retelling or repetition of the trauma."

"You're afraid of candles?" Salina chuckled. "How ever do you read?"

"I'm afraid of fire," I said, and she stopped laughing.

"This"—I waved at the table—"isn't enough to fix me, if I can be fixed, but it's something I can cling to when I need." *Which I need.* I hadn't fought or screamed at the maid—who wasn't Marin—who lit my lamps the night before, but only because I'd wrapped the sheets so tightly about my fists that I'd torn holes in it. As soon as she left the room I'd blown them all out . . . and then nearly broken my toe trying to get back into bed without the benefit of Sin's night vision.

"That's a nice gesture," I added, standing up and turning my chair around so we faced each other properly. "She wasn't of your house."

"No, but she was of yours," Salina said, touching the silk ribbon on her arm. "I know you were teaching her to read. I was sorry to hear she broke her neck falling down the stairs."

"A freak accident, really," I said lightly. "It was the skirts that did her in." I met Salina's questioning gaze and looked away. "I've ordered the servants to hem theirs."

"I don't understand why that led to you and Eld falling out, or was that due to the Masquerade?"

"I think we were looking for an excuse to have it out?" I ran my hand through my braids, felt the freshly shaven skin beneath them. "Marin provided the spark and the rest went up like a matchbox."

Salina rolled her eyes and her mouth quirked. "It's a juicy enough story that half the nobles have bought it and the other half think it some fling between Lucrezia and the two of you. Since I'm not that stupid, are you going to tell me what really happened?"

"You're not? That stupid?"

"Fuck you, Buc." She grinned and crossed her arms. "Are you going to tell me or not?"

"It's not a pleasant story."

"I didn't figure," she said, pronouncing the *g* with that strange lilt half the rich had. "You look like you haven't slept in two days, your entire house is in white mourning while you're in black—very becoming by the way, although I fear trousers are already on their way out—and Eld isn't speaking to anyone. Nor has he been seen since your servant died, and the Chair's strutting around like an alley cat that's caught a fat hen. None of that screams happiness for you."

"Or for Marin."

"Gods," Salina breathed. "It wasn't just a fight, was it?"

I shook my head. "It was an assassination attempt."

"That failed, thankfully."

"Maybe, maybe not." I tilted my hand back and forth. "Sometimes a wound doesn't kill you outright. Sometimes it festers and you're left dying for days."

"Surely it's not that bad."

"I don't know," I said, looking up from my shaking hand. "You tell me."

"I always thought you were just an arsehole," Salina said when I finished telling her about the previous day.

"Thanks?"

"About the children." Salina leaned forward, her eyes bright with unshed tears. "All that time, whenever I would even begin to bring it up you always acted like you didn't know what the bloody sands I was talking about."

"I didn't. Repressed memories are like that, according to Kolka."

I hadn't told her about Sin; only Eld knew about that. And Sicarii. And the Artificer. It was too many, and though I liked Salina, I didn't trust her. I'd made Eld earn my trust and he'd still betrayed me in the end. Perhaps Sister would have as well, if she'd lived longer. The thought hurt and I began tapping my thigh to the beat of a metronome only I could hear.

"Until you confronted Eld."

"He'd been lying to me about my informant," I reminded her. "Which opened up the floodgates."

"You'd been lying to him, too—"

"Whose side are you on?"

"Yours, of course." Salina tapped her chin with a lacquered nail. "Are we alone?"

"As alone as we'll ever be," I confirmed. No Eld. No Sin.

"I mean," she said slowly, shifting her eyes perceptibly to the fireplace, "are we alone?"

"Oh, that." I grinned. "I left a little gift for the next would-be eavesdropper. We'd know if we weren't alone."

"What?" Salina's eyebrows disappeared into her hairline. "Buc," she hissed, "you can't do that. You aren't supposed to know the Doga's listening!"

"Then she shouldn't have sent her Secreto into my bedchamber," I said.

"Who killed Marin? Who poisoned your informant and tried to kill Eld with him?"

"It wasn't me, if that's what you're hinting at," I growled.

"Easy. I'm not accusing you," she said gently.

"I saved my informant, though he's not happy about the abrasion required to scour the poison off his skin." I'd been puzzling over how to make sure Govanti didn't go up in flames at his first sip of water when a messenger had come from the Artificer with instructions. Apparently Eld had gone in search of the man after I ordered him out of the palazzo. Knowing Eld, he'd done so at considerable cost to his mortality, but if he thought that would mend the rift between us, he'd been mistaken. Not that he'd tried to follow up on it. Just like the man.

"I know you wouldn't do anything that could risk losing Eld," Salina continued. "He's a fool to have done the trick himself," she added.

"I wish you'd have told him that three months ago," I muttered. She made an expression and we both laughed. I didn't feel much like laughing; it barely sparked anything inside me, but I couldn't deny it felt better than not.

"Who set this all in motion?" she asked.

"That's the ten-thousand-lire question," I said. "Who stands to profit from Eld dying and me being alone?"

"Someone who knows you two are tied at the hip. Were tied at the hip," Salina amended, reaching out and patting my knee. "Or someone who wanted one less seat on the Board."

"I've narrowed it down to four or five," I said.

"This Sicarii person?"

I nodded. "She or her cronies definitely did the legwork here. The question is, did she know what she was doing or was she taking orders?"

"From the Chair?" Salina asked.

"Potentially."

"Who else? N-not, not the Empress?" she choked.

I snorted. "If the Empress wanted me dead I think I'd be dead already. She'd have her Imperial Guard surround the palazzo and destroy it with cannon fire. Gods, she could probably bombard me from her fortress with mortars right now and not a damned soul would do anything about it."

"That's true."

"If it's not Sicarii or the Chair, then it's likely the Doga or the Gods. The Doga doesn't make a lot of sense, but she knows enough to make the list," I added.

"The Gods?" Salina hissed.

"I don't think it's the Gods . . . in some ways it'd be easier if it were." I pulled a kan cigarillo from a drawer in the table.

"Since when did you take up smoking again?"

"Next you'll lecture me on drinking and keeping the company of strange men, 'Lina," I said with a laugh. I left unsaid that without Sin, kan was the only thing keeping my thoughts from driving me mad. "Gods or no, I'll find out in the end."

"You sound like the Buc who walked into the library last summer," Salina said with a smile.

"Good."

"You know," Salina said, tilting her head as if studying me. "Maybe you never really were the arrogant, unfeeling arsehole I thought you were back then, or after the fire killed all those children."

"Oh?" I put the cigarillo between my lips and bent over the candle, forcing my hand to keep an even beat against my thigh despite the terror clutching my chest. The cigarillo lit. Drawing deeply, I held the smoke in my lungs, let the kan seep into me, then exhaled in a billowing cloud. "Do tell."

"I'm serious," she said. "You grew up on the streets, lived cheek by jowl with harshness and violence. That kind of living doesn't leave you with much freedom, least of all the freedom to catch your breath, think past the next day, and see potential alternatives."

"Eld was my alternative," I whispered.

"Exactly. He gave you that opportunity to catch your breath, to read, to find wisdom"—her lips quirked—"or knowledge, at least."

I cursed and she laughed.

"What I'm trying to say," she continued, "is that you have options to consider now. Maybe since circumstances have changed, perhaps you have changed, too?"

"Gods," I said, taking another drag on the cigarillo. "I hope you're wrong."

"You do?" Salina frowned. "Why?"

"I'm not wearing mourning white," I said, my thoughts distilling as the kan slowed them down, "because white shows bloodstains." I ground out the rest of the cigarillo on the tabletop, scoring the fire-maple surface. "Black doesn't. Black hides all manner of things."

"What are you going to do?"

"The old Buc would have found a stiletto and a throat and she wouldn't have stopped cutting until answers or blood spilled out." I stood up and stretched, feeling the blades pressing against my sides, the small of my back, and my wrists. I couldn't keep the smile from my mouth. "At the moment? Either would please me, but the Cordoban Confederacy have a saying they use when trading that I really like. . . .

"Why not both?"

53

"You shot me!" Rafiro gasped, writhing on the alley's broken cobblestones. His bicorne lay beside him, his dark hair a disheveled mess that matched his bloodshot eyes. He glared up at me, holding his knee. "You stupid bitch, I ought to—"

Damn. I clicked my tongue and reached for another lead ball. The constable, the blue who had first given us Sicarii's name, hadn't been walking steady when I found him and followed him into the alley, where he searched out a dark place to take a piss. Now that I'd put a round into his knee, he'd be even worse. With Sin's strength, the steel bands bracing the slingshot's frame were an enhancement. Without him, I could barely pull the thing back far enough to do much of anything. It'd been enough to knock Rafiro on his arse, but the booze—I could smell it on his breath from here—had helped. It hadn't been enough to break his leg properly, which was what I'd intended. His hands moved. I pulled back as hard as I could, not reaching quite half draw—and shot him in the other leg.

"Oww!" he howled, falling onto his back. "Ye kneecapped me. Crippled Rafiro!"

"You shouldn't have reached for that pistole in your boot then," I told him, my voice loud in the space between his cries. "There's no one around to hear you screaming and even if there were, they wouldn't care. Still"—I sighed, slipping another round into the pouch of my slingshot—"it's growing tiresome."

"D-don't. Don't," he pleaded. "What do you want? I've a little set by from bribes. It's yours," he gasped, grinding his crooked kan-whitened teeth together. "Want me to arrest someone? Name them and I'll do it." He sat up, breathing hard, tears bright in his dark eyes. "I'll arrest the Doga herself if you stop fucking shooting me."

"Hmm, that could be interesting."

"Th-the Doga?" He winced. "I was jesting, sign—"

"—ora," I finished for him. I had a streetlamp at my back and from his vantage on the ground, all he'd be able to see was my outline. He didn't need to know my age. I'd prefer it if he didn't know my sex, but there was nothing to be done there unless I wanted to pretend to be a lad whose balls hadn't dropped yet.

"Signora, what do you want?"

"Information is what I came for, but you've just given me an idea," I told him. "I've someone I want you to arrest."

"Gods," he whimpered, probing his knee with two fingers. "Who, signora? I'll have them picked up before dawn."

"Sicarii."

Rafiro's crying cut off like he'd had his throat slit. He looked up at me through his greasy locks, salt-and-pepper stubble on his chin turning him into an old man. He drew in a ragged breath and shook his head. "Where'd you learn that name, signora?"

"A blue told me."

"One of us?" He wiped his mouth with the back of his hand. "I don't believe you."

"I don't care if you believe me or not." I tried not to laugh and had to fight with my tongue not to tell him he'd been the blue with the loose lips. He'd sent the prostitute after Eld and me with the information that led us to the Mosquitoes' maestro. We could have easily been immolated along with the beggar king—it'd clearly been a setup. The question was, who had done the setting? I had a suspicion. *Now let's hear you confirm it.* "You made me an offer and I'm taking you up on that."

"Now you're jesting," he said, a wheezing laugh shaking his shoulders. "You'd do as well to cut my throat here and now as ask for that."

"I'm thinking on it," I admitted. Between the drink and both badly bruised knees, I figured he wasn't going to be pulling off any fancy calisthenics and attacking me or trying to run away, so I slipped my slingshot back into my jacket and drew the stiletto I always left unblackened. Twisting it through my fingers so it caught the light, I took a step forward and he tried to slide away.

"S-signora, no!"

"You say you want to live, but you won't give me what I want."

"I can't! I'd die trying," he said, spittle flecking his lips. "They'd kill me before I got within a dozen paces of them."

"Who would?"

"Sicarii. Her gangs. What's it matter?"

"All right, all right," I said, catching the hilt in my hand and pointing the blade at him. "You can't arrest Sicarii, but you can tell me who you work for."

"Servenza," Rafiro growled, reaching for his knees again. "I'm a constable, you bloody fool."

"No shit," I said. "You're the fool. I just kneecapped you. Alone in this alley. You see anyone else?" I turned a slow circle, arms outstretched. "What's to stop me from ending your miserable life here and now?"

"Nothing," he whispered.

"Nothing," I agreed. "Save what you tell me. So—"

"I'm just a constable, I swear." He screamed and grasped his cheek with both hands, then made a noise in his throat when they came away bloody.

"Lie to me again and the next blade will be through your throat." I'd tossed the blade I had tied to my left wrist while he'd been focused on the stiletto in my right. I'd grown too used to Sin's preternatural accuracy; instead of pinning his collar to the street, I'd sliced his cheek open. It could have just as easily been his throat and that would have taken any answers he had along with this life. "You won't see that one coming either," I added.

"I work for the Doga," he said slowly, blinking as he tried to stare up at me and caught the streetlamp instead. "S-secreto."

"Bullshit," I snapped. "I guess you don't want to live. . . ."

"Her," he hissed. "I am Secreto, but I serve her. Sicarii." He touched his face and winced. "You knew that already, didn't you?"

"It was the only explanation that made sense," I said. "But nothing that should make sense has made much at all lately, so I had to know. How many others work for Sicarii?"

"I don't know. I don't!" he yelped when I took another step. "Would she tell me? I'm just another blue under her thumb."

"But the gangs all work for Sicarii."

"If they don't, they're fighting for their lives against the ones that do," Rafiro agreed. "Not too many left, being honest. Another fortnight and they'll all be serving Sicarii one way or the other."

"What's your stake in all this? If Servenza falls—" I snorted. "The audacity to think that some insane creature and a bunch of street gangs are going to take down Servenza and with it the entire Empire. . . ."

"Not just gangs. Constables. Soldiers. Sailors." Rafiro chuckled mirthlessly. "You don't know how many of us there are. I don't know either, but you know even less."

"Fine. Say Sicarii succeeds: What does a constable gain from that? Servenza pays your salary."

"And it's a shit one," he spat. "Sicarii will have need of someone to keep the folk in line when she takes power. I am irredeemable."

"You mean irreplaceable?"

"Aye," he said, pointing a shaky finger at me. "That." He wiped at his mouth again, leaving bloodstains in his stubble, and sat up straighter. "I've answered your questions, signora. What comes next?"

"One more question," I said. "How do you meet her? To get your orders?"

"Street rats," Rafiro said. "They used to work for the gangs, now they work for Sicarii."

"Sounds like half the city does," I muttered.

"Are you talking to yourself?" he asked hoarsely.

"It's too quiet in my head of late," I said, glancing at him. "You say street rats, but I hear children."

"So?" He barked a laugh and edged himself up a little higher, his right hand slowly making its way past his ruined kneecap. "What's it matter?"

"The problem with this world is we don't give a shit about how we got here and we don't care where we're going. In turn we swallow all the lies the Gods feed us and we exploit the little ones around us without a thought for what types of people they will be when we're old."

"Probably turn into someone like me. Or yourself. I don't understand?" Rafiro said, sounding genuinely puzzled.

"I know," I said, nodding. "Let's keep it that way."

The stiletto leapt from my fist in a flash of silver lightning and Rafiro jerked and fell back, the pistole he'd been reaching for falling out of its boot holster. He tried to grab the blade buried in his chest. Brow knit in confusion, he coughed a bloody spray that stained his chin red.

"I know where the heart is," I said, walking toward him. "A little lower and more to the center than most realize. It'll take you a bit to bleed out. Faster if I pull the blade, but . . ." I shrugged. "I have to pay a few more calls and it's rude to show up with someone else's blood all over you, isn't it?"

Rafiro opened his mouth to answer, then his head fell back, slapping onto the cobblestone with a meaty thud. His body spasmed and a harsh gurgling sound came from his throat as he began to choke on his own blood.

"Glad you agree," I told him, kneeling beside him. His eyes

flicked to me, past me, then back to me, but I wasn't sure if he was still seeing or not. I reached into his jacket pocket, where I found what I expected: a few kan papers and a match. "You tried to get Eld and me killed. That I could almost forgive—I mean, you're not the first, after all." I continued searching him; his other jacket pocket held something heavy and metallic.

"It's what you and others like you are doing to Servenza that earned you that blade. Eld was right, turns out I was ignoring those I was trying to help, all in the name of trying to help them. That's the danger of being brilliant, sometimes you're too damned brilliant for your own good." I looked at what I'd pulled from Rafiro's jacket and cursed.

"You weren't lying after all, you dumb bastard."

The sigil of the Secreto lay heavy in the palm of my hand, twin to the one I had in my own pocket. My mind began racing, dozens—scores—of disparate thoughts competing for my attention. What does this mean? The question kept surfacing between every other thought and I could feel the beginning of a headache. I grabbed one of Rafiro's rolled kan papers—he wouldn't be needing it—and struck the match against the cobblestone. Puffing the kan alight, I drew in a deep lungful and let it out as I stood up.

"What else were you telling the truth about?" I asked Rafiro. He didn't reply and I realized there was an awful lot of blood fanning out around his head, framing it against the street. "Shit," I muttered, blowing smoke out.

"I might have been a little hasty."

54

I walked out of the alley with my lungs full of kan and my mind full of questions, with answers beginning to rise out of the maelstrom. Adjusting my jacket, I began heading for the nearest canal. In summer, the city came to life at night, when the heat was almost bearable, but in winter, with a storm's wind blowing in, there was no one around. My bootheels echoed off the street in rhythm with the thoughts in my head. Rafiro was Secreto, one of the Doga's most trusted officers. How could she not know he'd turned his coat? Then again, he was a kan addict, so maybe her judgment wasn't as sound as I thought. *Or is she working for Sicarii, too?* But why the assassination attempts? I shook my hair, gathered into a single, loose braid over my shoulder. It didn't make sense. She had nothing to gain—she already had Servenza. Unless . . .

The sound of horse hooves and the rattle of harness interrupted my thoughts. I glanced behind me and saw a carriage approaching. A lantern hung at each corner; two hulking men sat up high behind the driver with a pair of blunderbusses. As it reached me, the driver pulled the carriage to a halt, the street suddenly going silent. I could just make out the sigil worked on the carriage door: a gilded kan leaf. One of the windows slid open and a familiar voice, full of arrogance and authority, called out.

"Get in the carriage, Sambuciña."

"I think I'll pass, Chair," I told the old woman. "It's a lovely night for a stroll."

"There's a warrant out for your arrest," she said. "If you want to stay out of the Castello, you'd be wise to get in."

"Warrant? For what?" I purposely avoided looking back into the alley. Killing a blue was definitely worth a trip to the Castello, whether they were on the take or not. To say nothing of the fight with the Veneficus the day before. I didn't think any could trace those to me, but the past few days had shown me my fallibility, so I climbed into the carriage.

"Take us out of here," she commanded the driver. "You know where to go." Looking at me, her eyes liquid in the faint light cast from the lamps outside the windows, she leaned forward.

"You've much to answer for, girl." The carriage lurched into motion. "Are you going to thank me for keeping you out of jail?" A black, fur-trimmed shawl, or perhaps a robe, was draped around the Chair's shoulders. She inclined her head, her white-streaked black hair tinkling with the jewelry threaded in her locks. "I know how much you hate politeness."

"I hate falseness," I said. After a beat, I said, "Thank you." I was surprised to hear that I almost sounded like I meant it.

"It was nothing," the old woman said.

I felt my mouth curl—*nothing!*—and the guards flanking her both shifted.

"I can't let the Company be dragged through the gutter," she continued as if oblivious to the temperature change in the carriage. "It pains me, but you're part of the Company. Therefore, you're under my protection . . . for now. It's why I've not interfered with Eld's foolishness."

"Foolishness?"

"Hiding after your tiff like a little girl who lost her mother's favorite amulet. It's given rise to the type of rumors that could land you in the Castello and could be easily fixed, save he's gone to ground, so only you and I know he lives."

"What's Eld got to do with me?"

"Rumor is you and he had a falling-out over your dead maid. With Eld missing, the rumors have grown to suggest you offed him, too." She sniffed. "Whatever romantic frippery is between the two of you, now that it's spilled out into the open, it needs to end. These rumors have given the Company a black eye."

"We wouldn't want that," I murmured. I wondered which servant was giving the world a front-row view into our home. *I'll have to ask that kitchen maid . . . she's supposed to be feeding the Chair only the stories I want her to hear.* I'd have a word to the maid and Glori, and between them would ferret out the rat. Or rats.

The Chair's silence was loud. She adjusted her shawl with thin, bejeweled fingers. "You need to atone for these rumors."

"I do, but Eld doesn't?" I snorted. *Figures.* "That bullshit aside, how do I atone, O great and mighty ruler?"

"You really are a child." The Chair's eyes were bright in the lamplight. "I was going to say you had to atone because you led and he followed, but perhaps I didn't have the right of it."

"In my defense, it's been a long couple of days," I said. "I—I apologize."

"Good. I'm glad you found the words, even if they had to be dragged from you." The Chair coughed into a silk handkerchief and muttered something about the weather.

"How do rumors, fanciful at best, lead to me in the Castello?"

"Her Grace has gone too far of late, insinuating herself into Board matters, working the shareholders through intermediaries like I'm too much of a novice to see her hand there. This, I've tolerated, but now she's signed a warrant for your arrest without consulting me."

"The Doga did what?" I sat forward in my seat. All the supplies required for Serpent's Flame were ordered in her name. Her Secreto work for Sicarii. "Why?"

"Haven't you been listening, child?" the Chair asked. "I can't ignore an assault on the Company, whomever it's directed at, and she knows that. The woman's acting like she wants to be removed. She's forcing me to see her gone or else rein her in so hard she'll never mind the bit in her mouth again.

"I'd take this to the Empress herself if I could. Unfortunately, a warrant for your arrest isn't enough evidence to show that the Empire must needs intervene."

"I might have something," I said. The Chair's eyes shot to my own so swiftly that I'd half palmed the dull blade I kept strapped to my wrist before I caught myself. In the poor light, and wearing all black, neither guard noticed. She should have paid more for brains instead of muscle. "But it makes no sense."

"Girl, sense is something I've seen very little of when it comes to you. That you'd fail to recognize it in others would not surprise me. Why don't you tell me and I'll explain it to you?"

"Has anyone ever smashed the bullshit you spout back down your throat?"

Both guardswomen moved, gauntleted fists raised. The Chair made a noise and they froze. We all stared at one another, the only sound the clip and clop of horse hooves.

"A few have tried, Buc. There's always those that think physical violence is the weapon of first resort."

"Funny coming from the woman riding around with all the muscle and firepower lire can buy."

"Unfortunately," she said with a shrug, "those types I was just talking about only recognize messages of the same." She settled back in her seat and the two guards sat back down. "Now, what were you going to tell me before I pricked your pride?"

"Have you—" I was unable to keep my voice from dropping, and hated it. "Have you heard of Sicarii?"

"Sicarii," the Chair said in her normal bell-like tone. "Sicarii, aye. I'm familiar with the name. I'm told they're some gang leader or such who is trying to unite the gangs." She chuckled, but her face didn't change expression. "The last to try was some old whore named Bloody Waters." She chuckled at the name, likely unaware she'd butchered it.

Blood in the Water was old, but she wasn't a whore. *I don't kill whores.*

"Killed by one of her own," the Chair continued. "Happens

every so often. A rat decides the rest are mice and that means they get to rule the gutters." She waved a hand. "Either another rat comes along to put paid to that fiction or else we send in a ratcatcher."

"Sicarii is many things, Chair, but she's no rat. Half of Servenza is hers, from the mice you don't see to the blues, maestros, merchants, and any number of would-be assassins." Now I laughed. "I thought you said I was the one without any sense." I leaned forward. "Even some of the Secreto work for Sicarii!"

"Say on," the Chair commanded, her eyes flashing in her stony features. "All of it."

So I told her. Most of it. Some, really. As much as I would tell anyone. Perhaps a little less. She had insulted me, after all.

"What doesn't make sense is that Sicarii could have infiltrated the Doga's ranks that deeply and the Doga not be aware of it," I concluded. "The other problem is the attempts themselves. Sicarii doesn't do half measures and from what I've seen, she's damned smart. How is it that the Doga's still drawing breath?"

"I understand why this doesn't make sense to you," the Chair said. I bristled and she reached a hand halfway out across the aisle. "No, I mean it. Why would it, when the Doga made an offer you couldn't refuse in exchange for you finding out who was behind the attempts?"

"I didn't say that," I growled.

"No," she agreed, "you didn't . . . but are you going to call me a liar?" Her lips quirked. "I thought not. I wondered why you weren't busy trying to turn the Board against me before I set you on the first ship sailing north."

"Can the Board be bought?" I shot back.

"I could almost like you," the other woman muttered, half to herself. "Don't you get it, child?" She nodded toward the direction of the Palacio. "This is all the Doga's handiwork."

"I'm not certain Sicarii would play second to her," I said. "She's insane."

"Of course she is. You'd have to be, to get into bed with that

woman. Oh," she said, holding a hand up to her mouth. "I forgot."
I blushed and her mouth widened into a genuine smile, almost as
if the old bastard could see my skin in the dark. "The assassina-
tions are fake, girl. Meant to make the Doga look blameless as all
comes apart like a sack tied with broken thread."

"Why let the city she rules fall apart?"

"Power," the Chair whispered. "She'll let this Sicarii turn the
streets into one big riptide, threatening to pull us all out to sea . . .
so that when she expands her forces, the Empress will believe it's
in response to this new threat."

"If Sicarii is working for her, though, she'll have two armies,"
I said, hearing the satisfying clicks in my mind as more pieces of
the puzzle slid into place.

"Precisely," the Chair said, sounding surprised. "Neither would
have a hope against the might of the Imperial army, but they don't
need to fight the entire army."

"Gods' breath," I choked. "Just the Empress's Imperial Guard."

"Aye. And the Servenzan army lies garrisoned on the coast of
the mainland. They're the largest contingent of the Imperial army,
and none would wager they would side against Servenza herself."

"Have they ever rebelled before?" I asked. "I don't recall ever
reading about it."

"You wouldn't," she said dryly. "There's history that's recorded
and then there's the truth, and rarely do the twain meet. Ancient
history, in this case. I believe there is a book on it hid within our
library, the only one of its kind."

A book? One of a kind? I bit my lip. *Focus, fool.* The Chair
knew my obsession with books; everyone did. That she mentioned
it now was meant to obfuscate or distract. Ah, I just did her a
massive favor.

"There's your atonement," I told her. "The information you
needed."

"Agreed, but it's not going to change my mind about you." She
laughed, chimes ringing in her throat. "Things are moving apace.

I don't need you hanging around fucking things up. I'll take steps to remove this Sicarii from the equation and I'll remind the Doga who invented the word 'machination.'"

"I always knew you were old, but I didn't know you were so old you created the Imperial tongue."

"Is that meant to be clever?" The Chair's tone dripped condescension. "You want to hear me laugh, tell me a joke. Until then, you'll do as you're told." She shrugged beneath her shawl. "It seems," the Chair said, her tone sending gooseflesh racing across my skin, "everyone is in need of a reminder of who the real power is in Servenza. In the Empire itself. It's all built upon the Company's coin," she growled. "Every fucking brick, and they'd do best to not forget it."

"Her Grace has."

"And that's why we're speaking tonight," the Chair said. "I told you once that I demanded loyalty. That wasn't a lie. I also told you I was sending you away and I wasn't lying then, either. A ship from Colgna put in earlier today. Once it's done refitting it sails north."

She jabbed a jeweled finger at me. "You'll be on board when it does or I'll send Eld to some flyspeck island in the Shattered Coast and you'll hang for his death like the Doga wants."

"You wouldn't do that," I whispered, clenching my hands into fists to keep them from a stiletto . . . or her throat. "You said so yourself. Not and see the Company dragged through the gutter like that."

"I can tolerate a surprising amount of shit if it's on my terms," the old woman said with a smirk. "I'll need a bath, aye, but I've any number of servants to draw one for me. Can you say the same?" She leaned forward. "That's what loyalty is, Buc. That's what I demand."

55

"You wish to see your accounts, signorina?"

"You took your sweet time getting here," I said, turning around in the comfortable leather chair at the junior maestro's desk. His dark eyes flashed—I'd usurped his seat—but his mouth twisted into a grin so wide it couldn't be true. I nodded toward the high, stiff-backed chair meant for patrons. "Have a seat."

"The signorina jests," he said. I gave him an equally false smile and said nothing, and after a moment he adjusted his gilded waistcoat and sat down, crossing his legs. "Your accounts?"

"I have none here," I said. "You only hold the gold of the older families and mine was as fresh minted as the lire in your drawer." I drew out a sack and tossed it on the desk. "Gold has a sound to it, doesn't it?"

"Signorina . . ." He dry-washed his hands and tried to look into my eyes to convey assurance, but I saw his tongue dart between his lips. I'd unsettled him. "I don't know where that came from, but if you have no account here, then I'm afraid I can't help you."

"It's really more about me helping you," I told him, kicking my feet up onto his desk beside the gold and crossing my polished boots. "This gold is going to take that anchor off your shoulders." He arched an eyebrow. "I'm going to take care of your gambling debts," I said, trying not to sigh. *Gods, he's a thick one. No wonder he lost so much.*

"I mean, just think, maestro, if your father-in-law knew you were using clients' coin to fund your . . . shall we say, your 'fondness' for gambling?" I scratched my chin. "Some would call it an addiction."

When I nudged the bag with my boot, it jingled. "You can stop at any time though, aye?" I nodded. "'Course you could. No need for the chief maestro to know about your fondness for gondola races."

"H-how did you know?" he choked, the color draining from his face.

"It's my business to know," I told him, flashing the sigil of the Secreto.

His eyes popped and I sat up, swinging my feet back down to the hardwood floor. I'd chosen a dark-blue outfit today, so deep a blue it was almost black, save for the brass buttons on my jacket. Not quite as close to black as the Secreto's uniform, but close enough to fool any who hadn't seen a Secreto up close. The Doga had warned me about showing off the sigil, but given that she was trying to kill me and overthrow the Empress, I was disinclined to acquiesce to her request.

"I'm doing you a favor, maestro. Now you're going to do one for me."

"W-what?" He cleared his throat, sweat beading across his forehead. "What do you want?"

"I don't want to pull an inside job, if that's what you're thinking," I said. He frowned. "That wasn't what you were thinking? Are you sure you haven't wondered if you couldn't hire a couple of thugs to strong-arm you and make off with half the vault's coin?"

I laughed as his bravado wilted. "Secreto know everything." I wagged a finger. "I wouldn't try it, though, boy. You haven't the brains for it."

"Tell me what to do," he whispered, his voice catching the back of his throat, "and I'll do it. I swear."

"I just want you to help me shift some funds around," I said. "First . . ."

"None of this makes sense," he muttered when I finished. "Moving coin through these accounts makes them more difficult to trace, more hidden, true—" He glanced at me and looked away, licking his lips. "But, signorina, they're still in the same name!"

"You're not wrong," I said. I picked up the bag of gold and hefted it so that the coin jingled loudly. "Do it anyway."

Rounding the table, I drew a blade and he yelped. "Shh," I whispered, holding the stiletto in one hand, the gold in the other. I put my mouth beside his ear. "The ways of the Secreto are mysterious, maestro." I ran the edge of the blade down his cheek, and though it was too dull to cause harm, he jerked away, making another noise in the back of his throat. "So do it anyway. Do it now."

Out on the street, crowds moved like an endless sea, everyone drinking in the unexpected sunlight. The clouds that had been threatening rain had moved on and while their darker, more ominous cousins were on the horizon, the morning was as beautiful as Servenza got at this time of year, and everyone was out to enjoy it. My heart was a thick lump in my throat and every fiber in my being cried out that I should draw steel, but I ignored the feeling as best I could, tapping my thigh to a beat only I could hear as I joined the wave of humanity. I'd never been afraid of crowds before; they were a wave I could ride with the best of them, having grown up in the crowded sections of the Painted Rock across from the Tip. Without Sin's protection, my mind whispered of all the opportunities not to hear whispers or pickpockets, but to be attacked, knocked down, run over.

Stop it.

My mind stopped tripping over the possibilities, but the fear remained, embedded in my bones. I tapped my thigh more slowly, focused on my breath, and gradually, it all helped. If only it cured. Something swirled in my mind and I pushed it down. Hard. *That's not healing. That's death.* Without Sin I was afraid, but without him, my mind was clear and I could see what Eld had seen, what I'd failed to see these past few months.

Servenza was rougher than I remembered. The people around me weren't wealthy, but they should have had enough coin to buy clothes that weren't threadbare and faded where they weren't patched a dozen times over. The populace always smelled outside the finer Quartos, but now the stench hung in the air like rot and all bent beneath its weight without seeming to notice. Here and there children darted through the crowd, most with no shoes. Not an unfamiliar sight in the Foreskin or even the Tip, but in the Mercarto or Painted Rock? *Something is wrong. It's been wrong for a while.*

A new smell pulled me up short and the woman behind me spat a curse when she ran into me and I didn't budge. She cursed again and disappeared into the throng while I made for the little cart on the corner where a boy and girl whose dirty-blond hair and matching thin features proclaimed them siblings. A dozen people stood in line, and getting a better whiff, I understood why. The cart was small, barely the size of a table, with a rough, metal chimney funneling flames up beneath a wide, metal bowl that the girl stood behind, sweating freely despite being in her shirtsleeves. She used a wide, flat ladle to stir noodles, broth, peppers, and a dozen other ingredients I didn't recognize, dipping the pan to cause flames to shoot up occasionally. Every blast sent a wave of deliciousness into the air. Beside her, the boy scooped out a small bowlful and passed it to the waiting patron, pocketing two coppers in return. Other customers stood nearby, finishing their servings, while those who hadn't eaten yet waited for empty bowls to be returned to the children.

When was the last time I thought about food? With Sin, I'd eaten of necessity. A lot. All the time. I couldn't recall ever enjoying it or even considering what I was putting into my mouth.

Gods. I'd always had a nose for tasty food, but was that a necessity? Apparently not to him. He killed my love of food like he
wiped out my need for kan to slow my thoughts. Bastard.

I found myself standing in line, listening to the artists in front
of me debate how to use the bottom floor of the building they
rented, which seemed to be just beyond the cart.

"Maybe we should talk to the Sin Eaters? They've been bringing in crowds."

"For free healing and to speak to loved ones leagues away, not
to look at art. We can't afford them and even if we could, none
would go upstairs. I don't know why I let you talk me into renting
the whole damned building. If we can't get people to look at our
canvases on one floor, what will two accomplish?" one asked. "I
told you we should have set up on the bottom floor."

"If they don't have to strive to find the art . . . then what's the
point?"

"Making coin? Not starving to death."

The first laughed. "You'd be right about starving if this cart
wasn't here."

Despite the line, I made it to the front in no time, partially
due to the fast service and more to do with how quickly everyone
shoveled the noodles down their gullets. The girl's attention was
on her cooking, but she spared a smile for me when I slipped the
boy a silver instead of a cupari, and he handed over the bowl with
a spoon and noodle sticks so quickly I nearly dropped it.

"Gods, you make this from that?" I asked around a mouthful
of noodles.

"I do, signorina." She bowed her head, eyes never leaving the pan.

"Have you thought of charging more?"

"Every day," her brother muttered.

"We cannot and keep our custom," she explained. A man waiting for his bowl glared at me and I shifted to the side. "Carts such
as ours cannot command more than a few cupari. Charge more
and the patrons that can afford more will never come because

they're sitting down at one of the taverns or the like. The rest can't afford more and will pass us by."

"So you need a shop," I said, slurping up noodles.

"And coin to afford it," she said.

"'S not cheap," her brother muttered around the smile he offered, along with a full bowl, to the waiting man. "Hard to find a place even if we had the coin."

I nodded and turned away, lifting the bowl to my lips to drink the broth. *Damn.* I couldn't stop myself from moaning. When I lowered the bowl I saw the two artisans entering their building still arguing about how to attract patrons.

"I've an idea," I told the young chefs, turning back.

"What's that, signorina?"

"I know of a building with a space sitting idle. You wouldn't have to move far at all. . . ."

I told them what I'd overheard and explained my plan to have the artists move downstairs, put the pair of them upstairs. With gear fans properly placed, they could pump the smell of their cooking into the streets, which would attract patrons with enough coin to want to sit down while they ate. Said patrons would have to walk through the artists' gallery to find the food.

"Everyone wins," I finished.

"It's a wonderful dream," the girl said, her smile not quite reaching her eyes.

"If we were fecking rich," her brother said out of the side of his mouth.

"Jaimi," she growled. "Keep a civil tongue in your head. Apologies," she added.

"None needed." I slipped my hand into the other bag of lire I hadn't shown the banking maestro—he'd been even cheaper to buy than I'd planned—and began counting gold coins onto the edge of the cart, using my body to conceal the amount. If my schemes went as planned, the banker's debts would get paid one way or the other, and if they didn't—fuck him. "I'm going to back you. Here and now."

"Be serious," the boy said, his eyes the size of oyster shells.

"I am," I said. I kept counting and the pair's jaws kept gaping wider. "Go pitch my—your idea to those fool artists. . . . The woman has some sense at least, so aim for her. Don't take their first offer. Pay them and put the rest . . ."

Some of the people behind me started to mutter as the line grew longer. I turned slightly toward them and flashed my Secreto sigil, hiding it from the siblings. The patrons quieted and I turned back. "Wait a fortnight to open," I finished. "Use the coin and time to prepare, but wait the full fourteen days."

"W-why?" the girl stammered.

"You'll understand, soon enough," I promised. "In the meantime, hide that"—I nodded toward the coins—"and enjoy your final service in this tiny-arsed cart." The girl swept the gold off the cart's edge and into her front apron pocket, the fabric dangerously close to bursting open from the weight.

"Savvy?"

"S-savvy," they said, both stuttering, looking poleaxed but excited.

"Wonderful."

Eld had been right; I had been ignoring the situation of those on the streets. I couldn't save all of them; I still needed to stop Sicarii. And the Doga. And take down the Gods. But I could help those I stumbled across. That was part of it, the part that would have brought a smile to Eld's lips and made him stand taller. *You stupid bastard.* I swallowed the lump in my throat. The other part was that helping others had its uses.

"Can I beg a favor of you?"

"Anything, signorina!"

"I've a friend I was supposed to meet, but something's come up. Could you possibly spare your brother here to run over to the Spired Quarto and give them this letter from me?" I slid the letter from my jacket. "You won't be able to miss him, he's a funny little sort of a person with strange spectacles. Tell him Buc sent you." I held the letter out and faked an exclamation. "Now that I think on it, he may be able to help you with the gear fans I mentioned for your new place—"

"I'm so very sorry to hear of your loss," the woman in crimson judicial robes said, rising from behind the bench.

"So you said," I muttered, burying my face in my handkerchief, which I'd wet with water before entering the legal office. Blinking back tears, I looked up. "If you meant it, you'd help me. The priestess at Baol's cathedral said you would help. I paid her!"

"Signorina . . . I appreciate the custom our Dead Gods provide, but the priestess isn't an expert in common law and I'm afraid the section on the succession of fortunes is quite clear. I'm sorry I can't be of more assistance, but unless you have incontrovertible proof that the dates on the signature page are wrong, then I'm afraid things stand as they are."

"W-what proof would I need?" I asked, blowing my nose loudly.

"In this case?" The woman adjusted her wig, her lips twitching as she tried to tell me what I already knew. Hoped I knew. "Your. Erm. Father."

"I don't understand," I said, frowning.

"He'd need to be here. To testify that he wasn't in fact . . . dead?"

"You're making mock of me?" I asked, my voice climbing with my eyebrows. I was right. "In my moment of despair and distress you wish me to go drag my father's corpse from the mausoleum because my scheming brother reworked some dates on a piece of paper?"

"Signorina, I—"

"I'll not be made a jester's fool," I cried, leaping out of the chair and stomping loudly across the hardwood floors. "I won't!" I shouted, opening the door and storming out. As soon as the door crashed shut behind me I wiped my tears away and jogged down the stairs. Out on the street, the afternoon shadows told me I was running out of time, but I'd had to be sure the book I read had its facts right and that some law or other hadn't cropped up since that would invalidate my plans.

I was still grinning to myself when I saw a boy with the fuzzy hair of one who'd just had his head shorn from having lice try to dart between two women. He knocked into the heavier one and went down onto his side in the muddy street, grasping at his bare ankle and shouting that she'd hurt him. The woman told him she'd hurt him again if he didn't shut up, and her companion told him it was all he deserved for running around like a fool. What neither noticed was the small purse he held tight against his body, directing their attention to his other hand as he made a show of rubbing his foot. He kept it up for a few moments after they left, still sneering at him, then jumped to his feet, a spring in his step and a whistle on his lips.

"You!" I grasped his shoulder and spun him into the alley, pulling him back just before he slammed off the brick wall. "Think you're clever, nicking purses off unsuspecting ladies?"

"I'm sorry, officer," he whimpered, shrinking back. He'd taken my dark-blue coat and trousers and brass buttons as that of the blues. "They dropped it, is all. I was going to return it!"

"An' here I thought ye was a clever lad," I said, letting some of the streets creep into my voice. "Fuck their lot."

"Sirrah?" he asked, raising his eyes. "That is, I mean, signorina? Officer?"

"Let's see how clever you really are," I said, squeezing his shoulder. I could feel his thin bones beneath the threadbare jacket he wore. *Let's see if I'm as clever as I think.* "What would you say if I asked you what the drowned do?"

All the tension leeched from his shoulders and he straightened up, grinning. "They rise, officer."

"That they do lad," I said, "that they do." I dug out a scrap of folded-up paper that had a mark on the outside. "You know what this means?" I asked, showing him the blade I'd drawn in ink on the outside. I didn't need Sin's perfect recall to see it in my mind's eye, flecked with blood from the girl I'd killed. *Another debt I need to call due.*

"I—I do, officer," he whispered, his wide eyes flicking back and forth from me to the blade.

"I've orders, so I can't return to the . . . you know where," I said, dropping my voice. He looked around, but no one had followed us into the alley. Because no one gives a shit about little boys being pulled into dark alleys. I added that fury to what was already simmering inside me. "Can you deliver it for me?"

"I can try, officer, b-but, they won't let me in," he said. "I'm just another eye for Sicar—"

"Easy!" I hissed. "No need for names." I pressed the paper into his hand. "You don't need to give it to her personally. Just get it to one of the leaders and make sure they see the mark. They'll take care of the rest."

"They will?"

"They will," I assured him.

I'm counting on it.

Dusk was a muted purple as the sun slipped below the buildings when I crossed back into the Blossoms Quarto. I glanced over my shoulder, but I'd lost the two tails I was sure of in the Kneeling Quarto when services let out. Hopefully not so lost that they didn't find the clues I left behind. With night approaching the streets weren't quite barren, but the swirling wind promised that the storm was finally arriving, so only a few were about. I stepped around a light pole just before I ran into it, as if I hadn't realized it was there, then ducked into the nearby alley.

"Buc?"

"It's me, little one," I told the girl, moving deeper into the shadows afforded by the palazzo walls on either side.

"I thought you forgot."

"Never," I told her, dropping to a knee. "You've got another patch on your dress."

"Fell playing," she said, her pale skin bright in the dim light. "Mama was upset, after you'd just bought it for me."

"She bought it for you," I said.

"You gave her the coin."

"Think of it as your wages for work well done," I said. I stood up. "Speaking of . . . do you have it?"

"I hid it back here," the girl said, turning and moving deeper into the alley. She pointed at a long, thin, cloth-wrapped bundle leaning upright against the wall. "It was heavy."

"Was it?" I unwrapped the hilt, and drew a few fingers' length of steel from the sheath. "They weren't lying," I muttered.

"Who wasn't?"

"The person who made this," I said. "Folks will say a lot of things, little one. Especially if they think it's what you want to hear and they stand to gain. Sometimes they'll do it on purpose, but often it's by accident."

"My mama says it's wrong to lie."

"It's wrong to lie to your mama," I told her. I brushed her thickly braided blond hair back over her shoulder. "It's not always wrong to lie to others." I let the blade slide home and rewrapped the cloth around the hilt. "You should listen to what folks have to say . . . and then make sure you see it with your own eyes That's how you know who is telling you the truth. Who can be trusted."

"I trust you."

"You should," I said, making a coin appear in my hand as if by magic. "I do what I say I will." I handed her the coin and offered her the bundle. "I know this is heavy, but would you be able to carry it a little farther yet?"

"You want me to take it in by the kitchens?"

"Too damned clever," I told her, smiling. "I do. Nan may have something set aside for you, if you're lucky."

"Stone fruit?"

"In winter?" I asked.

"You're rich. Rich have stone fruit all the time. Mama says you eat all the fruit so we have to have porridge and fish heads."

"I can't argue with that logic," I said, my smile slipping. "But if I'm rich today, it's so that you will be tomorrow. Do you believe me, little one?"

The girl looked up at me, and nodded slowly, clasping the bundle closely to her chest with both hands. "I trust you," she repeated. "Even if Mama says you're an arsehole."

I laughed, shaking the unshed tears from my eyes. "She's no liar. Run along now, little one, or Nan will eat all your peaches and leave you with a crying tummy."

"She won't!" the little girl said, turning and running away from me. "She said she won't ever hurt me!"

"She won't," I agreed, speaking to myself. "I won't either."

56

"Are you staying in for the night?" Glori asked, shutting the door behind me. She'd aged a dozen years in the days since Marin's death and she'd looked old enough to be a grandmother before her granddaughter had been murdered. Not that she knew the details; like everyone else, she thought Marin had tripped and broken her fool neck—I'd made sure only the girl's face was visible beneath the shroud. Glori had cursed Marin's name when I told her, crying even as she said it. Now she looked like the shell of the woman who used to have no trouble giving me the rough side of her tongue when I showed up with my clothes muddied. Her tanned skin had faded until it nearly matched the color of the ribbon tied around her arm.

"I am," I replied, unbuttoning my jacket and handing it to her. I waited for her to comment on the soup stain, but her gaze passed over it without noticing it. "Did I receive any letters?" She shook her head and I bit back a curse. I was right and I'd wished I'd been wrong. Repeating my trick with the street rats and appropriating Sicarii's runners had been a way to test what the Veneficus had let slip, but it seemed they were taking their orders from her as well. Of course, I'd planned for that possibility, but it still didn't make things any easier.

"Thanks, Glori," I told the older woman. "No need to wait up."

"What if sirrah comes home?"

"I told you—" I took a deep breath, swallowing the scalding anger on my tongue. *Her granddaughter died because of you.* For a moment I thought Sin had managed to wriggle free from the mental restraints I'd put in place, but no, the thought was my own. She died because she didn't listen. Marin's mistake had been one I could almost forgive: love. A year ago I'd have called it a weakness, but there was a certain sort of dumb, brute strength in love. Like all mindless muscle, it got you killed, but sometimes it did good before you drew your last breath.

"I told you, Glori," I began again, "Eld isn't coming back. Ever."

"Signorina, if this is because of Marin"—Glori's voice fell to a whisper—"then—"

"It's nothing at all to do with Marin," I lied. "Sometimes friends grow apart, that's all. Just shit timing," I added with a smile I didn't feel. Turns out mixing a lie with the truth does little to dull its bite.

"Signorina?" My eyes flashed and Glori inclined her head. "As you say, signorina. I hope he returns, all the same."

I nodded and strode away before she could see my expression, the echoes of my bootheels chasing after me.

"Hope is the hidden blade against your throat that you never realize is there until it cuts," I whispered. It'd cut me deep enough that if it were real I'd have choked on my own blood. A part of me still wondered if that wouldn't have been the greater mercy. *First, justice.* But that wasn't right. Justice would come, but first: revenge.

First, Sicarii.

There was a mustiness in the air of my bedroom that hadn't been there when I left, accompanied by a whiff of something sharp and metallic. Gunpowder. I let the blade strapped to my wrist beneath my shirtsleeves slide into the palm of my hand as I studied the organized chaos of my room. Books in random piles; plywood boxes with exploding skulls burned into the sides; match cord wound in tight bundles here, cut into pieces there; scattered everywhere, ropes and pulleys lay in coils and tangles. Nothing out of place and yet . . .

As I walked nonchalantly across the room, complaining out loud about the lack of a fire in the middle of winter, I noticed ash stains on the marble floor. I opened the secret passageway to find the Secreto captain lying in a heap, a puzzled look on the half of her face that hadn't taken both barrels of the sawed-off blunderbuss I'd rigged days earlier. The other half was a mess of blood and brains, with a white shard of bone jutting out of the vermillion puddle. Gunpowder hung in the air, stinging my nose and nearly overpowering the sickly sweet, almost rotten stench of brain fluid. The double-barreled 'buss, I saw, was still wedged firmly in place, still hidden from casual inspection

Slipping my blade back into its sheath, I stepped into the passageway and touched the dead woman's outstretched hand. Cool, but not cold. She had known I was coming and meant to wait for me, but she hadn't been following me herself. Lucky she came alone. I stood up and something caught my eye. A scrap of paper, a few paces from her body, just outside the congealed pool of blood.

Her Grace doesn't go where you will . . . you come to her. Do not go to the Lighthouse. Present yourself and the proof you claim to have of Sicarii to her at the Palacio. You have until morning.

    P.S. Lose the bells and wire, our eyes see what Her Grace wills, our ears hear what she wills. Traps and tricks won't stop us.

The sigil of the Secreto was half-pressed into the page, the rest smeared across it as if the hand doing the pressing had been suddenly ripped away.

The hammers of the blunderbuss had been tied back, along with the trigger . . . tied with an impossibly thin line to the trip wire that led to the bell. Cut the wire, and the hammers dropped. *Boom.*

"There are traps and then there are traps," I muttered.

I slid the fireplace back into the wall, realizing for the first time that there was a dinner tray on my nightstand. One of the servants must have been sent up with it while I was still giving Glori my things downstairs. I wasn't hungry. My breasts ached against my gown, and that, combined with the strange unease I felt, had me suspecting my time of the month was coming. Another pleasantry Sin had saved me from. Damnable timing. Then again, it might be that little extra bit of pain and rage I needed to make everything I dreamed reality.

My mind raced with the dozen plans and plots I'd set in motion today; I dug around in my pocket for some kan to ward off an impending headache. I pulled out two rolled papers, felt for more, and bit back a curse. I'd been smoking the stuff practically day and night—it was the only way I'd been able to bring all the disparate bolts of lightning flashing through my mind together into the scheme that I was, Gods be damned, close to pulling off. Now I was almost out.

"If you're going to do this, you're going to need your strength," I whispered.

Setting the kan aside, I sat on the edge of my bed and took the cover off the bowl on the tray, revealing Nan's fish-bone stew. A hunk of bread sat beside it. I ate mechanically, spoon in one hand, the other tapping out a beat on the side of my leg. *Why am I on a knife's edge?* Everything had gone according to plan. Almost everything. I hadn't counted on the Dead Gods and Sin Eaters refusing to leave their sanctuaries. The letters I'd sent in Sicarii's name should see to that. I hoped.

So what had me wanting to stab everything around me and run for the first hole I could find? Beyond my impending period, of course.

"Eld?" I tasted his name on my lips, all bitter with no sweet to chase it. The sharp, stabbing pain I'd felt when I realized the full extent of his betrayal had settled deep into my chest, becoming a dull throb that pulsed with my heart. Hope had fled when I sent him out the door. I was not one for half measures and I think, over the years, I'd converted Eld to the same. When he left, I knew, deep down, that he wasn't coming back. If he tried, I wouldn't let him. So it wasn't Eld.

Sicarii.

I felt a shiver run down my spine. She knew so much about me, almost like she'd crawled inside my head. Somehow she anticipated every move I made and lay in wait. Ambush after ambush, and when I'd finally gone after her and sniffed out her lair, it'd turned out she'd let me win that particular battle so she could make a stab at ending the war.

How?

I set the soup aside and used a candle to puff alight one of the cigarillos. My lungs burned with kan and my thoughts slowed and settled so I could consider what was gold and what was dross. *Sicarii knows me. Knew me before all this started.* The Artificer had told me as much.

"She wants you to suffer, Buc."

I took a drag of kan and blew out a ragged smoke ring, watched it form, then drift apart, my mind plucking at the strands of a tapestry I could just barely make out. She wanted me to suffer, but she had tried to murder me several times over. How hard did she try, really? I grunted. At the time, in the moment, they'd seemed like avid fucking attempts and yet—how close had I really come to dying?

"If Sicarii knows me, then she took that into account," I whispered. "What would I do, if I were trying to kill me?" The first attempt would have to be overwhelming, while my guard wasn't as high. I nodded, sucking down the last of the cigarillo and coughing out a stream of smoke. She wanted me to suffer. "Which means," I said out loud, "that she didn't intend to kill me. Just wound. Or distract?" I ground out the cigarillo.

Only after I'd fended off repeated attempts, tried to chase her down at the Masquerade, and followed up by searching her out had Sicarii changed tactics. She went after Eld through Govanti, and by going after Eld, she went for the heart. *My heart. That's the key to it.* Somehow, Sicarii knew how I felt about Eld and that meant she either knew us before—unlikely—or was fed information by the Chair or the Doga. Or Salina. Given what I'd learned in the last day or so, I was leaning toward the Doga.

Whatever Sicarii wanted, I was only a piece of it. The rest had to tie into the Artificer and the assassination attempts on the Doga—feigned or otherwise—and the unification of the Servenzan underworld. All of that screamed something larger than hurting Sambuciña "Buc" Alhurra.

I knew I was missing something, could see the blank space on the tapestry I'd woven in my mind, but I was damned if I could find it. It was that uncertainty, the unknown that scared me. *That's it. Fear.* Only, the feeling, tight in my chest, wasn't quite fear, it was too swift, too fleeting, here one moment and gone the next, but promising to return. *Panic.* I'd felt fear before, sure, I was no fool, but that fear had been muted by the arrogance of youth. I'd never worried about dying, not really, not when I knew my strengths and saw everyone else's weaknesses. Chan Sha had nearly caught me out on her ship last summer, aye. The Ghost Captain had come closer still, several times over. I'd felt fear there, real fear, but not this sense of impending doom. This heavy, sunken feeling deep within me that pulsed with terror.

"What the fuck are you afraid of losing?"

The question caught me off guard and I slumped back into my chair, considering. I'd lost the children in the factory. I raised a finger. I'd lost the Board, for all intents and purposes. Another finger. Eld and Sin, done in by their own betrayal. Third and fourth. Then . . . that was it. Everything I'd had going for me when we returned from finishing off the Ghost Captain—in two seasons I'd managed to lose it all. Aye, my dream was still there, my promise to Marin and Govanti and the rest, but if I lost my life, those promises might as well have never been made. Which meant . . .

"Nothing." I whispered the word and felt something other than pain or panic shoot through me. "I've got nothing left to lose."

I'd been dancing to Sicarii's tune, letting her call the steps. Now, after everything I'd put into motion, we were playing a new game. One of my choosing, and most deliciously of all: Sicarii had no fucking clue. She thought she was still the composer, still the one with the cards up her sleeves. I chuckled. That was exactly what I wanted her to think. You want to win? Let a person believe you're going to play one game, then play another. Change the rules. Better yet, create them.

I laughed hoarsely.

"Tonight, I deal the cards."

I reached for the last rolled kan paper and hesitated, let it lay there. I didn't need it. I couldn't see everything, but I could see enough.

"And I'm dealing off the bottom."

57

"Signorina, a box was just delivered for you," Glori said, backing into the room. She glanced over her shoulder. "Oh, I thought you were staying in tonight, signorina."

"I am," I lied, studying my reflection in the mirror. "I've an important meeting in the morning and I want to make sure I look my best, so I'm giving a few outfits a try. What do you think?"

"Crimson is very becoming on you," Glori said.

"It is, isn't it?" I buttoned the single button that held the tight-fitting top of the jacket in place; the bottom flared at the waist.

"I worry it's too loose for your frame," Glori added after a moment.

"Wants tailoring," I agreed. It did want tailoring if I was going to walk about like a normal lady. Luckily I'd never been normal and had no intention of starting now. If anything, I hoped it was loose enough for what I needed. "You said there was a package?"

"A rather large box, signorina."

"Where from?"

"The messenger said the stamp was of Normain, signorina."

"Ah, bring it in, then," I said. "I like presents."

Glori glanced around the clutter in my room and sniffed. "I'm not sure where to tell them to put it."

"Beside the bed works," I said, turning back to the mirror and adjusting the stiletto tucked behind my black belt so the hilt was out of sight. "I can use it as a stepping ladder if I need to."

"As you say," Glori said, some of the old fire returning to her voice. Without turning from the mirror, I watched her gesture two of the younger servants into the room; they were carrying a box the size of an armchair. "Place it there," she said, indicating an open spot beside the bed, nearly the last place in the room where one could still see the floor. "Carefully, mind!"

The box still made a dull thump when they set it down. Dust shot from its sides and both men coughed, beating at their jackets as they left.

"Thanks, Glori." I grinned in the mirror. "You can have the night, then, but before you go do you know where my—"

"Knives and slingshot are from your outfit today?" The old woman nodded. "I'll have them sent in, signorina, though I must confess that I don't quite grasp their meaning."

"You don't understand what a stiletto is used for?"

"I don't know why you'd take one to a meeting, is all."

"Oh." I chuckled. "Sometimes I let on it's to make men nervous, other times to intimidate women, but the truth is, Glori"—I turned away from the mirror—"I carry them to remind me that my mind is a blade that can draw blood if I want it to. In the meetings I've been in of late, that's been worth remembering."

"I . . . see." Glori ran a hand through her thinning grey hair and inclined her head to hide the confused look on her face. "If that's all, signorina, I will leave you to open your present."

Once the door was closed behind her, I crossed the room to the wooden box and used a stiletto to work the top free. I'd seen boxes like these before, in Sicarii's lair. The Normain stamp confirmed who it was from. Open, the box contained a mass of metal packed in straw, with a sheaf of papers on top. I snatched them up, revealing gearwork beneath them.

"What in the Gods' names did you bring me?" I whispered, studying the folded metal wings and bits of dark silk jutting out of a bulging backpack.

I riffled through the papers, drawings, and schematics diagrams with arrows and notes in a tiny, cramped hand. I flipped to the last page and saw now-familiar writing.

Buc,

The storm is about to break. Figuratively and literally. Lightning like cannon fire, driving rain, and fog will cover Servenza if my instruments are to be believed. Your bait worked. Both of them. Even with the rain, Sicarii is coming. What's her saying? "The drowned rise." Fitting, given the circumstances. Be wary of her, Buc. You and she may have similar aspirations, but you've always been a lone shark and she has a thousand lives and a crew at her back to support her now.

I've sent what I could . . . not quite what you asked for, but it should do the trick. Read everything I've provided twice! Once you have the fit down, none will know if concealed beneath a loose enough jacket.

Everything is set. On the second ring. I'll see you when it's over, one way or the other.

—Artificer

I turned back to the beginning of the notes and began to see how the disassembled gearwork was meant to fit together. Something about the pages tugged at my mind, but I pushed whatever it was down and turned to study myself in the mirror. I wore a bloodred jacket and trousers of a red so deep they were almost black; my pink undershirt looked like it had been drenched in blood that hadn't quite come out in the wash; and my wide, floppy hat with a feather through the brim gave me a roguish air. Enough, I hoped, to fool any that might see me until it was too late. My eyes looked tired in the light, my skin ashy—I'd been neglecting my creams, but if the Artificer was right, a quick layer over my face and the cold rain would take care of that. I shrugged out of my jacket and reached into the straw, pulling out the harness. According to the diagram, that went on first. Then . . .

I buckled my sword belt on over my other belt, the thick, short blade feeling heavier than I remembered. Between that, the repeating crossbow I'd tied around my shoulder so it hung beneath my armpit, and the gear the Artificer had provided, not to mention my other knives and slingshot, I felt as if I were wearing a diving suit. Luckily, the weight was fairly well distributed so I could move naturally, and with my oversized jacket on top, I looked as if I were moderately plump instead of concealing an armory. I ran through everything in my mind. If I was still alive tomorrow, the steps I'd taken earlier would pay dividends. But first I had to make it to tomorrow. First, I had to survive Sicarii.

I'd made my plans with one idea in mind: revenge. I'd gone over the Artificer's notes multiple times, sure I was missing something, but whatever it was, he'd given me enough to have a fighting chance. A faint one, but real nonetheless. The word "hope" flitted through my mind and I stomped on it, hard. Sicarii had all the gangs of Servenza at her beck and call. She had plenty of the Artificer's toys, too, and more besides: she knew me; I didn't know her. Knowing your enemy was as important as knowing the ground one fought on. Since I didn't have the one, I'd have to settle for the other.

Thunder rumbled in the distance. Best get to it. I stepped around boxes and over match cord and slid the fireplace away, again revealing the dead Secreto captain and the passageway beyond. I'd have to remove the body soon or it would attract rats, but it'd keep for the moment. She was staring at me with her one good eye. *Stare all you want, you won't be warning the Doga, which means Sicarii won't see this coming. Until I want her to.* Thunder rumbled again, louder, shaking the palazzo. Even with the oil worked into the leather of my jacket, I was going to be soaked through in minutes.

The drowned rise.

Sicarii's catchphrase made me pause halfway in the passage, something tickling the back of my mind. Frowning, I retraced my steps to the Artificer's notes, pulling out the page with his letter.

The drowned rise. Fitting, given the circumstances. *Be wary of her, Buc. You may both have similar aspirations, but you've always been a lone shark and she has a thousand lives and a crew at her back to support her now.*

"'She has a thousand lives,'" I whispered. "'And a crew at her back to support her now.' Thousand lives. Crew." Electricity shot through me, making my skin break out in gooseflesh. I would have fallen if I hadn't caught myself against the bed as a dozen epiphanies slammed together in my mind in a violent storm of realization. I knew who Sicarii was. I knew my enemy.

"You." My voice was harsh, ragged as the breath in my lungs. "You," I repeated. I stood up, let my hand caress the hilt of one of my blades, and growled. "The drowned rise, but do they burn?" I wasn't sure, but I meant to find out.

"I'm coming, bitch."

58

I watched shadows flitting across rooftops through my spyglass. Gears hissed as I twisted the aperture, intensifying its focus until I could see a figure, rope coiled over one shoulder, grasping a chimney to hold position in the wind. A gust sent another sprawling behind the first. The Artificer had claimed the telescope could see in the dark, drawing in light from the stars and moon overhead, but with the storm rolling in like a heavy-handed behemoth, the night sky was a smear of black paint. Full dark, no stars. Still, the scope was better than the naked eye, albeit less effective than if I let Sin free. I felt him stir in my mind and quashed him before he could try anything. When I stood up from behind the pillar I'd been using as both shield from the wind and perch for my glass, the storm's tendrils whipped around me, tugging at my jacket and playing with my loosely braided hair.

Servenza's Lighthouse was a massive gearwork contraption, wrought decades before, when Ciris wormed her way into the Kanados Trading Company with gifts of technology and mages. It towered above the city, fully three buildings taller than the nearest prayer houses of the Kneeling Quarto. Shining nearly all day and night, in almost any weather, lit by the sun or flames and using mirrors to twist and amplify its light. Its lanterns were dead now—no one was foolish enough to weigh anchor in a breaker of a storm like the one approaching, and being up this high, exposed to the elements, wasn't worth the danger. Unless you were me.

I stalked across the top of the Lighthouse, then jumped down from the brick-lined lip that ran around the edge, a full head and shoulders taller than the sundial that lay atop of the Lighthouse's lantern house. The gears within the contraption strapped to my back clicked together. I put my hand through the leather straps and adjusted it so it sat evenly between my shoulder blades. Running my hand along an hour marker, I stepped onto the sundial's face. Until tonight, I'd no idea there was a sundial up here. I wagered none but sailors and the guild who kept the Lighthouse knew. I guess I shouldn't have been surprised that the Gods would create a thing of beauty that could be enjoyed by few while the masses begged for scraps below.

Still, it had its uses. I bent down and ran my thumb carefully along a trip wire that ran from the brick wall to the hour marker. I'd inspected the rest, but between the wind and occasional rain, I was taking no chances. Satisfied, I marched across the roof toward the gnomon in the center. I'd wondered what that was, thrusting up into the sky from the Lighthouse's roof, the few times I'd had occasion to leave Servenza and return. It was one of the highest points in the city, along with the Doga's Palacio, the Castello, and the Dead Gods' cathedral. It was impossible to miss, and nearly as impossible to get to, which is why I'd chosen it for the battle to come. Discovering the sundial had given me answers to one of the questions plaguing me: how to defeat a crew when I was a crew of but one?

Sicarii had numbers, aye, but by forcing her to come to the Lighthouse, I controlled the territory, which meant I had a shot of controlling the flow of what was to come. She'd have to split her gangs up so as to not attract the attention of any who weren't under her thumb while her forces were clambering across rooftops to reach the only entrance that was accessible from the outside. They could have broken into the building and taken the internal stairs, but she'd taken care to remain anonymous to the populace at large, so I'd a feeling she would not attempt such a public act. Instead, her gangs would do as I had done, using the ladders that ran up the outside of the tower on either side, which afforded access to the lantern room and the rooftop above. In so doing, her forces would be slowed, giving me the time I needed to work my magic. Sinless, but magic of a kind nonetheless.

The wind caught at my cloak and made my eyes tear. I let my hands travel across the hilts of my blades, slingshot, and crossbow, eyes fixed on the spot that would tell me when Sicarii arrived. Lightning rent the sky from horizon to horizon, followed by the rocking boom of cascading thunder. Still, beyond a few drops, the storm held itself at bay, as if holding its breath for what was to come. As well it should, because if half went as I planned, Servenza would never forget tonight. Neither would Sicarii. It'd be her last night on earth.

I waited. And waited. The wind's howl grew in pitch, raindrops slapped me in the face, and lightning turned night into day. Sicarii didn't come. I was just beginning to wonder if I hadn't made a mistake when I saw a white ribbon flash, dancing on a wire in the dark. Someone had tripped my first wire. More ribbons waved along the lip of the brick wall, warning me that Sicarii had sent some of her crew up the other set of stairs. I felt my mouth creep toward a smile. I hadn't dared hope for that, and yet . . .

Your first mistake.

A few moments later a small figure, likely a child, appeared at the head of the stairs directly across from me at the far end of the Lighthouse's roof two score paces away. They glanced around and, though I couldn't see a signal, must have given one, for then a pair of men, hulking brutes who towered in the darkness, appeared. Between them stood another who kept them on their toes; as they advanced, each giant glanced frequently at the one they escorted. Lightning crashed, illuminating the hooded figure, and I knew, in my bones, who it was.

Sicarii.

I stepped out from where I stood in the shadow of the dial and Sicarii and her henchmen stopped. Other figures darted up the stairs and fanned out behind them. A dozen, then two score, then more, many more, until they filled the space behind the leaders, who had remained still the whole time. At last they moved toward me, the hooded figure first, the henchmen beginning to follow, then stopping at some gesture I missed in the darkness.

Sicarii walked with a slight limp, her left leg lurching after her right. She kept walking until we were a dozen paces apart, the only sound that of wind and rain and lightning and thunder growing ever closer. Slowly, she spread her arms high and wide, tilting her head.

"You're not wearing a dress," I called.

"Dress?"

"Aye, at the Masquerade? You said we both wanted revenge and that a red dress wouldn't be amiss either."

"Ah, but my jacket's red, as are my trousers, and that will do," Sicarii shouted back, her rasping voice cracking on the final word. She dug into her jacket and pulled out a letter. "You're not the Doga come to parley either."

"Aye, but I've a blade with a name on it and that will do," I said.

"Sambuciña 'Buc' fucking Alhurra," Sicarii said, her voice like the sound of a spade across a coffin. "Always a blade and a mind of where to stick it." She shook her head and chuckled, but there was nothing funny about the sound. "Like a mule-headed fool, but then again, if you kept your mind on things other than a knife, perhaps we wouldn't be standing here this night."

"I'm not sure I agree with that. My mind brought me here, and you as well. Right where I wanted you."

"If the Doga wanted to meet with me, she would have had me to her Palacio." She tore the letter into pieces and let the wind carry it away. "As she's done many times before," Sicarii said.

"So you admit collusion?"

"She'd own to the term, but is it collusion if I was the one calling the shots?" Sicarii shrugged beneath her flaring jacket, the ends flailing around in the wind. Twisting her head again, she

432 • Ryan Van Loan

took half a step toward me and paused. "You want revenge, don't you, Buc?"

"I want to draw steel 'cross your throat, sure."

"Of course you do," she said, nodding. "That's why you're here. Why you thought to lure me here to this Godsforsaken Lighthouse. I understand it," she added, clasping her hands together. "None better. Up here, to have your revenge for all to see if they would but raise their eyes." Her laugh sent a chill down my spine. "You of all people should know. In Servenza, none raise their eyes very far. They've learned the lesson of the Doga and the Company long ago: eyes down and live, eyes up and die."

The gang members behind her growled, a few throwing their weapons up into the air. Sicarii silenced them with the wave of a hand.

"You want to kill me, Buc?" she asked. "You'll have your chance, I promise you that. But before you do, don't you think you ought to know why you want me dead so desperately?"

"I think I've an idea," I said dryly.

"Half of one, at any rate, but half measures aren't your style, aye?" She laughed and spread her arms again. "Come closer and let me paint you the full portrait. No? You'll make me lose this rusted-out voice, shouting?"

"My heart bleeds."

"If it does, it's because I fucking pricked it," Sicarii hissed. "You returned to Servenza the hero, thought you had your whole damned future in front of you. You and that brute beside you, but you didn't reckon with me."

"Reckon with a gnarled, washed-up wreck of a ship that has to hide behind cloaks and darkness?" I shrugged. "Not worth my time."

"No doubt, no doubt," Sicarii said, pacing back and forth in front of me. She glanced at me and I saw a glowing eye staring from beneath her hood. "The children weren't either, eh? Not worth your time?"

"What children?" I felt my chest tighten.

"The ones that you burned alive," Sicarii hissed.

"I didn't do that."

"Of course you did," she snapped. "You owned that factory, owned the schematics, owned the child labor, and I'm here to tell you, you own the blame, for all of it."

I wobbled on my feet. My nostrils filled with the smell of ash and soot and flame as images flashed through my mind. Of the little boy I'd tried to save and the countless others I hadn't. Of Sister.

Sicarii jabbed a hand toward me. "My eyes and ears told me what a wreck you were in the aftermath. Cramming so much machinery together—it was sure to catch fire eventually. I just helped it along."

"You?" It wasn't my fault. I knew that wasn't quite true: I'd never thought to ask if they were using children on the floor, I had plenty of blame to shoulder, but I hadn't condemned them to death. The weight that had pushed me to the edge of insanity—killing the ones I'd thought to save—slid from my back. Onto the scale of my revenge on Sicarii.

"Me," she purred. "I set the spark that burned your mind. I dripped poison into the Doga's ears, turning her from an erstwhile antagonist into a willing ally. She practically gave me the streets and never blinked when I took her Constabulary besides. Through her, I bought half the Company's shareholders and blackmailed the rest to pressure the Chair."

"That's why the Chair wouldn't bend no matter the machinations I came up with," I muttered. I'd thought Sicarii a step ahead of me this whole time, but I'd been wrong. She was two steps ahead. Doubt seeped in. *If that's true, did I plan this or am I still dancing on her strings?*

"Precisely. It was amusing, watching you struggle from afar, unaware that the path you trod was one I laid, cobblestone by cobblestone, all leading to misery and defeat." Sicarii's eye burned brighter, as if feeding on the fire in her voice. "I'd have killed you already, but I wanted you to suffer the full measure before you breathed your last. And . . . I confess you've something I covet."

"Two eyes?" I asked.

"You always were an insolent cunt. But tell me, girl, how did it feel to watch Eld burn to death trying to save one of your little fish. Another child you couldn't save?"

"Motherfucker," I breathed.

"That was all me," Sicarii growled, mistaking my reaction.

She doesn't know.

Something eased within me. I hadn't murdered those children and while Sicarii knew me better than should have been possible, she didn't understand me at my core. True, Sicarii had won most of the battles thus far. I'd known that when I'd drawn my plans up—that I was facing an adversary that was perhaps the most formidable I'd ever encountered. Which, after last summer, was saying something. But—But I hadn't realized I was even fighting a war until recently and that had given her several advantages, since removed.

Still, I wasn't a fool. I was without Eld, without Sin, vastly outnumbered, and Sicarii seemed to have a preternatural sense of what I would do before I did it. Only, she'd just proved herself fallible, and if she had made one mistake, and a rather large one in the scheme of things, then she was capable of making more. I was only too happy to show her how. *I have a chance.*

"I cut that stupid girl's throat, as a party favor of sorts," she continued. "The rest, I improvised." Her voice dropped low, like a guttering flame. "Did he go up all at once or in spurts?"

Another mistake.

"At first," I said, ignoring the joy in her voice, "I thought the Doga was behind the Serpent's Flame trap on Govanti. Or else the Company." I shook my head. "They didn't understand the depth of my friendship with Eld, though, not really. Certainly not enough to ken how important his life is to me. Salina, perhaps, but I knew it wasn't her."

"You're not unintelligent, in your own way," Sicarii acknowledged.

"Truth is, Eld and I haven't been all that close these past few seasons. I'm sure you know that," I added, the smile frozen on my face. Inside, I was a violent inferno, a volcano of epic proportions, waiting to explode and rain molten revenge down on the lot of them. These were merely the tremors before the eruption.

"The Company's seen firsthand that we aren't close now. The Gods?" I shrugged. "If they wished us dead, they've had the opportunity more than once. I admit, your trap had me flummoxed." I took a breath and steadied my shoulders. *Now*. It was time.

"The only other two who saw Eld and me close enough to know the depths of our friendship died last summer. One's a rotting skeleton on a Godsforsaken flyspeck of an island and the other washed out to sea.

"But the drowned rise . . . don't they, Chan Sha?"

Chan Sha recoiled as if struck. She swept an arm out and pointed at me. "I could have killed you a dozen times over, but you've something you stole from me. A gift you never deserved, one you squandered to be rich and noble, to be one of them. I came to Servenza to take what was taken from me, from all of you! The Empire, the Company, the Gods, Eld, and you." Her voice broke. "I'll have my revenge," she growled.

She tossed off her hooded jacket and sank into a crouch. Lightning rent the night sky, showing her hair, shorn tight against her skull, and gearwork rising over her back. She flung her arms out and metal limbs shot out from the gearwork, scything blades hanging over her like spiders' fangs.

"But first I'll pry Sin from your mind with my own hands!"

Thunder rolled across her words and as the skies opened above us, she thrust her arms up into the air.

"Make her bleed!"

59

The gangs of Servenza rushed across the Lighthouse, howling their battle cries, lightning flashes glinting off scores of weapons. All pointed at me. They'd been fanning out while Sicarii and I spoke and now sprinted toward me in a semicircle. Right into the trip wires I'd set. Number 219. *Pyrotechnomancy, Maestros of Powder and Flame* was a book I'd read a few years back, though luckily I'd recently procured a copy for my library at my palazzo. I'd never had a chance to put it to use . . . until tonight.

The face of the sundial erupted in hissing flames that leapt up in gouts, turning the front rank of my enemies into a screaming, writhing mass of human torchwood. Their charge faltered, howls lost in the thunder above. The flames caught the match cord I'd interlaced around some of the time markings, and the floor exploded in a violent burst of gunpowder that sent bodies flying.

I saw all of this in my peripheral vision; my focus remained on Chan Sha. Her glowing eye shifted down, likely marking the smoking match cord at her feet. One of the brutes beside her tackled her just as the nail-filled keg exploded. Damn it. The Lighthouse shuddered; I lost my footing on the rain-swept tile and smacked my head off the gilded gnomon. Blinking back tears, I saw the other brute disappear in a blast of flame and iron—what was left fell to the ground in ragged, smoking pieces. All around the sundial explosions rent the air as the first waves were eviscerated.

A pause in the storm above gave way to an eerie silence atop the Lighthouse—the first wave of traps were spent and the gangs were still gathering themselves back together. Howls, snarls, and gunfire rose from the streets below and a lookout shouted from the stairwell.

"Sicarii—mages are fighting in the streets! Veneficus and Sin Eaters. They're surrounding the Lighthouse!"

"Well, that didn't go according to plan," I muttered. I'd sent letters to both the Sin Eaters and the Dead Gods, hoping that one side or the other would show up and I could use the knowledge they wanted as a bargaining chip to get them to fight Sicarii's crew for me. Apparently both groups had arrived and were now busy killing themselves below rather than up here. Damn it.

"You've started a holy war," Sin said, his voice loud in mind.

"How the fuck did you get free?"

"Bumped your head and I slipped out," he said. "Buc, what have you done?"

"The war was going on since Ciris woke."

"Not like this. Always proxies before."

"Sicarii set this in motion when the Veneficus killed those Sin Eaters."

"Do you know what this means?" he asked, ignoring me. "Open warfare will push the whole world into blood and flame."

"You always knew my plans," I reminded him. "Hush now, I don't have time to lock you back up. I don't want your magic."

"Buc—"

The gangs were more cautious this time, a few of the Sharp Eagles leveling muskets with impossibly long scopes, and here and there I saw versions of the Artificer's crossbow pointed at me. The rest walked forward, watching where they put their feet. A muzzle erupted in flame, a bullet whined past my ear, and I didn't stick around to see the rest. Flinging myself backward, I vaulted over the edge of the sundial as more gunfire rang out. Bolts caromed off the metal and ran screeching into the storm.

I tore around the side, hands going for my own crossbow. I hadn't dared plant more explosives this close to the dial, not unless I wanted to take the entire roof down, and me with it. My breath was in my throat as I came around the backside of the dial just in time to see the first gang members, running now, hit the wires I'd rigged with razors and oil. A woman went down with a scream and another behind her went arse over heels, her screams cut off when the ones running behind her trampled her.

It was chaos.

Rain and thunder providing a ragged chorus, lightning illuminated everything in flashes: men and women sliding on the oil-slick roof, breaking arms and ankles as their compatriots ran them over; others found their limbs flayed by razors strung across their path. In moments half the sundial was covered in blood and oil. I jumped on top of one of the hour markers and leveled my crossbow.

"You want me? Come and take me!"

The weapon jerked in my arms and a tall man with a ragged patchwork cloak flapping in the wind twisted and fell. The woman behind him, in a bright-white jacket and trousers, clasped her face as if she'd been bitten. A man's head snapped back in a spurt of blood and motion. My fingers worked the trigger, finding a rhythm: *tat-draw string-load bolt-tat-draw string-load bolt-tat*. The gears whistled with sharp puffs of air as I poured bolts into the attackers. *Click click click*. I plucked the now-empty cylinder from beneath the bow and flung it at the mob, now only a score of paces away. I grabbed another cylinder from my belt and snapped it into place.

I worked the trigger as fast my fingers would go, and the dead and wounded began to pile up in front of me, funneled together by the sundial's arm on one side and the lip of the roof on the other. As fast as I shot, more came running, urged on by Chan Sha's hoarse, maniacal shouts. I dropped another cylinder and loaded my last one. These weren't soldiers and I'd hoped they would break, but I was just a lone woman and they were fool enough to think they could kill me. I hadn't wagered on their fear of Chan Sha–Sicarii either. They weren't going to stop unless I was dead or they were.

Or Sicarii was.

Lightning hit the jutting rod above the stairs, returning the world to daylight in a hissing crack of electricity, and a moment later the Lighthouse shook violently. My world flipped and I lost my grip on the crossbow as I fell, slamming off the sundial's face. The hilt of my sword buried itself in my side and I felt something crack. Pushing myself back up, I saw Serpent's Flame leap into the night from across the roof, telling me that the match cord I'd wound around the lightning rod and down the far staircase had finally reached the bombs there. With luck, the rubble would block the landing and cut off further reinforcements.

"Artificer!"

Chan Sha came to her feet, shoving aside the dead henchman who'd shielded her from the earlier blast, screaming the Artificer's name again and again the whole way up. She wobbled on her feet, then shook her arms, flexing gloved fingers that glinted with burnished alloys. The gearwork mechanism on her back hissed as the metallic arms rose around her, blades spinning in the storm light once again.

"It seems I need a word with my inventor," she growled. "What are you lot waiting for?" Her spiders' fangs waved them forward. "Kill the bitch!"

"Hey! That's my line!" I shouted.

Chest heaving, I sprinted around the sundial and ran right into a mob waving cudgels and cutlasses, spears and stilettos. A pistole went off in my face, the heat and light blinding me, and I felt something rip at my jacket. A familiar burn coursed through my eyes and time began to slow.

NO!

"You don't get to control me anymore," I growled, pushing Sin away.

Time leapt back and with it came a man and woman charging ahead of the rest. I drew my short, thick-bladed sword without thinking. Even without Sin's magic, I had muscle memory to fall back on and if I didn't move as swiftly as I did with him, I moved fast enough to bury the blade in the man's chest, riding him down to the ground so the woman's wild swing cut only air above me. Grasping her boot, I pulled hard, throwing myself back to make up for my lack of strength. Her head slapped off the ground like a rotted melon and she sat up slowly with a moan. I was already up, pulling my sword free, and I buried it in her neck, blinking at the sudden warm blood that peppered my face. She fell back, pulling my sword out of my hands, and I had no chance to recover it because another dozen were racing toward me.

"Gods—damn—it," I gasped, my limbs on fire. I couldn't keep this up. There were too many of them. *Have to get to Sicarii.* Shedding my jacket, I pulled a knotted rope and the half-dozen pistoles I'd tied against my side swung loose, hanging on cords that attached to the Artificer's gearwork machine on my back. *Thanks for the idea, Chan Sha.*

I caught one and leveled it, hesitating until a woman in a sleeveless vest filled the front sight, then squeezed, closing my left eye to protect some of my vision. The pistole leapt in my fist and her head disappeared in flame and smoke. The barrels whizzed, whipping over, and I fired again. Dropping the empty pistole, I caught up another and fired. Again. And again. And again until they broke, leaving me, for a brief moment, in command of the field.

Wheezing, I drew twin stilettos, blades a palm longer than I normally used, but razor thin; they wouldn't tire my arms like my sword had and they'd give me the reach I needed to keep from getting stabbed to death while going for the wench. At least that was the plan. Drawing a deep breath that made my injured ribs scream, I took off in pursuit of the ones who had fled.

In pursuit of Chan Sha.

60

The storm unleashed its full fury as I ran, thumb-sized hail pelting down, wind lashing at everyone atop the Lighthouse, lightning the only illumination. Thanks to the remaining trip wires, which were still being sprung, and the havoc I'd already caused, Chan Sha's gangs had lost all cohesion. I was just another shadow in the chaos—but one with steel teeth—and I danced amongst the gearwork and markers, ducking and weaving in a pattern I'd created for this occasion.

The problem was, my dance partners were too many.

I slammed into a man who was more a boy and he grunted, trying to scream, but I already had a stiletto in each lung and all that came out was a blood-filled, frothy gurgle. I stepped back and he collapsed, leaving me just enough time to reverse my grip and rip off half of a woman's face with one slash before she tripped over the boy's body and her head met my knee. I leapt over them, knee clicking as I ran, taking a wide loop around the sundial to try to come at Chan Sha from the side, if not behind. In the next minutes I took a slashing wound to the leg, had a woman bury a small knife in my calf before I killed her with it, plugged both wounds with pistole patches and scraps of linen, took another cut to the forearm, and nearly lost the gearwork on my back to a pair of ax-wielding women who, in a lightning flash, looked enough alike to be sisters.

Here and there gunfire blasted through the hail and rain, but how anyone could see more than a few paces in front of them to aim, I didn't know. With all the different gangs involved, old enmities ran deep and if Chan Sha wasn't careful, she was going to have a civil war on her hands. She seemed to have the same realization at nearly the same moment because I heard a change in the tone of her screamed orders, but she'd have to have the Gods' luck to be understood over the maelstrom. My hair was plastered to the side of my face, my eyes reduced to slits to keep some modicum of vision, and my oil-treated leather garments were soaked through and clung to me like a diver's suit.

A tall woman with only one pant leg appeared out of the storm and plowed right into me. I went down and her weight drove the breath from me as my ribs screamed. I managed to drive a boot into her crotch so hard that I heard her yelp above the wind and rain. She rose, sword in hand, but before she could strike, something hit her in the head and she fell in a heap. I took a breath and the pain was exquisite. Spots flecked my vision, the world around me growing hazy.

"Buc!" Sin's voice snapped me back to reality. A reality filled with lancing pain in my leg and fiery tendrils down my arm. "Buc, get up or you're as good as dead!"

"I told you to shut the fuck up," I growled, stumbling to my feet. I drew in a ragged gasp, then bent and collected the blades I'd dropped in the collision. The dead woman had a hole in her head but I didn't have time to thank whomever shot her instead of me. Another dance like that one and I'd be out of the fight. I had to find Chan Sha now.

"If you didn't have me trying to stitch you back together from the inside out, you wouldn't be able to stand right now, let alone fight Chan Sha. Let me help!"

"No." I shook my head. "I'd rather die my own woman than live as an unwitting servant to you."

"That's not how it works," he protested. "You never gave me a chance to explain."

"There's nothing to explain," I told him. "You have your nature, I have mine. Now. Fuck. Off."

"Stupid, stubborn, silly woman—you're going to get us both killed!"

"Aye, likely," I agreed, taking off at a lurching run. "But first I'mma kill Chan Sha. Let's dance!"

I cut down another group, with sigils of tridents I didn't recognize, collecting another slash across my arm, higher up and deep enough to expose muscle. I lost one stiletto to a fat bastard's prodigious stomach and snatched up a boarding cutlass as a quick replacement. It weighed a ton but once I got it started, the weight of the blade took care of things. Thrice when someone got the drop on me, someone else got the drop on them, leaving them lying in crumpled heaps with holes through their heads. The first two times I thought it an accident, but after that, I wasn't so sure. Perhaps someone was using the battle to settle their own scores. *S-so long as it's not me, I don't care.* My breathing howled in my ears like a wild beast beset by hounds; my chest was fire, my leg fire, my arms bloody with stinging cuts. All was pain and I used it to deliver the message of the streets: when someone hurts you, spread the pain.

61

A woman punched me in the side; I had been focused on finding Chan Sha and hadn't even tried to shield myself from the blow. I couldn't keep the cry behind my lips when my abused ribs cracked again. Her wicked grin disappeared as the cutlass she hadn't seen coming crashed through her skull and I laughed as she fell, because if I didn't, I'd have cried from the pain. There was something warm on my lips and when I scrubbed at my mouth with the back of my hand, it came away bloody. Breathing was suddenly a real effort.

"She wore brass knuckles and broke your ribs. You've got a pierced lung," Sin whispered. "Please let me help."

"Fuck off," I said mindlessly. "I need to find Chan Sha!"

"Find her you have!"

Chan Sha leapt down from the gnomon's tip, her followers scattering to give her room to land. When she stood up, she spread her arms, and the mechanical limbs sprouting from her back spread with them, scything blades bright in the flashes of lightning. She looked wilder than she had when this all started and blood dripped from her clothes, but I didn't dare hope it was all her own. The entire roof was a charnel house, blood, oil, and water coating everything in a thousand tones of crimson.

"No more words, Buc. Blades only."

She swept toward me and I leapt to meet her, sending a stiletto at her face with an underhanded toss that she deflected with one of her mechanical arms without breaking stride. I drew my longer stiletto with my left hand, steadied the heavy cutlass in my right, and did the only thing I could do: attack.

Muscle memory is an underrated thing. In the months with Sin I'd practiced for hours—it was, truth be told, rather easy. Muscles that never tired, bones that didn't break, and a mind that remembered everything. I could learn entire books of fighting techniques in half a fortnight, committing them to memory with Sin. Despite Sin having returned, he couldn't do anything but seethe without my permission. I was going to fail on my own terms rather than win on his. I didn't have a God's strength and speed, but I had the memories, in muscle and mind, and in the first moments that was almost enough.

Sliding around one of Chan Sha's gearwork arms and its questing blade, I sent another reverberating back toward her face and followed in low, blades flashing. I tried first one pattern, then another, seeking the soft flesh behind her metallic spiders' fangs. Sparks flew up, hissing in the rain, but now that I was in close, I didn't have just the gearwork to deal with. Chan Sha's twin dirks punched toward me and it was all I could do to keep from being run through. If I had memories, she had memories, too.

We broke apart then, one of her gearwork limbs dragging on the sundial behind her, more sparks trailing in its wake. I had taken another wound, across my other thigh, not deep, but painful and worrying: I was losing too much blood to keep this up for much longer. I drew in a harsh breath, then another, and she attacked again and this time I merely tried to survive.

My blades moved like whipcords, my mind directing them without thought. *Parry here, block there, twist and fall back, sidestep— stumble, thrust.* It wasn't enough. I was driven back, heart screaming in my throat, lungs unable to draw full breath, every rattling gasp flecking my lips with blood. Chan Sha crowed, rushed forward— and slipped, and I nearly took her head off with my cutlass, instead shearing through the metallic appendage she managed to throw up just in time. The cutlass was ripped from my hand so I punched her instead, right in her false eye.

"Ouch!"

"Burns, doesn't it?" she gasped, stumbling backward a dozen paces.

"How?" I shook my hand. It felt like I'd punched a live coal.

"Magic."

"F-fuck your magic," I said, my words loud as the storm suddenly ceased save for a soft drizzle and now-distant thunder.

"Speaking of . . . where's yours at?" Chan Sha asked, reaching up and adjusting her glowing eye. "Surely you're better than this? Or did you blow your load killing all of my crew?"

"Saving it all for your pretty face," I told her.

"Then let's see it," Chan Sha growled, dropping into her familiar crouch.

Only half of her limbs were still working, but I'd begun to wonder if I could have taken her with Sin, let alone without. My arms were wooden, barely willing to listen to my exhortations to fight; my good lung was beginning to feel heavy, too, and the rest of me was all pain and fire. I didn't have much left to give. This was it. The final charge.

I'll die . . . but you first.

A clanging sound drew both our eyes. Three of them, anyway. A hook wrapped around a chunk of iron hit the lip of the rooftop and rolled to a stop; a braided hawser line led up into the dark sky. A moment later a broad figure slid down the cable, tricorne tumbling from his head and strawberry-blond locks spilling out to frame a familiar face.

Eld.

"It's good to see you, Buc," he said with a grin that sounded genuine, but in the bit of starlight that was beginning to peek out, I could see the lines of strain on his face. "Is that our old pal Chan Sha I spy?"

"Still making bad jokes, I see," she growled.

"Aye, but none as bad a joke as you are. Revenge? For what?" He snorted, moving forward at an oblique angle so that he got closer to me without seeming to walk much at all. Lightning flashed and I saw a massive balloon up above, air venting from half a dozen holes as the sides sank in on itself. The line Eld had roped in began to quiver and the lump of iron screeched as it was pulled toward the edge. Eld paid it no mind, just kept walking. As he drew closer, I saw the long musket strapped to his back, with a telescope attached to the barrel, and suddenly realized who'd been felling those who would have done for me if he hadn't done for them first.

"Go kill your Goddess if you want revenge," he said, sliding the heavy rifle into his arms.

"You sound like her," Chan Sha said.

"I learned from the best," he said simply.

"If that were true, then you wouldn't be about to die, wasting your fool life on a Godsforsaken roof fighting a war that few will know of and none will care about."

"Some things are worth dying for," Eld said. He tossed the musket up in the air, caught it by the barrel, and swung around, letting it fly—

"Friends are one of them!"

—straight at Chan Sha.

"Then die, both of you," Chan Sha said, sweeping her hands in front of her. Her remaining metallic arms crossed, catching the heavy musket and sending it spinning away. The blow clearly damaged the arms, which now hung uselessly. She waved her gang forward. "Kill him! Bring her to me! And someone get me another Spider!"

She disappeared in the horde that surged around her, clamoring for our blood. Eld drew his sword, swept me up in his free arm, and ran, with the remains of the gangs of Servenza hard on our heels. It should have hurt. It did hurt, a little, but the pain was a pinprick, overwhelmed by the warmth that suffused me. I'd

been alone for most of my life and then, when I'd thought I was
alone no longer and secure in that feeling, I'd had that taken from
me as well. Now, against all odds, I wasn't alone anymore. I had
Eld.

"Any ideas?" Eld gasped.

"I thought you had one, since you swept me off my feet."

"Well, you didn't look up to running," he said. "And my ride
seems to have sunk," he added, as the balloon contraption disappeared below the roof of the Lighthouse, heading for the canals
below. "But if I keep going in this circle, we're going to run into
the other end of them."

"There." I pointed in the growing starlight. "By the edge of the
gnomon. There's a bit of a blind corner there. If we can stop them
there, turn them, we can make for the edge of the roof. I have a—"

"Plan," he finished. "Aye, I know." He flashed me a grin, his
blue eyes warm in the darkness. "You always do, Buc. All right,
here we go."

Setting me down carefully, Eld swung his sword back and forth,
adjusting his grip and rolling his shoulders. As the pounding feet
came nearer, he casually drew a short, four-barreled pistole from
the pocket of his powder-blue jacket. As the frontrunners rounded
the now-pitted edge of the sundial, he fired. A man screamed,
clutching at his face; the figures on either side of him crumpled
completely. Eld rushed forward, sword flashing, and I swapped
my cutlass for my slingshot, shoving the blade through my belt.

One. Two. It took everything I had to draw it back, the steel
bands reinforcing the wood proving too strong for me unless I
threw my full weight backward, stretching and releasing in one
motion. It was awkward, but effective. *Seven. Eight.* Eld stood
like a stone against the incoming tide, breaking all upon him. I
searched out the few rogue waves that escaped and snuffed them
out. *Fourteen. Fifteen.* My arms screamed. Not my arms. Sin.

"He needs you, Buc!"

I let the slingshot fall and saw Sin was right: the tide was proving too much. Eld was being forced to move back. He fought it, moving no more than a pace at a time, his sword a blur, but he was growing slower with each swing. I dropped the slingshot into my pocket and drew the cutlass, needing both hands to keep it steady.

"I'm coming, Eld!"

He must have heard me, because he danced back a few paces, turned, and then moved so that he could protect my right while the gnomon shielded my left. I lurched into a run and slammed into the burly man who was trying to lay Eld's face open with a claw hammer. We both screamed, but his was louder as I laid him open from clavicle to bulging stomach. I rebounded and somehow Eld caught me with one hand while wielding his sword in the other. I steadied myself and then set to, both of us going at it hammer and tongs.

Our enemies swarmed around us and in moments we became an island surrounded by howling, screaming masses eager for our heads. Eld and I were back-to-back. He drew a pistole and fired it point-blank into the crowd, the rotating barrel affording him a quick second shot that opened up enough space around us for a momentary respite.

"We have to get to the edge of the roof," I gasped out.

"Then what?" he asked, drawing another pistole from a pocket in his coat. "I told you, my ride's sunk."

"Then, we jump."

"Free-fall suicide?"

"No, we fly."

Eld shot me a look to see if I was serious. I was, sort of, but I wasn't sure if it would work, not with the two of us.

"You have to trust me."

"Of course I trust you." His face lit up with a smile. "Always have; always will."

The tide surged around us again and we fought, backs pressed together, slowly working our way, step-by-step, toward the far edge of the roof, each pace paid for in blood. I found myself facing half a dozen men wearing those fucking chain-mail jackets of the Krakens. Knowing I had no energy left to swing my cutlass, I elbowed Eld.

"Pistoles and switch."

"Catch!"

Eld tossed a pair of pistoles over his shoulder and I dropped the cutlass, catching the weapons by their barrels. Flipping them, I fired, felt them buck in my fists. Smoke and flame obscured my vision as Eld and I spun in a tight circle, keeping our backs together. When the smoke cleared, the Krakens would find themselves facing a relatively fresh swordsman instead of a tired, ice-picking woman. The barrels hissed as they swung over, gears grinding, turning fresh barrels into place. I fired the one in my left hand and saw a woman sit down hard, her chest bloody, then took off the top of a man's head; he fell, tripping another man.

The swirling mass of humanity facing us surged forward. Suddenly Eld hurled his sword like a spear, making everyone flinch, and leapt up onto a pile of bodies. He shed his jacket, revealing massive, twin rotating blunderbusses with pistole grips—they were tied around each shoulder so they'd hung beneath his armpits. Eld whipped them up into firing position, their large barrels looking more like cannon-pistoles.

"Who wants to die next?" he roared.

"Shockingly few takers," I muttered, my voice loud in the silence.

A blunderbuss at this range was a fearsome thing, easily capable of tearing someone limb from limb or crippling a dozen people with each shot. And Eld had eight of them between the two weapons.

Growing up on the streets, death was a constant companion and a cheap one at that, which is why so many joined the gangs and why so many had been willing to die tonight. Still, there's catching a blade in the chest and then there's having your arm sawed off by hot lead. One you can wrap your mind around; the other haunts your nightmares. Judging by the silence and lack of motion, those still standing had vivid imaginations.

"Kill the pair!" Chan Sha's howl filled the silence, drawing every eye to where she once again stood atop the gnomon's point. Fresh mechanical appendages, these equipped with scimitar blades, rose behind her shoulders.

"I know you have a plan, Buc," Eld said. In the distance, the bells of the cathedral began to toll.

One.

"This time I have one, too."

"You do?" I asked, one part of my mind listening to Eld, the other part looking for a way to make it the score of paces we needed to reach the lip of the roof. Chan Sha began screaming threats when none of her forces charged. "Beyond sailing some magical-arse balloon in the middle of a storm to try to stop a gang war the likes of which Servenza has never seen, while taking on a maniacal madwoman, all to save some slip of a girl?"

Eld's laughter broke my concentration. I looked up and he was right there, his gaze melting into my own. "I'm so sorry, Buc. Sorry I lied, that I let magic and Sin and the rest keep us apart." He pulled me to him. "If I hadn't been such a fool, we could have faced the factory, and all of this, together."

"We're together now," I told him, speaking into his chest, breathing him in. Past the gunpowder and blood and sweat, he was there: clean and wholesome.

"Aye. We're together now."

"The woman, man, or child what brings me the girl still breathing I'll name my second!" Chan Sha shouted. The cathedral bells tolled a second time, pealing out across Servenza.

"Eld! We need to go. Now!" I pushed him but he didn't move.

"I love you," he whispered.

"W-what?"

"I'm sorry about that, too. I should have told you when I began to feel something more than just friendship, Buc. I—"

A whistling sound filled the air and Eld looked up, above the gang members who were beginning to shout and curse as they worked themselves up for another charge. Lightning flashed, illuminating some sort of winged creature and the bombs it was dropping.

"Part of your plan, Buc?"

"Aye."

"You're not using Sin. If you were you wouldn't need whatever that plan is," he guessed. "You're afraid of Sin and the power he offers, ashamed of using it . . . because of me. Buc, you're the strongest person in the world. You're stronger than Sin, stronger than his Goddess. Use that strength. Use him. You'll need it all. There's nothing to be ashamed of."

Eld looked down at me, his eyes filled with tears. "Last time we faced Chan Sha," he whispered, "you saved my life." He bent down and kissed me.

I wasn't prepared for the surge of electricity and warmth his lips sent racing through me, but I didn't need to be. I kissed him back and tried to pull him closer, but he caught my hands in one of his own. Tears fell down his cheeks as he pulled back. I opened my mouth to ask what he was doing even as he began to move, wrapping me in one arm, leveling one of the blunderbusses in the other. The whistling was growing louder, turning into an angry scream.

"Now it's my turn." When he pulled the trigger, the massive gun leapt in his fist and bodies flew through the air, some dead, others fleeing. Eld ran for the edge of the Lighthouse roof, jumping onto the lip of the brick wall.

Then he threw me over the edge.

As I flew I saw Eld, standing on the lip, fire spouting from his fists as gang members leapt toward him from every side, steel and fire filling the air around him as he faced down Chan Sha and the gangs of Servenza. Falling toward them all were the bombs filled with Serpent's Flame that the Artificer had dropped at the second tolling of the bells. Dropped on my command. Dropped on Chan Sha. And now . . . dropped on Eld.

"Nooo."

Wings shot out from the gearwork strapped to my back, triggered by my sudden momentum, and I was flipped violently around as the Artificer's glider sought to stabilize itself. Something inside me broke and I tasted blood in my mouth. A lot of it. Everything was a blur; the streets rushed up to greet me, the canals reflecting the gunfire and now bright starlight. The wings kept growing and suddenly my plunge turned into a graceful swan dive, and then I began to rise, the gears twisting the wings back and forth, capturing the wind.

Eld. I can save Eld.

I reached for the straps, intending to steer as the Artificer's notes had indicated, but could make no headway against the powerful thermals I was caught in, no matter how hard I strained to turn the glider. In moments I'd left the Lighthouse behind and Servenza with it, the dark waters of the Crescent shimmering beneath me as I glided out over the bay. Suddenly night turned into day as the Lighthouse exploded behind me in a violent conflagration of bombs and fire and screeching gearwork. I tried to twist my head, to see, and couldn't, but realized I didn't need to, as the waters of the Crescent provided a mirror for the destruction that I had wrought.

Have to turn around. Need to save Eld!

"Sin! Give me strength."

"You said you'd do this on your own," he whispered in my mind.

"For me, aye, but for Eld? I've already sacrificed myself once for him, I'll do it again."

"I know you would," he said quietly. "But he's gone, Buc." He hesitated. "Eld died to save you."

"He's not dead!" I growled, thrashing around in the straps. "Now turn this fucking hunk of steel around. I command it."

"If I did that you'd die, too. Either from all the damage you've taken or else from the flames, if you were able to reach what's left back there."

"Turn around! I have to save him!" I screamed.

I kicked hard, whipping my body back and forth; the glider caught the wind from the wrong direction and suddenly we spiraled. My head slammed into something hard and my vision swam through inky night and blurry stars. Darkness swallowed me.

62

I came to with tears in my eyes and a burning in my lungs. I blinked to clear my vision and realized I was heading straight for a small rocky outcropping in the Crescent. I was about to chastise Sin for healing me—I recognized that burning as his work—but, remembering the blood in my mouth and the strange, heavy feeling in my chest, decided to let it pass. Strangely colored light flickered off the water; the glider's wings were pulling in slowly, as if by command. Then I saw that it *was* by command: mine. My hands were on the straps, guiding it.

"Sin, what the fuck? I told you to leave me alone."

"You blacked out, Buc. I'm just getting us to the meeting point in one piece. Then you can do what you will."

I screamed when we landed and my wounded left leg cried out from the impact. We toppled over, landing awkwardly because of the wings. Half on my back and half propped up, I could see Servenza, lit up like the Festival of Lights.

"Eld!" Tearing at the straps, I pulled the gearwork apparatus off my back and dragged myself to the edge of the water, staring across the Crescent at the disaster I had caused. The top of the Lighthouse, fully engulfed in flames, broke and toppled over. What looked like sparks from a campfire flew up into the air, but I knew those sparks were massive beams and that if not for storm that had just passed, all of Servenza would go up like a tinderbox.

I love you.

Eld's words filled my ears, his kiss my lips, and that blissful moment stole my breath away for a moment. When I found it again, I screamed until my voice broke and my body with it, tears making me blind as I was racked with sobs, collapsing onto the gritty ground. I'd lost Eld once, and then, when I'd found him—no, when he found me—I'd lost him again.

Forever.

"I never got to tell him," I whispered, my voice strangled by grief and pain.

"Tell him what?" Sin whispered gently.

"That I loved him, too. He said it and I was so surprised and then it all happened so fast and I didn't and now he's gone and I didn't—I didn't say it! I didn't fucking say it!"

"Buc, he knew! You know he did. He knew you loved him and now you know he loved you."

"But I didn't get the chance to say it," I said, wrapping my arms around my legs. "Feelings are involuntary, but saying it is a choice. I missed it. I missed him."

I don't know how long I sat there, rocking back and forth on that scrap of land. It was a long while, I know that. The bells tolled the day of the month at midnight and the night was still black, with no hint of the coming of the sun, when the sound of the Artificer's gear-driven ornithopter beat a steady tattoo over the Crescent's waters. By then I'd cried myself hollow and though Sin's healing burned through me, I felt nothing at all. I'd started the night bent on exacting vengeance and now that was all that was left to me. I was just an empty husk. A husk with a burning ember. The ember was a word.

Revenge.

63

The Chair nodded to her serving man at the door, who stood ramrod straight in the shadow of the nearby pillar and didn't bow or look at her twice. Didn't acknowledge her in any way. *I'll have a word with Germo. I don't care if he's been running the household since I was a child: his underlings lack respect.* Suppressing her annoyance, the Chair walked into the drawing room. The woman waiting there was facing away from her and backlit by a roaring fire that popped and crackled. Something tickled at her nose and she sneezed, searching for the handkerchief in the pocket of her dressing gown.

"I'll flay the servant that's been lax about dusting in this drawing room," she said by way of apology. Not that she ever truly apologized, not even to the Parliamentarian. It was the fool woman's fault for insisting on meeting in her late husband's favorite room— she knew how the Chair had felt about Jerome. "Judging by the explosions that rocked half the city, it's been a busy night. . . . I was expecting you two bells ago. So tell me, Parliamentarian, do you have news?"

"I do."

I turned around and watched the Chair's white eyebrows climb up toward where her hairline was slowly ceding to age. Her thin braids—it looked like she'd had them redone not long ago— bounced as she shook her head, her parchment-thin skin darkening with anger.

"Fool child," she hissed. "What do you hope to accomplish? Bursting in unannounced, ordering my servants around, pretending to be the Parliamentarian?" I shrugged, and the tendrils of anger rippling beneath her skin bloomed, blood suffusing her face so that she was nearly as black as me. "Why do you have your face covered like a Burning Lands savage?"

"So many questions." I felt the thick silk across my face and smiled, not that she could see it. Not that I felt like smiling. But formalities had to be observed. "As for the covering, it is dusty in here, after all. For the rest? I wanted to have a talk, just you and I. One honest conversation."

"So you thought ambushing me in my dead husband's drawing room would be a good start?" The Chair snorted. "You're not that big a fool, girl."

"Neither are you," I told her. "A fool, that is. Anywhere else, the answers you'd give would be obsequious at best. But here? In the heart of your power, with none to hear, none to substantiate anything I might say later? If honesty can't be found here, then where?"

The Chair nodded slowly. "That's your angle; what do I get from this exchange?"

"Me out of your life."

"I'm already getting that," she said. "Remember? You sail north as soon as this blasted storm blows over."

"I've never liked the cold," I said. "Salina says there's a need for an inspection of the kan plantations out along the Shattered Coast. Since I was there just this past year, I'm a likely choice. In exchange, I'll give you the proof you need to hang the Doga. I can still be on that ship tomorrow and by the time I return summer will have come and gone."

"You want a plum assignment instead of the dregs I planned to serve you?" The old woman shrugged. "Done."

I canted my head. "Just like that?"

"If your proof is that strong? It's a cheap price and quickly paid."

"The price paid or the quality of the price?"

"What?"

"Never mind," I said, waving away her frown. All right, now that the personal is out of the way, onto business, shall we?"

"This wasn't the business you came to conduct?" she asked.

"Not by half," I told her. "Have you asked the Parliamentarian what she's been up to, with all her side speculations?"

"What?"

I stepped away from the fireplace, sweat dripping down my back, and she blinked owlishly, her gaze following me into the shadows.

"I had reason to look into some of her accounts recently—they're doing very well, by the way—and saw a number of short-term investments, high-risk, high-reward sort of affairs. They didn't make sense for her portfolio."

The Chair's lips worked soundlessly, then she clasped her hands together and shook her head. "I don't know what game you intend to play tonight, girl, but I'm the one that holds all the cards, so I've no reason to indulge your fancy."

"Come now, I thought we were having an honest conversation."

"That would require you to not be a Godsdamned obfuscator," she growled.

"True. Let me unfuscate . . . unobfuscate? Let me clear things up," I said.

"I don't think that's possible," the Chair said. "You've the streets in your bones and there's nothing so crooked as a street that runs through the Tip."

"Rebellion isn't cheap," I continued over her. "You were right about the Doga—she was plotting to overthrow the Empress using this Sicarii." The Chair's eyes lit up in the flames of the fireplace. "To do so she needed lire, and lots of it. Your Parliamentarian set up a number of accounts to help the Doga enrich her private coffers, to pay bribes to undermine the Board and to pay for the

460 • Ryan Van Loan

additional Constabulary she was trying to recruit beneath the Empress's eye. Hard to do that if she raised taxes, but with money off the books?"

The Chairs eyes narrowed. "Esmerlda would have no such need—"

"Next," I interrupted her, "you'll tell me you didn't know she was a worshipper of Ciris."

She opened her mouth, but choked on whatever word she was going to say and coughed, wiping at her nose with her silk hand-kerchief. Muttering again about the dust, she glared at me. "I agreed to a tell-all. Where's your proof?"

"In your eyes just now," I told her. "I said you were no fool and I think you've suspected. I think you found the path to bringing the Doga down trickier than anticipated, and given the number of ventures on your plate, you found reasons to look the other way. Old age creeping in?"

The old woman's eyes blazed as she drew her lavender gown tighter around her.

"If one were to go to a certain familial banker and seek out his son-in-law, who has a truly hideous gambling problem, they could find the same financial transfers I did," I explained.

"So you say." She licked her lips. "Esmerlda is no fool, either. I suspect they wouldn't find a damned thing."

"It's true, I paid off his gambling debts," I said.

"The transfers!" The Chair screwed up her lips, pulling at the neck of her gown with one hand. "They wouldn't find anything there."

"This parchment, with all of the account numbers, dates of transfers, and corresponding amounts, says otherwise," I said, pulling a thick envelope from beneath my jacket. "It's yours." I pulled it back. "But in return I want you to will everything the Parliamentarian owns to Eldritch Nelson Rawlings."

"Eld? Why Eld?" The Chair's frown said she didn't understand.

"Eld's dead." I bit my lip to keep from crying.

"What are you talking about?" She coughed into her handkerchief. "How? When?"

"Every single one of you thought to use us all as instruments of your will, tools to be cast aside when they are no longer needed," I said, ignoring her question.

"You. The Parliamentarian. The Doga. Sicarii. The Gods." My snarl was hidden by the silk mask I wore, but it must have shown in my eyes, because she took another step back. I bit my lip until I felt blood on my chin.

"That's where you fucked up," I said. "I've never been anyone's tool. You see"—I moved forward and she stood up straighter as if to protect herself—"I'm not certain you understand what you've done. I could forgive you for trying to use us, to use the factory fire against me, even though that separated Eld and me. Save that everything you did led to tonight.

"Those explosions"—I gestured past the wall, toward the heart of the city—"were his death knell. He's dead. And Sicarii with him."

"Everything begins to make sense," the Chair said after a moment. "You've lost your mind with grief and somehow you imagine seizing the Parliamentarian's fortune will assuage your guilt at your friend's death."

"It's not for me. It's payment for her betrayal of Servenza."

"I can't will her fortune to Eld," the Chair chuckled mirthlessly.

"You can if you're her benefactor."

"She'd never have—" the old woman began. She coughed, eyes narrowing above her handkerchief. "Wills made under duress are null and void."

"I'll let the lawyers fight it out."

"If Eld's dead, then what you ask makes no sense."

"It's the principle of the thing," I lied. I took a tired breath, letting my thoughts filter slowly through my mind. Between the past week and the fighting and losing Eld, my wits were a dull blade in want of a whetstone. *I can't afford to be dull. Not yet.* I pulled out a quill, a small inkwell, and a rolled-up piece of parchment and set them on the small table beside her. "Sign, and you own the Doga and the traitor in your midst, simple as that," I said.

The Chair's brow furrowed, but after a pause to wipe at the snot running freely from her nose, she reached for the quill.

"Mind you don't get your crud on the document," I added.

She glared at me, then scanned the document and gave a phlegm-filled sniff before writing her signature in a bold, flowing hand across the bottom of the parchment. I blew on it carefully in the absence of sand and a blotter, rolled it up, and slipped it back into my pocket.

"I tried to play your game, you know," I told her. "I thought the way to win was to play it better than all of you, never realizing that by taking a seat at the table I'd already lost." Quenta and Marin shone bright in my mind. "Worse," I added, "due to the Doga's greed, and mine, Sicarii nearly succeeded. Nearly upended everything I've worked my life for. That should have been what brought me here tonight, but it was Eld."

I sighed.

"It was all for Eld."

"Very touching," the Chair said, edging toward the door.

I pulled a sheathed sword from beneath my jacket and she froze. I almost laughed at her expression as I lightly tossed it to her. "Recognize it?"

She caught the weapon and held it awkwardly for a moment before half drawing the blade. Her eyes widened. "Th-this is my husband's, Jerome's, from his service in the navy." She looked at me. "But it's hanging over the mantel in my library."

"Is it?"

"Is that—is that blood on the blade?" She touched a spot of what looked like rust on the steel; her finger came away red.

"It is," I told her.

She coughed hard and took a rasping breath, staring at her hand. "Whose blood? Eld's? Sicarii's?"

"The Doga's," I said.

"What?!?" Her gaze flashed to my face, to the blade, and back, horror rising in her expression. "What have you done, you foolish child?"

"Think how surprised she was," I told her.

I could still hear her screaming for her Secreto after Sin and I had broken her legs with my slingshot. I told her of the traps I'd laid in the passages around her room, made it clear none were coming for her. The chaos she'd sought to create had come home to roost. She confessed to everything but even as she talked, I don't think she believed what was happening. Not to her, the Doga of Servenza, cousin to the Empress of the Servenzan Empire.

She believed when I ran her through, though. Reality has a way of asserting itself. So does a foot of steel through the ribs.

"You're mad," the Chair gasped.

"No. Sicarii was mad. The Doga was mad. You're mad, in your own way. All of you driven insane by power and its pursuit." I chuckled. "The Doga's dead, aye, but you're focusing on the wrong details."

The Chair sniffed and wiped at her nose. "Elucidate me."

"Have you heard of a new invention called forensics?" I shook my head. "Probably not, since the Artificer just invented it a few months ago. It can match the little swirls off your fingers"—I held up my hand and wriggled mine—"to other things you've touched. Now those swirls are all over the weapon that murdered Her Grace, the Doga of Servenza."

The old woman collapsed into a nearby chair, sword clattering to the ground. Her cheeks had undergone a transformation during our talk; now they hung pale and lifeless as she crossed her arms. "What do you want?"

"You have to understand just what it is I've done. The Doga's dead, by your hand or as good as, the murder weapon bloody with your prints. The Parliamentarian left enough documents behind to suggest she was the real Sicarii, the one bribing the gangs and bending them to her will—at your direction. She murdered the captain of the Secreto. . . .

"Well, actually, I did, and let me tell you, that sister was a pain in the arse to cart halfway across the city, missing head or no. But I framed the Parliamentarian—"

A thump outside the door drew our attention. The Chair looked at me, her eyes asking a question.

"Oh, did I forget to mention? That blood was the Doga's . . . and your manservant's."

"W-w-w—" she wheezed.

"I couldn't just stab you or shoot you full of holes, as pleasant as that would be," I told her, leaning forward. "I wanted to put Serpent's Flame in the doorjamb instead of mere poison, but that wouldn't fit the story we've just crafted, you and I."

"W-why?" she choked, falling off her chair and rolling onto her back on the floor.

I pulled out a different piece of parchment and slowly unrolled it. "You know," I told her, "the forger was right, she really was worth the coin. I could have had her forge your signature as well as this little beauty and Jerome's sword—the real one is still over your mantel, by the way, I'll collect it on my way out—but then we'd have missed our little conversation."

I dropped the paper, watched it float lazily down beside her, and squatted next to her. The Chair's dark eyes blinked at me, trying to focus. "It's your confession. To everything. The financial troubles you've been having—"

She coughed and I laughed. "Aye, you're doing well, though your accounts have been altered recently to look otherwise. That, along with your desire to supplant the Doga and the realization— too late—that Salina sniffed out your plot and turned the Parliamentarian over to the Secreto, led you to assassinate your ruler."

I stood up and walked over to the fireplace.

"These"—I pulled out a thick sheaf of papers and tossed all but one into the fire—"are another matter entirely. A little something to keep you guessing as you drown in your own fluids."

I bent over and let the single piece of paper catch aflame, and then carefully stamped it out. Sin better have been right that the cipher wasn't too complex.

"You all did this to yourselves," I whispered. Behind me the Chair made a throaty protestation that sounded like a drowning woman gasping her last breath before sinking beneath the waves. I slid the fireplace aside on hidden runners, exposing the secret passage, and stepped inside. I had one more task before morn.

"The work is mine, but writ in your hand, signed in blood." Behind me the crack and pop of the fire was the only reply.

Epilogue

———— ∞∞∞ ————

"Buc!"

I stood up from where I'd been leaning on the seawall to watch Salina navigate the floating docks in her amber skirts. She held two drinks out in front as if they would help her keep her balance. And maybe they did, because she didn't slip despite her heels and the rough surf. She surprised me by setting both steaming mugs down atop the wall and enveloping me in a hug.

"Oof!"

"Buc, I'm so sorry," she whispered in my ear. "He was such a good man." I could feel the dampness of a tear on her cheek. "The best."

"The best of all of us," I choked. I pulled back and she let me go. "Did you—?"

"It's all taken care of," she said. "Here. Kan for me and tea for you," she said, reaching for the mugs. "I know what kan does to your mind."

"Actually, I'm spent, Salina. Would you mind switching?"

"Of course not," Salina said, suiting the action to the word.

"You know, the last woman who switched glasses with me ended up poisoned."

"Thanks, Buc," Salina growled, stopping so fast that tea sloshed onto her sleeve.

"She came back to life," I said with a shrug. "The harbormaster?"

"Oh, that's right." Salina snorted. "Did wonders for her temperament."

"I bet."

I took a sip of the kan and felt its false warmth and energy course through me, Sin mitigating its effects on my thoughts. We'd had a conversation, he and I, and the days of him being in control in the background were over. I called the shots. He hated it and I had a feeling the war between us wasn't over, that this was merely a cease-fire, but I had nearly taken down Sicarii and the massed gangs of Servenza without him. I could do so again.

"Not if you want to defeat the Gods, you can't."

"So you're open to turning traitor, Sin?" I smiled in my mind and he shivered. He knew that after last night, I was what I'd always professed to be: emotionless. "Either way, you betray me and I'll lock you away like before, but this time I'll throw away the key."

"You wouldn't."

"You know I would."

"You and Eld," Salina said, breaking into my thoughts, "have been reported missing and are presumed dead, along with hundreds of others caught in the Lighthouse explosion. Your funds were transferred into the account you provided."

"Listing you as executor."

"Only in your absence," she agreed. She took a sip of tea and glanced at me over the rim of her mug. "The balance is, uh, much more sizable than I imagined."

"The Parliamentarian was generous," I said with a shrug.

"She was a traitor, consorting with Normain to overthrow the Doga."

"Aye, but a generous one." If I'd had any emotions left, I'd have grinned at the success of the false papers I'd left in her study. That is, if I'd wanted Salina to know the truth. "How's the Empress taking it?"

"Word is she's ordered a season of mourning for her cousin."

"Time to raise levies, more like."

"Aye, I'm afraid so. Speaking of treason . . . I don't understand why you set me up to win the vote for Chair when it could have been you."

I leaned against the seawall, watching the ship before us making ready to set sail, and shrugged. "The Chair passed suddenly and we needed a new one."

"The same night the Doga did. The Imperial Guard have surrounded her palazzo and none have been allowed entry."

"They say trouble comes in threes," I said.

I laughed at her expression. "The Chair wanted the Doga removed, Salina. When I told her"—I shrugged—"she laughed so hard she choked. To death."

"She did not!"

"Well, she's dead, and none can say it was foul play, so that's as good a story as any other." I took a sip from my mug. *And now the Empress thinks she has you to thank for staving off open rebellion.* "Best watch out what jokes you listen to in the future, now that you're Chair."

Salina chuckled. "But you should be the Chair! This is everything you've been working toward."

"It was," I agreed.

I thought about how I'd fucked up over the course of the past year, how I'd gotten caught up in the very thing I'd set out to destroy. It'd been easy to imagine that once I took control of the Company that I'd be able to change everything, but now I knew the truth. I need to get away from all of this. I'd given Salina instructions on how to break free of the Sin Eaters' grip. It'd be difficult and messy at first, but with half the Servenzan branch dead as a result of fighting the Dead Gods, with the Empire and Normain at one another's throats, Salina should be able to steer a path clear.

My own path was looking rockier than I'd imagined. I thought I'd scaled the mountain, but it had turned out to be a hill. The real summit still lay before me and I was just beginning to realize how much farther I had to go, how much more was left. I'd do it,

I'd come too far, scaled too high, to turn back, but I couldn't win my war seated behind a desk or on a throne. If Sicarii had taught me one thing, it was the value of working from the shadows. After losing Eld, I felt like a shade of my former self, ground down to the essentials and ready to do what was required.

"Salina, you'll be far better at doing what is needed here than I."

"I hope I'm worthy of your faith," she said dryly.

"I know you are," I said. If she wasn't, well, the Doga had given me enough before the end that even if I had somehow massively misjudged Salina, she wouldn't be able to step very far out of line before I could snap her back. I hoped it wouldn't come to that. She was the closest thing I had left to a friend, but there was no one and nothing left that I wouldn't sacrifice, in the end. Whatever the cost.

"Another thing. Give Lucrezia the Parliamentarian's position."

Salina whistled through her teeth. "Rewarding one of the sharks who had eyes for Eld? You're growing soft."

"No, it was never about Lucrezia." The ship I'd been watching, a massive galleon of Cordoban design, dropped sails and sailors began casting off lines. "She's dangerous in her own way, but it's a small way. Put her there and you won't have to worry about a situation like the one her predecessor created."

Salina shuddered.

"'Sides, do that and you'll earn an ally. Even being able to fill two seats and wielding our votes in absentia, you're going to need an ally."

"There it is," Salina said. Her amber eyes were bright in the sunlight. "I knew there was more to it than that." She frowned. "I'm not so certain she's going to give a fig about me."

"You're the Chair and your life is about to become very difficult. Everyone will want something from you—and from Lucrezia, if she is Parliamentarian. The woman will want for an ally, and who better than the Chair?"

Salina nodded thoughtfully.

"Artificer!" At my call, the short man detached himself from the wall a dozen paces down and joined us. Dusting off his dark, tailored coat that was buttoned to his neck, he dry-washed his hands and adjusted his spectacles expectantly. I pointed toward the Cordoban ship. "You're sure that's the one?"

"It is," he agreed.

"All right, go find Joffers and tell him to have the gondola ready. I told that captain we'd sail within the hour."

"As you say, Buc," he said, inclining his head before scurrying away.

"Do you trust him?" Salina asked.

"Gods, no," I snorted. "Trust no one and you'll never be disappointed."

"You're not wrong, but that's harsh advice to follow."

"The Chair's a harsh position," I told her, leaning back against the wall.

She followed my gaze and cleared her throat. "Are you sure about this?"

"I am."

"You . . . and Eld . . . have a year and a day to return before your seats on the Board will be forfeit."

"Should be plenty of time," I lied.

Eld was never going to see Servenza again, and neither was I. Not with the shadow war between the Gods finally coming into the light, Normain and the Empire on the brink of war themselves, and Eld's killer somehow slipping the trap I'd laid for her. A-fucking-gain.

A figure leaning heavily on a cane moved awkwardly across the deck of the ship I'd been watching, stopping every few paces to lean against the rail. They glanced back toward the docks just as the sun caught them in the face. Something glittered brightly where their eyes should have been.

"Today," I said quietly, "is my eighteenth birthday."

"Oh, Buc." Salina sighed. "I'd wish you well, but I'm not sure there's a present I could give you that would replace what you've lost."

"I've an eye on a prize. Won't replace a damned thing, but"—I shrugged—"it will do."

"Where are you going, Buc?"

"After," I said, watching Chan Sha sail away. *After my prize.* I wasn't sure how the bitch had escaped. Likely jumped and used her Spider to spear another building and climb inside before everything tumbled down. It's what I would have done, were I her. All that mattered was she still breathed. That my revenge was incomplete.

For several minutes we stood in silence; I kept my gaze on the ship as it grew distant, then blurry from the tears in my eyes.

Salina didn't understand. This was bigger than Chan Sha. It was bigger than empresses and kings and queens and parliaments and boards that all watched and did nothing. It was bigger than Gods who saw us as pawns to be used in their undying war. It was about justice. For Eld. For Sister. For the whole damned world. I thought the most powerful Company in this world would give me what I needed, but now I knew the truth: that kind of power corrupts, it spills poison in your ears, weighs you down with gold until you drown. Wielding that kind of power makes it impossible to mete out justice.

No, there was no justice in this world. And in the absence of justice, revenge would do.

The Selected and Annotated Library of Sambuciña Alhurra

Numbered and listed in order read, with notes by the reader. At the time of the events detailed in this volume, by her own count, Buc had read 391 books and an uncounted number of pamphlets.

11
Geniver Gillibrand
A Twist of the Tongue

Gillibrand may have poached her better lines from writers and poets and philosophers from throughout history, but she's not above a few originals of her own and even the weakest amongst them rival Ballwik's best.

Buc's notes: She has as much faith in what passes for truth as I have. Wonder what gutter she was swaddled in?

24
Yanton Verner
Disciple of the Body—Anatomy

Verner's magnum opus caused issues with the bookbinders upon its release, but if one wishes to understand the anatomy of the body in all its glorious complexity, one must study this work.

Buc's notes: Nearly passed this one over for want of a cover. There's a feel a book has, though, cover or not, that beckons, and I'm glad I

heeded the call. Else I might be emptying my guts over the side like Eld.
Easy crossing, my arse.

219
Hul Ferda
Pyrotechnomancy, Maestros of Powder and Flame

Hul made their living by selling fireworks displays to rulers of
various city-states for well over a decade before it was discovered
their name couldn't be found on any of the lists of maestros kept
by the pyrotechnomancy guilds of Colgna, Frulituo, Servenza, or
the other city-states. This was all the more embarrassing giving
Hul's superior displays. Having made their coin on the mystery
of their name and persona—in public they went masked, wearing
a deeply hooded cloak; features and gender were thus completely
obscured—Hul disappeared. Several years later, this work was released. While the guilds denounced it as full of false information,
many would-be practitioners (those who didn't blow themselves
sky-high first) made their living off Hul's learnings.

Buc's notes: I wonder why the army never took advantage of this?
Sure, it can send pretty lights up into the sky, and placed horizontal it's
not as effective as a cannon, but up close? It'd bring the Constabulary
or the Imperial Guard on the lighter side of said fusillade for certain.
Best leave it for now. Still, desperate times and all that . . .

286
Bocha Semsin
Flying Insects and Their Proclivities

Semsin's work isn't the first to dive into the world of the insect,
but it is the most comprehensive. She traversed the world from
north to south and all of the east, studying bugs, taking copious
notes, making numerous drawings of their carapaces, and taking
especial care to capture the detail in their wings. When travel to

the Shattered Coast became possible, she was one of the first to book passage, vanishing, like so many before her, into the foggy notations on the edges of the map table.

Buc's notes: I almost put this down at the start—but it could be worthwhile knowing which areas of southern Cordoban to avoid or that there's a morass between Normain and Colgna filled with a biting fly that will lay poisonous eggs beneath your skin. Even Eld didn't know that one, and he has surprising knowledge of all things biting.

371
Pavlia
On Hounds and Their Training

Pavlia kept the coursers of Normain's royalty for her entire life, having assumed the role from her father, who'd assumed it from his mother. While some claim Pavlia merely set down her father and grandmother's lessons, a careful reader will note that many of her advanced tactics, such as using treats to reinforce good behavior that is then built upon in increasing layers of instruction, seem to have come, whole cloth, from Pavlia herself. Her father and those who came before were fond of the whip, but after the first third of the book, Pavlia dispenses with punishment nearly entirely.

Buc's notes: No stick, all honey, eh? I feel like men need a firmer hand than that or they'll get uppity, but Eld's too damned polite to push back much. If Pavlia's tactics are sound, I need only tell him to do something he'd normally do already and then reward him for doing so? I'm not sure if this will have him eating out of my hand or not, but it's worth a try. Men and hounds . . . I should have made the connection sooner.

379
Kanma Siltriva
Silk and Sheets

Siltriva was a famed mistress to the Doge of Colgna before his untimely death sent her fleeing into the Princess of Frilituo's arms. When the papers learned of the wealth the Doge had willed to her and the Princess's heirs uncovered similar alterations to her will, there were questions of poison. Siltriva was exiled to the Free Cities, where she ran the most famous bordello in the isles. Even the most experienced salt will learn something between these pages, aye, and blush in the learning.

Buc's notes: I'm not quite sure what is meant on page seventy-five. Oh wait, there's an illustration on the next page. Damn . . .

382
Corewell
On Pain and Its Application

Half a century ago, Corewell was the maestro (*futuwwa* in Cordoban) of executions in the capital of the Cordoban Confederacy. One imagines, shuddering, that the man forgot more about torture than the rest of us have known. It is said that Corewell knew the methods to break every mind and every body, and how to keep a prisoner alive well past the point of endurance. Apocryphal, perhaps, but his famed execution of the assassin of the then-Doga's son was witnessed by her captain of the Secreto, who reported that the woman took a score of days to die, rasping at the end because she'd chewed her own tongue off.

Buc's notes: What the actual fuck? I don't think I'll be able to let liver past my lips again after reading about the hook-and-anchor keelhaul. Yuck.

384
Archo
The Distribution of Labor

Archo could be forgiven for being mistaken for a maestro in his own right, but in point of fact he was a clerk in one of the sundry mercantile guilds that cropped up before the trading companies consolidated power. Had his guild listened to his suggestions or read his later works, they might have been the ones reaping the benefits instead of the trading companies. A masterwork in logistics and operational efficiencies for those who don't mind a dry read, accompanied by, it must be said, rather bad illustrations.

Buc's notes: The bookseller warned me of Archo's politics on distributive labor, but it reads like good sense to me. I'd have thought everyone involved in shipping or trade would have read and implemented half these practices already. Gods, how much profit is left on the table due to simple inefficiencies in the operations of these warehouses, let alone the manufactories?

387
Franca Witi
Servenzan Antiquity and Architecture

Franca Witi was one of the first to question not just how but why architecture existed in its current form, and why it had changed over time. Witi discovered that many of the architects who oversaw the construction of grand structures like the Castello and the original reef forts on the northern coast of Servenza were illiterate and that there may never have been blueprints, or even written plans, for many buildings on Servenza and the Imperial Isle. Her studies and drawings are the closest we will ever come to knowing how they were designed.

Buc's notes: There's not just one, but two passages beneath the Castello's great wall where we could have walked if we had not been forced

out into that torrential downpour. If Eld finds out, he'll never stop in-
sisting politeness first is a policy I should adopt. If Witi is correct, there
are several points of entry beyond the main doors; honestly, for being
a prison the place has more holes than a block of Normain cheese. I
don't see any passages connecting to the cell of the Mosquitoes' maestro,
though. I'm missing something, I know it. I hate th—[paper is torn
here, rendering line unreadable]

391
Kolka
The Mind Fears the Body

Almost assuredly a pseudonym, this Southeast Islander woman
was a physiker caught up in one of the endless forays against the
Burnt. When medicine and even mage healing didn't cure the
ills of the mind, she began experimenting with that most novel
of cures: talking. Refining her work over the course of a decade,
Kolka gained fame after treating the son of the Crown Princess. Her work involved discussing the patient's trauma while
she distracted them by tapping a can against their leg. Her practices evolved from there, and briefly a sanctuary was established
on the Southeast Island's southern coast. Unfortunately, criticism
by other physikers of Kolka's refusal to include the body's essen-
tial humors in her treatments led to a loss of patients and income
and the clinic soon closed. When these same physikers refused to
accept her patients—all former soldiers or sailors—they were sent
to asylums or to the Shattered Coast.

Buc's notes: I could wish the woman was wrong, because I can feel
the fire in my bones, but there's something here, I think. I just wish it
wasn't so damned hard and that it wouldn't feel as if I'd read Felcher's
Discourse on Planetary Bodies *for the dozenth time after every ses-*
sion. My mind hurts and my heart aches and I just want this to go
away. All right, Buc, the only way out is through. Let's do this.

Acknowledgments

I don't know if I've ever been more excited to write a novel than I was for *The Justice in Revenge*. I also know for certain I've never had a more challenging novel to write. Second novel syndrome. The sophomore slump. There are a lot of names for this common occurrence in the creative arts, whether it be acting, music, or in this case, writing: the second work not being as good as the debut that got the artist noticed in the first place. I've seen some good theories on why that might be: pressure that didn't exist before, less time, no longer creating in a vacuum, etc.

This book was not my second novel, but it *was* my first sequel and the first time I wrote a book *knowing* that someone beyond my friends and family and agent were going to read it. You, dear reader, were going to read it. To that end, I put a lot into this novel. Loads of new characters, arcs, twists upon twists upon twists. Too much, in fact. Like the Swedish flagship *Vasa*, *The Justice in Revenge* was top-heavy. Thankfully, I've some of the finest shipwrights in publishing on my side and they helped me get her trimmed up and into fighting shape. If you enjoyed Buc and Eld's latest adventure, it is them you have to thank, and if you did not, the blame lies wholly upon myself. Here are a few of those shipwrights.

Melissa, my editor, to whom this book is dedicated. She saw the rocks through the fog when I thought I was sailing clear skies and helped pinpoint several key areas that made this book sing.

DongWon, my agent, who got me to trim quite a bit of my outline before I put fingers to keys, and who was in my corner every step of the way. DW said something about which character this novel really was about that brought it all into focus for me. . . . He's a genius like that.

My beta readers, Arnaud Akoebel, Dan Knorr II, and Kristine Nelson, who provided invaluable insight into some of the character arcs and helped me course correct when I was steering off the map. Thank you, friends!

TeamDongWon and Drowwzoo remain my faithful aunties and uncles, graciously giving me their sage wisdom on everything from writing to career advice. I wrote this book before *The Sin in the Steel* hit shelves but not before readers began to get their hands on it, and it's a tricky thing, writing for the first time while the outside world begins to slip in. Their steady hands on the tiller kept me true.

Penultimately, to you, dear reader. Thank you for coming back. Not only did you take a chance on an unknown, you returned, and that is what careers are built upon. I'm sorry for Eld, deeply and truly. He was never going to let Buc face Sicarii and the gangs of Servenza alone, no matter the cost. That we should all be so brave. I hope, when you've had a moment, you'll come back for the conclusion of Buc's story.

Finally, Rachel, who has to live with me. Living with a writer means sailing where the wind changes not by the day but by the hour, sometimes by the minute. A great scene laid down, another sinking beneath the waves. Reviews, business, marketing decisions, and sundry things that could make or break a career and nearly all but the page outside of your control. All of that weight has brought more than one writer low, but Rachel's always been there. She is, as I said in *Sin*'s dedication, never wavering. Thank you; I couldn't do this without you.

The shipwrights at Tor continue to astound, and there are so many to thank, I'll inevitably miss a few, but know that everyone there is the reason why this book is in your hands. Thank you to: Amanda Schoonmaker, senior contracts manager, who drew up the contracts. Nathan Weaver, managing editor, from whom all production floweth. Jim Kapp, production manager, who interacts with the printers, among other things. Megan Kiddoo and Dakota Griffin, production editors, who handle the different stages of production. MaryAnn Johanson, copy editor, who caught a bunch of continuity errors and kept me honest. . . . Anything you find in the lines that doesn't make sense I probably STETTED. Peter Lutjen, art director, has a fine eye; he commissioned the art and designed the cover. Lucille Rettino, vice president, associate publisher, director of marketing and publicity is, as I understand it, the boss of many who came before and a force of nature.

Especial thanks to Renata Sweeney, senior marketing manager, who headed up the marketing efforts this time around and is a tireless advocate for fine fiction everywhere, and to Caro Perny, publicity manager, who handles all of my appearances and gives me the same attention bestsellers receive despite my being a newb. I'm forever in your debt.

About the Author

RYAN VAN LOAN (he/him) served six years in the US Army Infantry on the front lines of Afghanistan. He now works in healthcare innovation. *The Sin in the Steel*, first volume in the Fall of the Gods, was his debut novel. Van Loan and his wife live in Pennsylvania.

@RyanVanLoan
www.ryanvanloan.com